Hunters for Hire

TOMORROW

SAMANTHA KANE

ELLORA'S CAVE
ROMANTICA PUBLISHING

What the critics are saying...

An Ellora's Cave Romantica Publication

www.ellorascave.com

Tomorrow

ISBN 9781419959608
ALL RIGHTS RESERVED.
Tomorrow Copyright © 2009 Samantha Kane
Edited by Raelene Gorlinsky & Meghan Conrad.
Cover art by Syneca.

This book printed in the U.S.A. by Jasmine–Jade Enterprises, LLC.

Electronic book Publication April 2009
Trade paperback Publication August 2009

TOMORROW

ॐ

Dedication

ဆာ

This book is dedicated to my family. I immersed myself in the Hunters for Hire world while writing this, so thank you from the bottom of my heart for putting up with my spacey behavior.

This book is also dedicated to two authors to whom I owe a huge debt of gratitude. Heather Holland created the world of Bounty Hunters, Inc. and then she let me come and play in her sandbox. So thank you, Heather, for holding my hand in my first foray into science fiction. I appreciate your guidance and your trust. And TJ Michaels was an outstanding partner in creating the Super Soldiers for the series. We were so in sync with one another and had such a good time working together. This book has been a joy to write and you two ladies were a big part of that.

Glossary

❧

Aboolan: The natural inhabitants of the Aboo System and its planets who moved on after beings from Earth moved in to mine the planets for their natural resources.

Aboo System: Home of the Aboo mining planets. Crystolium-rich planets located two Smith Gates from Earth.

Aboo Two: Second planet in the Aboo System where Amalgama, the capital city of the Amalgamation of Planets, is located.

Aboolan War of 2112: War that broke out when Earthlings invaded the Aboo System for the planets' natural resources.

Abyss, The: Section of The Web where prisoners are kept until transported to another planet or prison facility.

Amalgama: The capital city and chief headquarters for the Amalgamation of Planets. A large, dome-covered city located on the planet Aboo Two.

Amalgamation of Planets: The primary governing body of the galaxy.

Amaya: Cintealios capital city on the planet of the same name.

Aurelie: The Web's day shift cook.

Azo Eta: Planet very similar to Earth, located in the Secundus System.

Bounty-hunter class: Class of small ships, specially suited to carry and operate with only a small crew. Preferred mode of transportation of the bounty hunters, hence the name.

Bounty Hunters, Inc.: Organization of bounty hunters set up and run by Ulric Vonner. They work for large fees and at their own discretion and are neither good nor bad, though they will break the law when necessary in order to bring in a bounty.

Bulkhead Disrupting Charge: Fired from a normal missile cannon, the charge attaches itself to a target's shields, weakens the shields, opens a hole through the target's defenses and fires a concentrated charge into the target's hull. Inflicts major, concentrated damage to a ship's hull.

Cintealios: The warrior race. These beings are human/humanoid and live to conquer those who are weaker. Largest opposing force to the Amalgamation.

Comm-tabs: Buttonlike communication devices that are pressed to the skin behind the ear.

Constance O'Rourke: Supply handler for The Web.

Control: Small space station situated near the Smith Gate. Controls the energy field that operates the gates and determines where a ship will emerge from the wormhole.

Copper Arrow: Copper balls that expand into shafts of corresponding light; an arrow that explodes on contact.

Devil's Pit: Seedy neighborhood on Quartus Seven where The Web is located. Location chosen specifically for its rough appearance and dangerous atmosphere.

Dexter Smith: "Dex", The Web's computer geek. If it's electronic, he can figure it out.

"Doc": Holographic doctor in The Web's medical wing. He has numerous robotic shells that he can download himself into, to perform various functions.

Executioner: Ulric Vonner's personal bounty-class cruiser.

Gold Arrow: Gold balls that expand into shafts of corresponding light and act as a claw, anchoring target to whatever solid surface is behind it, such as a wall.

Halcion Cartiere: Top commanding officer of the Interplanetary Military Forces.

Hub: The heart of The Web, located at the very center. Also contains the Conference Room where meetings are held.

Hunter Pack: Small backpack that holds more than it appears to hold.

Icsantheze Dagger: Daggers created on the planet Icsanthia. Sixty-six centimeters total length from tip of the dagger blade to the end of the handle—fifteen centimeter hilt, fifty-one centimeter blade. The blade is curved like a serpent slithering across a surface, golden in color, with pale green streaks through the blade. Handle is wrapped in emerald leather.

Interplanetary Military Forces (IMF): The military power behind the Amalgamation that works diligently to protect the Amalgamation and everything it stands for.

Intergalactic Security Agency (ISA): The job of the ISA is to explore new worlds and collect critical intelligence on any alien species discovered.

Interplanetary Senate: Body of five hundred representatives from across the galaxy. Most major systems are represented in the senate—five representatives each—with a few exceptions.

Jacobi Smith (deceased): Discovered worm holes usable for faster travel times. The worm holes became known as Smith Gates in his honor.

Jiborui: Home world of Krys Xan, the Amalgamation of Planets' leader. Exotic planet that is home to humanoid, hermaphrodite beings who are tall and slender and have very sharp minds. Key in the production of many space travel inventions that have made traveling throughout the galaxy and colonizing new worlds easier.

Jump Drives: Allows the vessel to navigate through nearby worm holes, effectively reducing travel times significantly. (Note: Control must open the gate. Also controls to which neighboring system the gate connects.)

Krys Xan: Hermaphrodite from Jurgia and leader of the Amalgamation of Planets. He presides over the Senate and all its members.

Military Sciences Lab: Based on Earth, its purpose is to create and cultivate the ultimate soldier.

Nursotics: Robotic nurses.

Orbit Wisps: Spectral, universal snitches. They barter information for energy cubes.

PHD: Personal Holographic Device. When activated, it alters the hunter's appearance, aiding in acquiring a bounty.

Plasma Cannons: Can target an enemy ship's deflector shield and will drain the energy from the shield determinant to the size of the charge. If used on a small ship without a shield, it can slowly deteriorate the ship's hull.

Quartus Seven: Planet where The Web is located. Also known as The City Planet. Seventy-five percent of the planet's surface is covered by one continuous metropolitan area. The remaining twenty-five percent of the planet is covered in water. No indigenous life forms or plant life exist here.

Replicators: Basic replication of items such as food and clothing. Complex machinery cannot be replicated, though the replicator can retrieve items from storage compartments.

Sa-Ro Five: Largest agricultural hub in the Secundus System. This planet supplies food rations to many planets, including some from neighboring systems.

Scanners: Allow the ship's crew to scan other ships, space stations or planets for signs of life.

Sealy Garrison: Constance O'Rourke's assistant. If Constance isn't available, Sealy is the man to see.

Secret Sciences Police (SSP): Formed to ensure that no one toys with time travel or biowar sciences, to protect the Amalgamation and its interests.

Secundus System: System to which Quartus Seven belongs. Similar to Earth's system, Secundus possesses nine planets, many of which are uninhabitable due to extreme atmospheric conditions, though the use of atmospheric domes enables limited habitation of some of the planets.

Silver Arrow: Silver balls that expand into shafts of corresponding light and only work as a piercing weapon.

Smith Gate: Device used to access worm holes. It is located near the largest, most advanced planet in the system and significantly cuts down travel times.

Smith Hole: Proper name for the worm holes used by Smith Gates.

Spectra-shades: Special shades used to see Orbit Wisps.

Super Soldiers: Bio-engineered super soldiers, produced on Earth as supreme fighting beings.

The Web: Base of operations for Bounty Hunters, Inc.

Tomozava: A blue fleshy vegetable that is a cross between a tomato and a *zava* vegetable.

Tranq-ring: Ring that administers a dose of tranquilizer to a bounty/person/being but does not affect the ring's wearer.

T-Sdei Delta: The party planet. Located in the Secundus System, neighboring Quartus Seven.

Ulric Vonner: President and founder of Bounty Hunters, Inc.

Vanquiguard: Wristband that, when activated, creates an energy shield to protect the wearer.

Zava: Blue, tomato-like vegetable that is indigenous to the planet Azo Eta. Also known as *tomozava*.

Zeri: Night shift cook for The Web.

Prologue

ΣΟ

Welcome to the Devil's Pit. Home sweet home. My name is Ulric Vonner and I run The Web, the base of operations for Bounty Hunters, Inc. You need criminals found? We will find them. The crime doesn't matter. Remember that we don't work for free—our fees are high, but we always catch our man, woman, or whatever species it is that you're after. Of course, catching them and bringing them in are two different things. We may be scoundrels but we aren't without conscience.

I started this business fifteen years ago. Hunters come and hunters go, but that's life. No one lasts forever, not in this business. Each of my bounty hunters has his or her reasons for turning hunter. I don't ask what they are and I don't care. They war with their inner demons, carve out a living for themselves and then they move on—provided they survive their stint as a hunter. I don't get attached and I don't mourn their loss. I learned long ago not to depend on anyone but myself. Keep your friends close and your enemies closer, which is the primary reason I deal with the Amalgamation.

Behind every great power is corruption and the Amalgamation is no exception. However, they do pay well and I'm not without my own agenda. I fight to survive and to hold on to what little I have left. Bounty Hunters, Inc. gives me a purpose and a damn good excuse to move in the circles I do. It's said a man is judged by the company he keeps, so what does that say about me? In a galaxy fraught with danger, Bounty Hunters, Inc. will strive to satisfy all our customers—if it's in our best interests to do so. Though we may wear a veneer of legal process, we are bounty hunters and we hunt those we are paid to hunt. If in the process we bring down those who would do harm to others—so much the better.

What is a bounty hunter? We're just glorified rogues trying to make the best out of what life tossed our way. The galaxy is not without its flaws or its bad seeds and that's what we're here for—to do the jobs no one else wants.

The best way to learn about Bounty Hunters, Inc. and me is to first get to know the people who work for me. They are good people in their own ways, but if you cross them, be prepared to face the consequences.

Let the hunting begin…

Chapter One

೮೧

Tie wondered if this was the low point, the nadir of his life. Surely at this point all the forces of the universe would combine to thrust him in the only direction possible—up. He dodged around a trash receptacle and jumped over a pile of offal that at one time may have been a sentient being. For the thousandth time, he roundly cursed Ulric Vonner. Tie was one of the best hunters Bounty Hunters, Inc. had ever had and Vonner sent him on a shit assignment like this. He didn't need to chase petty little troublemakers down the filthy alleys of T-Sdei Delta. He didn't need Bounty Hunters, Inc., or The Web, or any of it. He was going to go solo after this assignment. Set up as an independent contractor and only take the choice jobs. Then he wouldn't need to work for the fucking Amalgamation.

Tie broke out of the alley onto a seedy street lined with low-end casinos and even lower-end hookers. He stopped and looked up and down the street. Fuck, he hated this planet. The other hunters flocked here when they wanted to play. Tie avoided it like the plague. Didn't the people here have any clue what was going on out there? Their hedonistic, suicidal lives devoted to pleasure and vice made him sick. He made himself sick. What the fuck was he doing chasing down the goddamn rebel princess for the fucking Amalgamation? Suddenly he saw her sleek, dark head darting in and out among a rowdy crowd of drunken IMF soldiers. Perfect, just perfect. That's just what he needed, some drunk private noticing one of the Interplanetary Military Forces' most wanted deserters in their midst.

Keeping his eye on his quarry's head, Tie strolled casually but quickly toward the group. He breathed a sigh of relief when he saw her run across the street and into another alleyway. He veered off to follow her and cursed silently when one of the drunken soldiers ran into him.

"Hey, asshole!" the young recruit yelled. He gave Tie a vicious shove. "You better watch what you're doing, asshole. Don't you know who we are?"

"Sorry," Tie mumbled. He backed away, his hands open in front of him in a defenseless gesture. "My fault, man. Sorry." Killing this little fucker would seriously delay this god-awful mission and put him on the IMF radar, so as hard as it was, Tie backed down. The soldier preened under Tie's feigned cowardice.

"That's right, your fault. Don't do it again, or you'll have the IMF on your ass." The little snot was posturing and taunting him, but Tie noticed a couple of his buddies weren't so drunk and were looking at him suspiciously. He revised his opinion of the group. They were a bigger threat than he'd originally identified. It would get messy if he had to kill all...he took a second to count them, all twelve, but it could be covered up.

He didn't doubt his ability to take them all. He was a genetically enhanced lab rat, a Super Soldier, or as the rest of the galaxy referred to them, an SS. He'd been bred in a test tube to be the perfect fighting machine. He could kill them all in a matter of minutes, with a minimum of fuss and not even break a sweat. He was bred to it and trained for it. The problem was and had always been, he didn't want to do it. It was the reason he'd deserted the IMF a decade ago and the reason they were still hunting him today.

"Hey, Morgan, back off," one of the soldiers told his friend as he looked up and down Tie's 1.9 meter, heavily muscled frame. "Don't mess with him." The one who had confronted Tie turned on his friend as drunks are wont to do and Tie took the opportunity to hurry across the street and down the alley after his quarry.

Princess Cerise, rebel leader. What a joke. Tie had gotten a pretty good look at her back at the space dock. She looked like she was about fifteen at the most. She was a tiny thing, skinny and delicate-looking, with an elfin face and a close cap of short, silky, dark hair. How the hell she had become the de facto leader of the rebellion against the Amalgamation of Planets, the primary governing body of the galaxy, he didn't know. She didn't even rule her own planet, Carnelia, anymore, damn it. The military and the mining companies had taken care of that back in the Aboolan War in the 2100's. It just showed how unorganized and amateurish the rebellion was, he supposed.

She couldn't be very smart either, because he'd found her exactly where the orbit wisp had said she'd be. Ordinarily Tie didn't like using the spectral beings for information. They'd tell you damn near anything for some energy cubes. But this one had spoken true. He'd found her on T-Sdei Delta's biggest space dock, recruiting for the rebellion as bold as brass. Well, not recruiting, exactly. He'd caught her in transit, apparently on some super-secret goodwill tour of the galaxy or some shit. She'd been well guarded, but Tie was SS. He hadn't had much trouble taking out her guards. And she'd made it even simpler by running away from them when he attacked. He guessed she thought she was protecting them by leading him away. He almost hated to bring in someone so stupid who managed to annoy the hell out of the Amalgamation on a regular basis. But money was money and he had a lead on Egan that was going to require hard currency.

Egan had been his best friend in the IMF, hell, in the whole galaxy and Tie hadn't seen him for almost ten years. Tie had been searching for him ever since he'd returned to Earth to help Egan escape, only to find his friend already gone, a deserter like Tie. Tie had gone to work for Bounty Hunters, Inc. a few months later and spent all his spare time and resources looking for him.

The thought of his best friend spurred Tie on and he rounded the next corner at a full run. When her foot connected with his jaw Tie was thrown off balance. He smiled even as his back slammed into the brick wall of the alley. The little rebel had actually managed to surprise him. Not many men in the galaxy could claim that honor, but this little girl had nearly knocked him off his feet. He calmly stood away from the wall and gazed at her where she stood panting about three meters from him. "I'm afraid you're going to have to pay for that," he told her softly and watched her large, almond-shaped eyes widen in alarm.

She thought she was hidden in the shadows but because of his enhanced eyesight Tie could see every thought as it passed over her expressive face. She was exhausted. Her face was drawn, her nostrils flaring with each heavy breath. Her wide eyes were so large in her face she looked almost like a caricature. They were a pure, mesmerizing lavender, royal purple for the princess of the rebels. Against her peaches-and-cream complexion and her dark hair they shone like jewels. They also blazed with an intelligence and acuity that made Tie add a decade to his earlier guess about her age, even though her frame was small. Her clothes were the formless gray uniform worn by people who have no idea how to avoid detection. Someone really needed to tell them that that was a giveaway in itself.

"Come, little rebel, come to me," Tie called out teasingly, as if she were a wary cat. "There's no need for all this running. We both know I'm going to catch you." Tie watched in admiration as anger stole over her features. No fear for the intrepid rebel princess.

"Fuck you," she snarled and, quick as the cat he had likened her to, she spun and raced off down the alley.

Tie laughed out loud. This assignment was proving to be entertaining after all.

Cerise's heart felt as if it were trying to pound its way out of her chest. She was so damn tired. Who was this guy? He was the best to hunt her so far. In the past, other hunters had been easy to escape with Regan's help and her guards. But not this one. This guy had been one step behind her the whole way, never letting her rest, never letting her get her bearings. He'd chased her across half the damn planet, it seemed. And she shouldn't have run from the guards, she could see that now. That had been stupid. But he'd come out of nowhere and it had been obvious to Cerise that he outclassed Regan's best bodyguards. She wasn't going to get them killed.

She couldn't believe how he'd taken that kick to the jaw. She may be small, but she knew how to take a man down. Regan had seen to it. That kick should have knocked him out. Instead he'd barely lost his footing. Cerise had been worried before that kick. After it she was downright scared. Then he'd taunted her. Taunted her! There was no way she was going to let him catch her. No way in hell. Even as she thought it, however, she could hear his footfalls growing closer, practically feel his breath on her neck.

Cerise felt a burst of energy sweep through her when she saw the bright lights of another crowded street at the end of the alley. She'd try to lose him again in the crowd. She was relatively nondescript for all that the planetary legends had her as beautiful as an avenging angel. She was short, skinny, looked half her age and dressed as plainly as possible. She could blend into a crowd easily, despite Regan's laughing assurances that, indeed, she stood out from any crowd. The pirate didn't want her traveling around, trying to build support for the resistance. If Regan had his way he'd lock her up like a porcelain doll and only take her out to wave to the crowd when they demanded a look at "their" princess. But this time she hadn't taken no for an answer. She'd threatened to sneak out without Regan's help, or her guards, and she'd meant it. Regan tried locking her up on his ship *The Rebel Bounty*, but he forgot he was the one who trained her—on his ship. The fifth escape attempt nearly succeeded and he'd had no choice but to agree to let her go out and meet some of the resistance leaders in this quadrant of the galaxy. Regan only controlled the resistance here in Secundus and the neighboring systems and even that was still a questionable control, although they grew stronger every day. And that was why Cerise had demanded he let her take a more active role. She was trying to help, damn it.

Cerise burst from the alley just as she felt a hand swipe down her back and across her ass, trying to grab her. He'd just missed her! She flew across the sidewalk, scattering the crowd and jumped onto the hood of a hovercraft, then off the other side, not even taking the time to go around it. She heard the thundering thud of his booted feet as he followed her over the vehicle. Several voices in the crowd called out after them angrily.

"Little rebel," he called tauntingly from behind her, his voice even. He wasn't even tired yet. Was he an android? She'd never seen one so convincingly human, but no man was this inexhaustible. Cerise felt her throat close with the fear choking her. He was going to catch her! This time she wouldn't get away. Just as the defeatist thoughts entered her mind, Cerise saw what she'd been looking for—a resistance safe house. There was one on almost every planet in the galaxy and T-Sdei Delta was no exception. There were actually several here and Regan had made her memorize their locations before he allowed her to come. The safe houses provided shelter and protection to members of the resistance who needed it and sometimes more, lending money and weapons if the situation warranted it. She'd thought it was a waste of time, but she'd done it to make Regan happy. She spared one disgruntled moment to think about the thanks she owed him. Again.

She hated to jeopardize the people inside, but there were probably several of them and only one hunter. Surely they could help her escape him. She raced for the small, brick building fronted by a little Aboolan restaurant.

"Don't!" he called out as she fell against the side of the building and yanked open the door to her right. "Don't do it!" She ignored him and raced inside.

The interior was dark, but not dark enough to hide the worn furnishings and seedy atmosphere. The few patrons at the tables looked up at her in surprise even as the woman working the credit machine started toward her.

"Help!" Cerise gasped, "Help me!" She didn't slow down as she barreled between tables toward the door in the back. "Stop him!" She didn't need to tell them who since she heard the door slam back against its hinges right behind her and those same thundering steps that had dogged her across the city followed her across the restaurant.

Cerise threw up her hands and thrust the back door open as she ran through it into a large room. One side was devoted to an industrial type kitchen, for the restaurant no doubt, and the other was clearly used as a dining room for family, staff and the temporary inhabitants of the safe house. The table there was full and half of the chairs were occupied by children.

"Princess!" one of the men at the table gasped as he stood up. Before Cerise could speak the kitchen door flew open again and the hunter came stomping in. There was nowhere else to run and Cerise spun around to confront him.

He was tall. She had gotten a brief impression of his height in the alley before, but hadn't realized how truly big he was until he stood before her dwarfing everything around him. He was even taller than Regan. His chest and shoulders were massive. Encased in a tight-fitting black shirt, his muscles rippled with every even breath. His huge hands looked as if they could break bones with minimal effort. When Cerise glanced at his legs her first thought was, *no wonder I couldn't outrun him*. His legs seemed endless, wrapped in their black leggings and knee-high black combat boots. Her heart leapt with hope when she saw he was unarmed. Her eyes darted up to his face and for a brief moment she felt a surge of astonished admiration. If only she had met this man under different circumstances. He was gorgeous, every inch of him. While his body was clearly a finely tuned machine, his face could only have been painted by the angels. All angles and square jaw, with wide, well-defined lips and deep-set eyes under heavy blonde brows—he was the stuff young girls' dreams were made of. Then he ruined the illusion by speaking.

"If you're done taking inventory of all my assets, Princess, we can get on with the capture part of our day." She almost didn't catch his words as she watched his wavy, caramel-colored hair swing against his shoulders as he surveyed the room.

"Capture my ass," she spat at him after his words sank in.

He stopped looking around the room and turned his eyes on her. They were a pale brown color and didn't look quite right in his face. "That's the plan, your royal rebelness."

Cerise could have bitten her own tongue off. She wasn't very good at snappy comebacks, although the entire crew of *The Rebel Bounty* had been trying to teach her. Regan said she was just too nice, as if it were a liability.

"Stop him," she told the men who had gathered behind her. As one, they moved forward to confront the hunter and he took a step back. Cerise smirked.

"I don't want to hurt any of you," he told them seriously. "I just want the princess. Give her to me and we can all walk away from this. Resist and I'll be the only who walks away alive."

The men hesitated at his words. He sounded so sure of himself even Cerise was nearly convinced of his invincibility. Then logic overruled. "He's bluffing," she told them, narrowing her eyes at him. "He can't take all of us."

Those disturbing eyes met hers again and Cerise shivered. "Are you sure of that, Princess? I know you don't want to be responsible for the death of any of these men. Do you? Or is everything I've heard about you wrong? Do you only care about yourself?"

Cerise was in a panic. He was right! She wouldn't be able to live with herself if any of these men died protecting her. She

24

tried to bluff. "They are willing to give their lives for the resistance."

He nodded as if in understanding. "Yes, but that's not the situation here, is it? I'm not fighting against the resistance. I just came for you." He sounded so calm and rational.

"It's the same thing," growled the man beside Cerise, the one who had recognized her when she first came through the door. She had a feeling she'd met him before, but couldn't be sure where or when. And yet this virtual stranger was ready to die for her? That didn't seem right. "No, wait—" she began.

"Leave my da alone!" a little voice yelled out as a small boy raced between the legs of a man on her left and threw himself against the hunter's legs. The boy gave a mighty kick to the hunter's leg and then fell down with a cry as he grabbed his foot.

"Kevin!" the man who'd recognized Cerise called out and he moved as if to grab the boy but the hunter was too quick. He reached down and plucked the boy from the floor, wrapping an arm around him so his little arms were trapped against his sides, his tiny back against the hunter's chest. A woman behind Cerise gave a strangled scream.

"Quite a little warrior you're raising here," the hunter drawled conversationally. His casual, relaxed tone made the hair on Cerise's nape rise.

"Leave the boy alone," she ordered him. He raised his eyebrow delicately.

"Why? What do you think I'm going to do to him?" Was that anger underlying his words, or annoyance?

"Please don't hurt him, please," the woman behind Cerise begged. Someone shushed her. Cerise didn't dare turn to look. She and the hunter were now engaged in a very dangerous standoff and she couldn't let her guard down.

"What do you want?" Cerise asked, trying to keep her tone as even as his.

"You," he said simply and Cerise felt a chill slither down her spine.

"I can pay you the bounty myself," she told him, praying that Regan would come up with the money. More often than not he found her a pain in the ass and told her so, but she thought he liked her a little, enough not to see her dead.

"It's not about the money." The hunter was standing still, ignoring the boy's struggles.

Cerise felt her traitorous heart begin a frantic tattoo. "Then what is it about?"

"It's about bringing in the bounty. It's about honoring my promises and fulfilling my obligations. It's about freedom and dreams and things you don't need to know about. But it all starts with you. I need you. And I will get you, make no mistake." His voice at last showed emotion. It seethed with rage and frustration.

Tie was furious. He never let himself get into these situations. How the hell had he let it happen this time? For Christ's sake, she thought he was holding the boy hostage. He was sick that she believed he would harm an innocent child. They all believed it. He had become the very thing he'd run from, the stuff of nightmares. He'd left the IMF, left Earth, left Egan so he wouldn't become the monster they all believed him to be. And now here he was, playing on their fears so he could turn this beautiful, courageous girl over to the Amalgamation. He hated himself at that moment. This was it. This was the low point, please, God, let this be the low point because he couldn't take much more, not even for Egan.

He'd played her with his little speech. From what little he knew about her—he hadn't done much research, she'd been so easy to find—she considered herself a shining example. She seemed like the type who always fulfilled her obligations, who took her responsibilities seriously like a good idealistic rebel princess should. He could tell by the look on her face he'd hit his mark.

"Let the boy go and I'll go with you." He should have felt elated at her capitulation, but instead felt curiously deflated.

"You first, then I release the boy." He was so goddamned convincing he scared himself. By the look on their faces no one knew he'd let them kill him before he'd harm one hair on the little man's head. Good. It meant he wouldn't have to take on da there, either. He had no desire to harm the boy's father, or any of these men.

The princess began slowly walking toward him and in spite of his better judgment, even as he felt the thrill of victory, he was filled with admiration for her courage. She was frightened, but she was holding her head high and trying not to show it.

"No, Princess!" One of the men grabbed her, not the boy's father. "You can't! If they capture you...what will we do? We need you. Without you the resistance will die. With you we finally have something to rally around."

She shook him off. "No, I'm not worth the boy's life. I'm just one person. Someone will rise to take my place. The resistance isn't about one person, it's about an idea, about freedom." She looked at Tie, captured his eyes. "It's about a dream. And perhaps the hunter is right. Perhaps it does start with me. Perhaps my death will be the spark needed to start the conflagration that will destroy the Amalgamation."

She meant every word. She was ready to die for her resistance. She was so young, so full of idealism it made Tie's heart ache. He almost let her go then. Almost dropped the boy and walked away. But something stopped him. Something told him he had to take this girl. That he was part of something bigger and that this path was where both he and she needed to go.

Tie considered himself a follower of philosopher Conor Stanislaus. In Stanislaus' most famous book, *Finding My Way*, the philosopher had written about these moments. He'd called them signposts. Moments that told you where to go even if you didn't know why. To ignore them was to court disaster. Tie didn't court disaster lightly.

Tie raised his free hand and held it out to the rebel leader. Without hesitation she stepped forward and took it. The electricity that raced through Tie at her touch confirmed his decision. He slowly wrapped his arm around her in the same way he'd immobilized the boy and then gently he let the boy down. When the child's feet hit the floor he ran forward into a woman's arms. She must be his mother. Tie watched the tearful reunion with curiosity. A mother's love was foreign to him.

Once the boy was free the men turned aggressively back to Tie and the girl.

"No," she told them calmly. "You know what to do."

The boy's father nodded. "Consider it done."

Tie wondered idly, as he backed out the kitchen door holding the princess, just what surprises she had planned for him. He felt himself grinning. He couldn't wait to find out. For the first time in a very long time he felt his feet were firmly on his path.

Chapter Two

ഌ

Cerise tried again to rattle the bars on her small holding cell. That damn hunter had dragged her across T-Sdei Delta and brought her onto this ship without another word after she'd surrendered herself to him. You'd think he'd appreciate the gesture a little more. She was hungry and tired and he kept ignoring her demands. She kicked the bars again in frustration. They were as thick as that hunter's head and hardly moved, even though she kicked with all her might. He could at least have a prison cell with bars that rattled, the damn man.

"You're going to break your foot, Your Royal Highness, and that might affect my bounty." The voice came from the shadows surrounding a hatchway on the right. Cerise was pretty sure it led to the bridge since she'd felt them moving not long after he locked her in here and marched through the hatch earlier. She was proud of the fact she didn't jump with surprise when he spoke, since she hadn't known he was there.

"Don't call me that," she ground out. "And I'm hungry. Aren't there some kind of rules that say you have to feed me? Or is even that humanitarian consideration too much for the Amalgamation?"

The hunter straightened from where he'd been leaning negligently in the doorway. "I'm not the Amalgamation. I'm the guy the Amalgamation hires when they're unable to do their own dirty work."

"Marvelous," Cerise sneered. "Your mother must be so proud."

The hunter looked unperturbed. "I haven't got one. A mother, that is. Never have. So that pretty much relieves me from any obligation to please one."

29

Against her will, Cerise felt a stab of empathy. "My mother died when I was young too. I'm sorry."

The hunter smiled pleasantly. "You misunderstand. I never had a mother, literally. You're looking at an example of the best that science can produce in a lab."

Cerise gasped. He *was* an android! She was shocked. He seemed so human. "You're an android." She shook her head. "I guess I should have known. No human could have chased me like you did and not be affected by it."

The hunter shook his head and looked at her with disappointment. "Sorry, no circuits in here." He tapped his chest. "Just flesh and blood. I'm a genuine test-tube baby."

Cerise was even more shocked. "I didn't think that was allowed, except for Amalgamation scientists and those SS drones the IMF grows on Earth."

The hunter just laughed. "Well I'm certainly no drone, so somebody else must be doing it."

Cerise was intrigued. Everything and anything that defied the Amalgamation could be useful to the resistance. "Who gr…"she paused in consternation. What exactly was the term for someone who was grown in a lab? "Who created you?"

The hunter nodded approvingly. "Good word, Princess. Created. Sounds better than grew. Grew sounds too much like I'm some kind of mold."

Cerise couldn't stop the lift of her eyebrows and the hunter laughed again. "Reserving judgment, are you, Princess?"

Cerise gritted her teeth. "Please do not call me that."

The hunter pulled up a chair until it was just out of reach of the bars, the back of the chair facing her. He sat down, straddling the seat with his arms across the back. He looked at her for several minutes and Cerise became self-conscious.

"What?" she asked, annoyed that he'd won their little standoff, again.

He grinned at her. "Why don't you like being called Princess?"

"Because I'm not a princess." Cerise hated having this discussion.

He looked surprised. "According to all my sources and half the galaxy you are. Carnelian royalty."

Cerise gritted her teeth. "I've never been to Carnelia. My family was dethroned almost three hundred years ago. I grew up poor and was raised just like anyone else. I look like your typical space mutt. It pleases people to call me Princess and in the right situations I don't object."

"And this isn't the right situation?" he asked with a lopsided grin. Cerise had to fight not to respond to it.

"Hardly," she said in her best royal tones. He just laughed.

Cerise sighed and moved back to sit on the cot in the corner of her cell. "So, hunter, have you got a name?"

"Why, Princess, I didn't know you cared." His tone was mocking as he rested his chin on his stacked hands along the chair back.

Cerise snorted. "Don't flatter yourself. I won't be calling it out during my next orgasm. I'm just tired of calling you hunter."

He looked positively startled when she said orgasm, as if he was shocked she knew the word. Cerise smiled for the first time since she'd caught sight of him at the space dock that morning. "Shocked ya, did I?" she asked smugly.

"The idea of you having an orgasm? Sure as hell did shock me. You don't look old enough or woman enough to have one."

His casually spoken put-down deflated Cerise's smugness. She fought to keep the hurt out of her voice. "I'm more woman than you can handle. You wouldn't have caught me today if I hadn't surrendered." Even as she said it Cerise knew it was a lie. It had only been a matter of time before he caught her. He was too good and she was too inexperienced.

He laughed because he knew it was a lie too. "How old are you, anyway?" he asked companionably. Cerise almost answered automatically. Oh, he was good at this interrogation thing. She'd have to watch her step with him.

"You first." Cerise settled back against the wall behind the cot. "You tell me your name, I'll tell you my age."

He cocked his head to the side and regarded her skeptically for a moment. God he was gorgeous. Too bad he was the enemy.

"You know I can just go pull up the information on the computer."

"Then why don't you?" Cerise managed to sound uninterested but he just answered with another of his killer lopsided smiles.

"Because I'm trying to figure you out."

His answer surprised her and she let it show. "Why? What's in it for you?"

He shrugged those massive shoulders and she felt her mouth dry up as the light caught the ripple of his muscles under the skintight fabric of his shirt. She tore her eyes away and looked up into his face only to find him watching her smugly. She frowned at him and his smile grew.

"Nothing. Everything. I'm trying to figure that out too." She was confused by his response. What was he talking about?

"Are you going to let me go?" she asked tentatively, hoping against hope that was what he meant. If she could convince him how important she was to the resistance —

"No." His flat tone and quick denial dashed her hopes. "No, I'm supposed to turn you in. I can feel it. Our paths have merged here and they lead to the Amalgamation. I don't know what it means, but we've got to play it out."

"Paths? What the hell are you talking about?" Cerise just shook her head. "My path is with the resistance. Your path is with the Amalgamation. Mine leads to freedom and yours to imprisonment and slavery."

"No." He spoke so quietly Cerise almost didn't hear him. "No, there has to be more."

Cerise sighed, but had no chance to answer.

"Finnegan," the hunter said, "my name is Finnegan."

Tie gave her the alias without thought. It was the name he'd been using for almost a decade, ever since he'd escaped the IMF. It was who he was now—Finnegan, bounty hunter and hunted. If he thought too much about it he got a headache.

"Twenty-five." Cerise Chessienne, heir to the Carnelian throne, spoke from the shadows of her cot. Her voice was light, feminine, slightly husky. As soon as he'd heard her speak today he'd known she was older than she looked. No child had a voice like that. It made his skin feel alive. He didn't want that. She may be a part of his path but she was definitely not in his plans. He was close to finding Egan, he knew it. He didn't need the deceptively fragile-looking princess interfering.

"So, Finnegan," she asked quietly, "are you going to feed me? Or have you decided to deliver me to the Amalgamation weak with hunger and unable to defend myself? That sounds like something an Amalgamation drone would do."

Her words grated, again. She didn't even know she was hitting all his weak spots. He'd fought so hard not to be one of those drones and yet life and circumstances, had put him back on that path. Why? He was trying to find his way, but god damn it, why did his way always seem to be this one? He stood up abruptly and saw her jerk in surprise.

"I'll feed you, but as long as you can talk you're anything but defenseless." He was talking about that voice of hers, but she thought he meant her words.

"I'm not exactly dangerous in a battle of words, Finnegan," she said, standing up and walking over to the bars of the cell as he moved over to the galley. He hit the button to slide open the concealing wall and the ship's small galley was revealed. He couldn't cook a full course meal on it but he could rummage up enough food to hold off starvation. "I know I'm not good at thinking on my feet. I do all right, but it will hardly protect me on an Amalgamation prison hulk."

Tie didn't want to think of her on one of the Amalgamation's huge, stinking prison hulks—nameless, faceless, defenseless. She was right. She had no way to defend herself there. He forced the concern out of his mind. She wasn't his responsibility. He programmed some basic rations into the replicator. It was hardly royal cuisine, but something told him she wouldn't complain.

"Why does the Amalgamation want you so much?" The question had puzzled him when Vonner had told him the bounty on her, but after meeting her he was even more mystified. She was brave, that was for sure, but not a great leader. People didn't follow her because she was a brilliant strategist, or a forceful presence. They followed her because of her birthright and her beauty and her kindness. None of those had ever won a war. So why were they so worried about her? What did the Amalgamation know that Tie didn't?

"I don't know," she answered evasively. "I guess they just don't like their displaced royalty running around badmouthing them."

Tie laughed. "You do more than badmouth them. It's a poorly kept secret that the rebellion is responsible for the recent explosions and shut downs at several crystolium mines."

"I had nothing to do with that." She sounded so earnest that Tie believed her.

"But I'll bet you know who did." He turned to face her and she wouldn't look at him. "Why do you hate the Amalgamation so much?"

"Why do you like it so much?" she asked, irritated.

Tie turned back to the replicator. "I don't. Can't stand it, actually. It's a corrupt, inefficient, militaristic oligarchy that has no care for the population which has to live under its dictatorship." He looked over his shoulder to find the princess staring at him in shock.

"Then," she sputtered, "how can you work for them?"

Tie looked away with a shrug. "They pay very well and it amuses me to let the Amalgamation periodically pay my salary."

"That's a ridiculous excuse for supporting a government that you hate. You should be using your abilities to help destroy them, not protect them!"

She sounded so angry, but Tie just couldn't match her fire. Once, long ago, he'd felt the way she did. But time and experience had taught him to temper his rage, to mind his own business and let the status quo alone. Now the most important thing was protecting his anonymity and preserving his freedom. He looked at her, genuinely curious as to her motives. "What do you hope to accomplish with this rebellion?"

"Freedom, the right of every Amalgamation citizen to live as they wish, to control their destiny and the destiny of the galaxy. To end this reign of terror and subjugation and to reintroduce the displaced millions to their home worlds. To end the forced enslavement of entire populations in the Amalgamation's never-ending hunger for crystolium." She was fervent in her dedication and for a moment Tie could see the woman the galaxy was pinning their hopes on.

"Oh, is that all?" Tie asked dryly. "Well, good luck with that." She sighed in exasperation at his sarcastic response but dropped the subject.

He walked over to the cell with a tray of food and motioned her back from the bars. She obeyed and he waved a hand in front of the lock sensor. The door popped open and he moved inside. The princess leaned back against the wall on the side of the cell and watched him.

"What's to stop me from killing you and waving your dead hand in front of that little box?" she asked curiously.

"Me," Tie told her without even looking in her direction.

"Oh yeah, right," she agreed, "that'd do it."

Tie had to grin at the resignation in her voice. At least she accepted his physical superiority. It would have gone hard on her and been hard for him if she hadn't. He turned to find her watching his ass. That made him grin too. She couldn't seem to stop herself from checking him out at every opportunity. He liked it. That he couldn't seem to stop himself from doing the same to her he didn't like. More than once during their earlier conversation he'd found himself wondering just what she looked like under those shapeless clothes. When he'd wrapped his arm around her today he'd felt how small and delicate she was, but he'd also felt the purely feminine indentation at her waist that flowed into soft hips. He bet she had small, perfect breasts, barely enough to fill his palm, sweet and soft and topped with pert little nipples. With shock he felt his cock growing hard for the little rebel. Who'd have thought it? This day was just full of surprises.

"Eat," he told her as he set the tray down on the end of the cot. She obediently walked over and sat down next to it. He wondered how long the obedience would last and exactly what she was planning.

She looked askance at the food on the tray. "What is it?" She picked up the flat, dull utensil and poked at a gray-brown blob.

"Food." He ignored her snort of disgust as he walked back out to the chair he'd been using and dragged it into the cell. As he sat down again he saw her take a tentative bite. After her first taste she shrugged and made a funny face but chewed and swallowed it.

"It looks disgusting, but it actually doesn't taste bad." She took another bite.

"So close your eyes," Tie told her and she smiled at him while she chewed. The smile brought out a little dimple in her right cheek. He'd noticed it earlier. It was the icing on the cake. She was officially the cutest princess he'd ever laid eyes on. Technically she was the only princess he'd ever laid eyes on, but he was willing to bet she would be the cutest if another one suddenly showed up.

She happily ate the rest of the food, unaware of Tie's growing admiration. He was a little awed by her ability to adapt to her present circumstances. Most women, hell, most men, would be devastated by her predicament. Captured, imprisoned, being transported to her death for a bounty and she still managed to eat basic rations with a smile.

"What are you up to?" he asked suspiciously. The princess looked startled by his abrupt question and then guilt flashed across her face before she could control her reaction.

"Uh huh," Tie nodded sagely. "I knew it. Confess now and I won't have to bring out the thumbscrews."

Her brows knitted in consternation. "Nothing! I'm not up to anything, I swear. What are thumbscrews?"

"An ancient method of torture," he informed her ominously and her face paled. It was Tie's turn to snort. "Oh, for Christ's sake, I'm not going to torture you. I can read you like a book. Whatever you're planning, forget it. There is no way you can take me down and no way are you getting off this ship unless you do."

She dropped the eating utensil on the tray angrily. "Well you can't just expect me to lie down and snivel my way to wherever you're taking me! It's my duty as a prisoner to try to escape."

He shook his head is disgust. "You watch too many vids. In real life, the helpless rebel princesses are exactly that— helpless. They sit quietly in their little cell and don't plot

37

useless schemes to escape their captor, who turns out to be a good guy just doing his job."

The princess stared at him in disbelief. "The good guy? You think you're the good guy? I've got news for you Finnegan, you're not. Only in your dreams."

Tie got up and carried his chair out of the cell. When he returned he picked up her tray, deliberately crowding her as he did so. He bent over, so close he could feel the heat of her cheek next to his lips. "Princess, you are too delicate to know what I dream about."

She turned the tables on him in the blink of an eye. She turned her face to his and their lips brushed. She didn't pull back from the contact before she answered him, the look in her eyes as they met his sending a shiver of pure lust down his spine. "Try me."

Chapter Three

ॐ

"What's the name of your ship?" Cerise asked idly from her cot as Finnegan did his best to ignore her. He was sitting over by the galley reading something.

Last night they had almost shared a kiss. Technically she supposed they had kissed. Right after she'd dared him, for one glorious moment, she'd felt the pressure of his lips on hers, his soft, hot, damp lips. It had been heaven, for about one second. Then he'd pulled back with a curse and stomped out of the cell. He'd refused to answer her when she yelled after him and eventually she'd gone to sleep.

This morning he was surly as hell. He'd stomped all over the ship, cursing anything and everything and had practically thrown her breakfast at her through the cell door, as if he was afraid to get too close to her. She'd tease him about it if she weren't so afraid he'd rip her head off.

Because of his bad mood she was shocked when he actually answered her question.

"The *Tomorrow*," he answered tersely.

It all clicked in Cerise's head then—Finnegan, the *Tomorrow*, paths merging. "Conor Stanislaus," she said. Finnegan's head came up sharply and he looked at her. She began to quote from Stanislaus' most famous work.

"Finnegan begin again. But like the average man, Finnegan had always said tomorrow, I'll begin again tomorrow. Until one day he woke up with the realization that there was no average among them, they were all extraordinary and tomorrow had arrived."

"You've read *Finding My Way*?" Finnegan asked suspiciously.

Cerise looked at him with disdain. "Clearly." Finnegan had the grace to look chagrined at his comment. "But I didn't start naming things after it."

Finnegan rose from the table angrily. "It's a great book, an amazing book. Stanislaus captured the feeling of imprisonment we all have, the primal urge to break free and forge our own path."

"Says the man who's taking me to prison," Cerise said dryly.

"I have my reasons," Finnegan growled from between clenched teeth.

Cerise stood up and stalked angrily over to the cell bars to confront him as he stood on the other side. "Stanislaus clearly says we cannot infringe on the freedoms of others in order to follow our own path."

"I thought you didn't like the book." Finnegan spoke slowly as he snapped off each word.

"You are infringing on my freedom," Cerise growled back as she clutched the bars and pressed her face against them.

Finnegan stepped closer until their faces were but a breath apart. "This is the path you chose, little princess. Unpleasant consequences are always a possibility on the paths we choose."

"Unpleasant for everyone but you!" Cerise yelled as she threw herself away from the bars in frustration.

"You have no idea how unpleasant I am finding this mission," Finnegan said, his voice low and vibrating with emotion.

When Cerise swung back around to look at him she saw him wave his hand in front of the sensor and push the cell door open. The look on his face made her take a step back.

Tie was so frustrated he could barely think straight. That kiss last night had nearly destroyed the control he was so famous for. It wasn't even a kiss really, just a press of lips against lips. But her lips had been so soft and pliant, with a sweet dampness that had seeped into his veins even as he'd stormed out of her cell. He hadn't slept a wink last night. He'd lain in his bunk and listened to every breath she took. He had turned off his auditory filter, the small chip embedded in his brain that allowed him to muffle his enhanced hearing to normal levels, just so he could hear her heartbeat in the adjoining cabin. When he closed his eyes he saw her face as it had looked when he'd kissed her. When he opened his eyes he could smell the soft floral of her perfume mixed with the womanly musk of her natural scent. It was a heady fragrance and he had no way to muffle it, no way to stifle his reaction to it, his reaction to her.

Why? Why her? Why did he react so strongly to this headstrong little rebel? She was nothing like the women he'd bedded over the last decade. Most of them had been very experienced, full-figured women. Women who were a handful in bed with large breasts and big expectations. Not princesses out to save the galaxy, innocent and so tiny she made him feel like a clumsy, lumbering giant, afraid to touch her for fear of hurting her.

"I don't want this," he growled at her, stopping just inside the cell door.

"Don't want what?" she whispered. She was frozen in place, her too-large eyes swallowing up her face.

"This," he said roughly as he gestured between them in frustration.

He felt her gaze like a caress as she looked down at the bulge between his legs, obvious in the tight leggings he wore.

"You'd better tell him that," she said a little tremulously.

Tie shoved a hand through his hair impatiently. "You push and push, don't you? One minute you're the innocent princess, the next you're a temptress out to drive me mad. How do you do it? And why the hell do I like it?"

"I am what I am." Her voice was stronger, more sure.

"What the hell does that mean?" Tie placed both hands on his hips and glared at her. At the gesture he saw her pupils dilate and her breathing grow slightly erratic. He looked down and saw that with his legs spread wide and his hands pulling the material of his leggings tight the size of his erection was obvious. The fact that his hard cock made her aroused wasn't helping him gain control.

He turned and walked quickly over to the peg on the wall that held her clothes. Tie pulled them off and threw them at her. They landed on the deck by her feet. "Get dressed," he ordered.

He'd let her use the head this morning and she'd showered. When she came out she wore nothing but a flimsy little tank top and a scrap of material that were obviously supposed to be underclothes when they grew up. They had a long way to go. She was a willowy dream come true in the almost clothes. He'd thought her tiny, but that was compared to him, he supposed. Her naked legs seemed long and lean, her hips small but shapely, her breasts the exact way he had imagined them, lovely and small enough to tuck into the palm of his hand. Her nipples had been hard from the shower and he'd nearly groaned out loud. Instead he'd silently escorted her back to her cell and marched off to the bridge after locking her in.

Tie had expected her to get dressed and when he came back an hour later and she was still unclothed he had almost turned around and walked back out. But the look on her face indicated she expected him to do just that, so he'd stayed. It was self-torture to not look at her where she sat on her cot, her back to the bulkhead and one leg stretched out over the side while the other was bent and her chin rested on her knee. The position gave him a perfect view of her nearly naked pussy every time he stole a glance at her. He hadn't tasted one bite of the breakfast he'd forced down.

"Why? Is there a dress code for Amalgamation prisoners? If this is to be my last day as a free woman I want to dress as I like." Her tone was belligerent, challenging.

"There's a dress code on my ship. Put them on." Tie was losing his patience.

"No." Her answer was defiant and when she turned away with a flounce and headed back for her cot, Tie's control snapped. He grabbed her arm and swung her back to face him so hard she spun around and slammed into him. Her hands automatically came up to rest on his chest and the heat of them burned through his thin shirt. Her startled countenance quickly turned to heated intent.

"Don't," he rasped, not sure which one of them he was talking to.

"I have to," she whispered. Then she rose on her tiptoes and, wrapping an arm around his neck, buried her hand in the hair on the back of his head and pulled his face down to hers. When she pressed her lips to his Tie tried to remind himself why this was such a bad idea, but he couldn't remember one single reason.

The warmth of her lips was like the sun on his face on a summer day and the press of her body to his as she leaned closer made his skin actually ache for her touch. He slid his tongue along her lips, almost afraid to taste her. Her mouth opened to him and he slowly swept inside. She tasted fresh and clean and sweet, like ripe fruit at its peak. The taste of her was so intoxicating he knew he'd never tasted anything like it and that he would crave it from this moment forward. Her kiss was untutored but passionate and Tie reveled in the certainty that she had never kissed another man like this. With a groan he wrapped his arms around her and pulled her tightly to him. It wasn't enough. It would never be enough.

The magnitude of his reaction to her was alarming. He'd never known such hunger for anyone. Even as his mind screamed at him to let her go, he thrust his tongue into her mouth, drinking her in, feasting on her taste, her touch, her reaction to him. From her moans and the way she trembled in his arms Tie knew she wanted him as much as he wanted her. The knowledge pushed him, drove him deeper into the madness of desire that consumed them both.

Finnegan lifted her off her feet and Cerise quickly wrapped both arms around his neck, clinging to him. God, she hadn't known, she hadn't a clue that it was like this. This was desire, this was lust, this all-consuming need to taste and touch and possess, be possessed. She wanted to melt into him, to feel him inside her, to know him, to own him. One of his hands came to rest on her ass and he lifted her hips into him. She could feel the press of his hard cock against her, but it wasn't right, it wasn't where she wanted it, where her body clamored for it. She wrapped her legs around his waist and then, ah, God, yes, there, the heat of his erection was branding her pussy, pressing on her sensitive clit. She had to pull away from the kiss, from his sweet lips, because her moan of pleasure couldn't be contained.

"Finnegan, yes, please," she cried out softly, rubbing against his cock, desperate for it, for him. She blindly sought his mouth again, but he pulled back, breathing heavily. She thought irrelevantly that he was breathing harder now than he had been after chasing her on T-Sdei Delta.

"Finnegan," she moaned, trying to pull his head down, but he resisted and she felt her legs slide down and off his hips as he lowered her to the floor. "No," she moaned, feeling the loss of that hard pressure between her thighs.

She opened her eyes and looked up at him. He was staring at her heatedly, clearly fighting the desire he still felt. She could see the moment he won the battle. His eyes hardened imperceptibly and his breathing became more even.

"No," she whispered, missing him already, missing the way he made her feel, missing his uncontrollable desire for her.

"Get dressed," he said softly, "please."

Tie turned and walked slowly out of her cell without looking back. Thank God she'd called him Finnegan. It had brought back the reality of their situation. He was a hunter and she his prisoner. This passion that burned between them was merely physical. She didn't know him and truthfully he didn't know her. Just as the image he presented to the world was false, the image of the beloved princess she projected could be a lie as well. He would never know. No matter how he longed to tell her his secrets and learn hers, the reality was they didn't have the time or the luxury. He ignored the ache in his chest at the thought as he once again sought refuge on the bridge.

Two hours later he returned to the galley beside the holding cell. Cerise hadn't spoken a word to him as he'd left that morning and he hadn't heard her calling to him as she had last night. She'd been so quiet he couldn't stand the suspense any longer. He had to check on her and make sure she was all right.

She was lying on her side facing the bulkhead, her back to him. She still wasn't dressed. It looked as if she'd crawled onto the cot and curled up into a ball right after he left and hadn't moved since.

"Princess?" he asked, hoping to get a reaction. It wasn't the one he expected.

"Will they rape me, do you suppose?" she asked conversationally as she rolled over onto her back and stared at the ceiling.

"What?" Tie was shaken by the question. He'd successfully avoided thinking about what would happen to her once he turned her over to the Amalgamation. He knew what they would do to her in order to get information about the rebellion from her. Rape was only one of the weapons in their torture arsenal. His mind rebelled at the thought of

Cerise being abused in such a way by some Amalgamation pig, probably while his buddies watched.

"No," he barked.

Cerise looked at him in surprise. "Really? That's not what I heard." She pushed herself up to a sitting position at the head of the bed, her back against the wall. "I can't really believe everything you say, of course, since Finnegan isn't your real name, is it?" She shook her head. "How stupid of me. I mean, I made the Stanislaus connection, but never took the next step." She turned to look at him. "What is it? Your real name, I mean."

He just stared at her, his frustration growing as he fought the urge to tell her.

"Not going to give it up, huh? Who are you hiding from?" She cocked her head to the side and he felt the intensity of her regard as a physical push. He couldn't stop the small twitch in his cheek at her intuitive assumption.

She nodded. "Yep. That's what I thought." She sighed and leaned her head back against the wall. "I'm sorry. I'm really screwing this up for you, aren't I? This whole paths merging isn't what it's cracked up to be."

Tie walked over the bars of the cell and waited until she turned to look at him again. "I will not let them rape you, Princess."

She smiled sadly. "Well, it's a nice thought, whatever your name is, but you won't be there, will you? You can put in a good word for me before you leave, for what it's worth." He winced and she looked wryly amused. "Can't do that either, huh? Flying under Amalgamation sensors, are you? How can you work for them?"

"I assume you don't mean philosophically." Tie sighed. "Technically, Bounty Hunters, Inc. works for them. That's who they pay and then I get my share." Tie wished she'd get up and come to the bars again. He wanted to be close to her, if only for a moment.

46

"Clever. And how you must laugh at them behind their backs." She gave him a genuine smile. "I know I would."

"Cerise." She looked at him questioningly. He didn't know what he wanted. He just wanted her. He needed to touch her. He stretched his hand through the bars and beckoned her over. "Come here."

She looked at him for several seconds and then seemed to come to a decision. She got up from the cot and walked slowly over to him. Her hips undulated with each step, her posture straight. "What is it, Finnegan?" she said softly, her voice husky with the same need he was feeling. The sound stroked over his skin like a feather one of his lovers had once used on him. It left him tingling and hot in its wake.

He pulled his hand back through the bars as she got close enough to touch, denying himself yet again. The need was too strong. If he touched her he wouldn't be able to stop. He knew that and yet it didn't lessen his desire. Cerise came right up to the bars and leaned against them, curling her fingers around them. "You've never called me by my name before. Say it again."

"Cerise." He heard the gravel in his voice, knew it for what it was. As inexperienced as she was he could tell Cerise knew too.

"I want you, Finnegan." She spoke the words reluctantly, but his heart sang all the same. "I don't know why it's you. Why you're the one who makes me feel this way and quite frankly I don't care." She raised her chin defiantly. "We both know I'm surely going to my death. I've never wanted like this before and I probably won't again. So take me Finnegan, take what I freely offer. You owe me. You owe me that much."

Tie couldn't stop himself this time. He reached out a hand and gently covered hers where it was wrapped around the bar. The contact was shocking in its intensity. He tightened his grip. "I can't." He spoke softly, but it didn't make his rejection any easier, for either of them. "It wouldn't be right. It's unethical. This desire between us, it's strong, true, but it's insane, Cerise. We would both hate me afterward and I'm about the last person in the galaxy I still like at this point. So, no. But I thank you for the offer."

She sighed and moved her hand slowly from under his, turning the movement into a caress. She crossed her arms defensively, but didn't move back from the bars. Looking at her feet she said, "I knew you'd say that. It's part of the reason I like you so damned much."

She didn't know it, but that almost made Tie change his mind. He couldn't remember the last time someone told him they liked him. Wanted him, admired him, feared him, hated him, but never liked. "I like you too." His words were soft and Cerise peeked up at him with a small grin.

"If I had more time, I'd wear you down," she joked.

Tie nodded, completely serious. "Yes, you probably would."

Tie put the palms of his hands over his eyes and rubbed as hard as he could. He was lying in his bunk trying to sleep. He was exhausted, emotionally and physically. He'd informed headquarters yesterday that he'd captured his quarry. Today Vonner had contacted him and told him they were expecting them at a prison hulk cruising the Hikoi system. There was no going back. He still felt that, for whatever reason, he was meant to turn Cerise over to the Amalgamation. But God, he didn't want to do it. The little rebel wasn't making it easy on him either. She was trying to drive him mad. Since that tender moment this morning when she had accepted his rejection with resignation Cerise had spent every minute doing whatever she could to push him over the edge.

He could hear her now, calling to him from her cell. He was sweating with the effort it took not to respond, not to go to her. It was more than desire, more than wanting her. He needed her. It felt as if his body was shaking itself apart trying to get to her. It was small comfort that she sounded the same.

His body was on fire for her, his skin so sensitive his clothes had begun to hurt him. He'd stripped and lay on his bunk nude, the air circulating through the cabin doing nothing to cool the flames. His cock was hard even though he'd already brought himself off twice since he lay down. The smell of his own cum mixed with the musky smell of her arousal in the air was making him crazy. He'd never, never felt this kind of sexual need.

His physical need for her was all wrapped up with his fear for her. His fear over what would happen when he turned her over to the Amalgamation. He was so damn confused. He wanted, no needed, to find Egan as much as he needed to be with Cerise. What the hell was that about? Egan had been his best friend for as long as he could remember. Finding Egan had been the focus of his life for ten years. He had known Cerise for less than two days. How could he feel like this? Why?

God he was tired and desperate. And Cerise kept calling to him. Her voice, her scent, her desire, her courage, her beauty, everything about her called to him. He wanted her. Just her.

"Finnegan, please don't leave me alone. Please. I need you. I need you." She paused and Tie took a deep breath even as he tensed waiting to hear her again. "I've never been with anyone, Finnegan. Please don't make me die without feeling that. I want to feel it. I need to be with you, Finnegan. I need you." Her voice was so quiet he had to strain to hear her. She sounded so lost his chest ached. He knew her pride was taking a beating, begging him like this. The thing was, he was almost ready to beg as well.

He heard her sigh. The sound tore through him like a knife and her next words drove the blade deeper. "Fine. I'll choose one of the guards. They won't say no. Surely one will agree—"

"No!" Tie was off the bed in seconds, racing into the adjoining cabin. Cerise sat on the deck next to the bars, her back against the bulkhead. She still wore her skimpy underclothes and she looked up at Tie in surprise.

"You will not fuck anyone else," Tie growled at her, stalking over to her cell.

Cerise didn't get up. "You won't...fuck me." She hesitated on the word and Tie felt his stomach clench with heat when she finally said it in that husky voice. "If I have to, I'll offer myself to one of the guards or another prisoner. Surely there must be someone who will take my damn virginity before I die."

Tie angrily waved a hand in front of the sensor and opened the cell door. "Do you know what you're saying? Do you know what they'll do to you?" Warning bells were going off in his head and he fleetingly thought of how ill-advised it was to stalk into her cell completely naked, but common sense was beaten down by frustration and anger and burning desire.

"No," Cerise whispered, watching him with her luminous lavender eyes wide in the semidarkness of night on board ship. "Show me. Show me what they'll do."

Tie hauled her to her feet roughly and pulled her into his arms. He held her so tightly he was afraid he was going to hurt her but he couldn't make himself let her go. He pressed his cheek against hers and spoke urgently in her ear. "Why? Why me? Why are you still a virgin at twenty-five, Cerise? You're smart, sexy, fearless, a fucking princess for Christ's sake. Why hasn't someone claimed you yet? Why isn't there anyone else to protect you?"

Cerise wrapped her arms around him as tightly as he held her. The short nails of her fingers dug into his back but the pain only heightened his desire, making him aware of the ache in his cock. She soothed her hands down over his back. When she spoke her breath blew against the side of his neck, across the throbbing pulse there and Tie shivered.

"There have been plenty of men who wanted to take the virginity of a princess. But they didn't want me, they didn't

50

care for me. And when I reached the point where I would have taken one of them just to get it over with, there were…people who wouldn't let me, people who kept those men away from me and told me it was important I wait until the right man came along." Her voice was soft, shaky. When she finished she pressed her lips against Tie's neck and he arched into the gentle caress. She spoke again. "When you're a princess, there are so many other considerations, Finnegan." She shook her head. "I have no kingdom, but to so many I have the responsibility of producing the next heir. I have to live an exemplary life and yet for what?" She pulled out of his arms and looked up, her eyes capturing his. "I'm a princess in a tower, Finnegan. And I want you to rescue me."

"Cerise," he said softly and her name on his lips was filled with longing, with awe and desire and acceptance. He could deny her no longer.

Chapter Four

ᔆᓍ

Finnegan leaned down and swept her off her feet, one arm behind her knees and the other around her shoulders. Cerise had no choice but to wrap her arms around his neck and hold on tight. She felt feminine and desirable in a way she never had before. Certainly no man had ever carried her like this. No man had ever wanted her so much. It was a heady feeling, a powerful feeling and she liked it. But her pleasure was laced with guilt and regret.

Finnegan seemed almost awkward as he took three quick steps to the cot in her cell.

"Couldn't we go to your cabin?" Cerise asked hesitantly.

"No time," Finnegan answered tersely and he dumped her unceremoniously on the bed. Before Cerise could get her bearings he was pulling her shirt off over her head and yanking her panties down and off her legs. In the blink of an eye she was nude, ungracefully splayed on the cot and dying of embarrassment as Finnegan stood back and stared at her. She started to reach for the thin blanket to cover herself, until she looked at Finnegan. He was breathing heavily, his eyes glinting dangerously in the half-light. She wasn't afraid. His hunger for her was ferocious. She owned him right now, in the way a woman owns a man who desires her above all else. In a move that made her give a surprised squeal, he threw himself down on the cot on top of her, his weight pressed into her. Somehow it managed to be arousing instead of intimidating, a welcome sensation not at all crushing or oppressive.

Finnegan groaned as he lay there against her and ground his hips into her. The pressure of his hard cock against her mons had Cerise gasping and suddenly she could feel every point of contact between them. His skin was so hot, the hair on his body coarse as it rubbed against her breasts and belly and legs. The sensation sent a shiver down her spine. Of their own volition her arms went around him and she arched into the heat and hardness of him.

She knew what she was doing, but, God, it wasn't at all what she'd expected. He felt so wonderful against her she forgot everything else. All she could think was his name over and over, all she knew was the reality of his hot flesh pressed to hers. She wanted to melt into him, feel him melting inside of her. She wasn't sure who made the first move, but suddenly they were kissing and Cerise was drowning in the taste and texture of Finnegan's mouth. Like the rest of him, his mouth was hot, so hot it nearly burned her. His kiss was perfect in every way—passionate, demanding, wet and oh so desperate. He kissed her like a starving man and Cerise fell into a boiling sea of desire. She met him as an equal in that kiss, showing him as best as she could how much she wanted him.

He groaned again and Cerise enjoyed the sound. She loved to hear him like that, overwhelmed by the passion between them. Her arms tightened around him and she wrapped a leg around his waist to hold him closer. The move brought the heat and hardness of his cock closer to her as well and it was Cerise's turn to moan as the moist, plump head bumped into her throbbing clit. His hands gripped her hips for a moment and then slid up her sides to cover her breasts and Cerise's world teetered crazily, out of focus for a second. She was gasping for breath and feeling out of her depth.

"Finnegan," she rasped, "stop. I..." she had to pause to catch her breath, "I don't know what to do. I don't..." Finnegan cut her off with another kiss. Something brushed insistently across her nipples. His thumbs? Her nipples hardened impossibly. Cerise dug her fingers into his arms and the feel of his straining, bulging biceps made her insides liquefy and she felt her pussy get even wetter.

She let go of his arms as if burned and then her hands were fluttering without purpose over his back. She was afraid to touch him, afraid of the strength of the feelings he stirred in her. Finnegan trailed his lips down her jaw to her neck as he let go of her breasts, leaving them cold and bereft. He ran his hands down her arms in a caress as light as air and took hold of her hands. He raised them over her head and used his own hands to wrap hers around the cold bar at the end of the bed. His hands slid away in a sensuous caress as he whispered against the dip between her collarbones.

"Just hold on, baby. Hold on while I love you."

Cerise could do little else as Finnegan began to devour her. There was no other word for it. He started there in that sensitive hollow and proceeded to lick and nibble every bit of her from neck to hip. His lips burned a path down her torso, his tongue leaving flames behind. When he kissed her breasts Cerise had never felt anything so devastating in her life. He was gentle at first, with small licks and open-mouthed kisses against the sides. When she thought she'd go mad if he didn't kiss her nipples, he finally placed his mouth over one and sucked it tenderly. Cerise nearly came off the bed. He didn't seem to mind. He bit her nipple softly and Cerise let out a little whimper before she could stop herself.

Finnegan chuckled and pulled back. He blew a hot breath across her damp nipple and Cerise arched her neck and bit her lip to keep from crying out. "Liked that, did you?" he murmured, more to himself than to her. "These are just as I imagined they'd be," he continued quietly, "so sweet and small and perfect. They warm the palm of my hand. And your pretty nipples, pink as a rose, they press so deliciously against my tongue." He licked the flat of his tongue over her hard nipple and then swirled the tip around it. It felt so amazing, his words were so amazing.

"They're not perfect," Cerise whispered. She'd seen Regan and the others with women before, big breasted women

54

whom they seemed to like to fondle and kiss. Finnegan looked up at her, his expression intense.

"They are perfect for me," he whispered and looked back down at her chest. As she watched he rubbed his cheek against her left nipple, the beard stubble there rough and arousing on the sensitive tip. He rolled his face against it, ran his nose over it and then opened his mouth and sucked it in again. Cerise moaned and arched into his mouth. Finnegan snaked one arm under her back, arching it for her and grabbed her hip with the other, holding her leg wrapped around his waist.

"Finnegan," she cried out, his name a curse and a blessing on her tongue.

She didn't remember doing it, but by the time he was sucking the thin, sensitive skin of her hip she had moved both hands down and buried them in his sinfully thick, silky hair. He had one arm wrapped up between her legs so that one leg hung over his shoulder and the other hand was holding her other leg behind the knee, bending it and pushing it off to the side. She was completely exposed to him and it felt so right.

"I've got to taste you, Cerise," Finnegan told her in a deep rumble that traveled up her spine with a tingle. "My mouth is watering at the smell of your sweet pussy, baby, and I've got to have some."

"Oh, God," Cerise groaned, his coarse words sounding like poetry to her love-drunk mind. "Yes, Finnegan," she urged him, pressing his head down, not sure what she was begging him for, only knowing it had something to do with his mouth on her there and wanting it desperately.

When his tongue licked her from entrance to clit, Cerise's whole body stiffened right before she bucked wildly against his face. Finnegan's hands tightened on her legs, holding her down and open and his dominance only made her pussy ache and throb more. She sobbed his name and Finnegan rewarded her with more — more tongue, more mouth, more pleasure. He murmured his approval against her, the words incoherent but their meaning clear. When he pressed a finger inside her, Cerise knew it was more than she could bear.

"Finnegan, I'm going to come," she panted, "oh, God, I'm going to come."

He pulled back immediately. His voice was shaky and rough when he spoke. "Have you come before?"

"Yes, oh, God, yes. I've done it myself. I mean, don't stop! God, don't stop." Cerise was babbling, she knew it, but all she could think was how much she wanted his mouth back on her.

"Can you come more than once?" Finnegan continued to question her and Cerise yanked at his hair trying to get him back at her pussy.

He resisted and Cerise cried out in frustration. "What?" she asked desperately, knowing he'd asked her something but unable to concentrate.

"When you…" Finnegan paused and Cerise heard him swallow and catch his breath, "when you masturbate, can you come more than once?"

Cerise didn't understand the question. What did that matter? "Yes, yes, I come more than once. Finnegan, please!"

At her words Finnegan pressed his mouth back to her wet and swollen pussy and Cerise cried out in relief. But now that he'd made her stop and think there was something she needed to remember, something she needed to do… Cerise's euphoria began to fade as she remembered. Then she looked down and saw Finnegan loving her with his mouth and she knew she was doing the right thing. She wanted this man, wanted him so much. He was beautiful, inside and out. She ran her hands over his warm, soft hair, the thin light catching the blonde streaks in it. He had thick slashes of dark blonde brows and below them his odd eyes looked up at her, a light burning, somehow, behind the bland brown of his irises. There was something he was trying to tell her with those eyes, but she couldn't figure it out.

She couldn't think at all when, their eyes locked, Finnegan took the tip of his tongue and ran it roughly over her aching clit. Cerise arched sinuously, silently asking for more. He pressed his tongue against it, once, twice and Cerise felt the pressure building again. His tongue slid down to her throbbing passage and then thrust inside, next to his finger. God, to have both his finger and tongue inside her, moving independently, thrusting and then pulling back until only their tips remained was the most amazing thing she'd ever experienced. She felt her muscles clenching around him, trying desperately to hold him inside. The rhythm soon had her panting and writhing, fucking his tongue, his finger, reaching for the climax hovering on the edge of her consciousness.

Finnegan's tongue slid out of her and Cerise moaned in anguish at its loss. But they turned to moans of pleasure when he once again licked and sucked at her clit, his finger driving harder and faster inside her.

"Come on, baby, come on," he whispered against her and she could feel his breath on her soaking lips, feel the words tremble against her.

"Oh, God," she moaned and his mouth latched onto her clit and sucked hard and Cerise cried out hoarsely as her shoulders curled up off the bed and she pressed his face against her during the most mind-blowing orgasm she'd ever had.

The pulsing went on and on until she saw stars and the entire time Finnegan continued to love her, slower, deeper, his tongue now pressing against her clit to ignite smaller explosions of pleasure on the heels of the first blast.

When it was over, when all she had left were whimpers and shivers, Finnegan slowly pulled his finger from her throbbing pussy and Cerise made a noise somewhere between pleasure and pain. He tenderly kissed her drenched pubic hair and then lowered her legs and moved so that he was lying between them. He braced his weight on his hands and stared at her until she could focus on him. She gave him a sleepy, dazed smile that turned into a gasp as she felt the first few centimeters of his cock slip into her slick passage.

He closed his eyes and Cerise could see his jaw clench as he stopped just inside her. "Tell me now," he ground out, "tell me no right now, or it will be too late."

Cerise lifted her legs still trembling from her climax and wrapped them around his waist, pushing him deeper. Finnegan stopped and his eyes flew open to pin her with a hot, determined look. "Say it," he demanded, starting to pull out. Cerise wrapped her legs tighter around him, fighting his withdrawal.

"Yes, Finnegan. That's a yes," she told him, reaching up and pulling his head down to her. Against his lips, tasting her own essence there, she whispered, "Yes, a thousand times yes. I am yours." Then she kissed him and in the next instant he thrust deeply inside her.

Tie had to stop after he penetrated her. He wanted to fuck wildly and deeply into her and cry out, *Mine!* But he forced himself to stop, to let her adjust to the feel of him inside her. He knew it had hurt, when he'd thrust so deep, so fast. She'd cried out and tensed around him, her hands clutching at his back, her nails digging into his skin. Her reaction only made him wilder. She was his in a way she had never, would never, belong to anyone else. He was the first, the only man to fuck into her, to feel the sweet, wet, unbelievably tight heat of her gorgeous pussy. He bit the inside of his cheek and suppressed a shiver at the primitive emotions that thought roused in him.

Pressing his face into the gentle curve of her neck Tie focused on breathing slowly and evenly, all the while feeling the decadently soft, slick walls of her pussy throbbing around him, holding him tight, pulling him deeper. The way she welcomed him, wrapped around him, it was as if her body was claiming him just as his cock had claimed her. He couldn't remember what it was like to fuck any other woman, couldn't imagine fucking another woman as long as he lived. Nothing, no one, would ever feel like Cerise, would ever own him as she did at this moment.

"Baby?" she whispered and Tie's heart contracted at the endearment. All his life he'd waited to hear someone call him that with a wealth of emotion behind the word. Cerise did. Cerise was the one.

He lifted his head and pulled back slightly to look at her. She smiled tremulously. "Um, I'm pretty sure there's more to this."

Tie looked at her blankly for a moment. She seemed expectant. "Aren't you supposed to move?" she asked tentatively. "Like this?" And then she thrust delicately up against him, pushing his cock deeper into her swollen channel, strangling it until it felt so good he wanted to cry. She rolled her hips and sighed with pleasure and Tie felt his control snap.

"Tell me it feels good," he told her roughly. "Tell me and I'll fuck you, sweetheart, the way you want." He kissed her neck without finesse, lust and the need to stake his claim on her driving him. He sucked the delicate skin right below her ear and Cerise gasped. He didn't stop. He sucked hard enough to leave a mark — a mark that would tell others, *stay away, this is mine.*

"Oh, God, Finnegan, it feels good," she moaned. "Fuck me, baby, please."

Tie jerked away from her neck and grasped her hip with one hand, using the other to brace himself on the bed. Then he began to fuck her, slow, but hard and deep the way he wanted. If she had cried out, if she had said stop, he would have. But she didn't and his soul and body sang with the thrill of having his woman want to be fucked the way he wanted to fuck her.

He looked up and felt a deep satisfaction at the look of pure pleasure on Cerise's face. Her head was thrown back, her eyes closed, her mouth open and gasping as her hips thrust up against him, matching his rhythm perfectly. Her nails dug into the muscles of his upper arms as her hands gripped him with a strength that was surprising and arousing. He needed to know, he needed to hear the words and how it felt for her.

"Tell me. Tell me how it feels to be fucked." His urgent whisper split the night that had been filled with their erratic breathing, the sound of wet flesh against wet flesh, the groans of effort and pleasure. Cerise's eyes flew open and her cheeks flushed bright red. Tie felt tenderness well inside him at her embarrassment. "Tell me how my cock inside your pussy makes you feel," he whispered, giving her the words, guiding her.

"I..." she stopped and licked her lips and Tie shuddered. "I feel so full," she said, hesitant.

"More," Tie whispered, changing the angle of his thrust slightly. Cerise gasped and her whole body shook. "Tell me how that feels."

"Oh, God, Finnegan," Cerise moaned, "so good. You feel so good."

"Yes, that's right baby, more." His hand squeezed her hip tighter and he fucked harder into her, pushing her up the bed. Her hands flew up and pressed against the wall behind her, bracing herself for his thrusts and Tie nearly came then.

"You're so big, Finnegan," she whispered brokenly, "so big and hard. But soft, like velvet. Ahhh," she moaned as she arched her back when he fucked particularly hard into her.

"Do you love the hard fuck, baby?" he asked. "I can be gentler." He softened his thrusts, going slower.

Cerise tightened her legs and pressed hard against him. "No, no, hard. I want it hard tonight. I need to belong to you, Finnegan. I need to feel like I belong."

"Oh, little rebel," he told her softly, bending down to kiss her tenderly, "you belong. You belong to me." He pulled back from the kiss and looked at her a moment before thrusting hard and deep again, making her cry out. "I think you like it hard, Cerise, and deep. I want to fuck you so deep you feel me in your throat."

Cerise let out a strangled laugh. "I don't." And Tie laughed with her. The laughter seemed to relax her and she began to fuck him smoothly, her pussy so hot and wet they slid together and apart like two halves of the same whole. She started to speak again and Tie had to remind himself to breathe.

"I love it, Finnegan, I love being fucked by you. Because you're fucking *me*, not some damn princess, but me, Cerise. You love it too, you love how hot you make me, how wet, how much I want it, want you. You want to hear it? I'll tell you. Fuck me hard and deep because it feels so amazing. I've never felt anything as good as your cock fucking into me. God!" She shivered as his control slipped another notch and his thrusts got wilder. "Yes, baby, fuck me like that, like you're going to die if you can't be in my pussy."

She suddenly tensed and Tie knew she was going to come again. She was going to fly apart in his arms. Feeling her come on his mouth and finger had been so good he'd nearly lost it himself, but this, this…already her inner muscles were jerking on his cock and he could feel his balls pull up tight.

"Oh, God, Finnegan!" she screamed and then she was coming, calling his name again, clutching him to her, wrapping her arms and legs around him so tight he became a part of her. And as much as he wanted to feel her orgasm, to watch her come, he couldn't because he was coming too. Coming deep inside her while she pulsed around him, pulling stream after stream from his cock inside the incredible heat of her.

When he could breathe again, Tie rolled off her, afraid of crushing her. She made a sound of protest and he turned on his side and pulled her against him, her back to his chest. He wrapped his arm around her tightly and threw a leg over her legs. "Mine," he whispered. Cerise's breathing was already even as she snuggled back into him, lost in exhaustion. "Mine," he said again, kissed the top of her head and faded into sleep.

Samantha Kane

Chapter Five

&

Tie woke in the middle of the night, hard and aching for her. Half asleep, he crawled on top of her and snuggled between her legs. She made a sound in her sleep, a mumbled protest, but Tie pushed his cock into her in spite of it. She was still warm and wet from their last fuck and Tie felt a thrill chase down his spine at the tangible proof that it hadn't been a dream. She was his.

Cerise woke with his name on her lips, her hips thrusting up into him before she knew what she was doing. In two quick hard thrusts he had her climaxing. The feel of her pulsing around him was intoxicating. Cerise blindly searched for his mouth and he kissed her.

This fuck was slow and intense. It was all wet, hot kisses as they were pressed together, sticky with sweat. They were chest to breast, pelvis to pelvis and his cock made a slow grind inside her pussy and against her clit. Tie murmured in her ear, words he didn't think about beforehand and didn't remember after. She was so sweet, so fucking desirable and God, how she loved to be fucked. Everything Tie did she loved. She reciprocated every kiss, every touch, every caress.

Being inside her was heaven. She was made for him. He'd woken feeling almost desperate to be inside her, needing her again painfully. But being inside her eased the ache, almost as if she were a drug that he craved.

The thought made him pause, something tingling on the edge of his consciousness. But then Cerise bit his earlobe and her voice trembled in a low cry as she came again and Tie could only fuck her desperately, absorbing her climax into himself, soaking up her spasms and cries and wet heat and

62

Tomorrow

then he gave it back to her. He ground into her and felt his
cock jerk as he fed her his climax, filled her with his seed and
his desire and his love.

When it was over Tie pulled away, scrambling off the cot.
He was breathing heavily, not from their exertions, but from
fear.

"What have you done?" he whispered and he winced at
the horror in his voice, at the accusation. How he needed her
to deny it. He was ashamed of the desperation in his voice, the
weakness behind his words. But he couldn't deny that
weakness, his need for her, not just her body but her love.
She'd shown him in so many ways tonight that she had
feelings for him, hadn't she? But the look on her face was not
the answer he craved. She looked guilty, ashamed, afraid,
pitying. Tie backed away from that look.

"Finnegan," Cerise cried out, undisguised desperation in
her voice. "No, don't go." But it was too late. He was already
gone.

* * * * *

"Carnelian Tears," Finnegan said slowly as he stood
outside her cell. The door was open but he didn't come in. His
voice was flat, dead.

It was morning. He had been gone for hours. Not gone,
really, but on the bridge, she thought. She'd been too cowardly
to seek him out. By the time he'd returned Cerise had cried
herself numb.

"Yes," she answered, her voice hoarse from crying and
weak with self-disgust. At the sight of him she trembled. In
spite of everything she wanted him again. Wanted to feel him
moving inside of her, possessing her as only he had, as only he
could.

"Carnelian Tears," he said again, "a hormone unique to
Carnelian women that can be released at will during sex to

63

enslave their partner to their will." He sounded as if he were lecturing at university.

Cerise chose to respond with anger instead of shame. "You gave me no choice. You wouldn't listen to reason."

"Order me to do something." Cerise jerked back at the harsh command.

"What?" she asked, confused.

Finnegan took a step closer to the cell door. With shock she saw that he was trembling, in anger most likely. "Order me to do something." His voice nearly cut her it was so sharp.

"Shut up," she told him just as sharply.

Finnegan cocked his head to the side and his expression cleared slightly. "I feel no compulsion to obey you whatsoever," he told her coldly.

"Too bad." She couldn't keep the bitterness out of her tone and Finnegan smiled cruelly.

"I don't think your hormones are working properly, Princess," he sneered and Cerise cringed. Not once last night had he called her that. Now they were back to it. How she longed to hear him call her by her name, or whisper baby in her ear in that sweet, desperate rumble. "According to what information I've found, Carnelian Tears were bred out of existence a hundred years ago."

She straightened her shoulders. "I'm not going to pretend to know exactly how it works. I can tell you that the only Carnelian women who have the ability now are royal descendants."

"Well, isn't that convenient," Finnegan drawled as he sauntered into her cell.

She'd dressed this morning, her mission accomplished. But she'd never felt so awful in her life. Finnegan was a good man and she'd ruined his life. He wouldn't be able to live without her now, whether he liked it or not, whether he liked her or not.

"You can't turn me over to them, Finnegan," she told him, finding it easy to keep the victory out of her voice. She didn't feel like the winner here. She felt as if she had lost so much when she saw the cold look on his face.

"Oh really?" he asked, feigning surprise. "I think I can. I think I will." There was anger behind his words, so much anger that Cerise thought her heart might be breaking.

She sat down on the cot and put her trembling hands between her knees. "You need me. Without me, you'll go mad. You'll wither and die."

Finnegan stopped pretending and let his rage show. "Damn you, Princess, god damn you. What have you done to me?"

"I'm not sure," she began, shaking her head and Finnegan cut her off with a curse.

"You don't know? You all but ruin a man's life, you think, but you can't give him the particulars?"

Cerise sighed and closed her eyes, but a tear escaped to run down her cheek anyway. Suddenly she felt his hands on her arms, jerking her off the cot. He shook her roughly.

"Don't try the real thing, Princess. I've had enough of your tears."

Cerise opened her eyes and she saw him flinch. His hands gripped her arms so hard it hurt. "Tell me," he demanded. "Tell me what you do know."

Cerise sighed again, the sound quivering. "You'll need me, physically. Like a drug addict. Without...without being with me, you'll go through the same withdrawal, but it will be fatal for you."

Finnegan laughed, the sound a little wild and very cruel. "Is that all? Well, you were a good fuck, Princess, but hardly addicting."

Cerise felt her heart shrivel and die at his words. Was that all she'd been to him, a fuck? Even though she had taken him out of necessity, she had thought he had feelings for her. He'd seemed to care and she knew she'd begun to care for him. But it was all a lie, just like Regan said. He'd always told her that men would lie to be with her. He'd been right of course, as always. Again she straightened her spine and accepted it. They were stuck with each other now and that was her fault. She wouldn't desert him, no matter how cruel he was. He was her responsibility now. And perhaps in time—

"Do I have to do what you tell me? Am I a slave to your will?" Finnegan's voice cut into her thoughts harshly.

Cerise shook her head. "No. You still have free will. At least I think you do. You seem to. All Mother's husbands seemed to have free will, if I remember correctly. I was so young when they all died, I can't remember very well. But no, I don't think your will is enslaved."

"Just my body?" Finnegan asked, his tone less than amused. He paused a moment. "How did they die?"

"What?" Cerise asked. She must be more shaken by their conversation than she'd thought. She couldn't follow his questions.

"All your mother's husbands. How did they die?"

"When Mama was murdered, they all died without her." Cerise turned away, the only real memory of the event one of being left all alone.

"How many?" The question seemed to be dragged out of Finnegan.

Cerise turned back to him. "What?"

Finnegan cursed. "How many husbands did she have when she died?"

Cerise answered hesitantly, not sure where this was leading. "Five."

Finnegan turned away from her for a moment. When he turned back he was composed. "Did she enslave them all with the Tears?"

Cerise considered the question and answered honestly. "I don't know. I was very young. I don't know what their situations were."

Finnegan nodded but didn't say anything more. He walked out of the cell without another word and Cerise sank back down on the cot, her broken heart pounding and her dreams in shattered pieces at her feet.

Tie reluctantly walked back to the big cabin where Cerise's cell occupied the back corner. He was shaking so badly he couldn't work on the computer anymore. He needed her. She was right. He was addicted to her. And he hated her for it. He hated her for making him feel again and then sucker-punching him with her betrayal. She was staring at him as he sank down into a chair at the table facing her.

It took a moment before her condition sank in. She was pale and he could see her hands shaking as she pushed her smooth, dark brown hair behind her ears. She stood abruptly and paced over to the far wall, leaning against it for support, her face turned away from him. It was then that the full impact of what she'd done hit him.

Slowly Tie got up and walked over. She'd closed the cell door herself and he unlocked it. She didn't turn to look at him as he walked in.

"Come here," he told her, his voice harder than he'd wanted, but he still burned with anger and the anger had a new focus now.

She shook her head.

"I said come here," he told her slowly, the menace in his voice filling the space between them. She turned at last.

Her pupils were dilated and her cheeks flushed. Her lips were pale. She'd folded her arms across her chest and tucked her hands under them. Tie held out his hand to her and she resisted for a minute before giving in and crossing the room, as if she couldn't deny him. When her hand slipped into his, Tie's knees nearly buckled with the lust that slammed into him, the thrill that shot through his veins straight to his cock. From the way her fingers gripped his hand and the erratic state of her breathing she felt the same thing.

Without a word Tie spun her around. She gasped as he yanked down her baggy, shapeless pants, baring her sweet curvy ass and long legs.

"What are you doing?" she asked weakly, not trying to stop him.

"Getting my fix," Tie told her roughly as he pushed her forward until her hands rested on the cot. He ripped open his pants and pulled out his aching cock with a groan. He placed it against her heat and the swollen folds of her drenched pussy. "And testing a theory." His voice choked off as he thrust inside her.

That was all it took. Cerise screamed and he felt her climax around his cock. She'd been so ready for him and he was so hard. He thrust into her through her climax and she kept coming around him, thrusting back against him with a sob. He spread her legs wider and slammed into her, holding his cock deep while he ejaculated with shivers of pleasure and relief. The feel of his cum inside her made Cerise moan and grind against him and he felt her walls squeeze tight around him as if to hold him there.

When they were both done coming they were breathless. Tie pulled away from her. The slide of his cock from the oven of her pussy left him cold and forlorn. She sobbed again as he pulled out.

Tie fell back against the wall beside the cot as Cerise fumbled with her pants, pulling them up unsteadily.

"Did you know?" he asked, almost certain of the answer. "Did you know that you would become addicted to me as well?"

Cerise wouldn't look at him. She shook her head and Tie had his answer.

"Oh, little rebel, what have you done?" he whispered.

They came for her two hours later. Tie hadn't told her when he'd gone to her that morning that the ship had been on autopilot last night and they had already docked at the prison hulk. There was no escape, no way not to hand her over without both of them dying. And Tie wasn't goddamned ready to die yet.

"Finnegan," she pleaded as the guards put restraints on her wrists, "please don't do this. Don't let them take me."

He couldn't answer her. It was all he could do to stop himself from killing the guards for daring to touch her. It was primitive and primal, this need to protect what was his. Logically, he knew it was another aspect of the Tears but that didn't make the feelings less powerful. Once they had her out of the cell, Tie walked in and closed the door, locking himself in.

"Computer," he said tonelessly, "lock cell door. When prisoner has been escorted off the ship, secure hull and engage autopilot for Quartus Seven. Do not open cell door for two hours."

"Yes, Captain," the computer said in its efficient, emotionless voice.

"What the hell are you doing Finnegan?" one of the guards asked, perplexed. "Don't you need to collect your receipt?"

"I'll notify Vonner of delivery," Tie said, gritting his teeth against the pain in his head as they led her away.

"Finnegan!" Cerise screamed as they led her onto the lift. She fought their hold, but she was no match for two Amalgamation prison guards. They handled her struggles effortlessly. She sobbed his name and Tie ran back to the cell door, grabbing the bars and shaking them. They loosened in the wall at his superior strength, but held fast. He reached his hand through the bars, desperate to touch her, to get her back.

Cerise reached her hand out to him as the lift doors began to close. "Finnegan," she sobbed and he felt the sound rip through his chest.

"Little rebel," he whispered, "what have we done?"

The only answer was the hiss of the lift doors as they closed.

Chapter Six

ℭ

"What the hell did you just say?" Regan grabbed the man by the throat and shook him roughly.

The pirate was a frightening sight. Tall, with sleek muscles that rippled with suppressed power, he wore his usual skintight black vest left partially unbuttoned to reveal a broad chest covered with wiry black hair. The hair seemed incongruous with the pirate's completely bald head. His skull was large, heavy, yet as sleek as the rest of him. His skin was pale, with a hint of exotic color, perhaps brown, although in a certain light there were some who swore it was iridescent green. The ridged scar that cut across his left cheekbone turned an angry red to match its owner's current temperament. His eyes, however, remained the same flat, dull brown, looking out of place in his arresting face with its sharp cheekbones, square chin and heavy black brows.

Regan was imposing enough when he was his usual utterly composed self. When he was in a temper, as he was now, he was a sight to behold. It took a great deal to drive him into a rage, but today's news had done it. He was famous across the galaxy for two things: his infrequent, violent bursts of temper and his almost obsessive loyalty to Princess Cerise Chessienne.

"Put him down, Regan, and let him tell us. He's not the one who took her." The pirate's second-in-command, Sasha, spoke up from the second level of the small bridge. *The Rebel Bounty* was in port at Sa-Ro Five, disguised as a small cargo ship. Regan and his crew were delivering a package all right, a big fat bundle of money to the small rebel contingent left on the Amalgamation's largest agricultural planet. They in turn were going to smuggle it out in produce shipments to various posts around the galaxy.

Regan lowered the struggling man to the deck with precision, his temper and his strength clearly held in check by the merest thread. "Speak," he ordered. The poor man he'd mistreated was struggling for breath as he collapsed on the deck.

"Hunter," he gasped, "Finnegan, I think. He got her on T-Sdei Delta. She gave herself up to him to save a boy. Two days ago. Word is he's taking her to a prison transport ship cruising in the Hikoi system. It's to take her to Aboo Two, to Amalgama for execution."

Even Sasha, who had been with Regan for almost a decade, took a step back at the cold fury on the pirate's face.

"We'll just see about that," Regan said quietly.

An hour later Regan leaned both hands against the wall of his cabin and gazed out the porthole into space. He sighed. Cerise's predicament was his fault. He should have kept a tighter rein on her.

He'd known the irrepressible princess for over seven years. She'd been just eighteen when she was escorted onto *The Rebel Bounty*. She had already made a name for herself on Sa-Ro Five for her support of the rebellion. The natives there loved their rebellious little orphaned princess. All Regan saw was the opportunity he'd been seeking.

Almost ten years ago he'd left Earth on the run, wanted for desertion and treason. The rebels who helped him off planet set him up with a small rebel contingent and a ship. In three years he'd parlayed that beginning into a legendary career as one of the most successful pirates in the galaxy. A pirate firmly in the rebel's camp. He had almost single-handedly turned a few malcontents into a viable resistance, with rebel army training camps in three secret locations. There was still a lot of work to be done. The resistance was still mostly unorganized except for his relatively small force. But he was on the verge of initiating talks with the Cintealios for monetary support and safe harbor.

He had his reasons for wanting to see the Amalgamation destroyed. And the young, beautiful, idealistic princess was going to help him accomplish it. She'd become more or less his ward and he molded her into a leader. He'd touted her as the natural leader of the new, republican Amalgamation and the galaxy had bought it, hook, line and sinker as the old saying went. The problem was, so had she and most of his crew. And on some days, so did Regan.

He hadn't expected to like her, but every day his admiration for her grew. Thrust into the limelight at an early age, into an uncertain future, a death sentence hanging over her head, she still managed to be sweet and kind and brave. She faced each day as if it were a new beginning, the beginning of something wonderful and over the years she'd made Regan start to think that maybe it was. She'd developed a crush on him the moment she came on board his ship and he encouraged it. He'd deliberately set out to tie her to him in every way he could, except the final, most basic way. He still had enough honor not to fuck her to control her.

He wondered where this course would take him. He was a meticulous planner and rarely was surprised by events. This event surprised him. Who was this Finnegan and what was his interest in Cerise? Regan knew he was a bounty hunter, but was he an independent or an Amalgamation assassin? Had he already delivered Cerise? Was she even still alive? At the thought Regan's hand curled into a tight fist. He had to believe this was a road they were meant to travel and that he'd be able to take care of Cerise, just as he had for the last seven years. Cerise was a firm believer in following your path and recognizing signposts.

The mechanism on the door to his private quarters hissed as it slid open. Regan turned slowly, feeling no threat from whoever was behind him. He shook his head as he thought about Cerise's devotion to Stanislaus' philosophy. He stared at the man himself as he strolled into the cabin.

Conor Stanislaus was an outlaw, like Regan, like most of the crew on his ship. He'd been on the Amalgamation's list of wanted thought criminals ever since *Finding My Way* was published. When Regan left Earth he was searching for someone — someone who was a believer in Stanislaus' rebellious philosophy, like Cerise. He'd hunted Stanislaus from one end of the galaxy to the next, hoping against hope he'd find the man he was looking for. He'd only found Stanislaus. Stanislaus had been a drunken wreck. Out of respect for the memory of his long-lost friend, Regan had picked him up, dusted him off, dried him out and hauled him on board *The Rebel Bounty*. At the time Regan never imagined Conor would become his closest friend.

"So you've located our lost little rebel princess, hmmm?" Conor asked as he sat down on Regan's bed. The man had no sense of personal space.

"This is your fault," Regan growled as he stalked over and kicked Conor's foot. "Get off my bed."

Conor yelped and yanked his feet out of the way. He was a match for Regan physically, just a few centimeters shorter than him and muscular. He was on the back edge of forty, his brown, curly hair showing salt and pepper at the temples. His light green eyes were surrounded by laugh lines and Regan could attest to the man's good humor. What Conor didn't have was Regan's superior strength, or stamina, or physical abilities. Or Regan's temper. Conor pulled his feet up and lay down on the bed with a grin.

Regan stood over him and frowned down at him. "If you hadn't filled her head with all that freedom shit and honor and walking her own path, she'd be safe and sound behind locked doors on this ship where I can keep her safe."

Conor sat up abruptly and flung himself off the bed. His arms spread wide as he exclaimed, "I didn't fill her head with that shit! Hell, I don't even believe it anymore. I told her it was shit, but you know her. She wants to see the best in everyone. She sees rainbows when it's clearly just rain."

When he stood up Regan got a good whiff of him. He wrinkled his nose. "Whose bed did you just crawl out of? You reek of sex."

Conor grinned again and Regan sighed. "A gentleman doesn't kiss and tell," he said.

"A gentleman doesn't fuck everything that walks and talks — and some things that don't."

Conor laughed outright. "Too true, my friend." He shrugged. "What can I say, I'm irresistible."

Regan raised an eyebrow. "No. You're persistent. There's a difference."

"Blasphemer," Conor told him congenially. "I have made fucking an art. They line up outside my door for a taste." He narrowed an eye at Regan in mock ferocity. "And don't think I didn't notice the change of subject." He walked over and put his hand on Regan's shoulder, for once serious. "You're worried about her, aren't you?"

Regan growled in frustration and paced away from Conor to punch the wall, leaving a dent in the reinforced synth-steel. Conor whistled. "Sometimes I forget exactly what you are."

At his words Regan's stomach clenched. What you are, not who you are. Even his best friend thought he was less than human. Regan took a moment to get himself together before turning back to face Conor.

"You were all in favor of her going out and recruiting, or whatever the hell she was doing. You encouraged it."

Conor defended himself. "They've got to see her sometime, Regan. She's got to be seen as active in the resistance, not just a mindless figurehead. There's already talk she's nothing more than a tool for your personal agenda. If you hadn't let her do it she would have found another way. A more dangerous way."

"More dangerous than getting captured by a bounty hunter?" Regan asked sarcastically.

Conor sighed. "She desperately wants an active role here, Regan. She needs to prove something."

"Not to me," Regan bit out.

Conor just shook his head. "To herself."

"It was a harebrained, ill-thought-out scheme and you know it." Regan could hear the frustration in his voice and winced. But this was his fault. Conor was right about one thing. He should have taken her demands more seriously. He'd sent her on what was supposed to be a short, simple meet-and-greet tour to pacify her, without adequate guards obviously. Regan wanted to hit something again. He should have been prepared for this. He should have guarded her more carefully. But he knew he couldn't have kept her from leaving him. He'd known that eventually his little bird would want to fly away from the nest.

Conor just nodded. "Yep, when you're right, you're right. But you went along with it. You know I'm about as useless as a whore on Jurgia, so it's your fault for listening to me in the first place." He sounded so forlorn that Regan rolled his eyes, amused in spite of himself by Conor's reference to the home world of the Amalgamation leader, Krys Xan. Jurgia was populated by a race of androgynous hermaphrodites.

"I'm sorry, Conor," he said, exasperated. "I hate to interrupt your daily identity crisis, but could I please have a brief moment for a little personal anxiety attack?"

"No." Conor's tone was teasing, but when Regan looked at him Conor's expression silently communicated the truth of his remark. "Everyone else can have anxiety attacks, but not you. It is not allowed, ever. You are the one who keeps this whole circus rolling. You want to see real panic? Just walk out there and tell them you're worried." Conor put his hands on his hips and cocked his head as he observed Regan. "And you are worried, aren't you?"

Regan turned to look unseeing out the porthole again. "Yeah, Conor. Yeah, I'm worried." And the truth of his remark made his stomach roil.

* * * * *

Tie lowered the unconscious guard to the deck. Once out of sensor range, he'd given the computer the override code, unlocked the cell and put his plan to rescue Cerise into motion. The prison hulk thought him long gone, the guards who'd taken Cerise surely spreading the news of his odd behavior. He'd had to wait until he'd intercepted the night code initiation on board the prison hulk to sneak on. He knew at night they had a skeleton crew and security was left mainly to the computers.

The wait had been the longest six hours of his life. He had to believe that Cerise was still okay. The usual protocol was to let political prisoners sweat it out until, by the time they came to interrogate them, they were already so scared they told the interrogation team whatever they wanted to know, in theory anyway. These rebels were notorious for their resistance to formula interrogation techniques.

Hacking into the ship's hull lock system had been relatively easy. The Amalgamation was so cocksure of their hold on the galaxy they'd become lax in security procedures. One of Tie's innate abilities that the IMF had encouraged with rigorous training was his ability with computers and other mechanized equipment. He could hack into almost any computer the Amalgamation owned. He'd opened a little-used cargo bay in a section of the prison hulk that was under construction. He'd turned off the warning system on the bay before opening it, so unless someone happened to walk in there no one should be the wiser. The *Tomorrow* was as safe and hidden as if it was docked at home on Quartus Seven.

He was halfway to Cerise's cell. He'd downloaded a grid of the prison hulk and committed it to his enhanced memory, another handy little gift from his breeders. He was sticking to the less-used corridors, service lifts and even repair ladders within the ship's bulkheads. He'd already made it up seven decks undetected. This guard was the first he'd encountered and Tie had taken him by surprise. He hadn't even had enough time to mutter a shocked exclamation before Tie incapacitated him. Tie didn't kill him. He was just a tiny little cog in the Amalgamation machine, a poor sucker like Tie had once been. He didn't deserve death. Tie grinned as he thought how disappointed his former commanding officers would be in that logic.

Two decks later Tie froze, hidden in the shadows of a cavernous storage bay. Something didn't feel right. He sniffed the air and listened closely. There, a whiff of scent unfamiliar here, something musky and foreign. And there, a smothered cough, so quiet an ordinary man would have missed it. Tie silently unholstered his laser, already set on stun. His usual method was to rely on hand-to-hand combat, but that was with known opponents. This threat was unknown. He could hear and smell more than one person out in the bay. He didn't know if they were armed or not. They were trying to be quiet. Actually, to the average ear and nose they would have gone undetected. They were good and obviously not supposed to be here either.

Tie heard a footstep less than a meter away. It was soft, quiet — too quiet. Tie counted to five and then spun out of his hiding place, his weapon trained on the threat. Staring at him down the barrel of a laser was Egan.

They stood frozen in place with weapons held on each other, almost within touching distance. For a moment Regan thought he was dreaming. It was Tie, but it wasn't Tie. This stranger's hair was shoulder length, not the military buzz Tie used to wear. And his eyes, left opaque gray with nearly white irises by the genetic enhancements, just like Regan's, were covered by the same dull brown contact lenses that Regan used to hide his identity as a former SS. Tie was bigger than he used to be, his muscles more pronounced. The deep grooves next to his mouth made him look hard, cold.

"Egan?" Tie whispered, his shock evident. Regan was startled for a moment. He hadn't heard that name since that fateful day he'd thrown in his lot with the rebels in a burst of laser fire.

"It's Finnegan," Regan heard one of his men say and his heart stopped beating for a moment. Could it be? Had Tie gone back to work for the Amalgamation?

"What are you doing here, Tie?" he asked softly. Tie looked at him as if he was looking at a ghost. He didn't answer. "Tie?" he prompted.

"Egan." Tie shook his head. "Jesus, I...I can't believe it. What...what are you doing here?"

Regan smiled gently. "I asked first."

Tie took a step back. At his movement Regan felt his finger twitch on the laser's trigger. He almost dropped the gun. Christ, was he actually going to shoot Tie?

"Do you work here?" Tie asked carefully.

"Do you?" Regan countered.

Tie slid over and placed his back against the wall. He quickly looked around and Regan could see him make note of each member of *The Rebel Bounty's* crew who had accompanied him. Tie hadn't lowered his laser either. Regan noted his precise movements with approval. Whatever he'd been doing Tie had kept in practice. He turned to look at Regan and seemed to come to a decision.

"No."

Regan relaxed. So Tie was going to talk. Good. When nothing further was forthcoming he sighed. "And?" he prompted.

Tie just tilted his head in a move that slammed through Regan. Countless times Tie had looked at him like that, conveying meaning without words—a necessity in the IMF, who frowned on emotions and personal relationships in general among their elite SS troops. He felt as if he'd stepped back in time as he answered Tie's unvoiced question.

"Me neither." Tie visibly relaxed. "Fancy meeting you here, then," Regan continued and Tie grinned at him.

"Regan," Sasha hissed, "hurry up with old home week. We've got to snatch the princess and be on our way."

Tie's smile crumbled. "Regan?" he asked, confused. Regan could see the exact moment Tie made the connection.

"Jesus, Regan," Tie breathed. "I didn't..." He was visibly shaken, but pulled himself together. "What do you want with Cerise?" He cringed and Regan could tell he hadn't meant to call her that in front of him. Curious.

"A better question is, what do you want with Cerise?" Regan took a stab in the dark and watched Tie's eyes flicker in that way he had when he was hiding something.

"You brought her here, turned her over to them." Regan spoke dispassionately, but Tie looked as if he'd hit him.

"No! I mean yes, but I had to. I'm here to rescue her." Regan almost laughed at Tie's sincerity, his earnestness.

"What a coincidence," he drawled, "so are we." He was thinking furiously. This could be very helpful.

Tie looked at him suspiciously. "Why?"

"I could ask the same."

Tie looked disgruntled for a moment. "That's between the princess and me."

Regan nodded in agreement. "That is my answer as well."

Tie huffed and blew a few strands of his hair into the air. Regan had never seen it this long. He'd never known how soft it looked, how golden and wavy it was. It looked good on him, the inner Tie revealed. He almost smiled at his fanciful, wayward thoughts.

"Regan!" The whisper this time was urgent. "They're two corridors over!"

Tie turned at the whisper and Regan took advantage to hit his wrist and knock the laser from his hand. Tie went down on one knee, holding his abused wrist and glaring at Regan.

"What the hell did you do that for Egan?" he asked, irritated, as he pushed back up to his feet.

Regan shrugged. "It's Regan now. And you did have a laser pointed at me. I'm afraid I had to take exception to that."

"I wasn't going to shoot you, for God's sake," Tie said in exasperation. "Not when—" He was interrupted when ten men dropped out of the ceiling scaffolding ten meters above them.

"Let's move," Sasha said, "and bring the pretty boy."

Regan smiled, his first genuine smile since he'd heard about Cerise's capture. "Oh, no, Sasha," he said happily, earning a frown from both Sasha and Tie. "Tie is going to rescue her for us, aren't you, Tie?" he asked and laughed at Tie's shocked expression. Regan began backing away from him, a plan already fully formed in his head. "You fetch her for me, won't you? We're just going to have some fun and you'll bring Cerise home for me."

Tie took a tentative step toward him, but Regan stopped him with a look. "I trust you," he told Tie and he watched Tie's expression clear.

"How will I find you again?" Tie asked as Regan and his men moved swiftly to the door leading away from Cerise's cell.

Regan looked back at him with a grin. "Don't worry, I'll find you, now that I know who I'm looking for."

His last look at Tie showed the other man melting back into the shadows, heading toward Cerise.

"Do you trust him, Captain?" Sasha asked suspiciously.

Regan couldn't seem to stop grinning. "I trust her with him as with no one else in the galaxy, Sasha. Completely."

Samantha Kane

Tie was shaken by his encounter with Egan. No, Regan now. Ten damn years he'd searched for him and wham! There he was sneaking aboard the same Amalgamation prison hulk as Tie, here to rescue the same princess—his princess. What was his relationship to Cerise? Were they lovers? No, Tie knew they weren't. He'd taken Cerise's virginity last night. So what were they? Was Regan the reason the Amalgamation wanted her so much? He was an even greater prize than the rebel princess. It made sense. The Amalgamation had to know he'd come looking for her. That meant if they hadn't set up traps for him yet, they soon would. Tie's mission took on new urgency.

The hulk was suddenly rocked by an immense explosion and alarms and foam fire sprinklers began to go off. When he heard the sound of running feet coming toward him Tie ducked through the nearest hatch, into what appeared to be a maintenance closet of some sort. An emergency crew was running back the way Tie had come, toward the direction Regan and his friends had moved. Tie understood. Egan, damn, he meant Regan, was creating a diversion for him. He hurried, running down the newly deserted corridor toward cell block C, cell 9580i. He wasn't going to have much time, not if what he suspected was true. If they were expecting Regan to come for Cerise it wouldn't be long until someone thought to send some guards to her cell to protect their newest arrival.

The gate to cell block C was open—that alone made Tie stop and duck into another hatch. He peered around the edge of the opening and watched the entry for a few moments. It didn't take long before he noticed surreptitious movement on the other side. They were already waiting for him. As soon as the thought went through his head, Tie knew it was wrong and he smiled. They weren't waiting for him, they were waiting for Regan.

Taking a deep breath Tie charged out of the hatch and ran full tilt for the open gate.

"The princess!" he yelled frantically. "Get her! Regan's on board and he's looking for her."

82

"Halt!" a voice called out and a laser blast split the bulkhead just past Tie's right shoulder.

Tie skidded to a stop and didn't have to feign indignation. "What the hell?" he hollered. "It's Finnegan, with Bounty Hunters, Inc.! I brought her in, you idiots."

A head poked out of the hatch to the left of the cell block's gated hatch. "Why are you here?" the guard called.

"God damn it!" Tie yelled, "I'm protecting my investment. As soon as I heard Regan was coming for her I hightailed it back here. I can collect the bounty on both of them."

The guard burst angrily from the hatch, followed by two friends. "Now just a minute. We were told that if we apprehended him we could collect the bounty. They never said anything about independents showing up."

Tie jogged over to the guards, watching for any defensive moves on their part. They didn't make any. He nearly shook his head in disgust over their incompetence. "We can split the bounty if you guys want a share. I just want some of the credit for catching the infamous Regan."

The guards eyed him suspiciously, more Tie thought because they didn't trust him to share the money than because they didn't trust him not to rip their heads off. More fools they, he laughed to himself.

When he stopped next to them Tie pretended to be winded from his run. "Whew! I ran something like three decks to get here when the alarms went off. Have you got hydration of some kind?"

"Yeah," one guard mumbled and turned away to reach for a bottle on the table just inside the hatch where they'd been hiding. He holstered his weapon as he reached for it and Tie used his distraction to kick out and disarm the other two guards. As they scrambled to right themselves Tie spun to face them, ramming his shoulder into the solar plexus of the man just turning in the hatch. Because of his awkward half-turned stance he was easily thrown back into the room, landing on the floor with a crash. He screamed in pain and Tie assumed he'd broken something in his fall on the hard synth-steel deck.

With one out of commission, Tie was free to face the other two. They spread out to either side of him in a classic two-on-one maneuver. They were so inept Tie was almost ashamed they'd been Amalgamation trained.

"Do you know what I am?" Tie asked conversationally, keeping both men in sight.

One laughed evilly and Tie nearly rolled his eyes at the stereotypical behavior. "A dead man," he said and his friend laughed while the one in the small room to the right moaned.

"Nope," Tie said shaking his head. "I'm a Gen8 SS, my friends, and I kill little prison hulk guards for breakfast."

The two guards exchanged uneasy glances. "Nice try," one said suspiciously, "but everyone knows no one leaves the SS. If you were a Super Soldier there's no way you could be a bounty hunter."

"No one leaves the SS with their blessing. But it's pretty damn hard to stop us when we get the urge to roam." Tie grinned at them. He hadn't been able to tell anyone that for years. But he was going to be on the most wanted list anyway, so what the hell.

The guard on his left decided to play the hero. He dove for Tie hoping, Tie supposed, to take him by surprise. He'd have had to be a lot faster to do that on one of Tie's bad days. Tie punched him hard in the temple, dropping him to his knees and kicked behind him, driving his booted foot into the stomach of the second guard who tried to jump him while he was occupied with the first. Tie took a moment to land another punch to the first guards jaw before turning and giving the second the same treatment. The entire fight lasted less than a minute and both guards were down, unconscious, but still alive.

"Mayday, mayday," he heard the soldier inside the small cabin calling for assistance. "Escape in progress, cell block C."

Damn, damn, damn. He knew better than to allow a man to remain effective enough to call for reinforcements. His time had just run out. Grabbing the lock sensor from the belt of one of the fallen guards Tie ran down the corridor.

"Help!"

"Please, get me out!"

"Freedom, I beg you!"

The prisoners from each cell Tie ran past called out to him. He hardened his heart to their pleas. He was here for Cerise, she was his priority. He counted off the cell numbers, 9560i, 9570i, 9580i. He stopped at the cell hatch and pounded on it, leaving dents.

"Cerise?" he called. "Cerise, are you in there?"

"Finnegan?" He heard her muffled response. "Finnegan! Get me out of here, damn it!" He heard a weak thud on the other side of the hatch. He smiled to himself. She sounded mad enough to spit. God she was wonderful.

He fumbled with the lock sensor for a moment and realized he was more affected by hearing her voice than he'd thought. When he righted it he punched in some simple codes. It was a sure bet these guards couldn't handle a complicated lock system. On the third try he unlocked the hatch and shoved the door open.

"Oof!" He heard Cerise hit the deck before he saw her. When he rushed in she was sitting on the floor glaring at him.

"You could have given me some warning!" she hissed at him. She started to get to her feet slowly and it was then that Tie saw how badly she was shaking.

"Oh, baby," he said softly and gave her a hand up. Her touch nearly undid him. He wasn't sure if it was the Tears or if he was just so damn glad to see her alive. He went to haul her into his arms and she resisted for a second or two before tumbling into him and holding on tight.

"I didn't know if you'd come," she said in a tremulous voice. "I hoped, but I didn't know."

"Of course I came," he told her, smoothing his hands up and down her back. "We're a team now, remember?" She nodded against his chest with a little hiccup.

Tie set her gently away from him, although it killed him to do it. "We've got to go sweetheart. Regan set off a blast to distract them, but it won't keep them away forever. The guards already called for reinforcements."

That got Cerise's attention. "Regan? Regan's here? Where is he?" She looked frantically behind Tie and he felt an arrow of white hot jealousy shoot up his spine until his head nearly exploded. He took a deep breath before answering her.

"I told you, he's setting up a distraction. I'm the only one here to get you out." Tie started to deftly undo the buttons of her prison uniform jacket.

"Regan sent you?" Cerise sounded bewildered. "But, he always comes for me himself."

That made Tie pause. "You've been in prison before?" That was news to him.

Cerise shook her head. "No, but I tend to jump into certain situations without thinking. Regan's always yelling at me about it." She smiled as she said it and Tie clamped down on the jealousy before it gave him another headache.

He resumed unbuttoning her jacket. "Well I don't know about the past, but I'm the one who showed up to rescue you." Tie heard the half truth fall from his lips and cringed. "Well, Regan showed up too, but he sent me to fetch you, as he put it, while he had a little fun."

"Oh." Cerise's voice sounded little and disappointed. Whatever she and the pirate were to each other, lovers or not, he was obviously important to her.

Suddenly she slapped at his hands. "What are you doing? Why are you undressing me?" She gasped. "You can't be thinking of fucking me now! We've got to get out of here!"

Tie laughed, although it was strained. "No, that's not why I'm undressing you, although to be honest, yeah, I am thinking about fucking you. Thanks to the goddamn Tears that's practically all I can think about." He took another deep breath and huffed it out, then bent over and yanked the prison garb pants down her legs. She was barefoot. "These clothes have most likely been treated with something that will set the sensors off if you leave this cell wearing them. If we don't want them to track us, you go as you are." After she stepped out of the pants, Tie looked up at her and groaned. She was wearing the same barely there underclothes she'd worn on the *Tomorrow*.

Cerise was looking down at him and she swallowed deeply. "They let me keep my underwear. I thought that was nice."

Tie stood abruptly. "Nice had nothing to do with it. By doing it they made you think nice thoughts about them. Therefore, when they came to question you you'd be more amenable to telling them what they want to know because you'd think of them as your new friends."

Cerise looked shocked. "I never thought of that."

Tie smiled ruefully. "I helped write the book, baby. Now sit down." She was shaking so badly she could hardly stand.

"I'm sorry, Finnegan," she said, her teeth chattering. "It's just that it's been hours since, you know…"

Tie grinned at her. "Yeah, I know. You need me, bad." She frowned at him and he laughed. "Seems I'm not the only one who can't stop thinking about it."

"Why aren't you this bad?" she asked crossly. Her eyes got wide as Tie pulled an old-fashioned hypodermic needle from a pocket in his leggings. "What is that?" she squeaked.

"The reason I'm not as bad off as you are." Tie told her and reached for her thigh. She covered it with weak, shaking hands.

"No!"

Tie sighed and got down on his knees in front of her. He could see tears swimming in her eyes and his heart ached. "Baby, its airomoxide. It will help."

She titled her head and he could see she was having trouble concentrating. "Isn't that what they give...?"

"Romheads and highboys," Tie finished for her, using the slang terms for users of the galaxy's most popular illegal drugs. "Yep." He grinned ruefully at her. "It also works, temporarily, on Ceriseheads."

She grinned weakly back at him. "And Finneganheads?"

"I sure hope so," Tie told her fervently. He reached for her thigh again and she shied away. He altered the course of his hand and stroked it up and down her calf to calm her. "Baby, it's the fastest way to get this into your system. I need you to be able to run in the next couple of minutes. This will help you."

"What's your real name?" she asked quietly.

Tie froze. This was the moment of truth. He found that it wasn't so hard to be honest for a change. "Tie. My real name is Tie."

"Just Tie?" she asked curiously.

Tie nodded, looking at her. She let go of her thigh and reached one hand up to stroke his jaw. "Okay, just Tie. Help me not need you so much, just for a little while."

Tie wasted no time. He looked down and pushed the needle in, releasing the drug into her. She gasped and then began to shake uncontrollably. She fell off the bed into his arms and he held her close. "It will pass, little rebel. Just relax and let it take you." In another few moments the shaking lessened and then stopped altogether.

Tie set her back up on the cot and capped the needle, sticking it back in his pocket.

"Why are you keeping it?" Cerise asked and Tie was relieved to hear how steady her voice was.

"If I leave it they'll know something's wrong. We don't want to give them any advantages." Tie moved toward the hatch, peering cautiously out at the hallway beyond. When he saw it was clear he motioned Cerise forward.

Cerise came quickly and Tie was reminded of the chase she had given him on T-Sdei Delta. He felt a wave of relief pass through him when she took his outstretched hand. He had her. He knew without a doubt he could get her off this ship and he knew she was going to help.

Chapter Seven

ഔ

Cerise took Tie's outstretched hand and his touch sent a shock of calm through her system. She'd been so frightened, so desperate for him and now he was here, he'd come for her and she knew he would get them both off this ship. There were no doubts in her mind. She trusted him completely.

"Ready?" he asked, looking at her expectantly.

Cerise nodded with a little grin. "As I'll ever be," she quipped and was rewarded with Tie's devastating little half-smile.

"That's my princess," he told her and pulled her out into the corridor behind him. He was walking quickly and his longer strides meant that Cerise had to practically run to keep up with him. She didn't protest. She wanted off this god-awful hulk as soon as possible. Then she heard them.

"Please, don't leave me!"

"The lock! For God's sake, open the door!"

"Please, please, take me with you!"

"Tie!" Cerise tugged on his hand, struggling against his hold. She stumbled as he refused to slow his pace. "Tie! We've got to set these people free!"

"No." His one word answer was firm and brooked no argument. She argued anyway.

"Yes! They're political prisoners like me, Tie. They've done nothing wrong." She refused to go another step and Tie caught her as she started to fall face-first to the deck as he pulled her along.

"We haven't got time," he growled. "I've got to get you out of here. Regan's ploy will only hold them off so long. Reinforcements are on their way."

"We have time," Cerise told him firmly. She grabbed for the lock sensor he still held in his hand. He pulled it out of her reach. Cerise pushed away from him and put her hands on her hips to glare at him. "If they're chasing sensor alarms all over this ship from an entire deck of escaped prisoners it will make it that much harder for them to find us. Better to be one tiny blip among hundreds than the only one on the screen."

Tie's look turned to one of calculating admiration. "Score one for Princess Know-It-All," he said quietly and then turned without another word and began quickly inputting codes into the sensor. One after another the doors to the cells up and down the corridor began to open and prisoners rushed out. One tried to grab Cerise as he raced by and almost negligently Tie reached out and knocked the man unconscious. Cerise turned to him with wide eyes as the man slid down the wall he'd been thrown against by the force of Tie's fist.

"Oops," Tie said and then addressed the corridor in general in a loud voice. "If anyone else touches her I'll snap their neck." After that the tide of released prisoners gave Cerise a wide berth. Cerise shook her head in admiration.

"Quite the knight errant, aren't you?" she said sardonically.

"I'm the only knight you've got, Princess," he said with a grin as the last door opened. He grabbed her hand again and dragged her through the open gate at the end of the cell block, stopping abruptly and shoving her behind him. "Hey, does that make me a consort now?" he asked conversationally as he punched in another code on the lock sensor.

"Oh, uh, yeah I guess," Cerise said a little breathlessly, finding all this running and grabbing and dragging a little wearing. "If you want to be."

The gate to the cell block began to close as the last of the prisoners rushed through the opening. Tie tossed the lock sensor over his shoulder with a grin. "Hell no, I want to be king." He grabbed her hand and took off running before she could answer him.

* * * * *

"Tie!" Cerise shouted at him right before he felt her shove him into an alcove with all her might. He'd been moving quickly, only two more decks to go before they reached the *Tomorrow*. Their good luck so far had him twitchy. It was never good when things seemed to go your way on a mission. There was always something waiting to trip you up right when you got cocky. The laser blast that blew a hole clear through the bulkhead next to him actually made him feel relieved. Then he got pissed. They weren't even shooting on stun. Cerise was unarmed, for Christ's sake, and he hadn't pulled a laser on the guards. Who the hell had ordered deadly force?

He looked around for Cerise and his heart stuttered in his chest when he saw her on the deck at his feet. Had she been hit? He'd only heard the one blast. "Cerise!"

"I'm fine," she bit out as she rolled over until she was plastered to the wall. She slid up first to sit on her ass, her back pressed against the wall, then slid the rest of the way up to her feet. It was a practiced, professional move and Tie was impressed. "What the hell are they firing?" she asked as she glared at the hole in the bulkhead that was nearly a meter wide. She ruined the effect of the move by swaying a bit on her feet and pressing a hand to her head.

"Lasers set on kill." Tie's voice was clipped as he tried to disguise his relief that she was unhurt.

"What are they trying to kill, a Pyaw randwulf pack?"

Tie grinned at her sarcasm. She had backbone, that was for damn sure. She wasn't fazed a bit. A thought struck him. "Did Regan train you?"

She looked at him, surprised. "Yes. Why?"

Tie shook his head. Clearly there was a lot between the two of them that he knew nothing about. Without thinking he asked, "Are you in love with him?"

"Yes," Cerise answered without hesitation. Then she slapped a hand over her mouth and looked at him with wide, horrified eyes. After a moment she moved her hand to whisper. "Why did I just tell you that? I didn't mean to tell you that."

Tie got a sinking feeling in his stomach. Not just at her answer, but at her admission. "Did you eat or drink anything after they brought you here?" She couldn't have been that stupid.

Cerise nodded and Tie suddenly understood why she had seemed to be going slower and slower the last few decks, why he'd had to help her down the last ladder and her increasing unsteadiness as she stood next to him.

"Well, Princess Know-It-All, I'm guessing they gave you a little truth serum to help when they came to question you, which probably was going to be right about now." He couldn't keep the disgust out of his voice and Cerise glared at him.

"Well how was I to know?" she hissed. "It was supper time. They fed all the prisoners and I thought it might be my last meal."

"It's a prison hulk, you idiot. You are a rebel leader. Didn't it occur to you that they might want to, oh, I don't know, interrogate you about rebel plans? Or about your best friend Regan?" Tie was so mad at her he could have shook her. Just then another laser blast split the hatch to the left of their hiding place.

"Eek!" A little squeak escaped Cerise and Tie couldn't help laughing at the sound. She glared at him harder. "It surprised me!" Tie just laughed harder. "Are you insane? That's it, isn't it? You've gone insane." Cerise sounded so put out that Tie had a hard time trying to stop laughing.

"No, I haven't gone insane," he told her, still smiling. "It's just that you are a piece of work. One minute you're tough as nails and the next you squeak like a frightened little girl. I never know what to expect from you."

Cerise started to tip forward like a drunken man. "Oh, God," she moaned. "Does this serum always affect people like this?"

Tie sighed as he caught her shoulder and held her back against the wall. "Only if you mix it with another strong drug like, let's say airomoxide."

Cerise frowned at him, concentrating hard. "But that's what you gave me."

Tie just raised an eyebrow at her wryly.

"Well, you should have taken into account that they might have given me something," she slurred, trying hard to maintain her dignity.

That's exactly what Tie was thinking as he shook his head in disgust, this time at his own poor planning. He shrugged off his annoyance. Well, this is what he had to work with. Adjust the plan and finish it. It was how he'd been trained. He looked around and found what he was searching for after only a moment. These prison bozos had picked just the right location to attack them. He looked over at Cerise. "Can you stand on your own?"

She shook her head. "I don't think so," she said and Tie adjusted again. He moved in front of her, barely shielded by the edge of the alcove. He pressed her against the wall with his back.

"Hold on to me," he told her and she wrapped her arms around his waist. "Good girl." He pulled out his laser and sighted on the control box in a corner near the upper deck at least fifty meters away. Once again he thanked his SS abilities, knowing he'd never have been able to sight and hit the target without enhanced eyesight and military training. He was about to fire when Cerise snuggled into his back and whispered to him, ruining his concentration.

"I love you, Tie," she said and rubbed her face against his back.

For a moment he was frozen. Did she love him? Was it the truth serum talking, or the Tears? Or just this punch-drunkenness that she had from mixing chemical cocktails? He forced himself to put it aside. First things first—he had to get them off this deck and down to the *Tomorrow*.

He sighted on the box again and fired. It blew up in a fiery explosion and the lights up and down the deck blinked and then went off. Tie could hear pandemonium erupt at the end of the corridor and one wild shot was fired. He heard someone yelling, ordering everyone to stand down and he quickly holstered his laser, spun around and hoisted Cerise over his shoulder.

"Tie!" she exclaimed. "I can't see anything!"

"Shhh," he hissed. "Keep quiet!" He began running as quietly as he could toward the hatch he knew was one hundred meters down the corridor to his right. He could picture the map of this level in his head. Behind the hatch, in the storeroom, was an access panel to a maintenance ladder that extended down four decks. He only needed to go two. Cerise was so slight on his shoulder he marveled at how she'd been able to take him when he fucked her so hard. He was amazed that he hadn't broken her in two.

"Can you see?" she whispered tremulously, clutching his shirt in tight fists as she held on. He was so proud of her at that moment. No complaints about the uncomfortable ride, just the practicalities.

"Yes," he told her, stopping and lowering her next to the hatch he needed. He didn't expound on his answer. She didn't need to know that what he could see was the map in his head, not the actual deck under their feet. He could see like a cat in the dark, but even that required a little light. Here, on an enclosed deck, there was nothing, the blackness as dense and impenetrable as stone. She let him set her down, but kept a hand clutched to his arm. Her trust in him was humbling.

"Hurry, Tie," she whispered, although she needn't have bothered. He, too, could hear the stumbling steps of the prison guards as they made their way awkwardly toward them in the dark.

Tie reached out and, as expected, encountered the outline of the hatch. When he located the latch he gave it a twist with a satisfied sigh. Nothing happened.

"Shit."

"What? What is it?" Cerise trembled beside him, clinging to his arm.

"It's locked." Tie felt for the lock mechanism and finally located the small box next to the door. It was encased in a tightly locked box of synth-steel, with no edges to grab a hold of to rip it off the wall.

"Oh, God," Cerise moaned. "Tie, what I said, earlier…"

Tie's stomach clenched. Now was not the time for true confessions. "Hold it, Princess, until later. Right now I've got to concentrate on opening this hatch."

Both hands were on his arm now. "But, if you can't, I need you to know —"

"Losing faith already?" he teased, his voice tense. "Don't worry. They haven't yet built a door I can't break down." He gently eased her away. "But you've got to give me a little room, baby, all right? Don't worry, I won't leave you, I promise."

"I know," she whispered and Tie could have moved mountains for her at that moment. He grabbed the latch and pressed while at the same time bracing his feet and pushing his shoulder hard against the hatch. He felt both give a little. He had to be as quiet as possible or he'd just ram his booted foot against the damn thing. He heard the synth-steel begin to whine as it gave way to his superior strength. He adjusted his hold and the angle of his shoulder, hitting the weak points of the construction. This was just the sort of situation he'd been bred for, wasn't it? Perhaps this was *the* situation, the moment for which he'd been created. The thought gave him a feeling of peace. He'd known meeting Cerise had been a signpost. Perhaps his whole purpose for being had been to protect Cerise, here and now — perhaps forever. The thought didn't alarm him. It instead gave a meaningless life purpose and it was that purpose that allowed him to shove the hatch until it almost opened. Only one spot proved reluctant, a lock along the lower edge of the hatch.

He stepped back and kicked at the hatch as he'd wanted to all along. He realized that even if they heard it, the guards were too far down the corridor to catch them before they disappeared. Without his knowledge of the ship, they'd flounder about looking for them in the dark. With one more mighty kick the door flew inward. At the sound there was renewed activity among the guards.

"Tie?" Cerise asked, her voice shaky, but not fearful. Never fear, not for her.

Tie reached out and pulled her to him. She clung to him, feeling her way up until she wrapped her arms around his neck. He straightened to his full height and her feet left the floor. "I've got the door open," he whispered into her ear. "Inside there's an access panel to another ladder. When we reach the ladder, I'm going to move you to my back and I want you to hold on tight. I'll carry you down. Understand?"

Cerise nodded against his shoulder. "Yes, I understand," she whispered and he ducked his head and moved into the storeroom. He located the panel without any problems and pried it away from the wall. He moved Cerise around to his back and she clung to him with arms and legs as he moved out onto the ladder. He could feel the abyss beneath them, a cold breeze blowing up the long access tunnel between decks. Cerise's arms tightened around his neck and he began climbing down.

97

* * * * *

"You let them escape?" Captain Ward's voice was low and menacing as he confronted the Commander of the Amalgamation prison hulk. The Captain had arrived with a small contingent of Super Soldiers mere hours after the escape of the rebel princess. Like most SS he was tall, extremely muscular and unnerving with his opaque eyes that missed nothing. Captain Ward stood out from the others, however, with his unusual shock of almost-white hair. The bridge felt suffocating with the SS soldiers monitoring all stations. They'd taken over the hulk as soon as they arrived without bothering to ask permission.

Commander Tsung stuttered slightly as he responded, taking a step back. "I...I'm not sure how they got away. Our security sensors showed no anomalies, no breach in security."

Ward raised an eyebrow, his anger palpable. "Of course, they didn't, Commander Tsung. We are dealing with Super Soldiers, one of whom is an expert in computer infiltration. If you run a scan, I'm sure you'll find a harmless system correction in the last twenty-four hours that falls outside of security parameters. Clearly, they rerouted your system to ignore the breach." Ward stepped closer until Commander Tsung could see his nostrils flare slightly with annoyance. "I notified you via comm link that they were to be considered extremely dangerous and you were to shoot to kill. Why were my orders not followed?"

"They were, they were," Commander Tsung rushed to reassure the taller, younger man. "But shooting to kill doesn't necessarily guarantee a kill. We weren't told that Regan and Finnegan were SS. They were too good. Isn't that what they're trained for? I don't have special ops troops here, just prison guards. If you were planning on securing the rebel princess here, proper measures and precautions should have been taken. I was not given prior notification to make the needed arrangements."

Ward stepped back with a deep breath. "No matter. Our information indicated that Regan and the hunter separated while still on board this hulk. It would have been almost impossible to capture them separately." Ward turned and looked out the viewscreen of the bridge, in the direction of the Secundus System. "I'm one step ahead of them. They'll have to rendezvous somewhere before heading for the rebel's headquarters. And I think I know where that somewhere is."

Ward turned sharply to pin the commander with his gaze. "I require some information, Commander. You will find a rebel on this hulk for interrogation, immediately." His voice lowered and the Commander grew pale under his stare. "Do not fail me again, Commander. If I lose Regan and the rebels because of your incompetence, you will learn the hard way not to disappoint a Gen10 SS."

* * * * *

Tie was glad the rest of the escape had been anticlimactic. He had easily climbed down to the deck where the *Tomorrow* was waiting for them. The ship was still undiscovered and he and Cerise had gotten aboard without meeting any more guards. When Tie opened the bay doors no alarms sounded. Even if they'd run a diagnostic on the security program to see if there had been tampering they wouldn't have found Tie's work. He'd rewritten the basic program to exclude this bay, so the computer didn't register it as a break in security. Simple, but effective. Hopefully Egan had someone competent with computers too, or Tie would be making another run on this prison hulk.

He sat in the bridge now, programming the ship for evasive maneuvers. He didn't dare try to get through the Smith gate now. Somehow they'd have to find another ship. The thought made him sad. He and the *Tomorrow* had been together a long time. She was armed and redesigned to his exact specifications. He might never find a ship as good as she was. And it was here he'd found Cerise—claimed Cerise. The thought sent a bolt of white hot lust into his cock, making it hard until he burned with an ache he knew only she could soothe.

As if he'd called her, she appeared in the open hatch of the bridge.

"Permission to enter, Captain?" she said teasingly, her voice still a little weak.

"Are you all right?" Tie asked, concerned. He partially rose from his seat to help her but she waved him back.

"I'm not going to pass out or drool all over." At his raised brow she sighed. "I'm fine. Well, better anyway." She moved slowly over to the seat next to him. There were only two on his small bridge. The *Tomorrow* was a very small, highly maneuverable bounty class ship with excellent speed.

Cerise turned eyes full of gratitude and curiosity to him. "What exactly are you, Tie?" she asked him quietly and Tie knew the real moment of truth was upon him.

* * * * *

Cerise watched his eyes go blank for a moment and was again struck by how out of place they looked in his face. Dull brown, they were flat and lifeless, so unlike the Tie she'd come to know.

"You've got it right," he said tonelessly. "I'm a what, not a who."

Cerise shook her head, confused. "What?"

Tie sighed and turned to face the view out over the bow of the ship. He slumped down in his chair and crossed his hands over his stomach. The pose was meant to be nonchalant, she was sure, but instead he looked like he was holding himself together, preparing for a blow.

"I'm a Super Soldier, Cerise, or at least I was."

Cerise gasped, unable to contain her shock. "But...but, you...how? How could you be?" She'd heard the stories. The

SS was filled with inhuman drones who killed without thought, without remorse. They blindly followed orders, were bred to be ruthless, unstoppable killers. That wasn't Tie. Her mind revolted at the very thought.

Tie turned to look at her, his eyes still lifeless though she could see the pain on his face. "Think about it, Cerise. Think about what you've seen."

His speed, his agility. His ability to see in the dark on the prison hulk. His strength, unlike any she'd seen before. He'd maneuvered on the hulk like a soldier, getting them out of the cell block and down to the bay where the *Tomorrow* had been docked without referencing any maps, but also without killing anyone. She'd seen him have ample opportunities to kill with impunity and every time he'd failed to do so. His kindness, his sincerity, his gentleness with her. The two sides seemed paradoxical, yet in her heart she knew he spoke the truth. She looked at him and realized that what she said next was extremely important. He tried to look cold, uncaring, but she could sense his tension, his expectancy.

"Well, I guess Super Soldiers aren't exactly what I've been led to believe." She spoke slowly, softly, gauging his reaction just as he was gauging hers. For a moment relief flashed on his face and then was gone.

"The Amalgamation likes to perpetuate the rumors about the SS. Having the galaxy fear their little lab rats suits them perfectly."

Cerise went with her first instinct. She reached out and gently ran her hand over his shoulder and down his arm. "You're not a lab rat, Tie. You're a human being."

Tie closed his eyes for a second before opening them and looking at her. "I'm a genetically enhanced freak, Cerise."

She shook her head roughly. "No, just a...a superman. They've made you better than the average human. There's nothing wrong with that, Tie." She smiled crookedly. "It just makes you a space mutt like the rest of us."

"I'm not a man, Cerise, super or otherwise," Tie said softly, sadness coloring his voice.

Cerise couldn't help it. She burst out laughing. "Oh, you're a man all right," she told him. "Trust me. I'm in a position to know this for a fact."

Tie looked at her, his face a picture of hope. "Is that how you see me? As a man? Or as some freakish genetic monster?"

Cerise gaped at him. "Good God, is that how you see yourself? As a monster?"

Tie sat up suddenly and reached for his eyes. Cerise's heart seemed to stop in her chest as she imagined him popping out an eyeball. But when he pulled his hands away and looked at her, she understood. "Your eyes," she breathed, awed at the surreal beauty of the luminescent gray, almost white, irises with a burning black pupil staring back at her. They looked...right. For the first time his face looked as if it was complete. "They're amazing," she said, staring into them, drowning in them.

Tie closed his eyes as if in pain. "They're freakish, Cerise," he whispered. "They brand me as surely as if they'd put an iron to my forehead."

She reached out and touched his cheek, then ran a fingertip over his eyelid. When she pulled it back he reopened his eyes. "No, they're beautiful. All this time, I knew. I knew there was something wrong with your eyes. They didn't fit. Now you look right, now I feel like I'm seeing the real Tie." She pulled back and tried to lighten the atmosphere. "So, can you see through my clothes, or shoot rays out of them?"

"What?" Tie asked, clearly taken aback by her question.

"Your eyes. Can they shoot death rays, or see through solid objects?" She could hear the eagerness in her voice. Damn! This was so cool. A real Super Soldier. And he was hers. The thought brought a rush of heat and wetness between her legs. One of the most powerful men in the galaxy, bred to be perfect and he was hers. Would be hers, soon, if the ache inside her and the trembling in her hands was any indication. She needed him and he, superman, Super Soldier, needed her just as bad. The thought practically made her moan out loud with desire. His strength, his agility, his stamina, all focused on fucking her and only her. God! She was nearly a puddle in the big captain's chair next to him.

Tie allowed himself a small smile next to her as he unconsciously leaned closer and the scent of him sent her pulse skyrocketing.

"I don't need to see through your clothes, I already know what's under them." His tone was suggestive and teasing and Cerise had to swallow before answering. She pretended to pout.

"I guess now that you've seen it, you're not interested in it anymore—" She didn't even get to finish the sentence before Tie had pulled her chair around and was tugging away the blanket that she'd wrapped around herself.

"That's not to say that when you're around I don't wish constantly that I could see through your clothes," he told her seductively as he concentrated on untangling her from the blanket. Underneath she wore nothing but the thin tank and panties he'd seen on her almost since they'd met. She thought he must be getting tired of them, but the gleam in his eyes when he looked at her dispelled that notion. God! To see those pale, otherworldly eyes glowing with desire for her. It was intoxicating. She couldn't stop staring at them. Tie glanced up and at her stare suddenly froze. He looked away.

"Do they bother you?" he asked. "I can put the contacts back in."

Cerise smiled at his show of vulnerability. He may be invincible, but she conquered him. Her smile dimmed a little as she amended the thought. The Tears had conquered him. She tenderly reached out and placed her hands on his cheeks, turning him back to face her. "No, they don't bother me. I told you, I think they're beautiful. I think you're beautiful."

Tie blinked slowly, once, twice. "Most women," he whispered, looking down at her mouth until she just had to lick her lips, which made him groan, "are frightened of me, of us. They don't think of us as men, but as machines. When I was still active duty, I had more than one cry at the thought of my touching her. One made me close my eyes the entire time we were together."

"Oh, Tie," Cerise breathed and she kissed him softly, tenderly, her lips barely brushing his. "I must be the freak then, because the thought of it makes me weak, I want you so much. So strong, so perfect, and mine. Your eyes make me wet just looking at them."

"God, Cerise," he groaned and he dragged her closer, to the edge of her chair, as he wrapped his arms around her and covered her mouth with his, driving his tongue inside to claim her with a wet, hot kiss. Cerise let out the moan that had been building there ever since he'd removed his contacts. Suddenly she had to see him, had to touch him, touch the power and strength of him. She grabbed the bottom of his shirt and began yanking it out of his leggings, pulling it up until he had to break the kiss. He jerked back and reached for his shirt, nearly tearing it off in his haste to be free of it. He threw it blindly to the side, uncaring where it went as he grabbed Cerise's hands, which had been reaching for him anyway. He pressed them against his chest, right over the flat, brown nipples there. When she ran her palms over them, enjoying the feeling of the hard nubs rubbing against her skin, he groaned as if in pain.

"Do you like that?" she whispered in wonder, still amazed at her ability to please him, to make him want her so much he groaned with it.

"Yes," he moaned desperately, "yes. Touch me, Cerise. Love me." He leaned forward and nuzzled her neck, his tongue licking over the pulse pounding there, licking up to the sensitive hollow behind her ear. Then he nipped her earlobe with his teeth. Cerise squeaked at the sting and his low laugh rumbled in her ear. In retaliation she pinched his nipples hard and he shuddered and his laugh turned to a groan. "Yes, baby, rough like that." His gravel-voiced command made Cerise shiver, caught up in the heat and impossible eroticism of the moment.

"Rough?" she whispered, her voice weak and shaky. She didn't care. She was beyond caring about anything except Tie, touching him and having him touch her. Her body was hot and swollen and throbbing in anticipation of feeling his cock driving inside her, fucking her until she screamed. At the thought her head fell back and her breathing became erratic.

Tie stopped and pulled away from her. She could feel his mesmerizing eyes studying her and she straightened her head to look back at him, trusting him with a carnal look of desire, of need. He caught his breath and then let it out in a rush. "I would give a thousand credits to know what you were just thinking about."

"Only a thousand?" she teased, not recognizing the wanton, husky voice as her own.

"A million," he whispered with that half-smile that had devastated her defenses from the first.

"I would give you all my thoughts for some of your secrets," she told him. His eyes grew hooded and she felt him pull further away from her, not physically, but emotionally. She couldn't hide her confusion. "Tie?"

"What secrets?" he asked, his voice no longer teasing.

"Just...just what else you can do. Is there anything else you're hiding? Like your eyes?" She saw relief flash through those eyes and the knot that had formed in her stomach released. Whatever he was hiding, she didn't care. In her heart she trusted him. She knew him as well as she knew herself, knew he would never hurt her.

"You don't have to tell me anything, Tie," she whispered. She gently pushed him back and smiled wryly when he let her, knowing that if he hadn't wanted to move nothing she did could have made him. His surrender was a kind of power for her, an aphrodisiac. She pushed until he was pressed against the back of his chair and then she climbed onto his lap, straddling him. His eyes glowed brighter as the skin along his sharp cheekbones grew taut with growing desire. "I was thinking about fucking you. Or, I guess, about you fucking me. The way you drive your cock inside me until I can't think, can't feel anything but its heat and hardness and how it feels to come with you inside me."

"Jesus," Tie breathed, his hands cupping her ass and pulling her down further until her pussy was pressed against the hot, hard length she'd been dreaming of. He looked up at her with a touch of amusement. "So you like the eyes, huh?" She could only nod as he manipulated her hips, rubbing her against his cock. "I have super hearing, too," he whispered, his voice a little rougher than it had been. "I can turn my auditory filter off and on with a mere thought. When the filter is off, I can hear things up to five hundred meters away."

Cerise felt her eyes widen in surprise. "That's amazing," she gushed, thrilled all over again at his enhanced abilities. "Anything else?"

Tie laughed and pressed her especially hard against him, making her gasp and thrust into him.

"Mmm," he said as he licked his lips, biting the bottom one as he moved her again in just the same way.

"Oh my God," Cerise said, shock in her voice, "I think I'm going to come and we're not even naked."

Tie licked his lips again, this time with a calculating gleam in his eye. "That first night you were here I lay in my bunk and I jacked off listening to your breathing, your heartbeat. Two times, just listening to you and smelling your wet pussy in the air made me come." He pressed her against him while he spoke, grinding his cock into her clit through their clothes. The images he invoked with his words and the proof of his desire for her rubbing her clit so hard and sweet made Cerise shake as she felt the first contractions of a climax.

"Tie," she groaned as she ground onto him. Her hands were pressed against the hard ridges of the muscles in his stomach, his skin hot and damp. She could feel his muscles shift and tighten as he thrust against her and she threw her head back, letting the climax take her, enjoying it.

"Yes, baby, that's it, come for me," Tie whispered as he moved against her just right, prolonging the rapture.

When it was over Cerise lowered her head and looked at him, basking in the hot, thick, lethargy that ran through her. She felt primed, as if the climax had done no more than prepare her for him. His indrawn breath spiked her anticipation.

"More," she whispered and Tie's responding smile was feral.

Chapter Eight

ೕ

Cerise's orgasm and her whispered demand pushed Tie over the edge. He'd been trying to be so careful with her, he'd been afraid of frightening her, driving her away now that she knew the truth about him. But now he knew the truth about her — she liked it, liked him, liked, no loved, what he was, what he was capable of. She wanted him more than anyone had ever wanted him before and he didn't think it was because of the Tears. He'd never thought he'd have this, a woman in his arms who knew about his past and yet still burned for him.

Without warning Tie grabbed the bottom of Cerise's flimsy little tank and ripped it apart from bottom to top. Cerise gaped at him.

"Oops," he said, clearly not contrite at all, "I guess I don't know my own strength."

Cerise narrowed her eyes at him and gave him a crooked smile that made his heart race. "Perhaps we should explore your other senses, just to make sure we're fully informed of your capabilities," she purred. She leaned into him, her breasts pressing against his chest, those tight, rosy nipples he loved branding him. She leisurely licked a path around his lips. "First, taste," she whispered and then she slowly insinuated her tongue in his mouth. He sucked it deep and Cerise's arms snaked up around his neck as her head tilted to the side, the better to plunder his mouth. The movements of her sharp, hot tongue exploring every corner of his mouth made Tie feel as if his skin were on fire. He unconsciously followed her as she pulled slowly away from the kiss, reluctant to let her go.

"Open your eyes," she whispered, "I want to see them." Tie obeyed and felt a satisfaction he'd never known before watching her pupils dilate as she licked her lips, overcome with lust at the sight of the eyes he'd always hated. "Now, sight," she went on. "Look at me." Tie let his eyes roam over her and his hands followed close behind. He pushed the thin straps of her ruined shirt off her shoulders and it fell to the floor unheeded. His hands ran down her arms, small but muscular arms, with warm skin, not too soft, the light coating of hair on them pleasant against his palms. He took a deep breath, inhaling her fragrance. She was wet and musky, spicy, as she'd been that first night when the scent of her was enough to make him come. Now he needed more. Needed what he'd had before but would never have enough of.

"You're supposed to be just looking," Cerise said, amusement lacing her words.

Tie looked up, unable to be flippant. He'd passed that point. "I can't. I can't just enjoy you one way at a time. You're a feast for my senses, Cerise—the touch, the taste, the feel of you. I want to breathe you in and live on you, to eat you for breakfast, lunch and dinner."

Cerise's smile faded, replaced by a look of wonder and stark need. "I can't help with the first, but if you need a little nibble now and then, well, go right ahead."

Tie didn't need to be told twice. He lifted Cerise from his lap and gently laid her down on the control panel in front of him. "Is that all right?" he asked, already pulling her panties down her legs.

Cerise shifted a little to the left. "I'm fine, now. There's one really big button here," she pointed vaguely to the right, "but I'm off it now." She raised her head and looked down at him where he sat between her legs which he had spread wide. He was staring at her pussy. "For God's sake," she groaned, "put your mouth on me already! I'm going mad." As if to punctuate her point she thrust her hips toward his face.

Tie ignored her. "Your pussy is so beautiful, Cerise. It's so pink and wet and swollen. Feel it." He grabbed her hand and pressed it against her, guiding two of her fingers into the folds there. She cried out and bucked against their joined hands. "Has anyone else ever been here, Cerise? Has anyone else seen how pretty this is?" He let go of her hand and ran a finger down the center of her slit, the deep well of her entrance nearly sucking him in, but he passed lightly over it, collecting and spreading the cum seeping from her.

"Tie," she whimpered. Her surrender made him wild. He wanted to feed and fuck, to possess her again and again. He replaced his finger with his tongue and Cerise sobbed. When she started to pull her hand away Tie stopped her. "Answer me, Cerise," he growled, his breath stirring the damp curls over her mound, making her shiver. "Has anyone else been here?"

"No, Tie, no," she cried, "only you. Please Tie."

Tie felt a savage possessiveness at her response. He pressed her fingers back against her nether lips. "Hold yourself open for me, Cerise. Open these lips and let me kiss you." When she obeyed, spreading the lips apart so that he could see every wet, pink millimeter, he leaned in and pressed his mouth against her, kissing her pussy the same way he'd kissed her mouth, his tongue delving inside and swirling around, tasting every soft, sweet morsel he could reach. He nibbled with his lips, teasing her and she moaned, thrusting her hips, fucking his mouth and Tie let the beast roaring inside him free.

Sliding his hands roughly beneath her Tie gripped her ass and pressed her pussy against his face. He devoured her, his teeth and lips and tongue licking and sucking and biting. He rubbed his stubbled chin softly against her tender skin and felt her fingers fist in his hair. He knew one of her hands was wet with her own cum and now it was in his hair and the thought of that sweet cream on him made him ravenous. He wanted it everywhere. He wanted to pick her up and rub that wetness all over his body. She was drenched with it. He could feel it begin to run down his chin and his hand automatically came up to catch it. He reached out and felt it dripping down from her

110

opening, running over the sensitive skin of her perineum, where he lightly tracked it with a fingertip, making her shiver. His finger kept going and he skimmed it over the tightly puckered hole of her ass, soaking wet with the overflow. This time it was Tie who shivered.

He rolled his finger in her juice, liberally coating it, and all the while Cerise moaned and sighed and held his mouth to her. She was on fire for him, his in every way and Tie knew he could do what he wanted with her. He could pleasure her however he wanted and she wouldn't protest. She trusted him. He would make sure she never regretted it.

When he gently pushed the tip of his index finger inside her ass, Cerise shrieked and tried to sit up. "Tie! What are you doing?" She was panting, partly from desire, but Tie knew it was also a little bit from fear of the unknown.

He kept his finger inside her and kissed her pussy deeply, pressing his tongue inside and fucking her with it in short, quick thrusts. She moaned and arched her back as her head fell back on the console. He pulled away briefly and lapped at the juice flowing from her with a rumble of approval.

"It will feel good, Cerise, trust me," he assured her, looking up at her as he traced her clit with the tip of his tongue. She looked down at him and then swallowed hard as she closed her eyes, her hips bucking, forcing his finger in a little deeper.

"Oh, God," she moaned, but she didn't protest.

Tie allowed himself a little smile of triumph before he went back to his feast. He pulled his finger back to edge of her tight, hot ring and then thrust a little deeper, a little harder, repeating the motion over and over. With each pull he gathered more of the cream that was now flowing liberally again, running down her seam, easing his passage into her sweet little ass. He groaned against her. He'd never dreamed he'd be able to do this to her so soon, but she was wild for fucking, wild for him. She'd let him do what he wanted, what pleased them both.

"Ahhh, God," she cried as he pressed his finger in all the way. "It's too much, Tie, too much!" She was fucking his mouth and his finger in short, hard, erratic bursts.

He pulled back and licked her gently again. "Slow down, baby, steady, smooth," he instructed her, softly rubbing her stomach with his free hand. "Fuck me smooth and steady, Cerise," he said again. "I want to make you come one more time before I fuck you with my cock."

"Oh, God," she sobbed and he watched her struggle to follow his instructions, her hips moving in counterpoint to his finger. When her motions became smooth and steady he lowered his mouth again. At the same time he thrust both his tongue and his finger inside her he pressed the thumb of his other hand against her clit in a matching rhythm. It took only moments before the combination set her off like an explosion. She arched her back and screamed as her thighs clamped around his head, her pussy milking his tongue. He pressed his finger into her ass and held it there, doing the same with his thumb against her clit, until the spasms of her orgasm slowed and she collapsed back against the console.

She lay there panting furiously, her legs and arms sprawled, useless. Tie could only smile at the picture she made, replete with sexual satisfaction. He loved to do this to her. She always seemed to be worried about something, never resting. Not until after he'd fucked her senseless. He could do this to her, for her. Slowly he sat up and took his hands from her. As his finger slid free, she groaned. He slid forward on his chair, gently pulling her downward as she lay on the console. Her legs widened to accommodate him between them until finally her soaking pussy rested against his chest. He moved himself then, rubbing his chest against her wetness, spreading it on his body, his skin melting at the contact.

"What are you doing?" she asked, her voice breathless. He could almost feel her body stretching again, flaring to life after the last little death, craving more. God, she was made for him. She never tired of fucking him, never.

"I wanted to rub your cum all over me," he told her as he looked down at the sticky residue coating his chest. He wiped a hand through it and rubbed it over his nipples. The feeling made him shudder with animalistic pride and desire. He leaned over and bit her thigh, not hard, but enough to claim and she purred in response.

"Fuck me." Her words were harsh, but the tone was tender, loving and possessive. Without a word Tie helped her up and she stood on shaky legs as he rose from his chair and removed the rest of his clothing. She watched each bit of skin revealed avidly, her lips parted, her tongue darting out to wet them when he finally kicked free of his leggings.

He sat again and motioned her to him. She came and understood what he wanted without being told. She straddled his lap again, but this time when he lowered her it was onto his hard, aching cock, nearly bursting with the need to fill her. As he slid into her tight sheath, so hot he felt the flames licking up his spine, he knew he'd found home at last. Here, inside Cerise, this was where Tie belonged, his path revealed. When he was fully seated inside her, he felt her hands on his face and let her raise his head until they looked into each other's eyes. Then she began to move. There was no doubt in Tie's mind what she was thinking then. She was right where she belonged as well.

As tender as he wanted to be, Tie couldn't hold back. He fucked into her hard and deep and like the times before, Cerise took it and begged for more. She slammed her hips down on him, her pussy so wet from her previous climaxes he could hear each thrust, the smell of their arousal drenching the air on the bridge.

"Harder, baby, deeper," she begged and she dragged his hand back to her ass. He thrust his finger inside and she cried out. "Yes," she sobbed as he began to fuck her with his cock and his finger in tandem.

Tie knew he couldn't last much longer. "Come again, baby, hurry," he gasped, tilting her forward slightly so that her clit rubbed against him with each thrust. "I can't wait, Christ, Christ, I'm going to come," he ground out, feeling the heat of his semen as it rose from his tight sac up through his cock.

"Yes, yes," Cerise yelled, "come inside me, Tie, God, yes!" She was fucking him so fast and hard, taking him so deep, loving every second of it and Tie couldn't hold back. His climax tore through him violently and he growled as he pressed into her so hard he was afraid she would ache from it later, but he couldn't stop. He could feel his cock jerk as he came into her, burning inside from the heat of his own cum and outside from the heat of her pussy.

As soon as the first stream of his cum hit her, Cerise blew apart. She cried out his name over and over, clinging to him, her arms around his neck. Their wet skin was plastered together, one more sensation in a moment overloaded with them.

The tears she cried in his arms afterward, as he carried her to his bed, bound him to her more tightly than her Carnelian Tears ever could.

* * * * *

Tie rolled out of bed quietly. He wasn't even sure what time it was. He rubbed a hand over his face, feeling the stubble there. Christ, he felt like he'd been fucking Cerise for days and he still wanted more. If this is what the Tears did to a man, no wonder just about everyone in the galaxy could claim some Carnelian blood. He pulled on a pair of loose pants that he'd casually thrown over a chair the night he'd first brought Cerise here. It seemed like years, but it was only a few days ago. A few days that had completely changed his life.

He walked quietly out of the cabin and headed toward the galley. He was so thirsty he could drain a lake and he wanted to have something for Cerise when she woke up. He smiled at the thought of her curled up in his bed, their bed now. He'd never have to sleep alone again. He stopped mid-step, just stopped as the realization hit him. He would never be alone again, period. Someone, somewhere would always worry where he was, worry that he was all right and miss him when he was gone. He felt unsteady on his feet and turned to rest his back against the wall. He tipped his head back and closed his eyes as he felt his throat choke up with emotion.

"I thought you two would never stop fucking."

The voice, low and bitter, came from the dim recesses of the open cell. Tie spun to face the threat in it. Regan rose slowly from the cot, his hands loose and open at his sides. Tie felt his tension ease slightly.

"When did you get here?" Tie wasn't surprised to see him, nor was he surprised he'd gotten on board without Tie realizing it. Regan had been trained just as Tie had and probably a little better than Tie considering Tie had spent half of his time in the brig for insubordination. And Tie had been so caught up in Cerise, in loving her, that he hadn't given a thought to security. He inwardly cursed. He was sure the pirate would have something to say about that.

"Around fifteen orgasms ago," Regan replied wryly. He stepped forward and left the cell, walking toward Tie. "How could you? She's a child."

"She's twenty-five." Tie tried not to be defensive. This was his chance to find out what the hell was between Cerise and Regan. "And why do you care? She told me you two weren't involved." He saw Regan wince slightly. That one had hit the mark.

"She's been under my protection for the last eight years." Regan was on the defensive.

Tie looked at him stony faced, but couldn't resist raising an eyebrow. "Yeah, good job on that, Regan. You're lucky I wasn't hunting her sooner."

The pirate took a menacing step closer to him. "Did you make her? Did you force her? Was that your price for rescuing her?"

115

Samantha Kane

Tie felt as if he'd been punched in the stomach. This man used to be his best, no, his only friend in the world. He'd known Tie better than Tie knew himself. And now here he was accusing Tie of rape. Tie was swamped by the nausea clawing its way up his throat.

"Is that what you think of me? Do you believe I could do that?" he whispered.

Regan blew out a frustrated breath and ran both hands over his slick skull. The movement was so clearly unconscious Tie knew instantly it was one he repeated often.

"I don't know. I don't know you anymore, do I? I trusted you with her! Was I a fool?" He paused and Tie could clearly see that there was more he wanted to say, but he wouldn't. "You're right," he bit out suddenly. "I should have protected her better. I should never have let her out of my sight." He was so disgusted and angry at himself that Tie felt sorry for him. "Why are you working for the Amalgamation?"

So that's where this was coming from. "I'm not." Regan started to speak, his face angry, but Tie wouldn't let him. "Technically I work for Bounty Hunters, Inc. Sometimes we take a bounty for the Amalgamation, but only as independent contractors."

"Jesus, Tie! What are you thinking? They've been hunting you since the morning I woke up and you were gone. Have you got a death wish?" He sounded so angry it took a moment for Tie to understand what he meant. He was worried about Tie.

"I came for you."

Regan froze and looked at Tie from hooded eyes. "What?"

Tie stepped closer until less than half a meter separated the two men. "A year after I left. I spent that year planning how to get you out. But when I got back, you were gone — deserted, a hefty price on your head. You ask me what I was thinking. What were you thinking Egan, to open fire like that?

116

To kill nearly ten SS and help a resistance prisoner to escape? You were lucky to get out alive."

Regan hadn't known. No one had told him Tie had come back. Perhaps no one knew. But Regan believed him. That was what Tie would do, something insanely heroic and stupid.

"Regan," he corrected without thinking.

"Egan, Regan, what the hell is the difference?" Tie snapped at him.

Regan jerked his head up to face Tie at his response. "There is a world of difference. Egan was a fool. A fool who believed that if he just followed the rules everyone would leave him alone and let him live his life. An idiot who was betrayed by a best friend, who ran off and left him to face the consequences. Regan is smarter than that blind fool ever was."

"Egan—" Tie began, but Regan cut him off.

"They tortured me for your whereabouts," he said conversationally, as he turned and walked casually over to one of the chairs at the small table near the concealed galley. "And when they realized I really didn't know where you were they busted me in rank and tagged me." He tapped his scarred cheek. "Tracking device." He grinned smugly. "Didn't work." Tie stumbled toward him, his face a white mask of horror. Regan was glad he was so horrified. Glad he was being eaten alive by guilt. He'd left him. Tie had left him with no good-byes, no promises and no hope. "Egan didn't get out alive. He wanted to die that day, so I let him. And Regan took his place."

He sat down as Tie stared at him with wide, glowing eyes. Suddenly the meaning of those pale eyes registered and Regan jumped up again. "Damn it! God damn it, she knows doesn't she? You told her."

Tie looked at him confused.

Regan pointed to his own disguised eyes. "Your eyes, damn it. She's seen your eyes."

"Tie?" a sleepy voice asked from the cabin doorway.

Cerise walked out of the bedroom to his right into the dim lighting of the galley, naked. Regan's heart stuttered to a complete standstill in his chest. Christ. God, she was fucking beautiful. He'd seen her in tight-fitting clothing before, when they trained and worked out. He'd known she was small-breasted, with long legs and a sweetly curved ass. He'd admired them from afar, as if she were a work of art in a museum, the princess so far above him he couldn't even touch the toe of her delicately arched foot. And now here she was, naked and flushed, her skin glowing with life and sexual satiation. In a flash he saw what had only been hinted at all those times he'd locked his arms around her as he taught her self-defense. Her back was long with a graceful arch that curved into high, round cheeks on a lusciously full derriere. She turned at his indrawn breath and his heart started beating again twice as fast as before. Her legs were long and the line of them led to the dark apex of her thighs and a small bush of tightly curled pubic hair with pale lips peeking from their midnight depths. Her stomach was flat, her breasts small and perfect, with ripe pink nipples gleaming hard and aroused in the faint light. She was fucking perfect.

He could smell her. Smell the sex on her and smell Tie on her. His gut was churning with anger, resentment and possessiveness. The last surprised him. He hadn't realized how much he'd begun to think of her as his. But his in what way? His ward? His protégée? His...what?

"Get your clothes, Cerise," he snarled, "we're leaving."

Cerise's eyes went round with dismay and she squeaked inelegantly. "Regan!" She instantly crossed her arms over her bare breasts and looked frantically around. Regan was about to offer her his vest when she turned to Tie and fell into his open arms. Tie's arms wrapped around her and she buried her face in his neck. As Tie's hand ran soothingly up and down the smooth, soft-looking skin of her bare back Regan felt his chest crack open and bleed regret. He was amazed he was able to maintain a façade of detachment. While he looked at them stony-faced, inside he wanted to fall to his knees and beg her forgiveness for all those wasted years. He wanted to confess...what? That he desired her and always had? That he admired her? He watched her hand slide up Tie's chest and around his neck in a caress that said everything. She belonged to another man now. A man he'd once called best friend. A man who had confessed to him in the dark of the night long ago that he loved him.

"She's not going anywhere with you, Regan." Tie's voice was cold, hard. Cerise didn't know what they'd been talking about before she woke up, but it had definitely set them on edge.

She knew she was being a coward, hiding her face in Tie's shoulder, refusing to face Regan. There were so many thoughts chasing around in her head, she didn't know which to grab on to. God, she was so embarrassed that Regan had seen her like this, naked and thoroughly fucked, climbing from another man's bed. Mixed with the embarrassment was a bone-deep sadness for something lost. She had always dreamed it would be Regan's bed she shared and now that dream was shattered.

Tears of guilt and regret filled her eyes. How could she think of another man when Tie had just made such wonderful love to her? Regan's order and Tie's response, made her feel fiercely loyal and possessive of Tie. She knew she could never give him up, but more than that she knew she would never want to. Was that the Tears talking, or her heart? Did it really matter anymore? She tightened her hold around his neck.

"That's up to Cerise," Regan replied, his tone as cold and hard as Tie's.

Cerise pulled her head up and looked into Tie's amazing eyes. "I can't go, Regan. I won't leave him." They were some of the hardest words she'd ever spoken.

119

Regan cursed and she cringed as she heard him kick over a chair behind her. "God damn it, Cerise! Are you going to give up everything we've worked for the last eight years because of one good fuck?"

Regan had never spoken to her like that before. He was so angry and somewhere in there she thought she heard a little hurt. Even as she clung to Tie she felt a thrill course through her at the thought of Regan jealous over her. She ruthlessly tamped down the feeling.

"Don't ever speak to her like that again," Tie growled, his body tense. Unconsciously Cerise began to mimic his stroke along her back, her hand running up and down along his spine. She felt him relax, but their caresses were affecting her in a different way. In spite of Regan's presence, she wanted Tie again. Her blood coursed through her veins, heat spreading outward from her core as her pussy was bathed in her wet response. The thought of Regan standing behind her staring at her naked back and ass, watching Tie's hands caressing her, was disturbingly erotic.

"She needs to get dressed." Regan's voice was deeper, his breathing a little ragged and he cleared his throat, stepping away from them.

Tie's hand suddenly dipped down and ran deliberately over her ass, making Cerise groan. She bit her lip after it slipped out, horrified. She felt Tie shake as he chuckled quietly. "I like her this way." His hand came to rest on one cheek, his fingers gliding softly over the crease, teasing her. She shivered and his arms tightened around her.

"You bastard," Regan said softly. "Do you know what you've done?"

Cerise wasn't so far gone that she didn't hear the threat in his voice. She'd heard Regan use that tone before, usually preceding a violent outburst. She pulled out of Tie's arms and spun to face him. "No, Regan! Tie didn't do anything. It was me. I did it." She hugged herself, ashamed. "I used the Tears on him."

Regan was breathing heavily, his chest rising visibly with each inhalation. His hands were fisted at his sides. She could see his eyes darting down to look at her, see him fighting the urge to do so until finally he gave in and starting at her feet he lingeringly caressed every inch of her until their eyes met. The heat of his gaze scorched Cerise and she stepped back, stunned. Regan wanted her? When? How?

Tie slid up behind her again, his arms gliding around her, his hands resting on her lower stomach just above her pubic hair. Tie's motion seemed to snap Regan out of his stupor. "Get dressed, Cerise," Tie murmured in her ear and she nodded, still in shock. She turned and ran into their cabin, frantically searching for her underclothes. She came out wearing one of Tie's shirts when she remembered Tie ripping her tank top off.

The two men were standing there glaring at one another when she rushed back out. Tie hooked an arm around her waist and brought her back in front of him. "She was meant for better." Regan's tone was harsh, accusing and Tie froze behind her.

"I was never good enough, was I?" Tie asked quietly.

Cerise was confused. What were they talking about? Good enough for what?

"She's a fucking princess. She's going to rule the galaxy when the smoke from this war clears. She needs a man who can rule at her side. Someone the people will respect and follow. Do you honestly believe a renegade Super Soldier is that man?" Regan's voice kept getting louder, his volatile temper rising with each word.

"Is that why you haven't taken her?" Tie asked softly, his hands slowly caressing her stomach and sides.

Regan hissed and stepped toward Tie and Cerise's hands automatically came up to stop him, slamming against his hard chest. Regan's gaze swung down and locked on hers. "Yes," he whispered, "God damn you, yes."

Cerise couldn't hide her shock. "Regan..." she gasped. Suddenly so many things fell into place. He'd always seemed larger than life to Cerise, his abilities greater than any other man she knew — until Tie. She'd always believed part of that was because of her feelings for him. And his eyes — the same flat, dull brown as Tie's had been. She'd often wondered how Regan managed to have such empty eyes with such a legendary temper. Her shock was replaced by anger and hurt. "Why? Why didn't you tell me?"

Regan's look was pitying. "To what end, Cerise? Only a few people know. It's not who I am anymore. And it wouldn't have removed the barrier between us. It would only have strengthened it."

"A barrier that exists only in your mind! God damn it, I had a right to know! To know who you are. To know how you felt. I am as much outlaw as you Regan. The Amalgamation wants me dead. Every day I evade capture is a miracle. I—"

"No!" Regan cut her off angrily. "It's not a miracle. *I* make it happen Cerise. *I* protect you. It's my responsibility. I keep you alive and safe so that you can be the leader you were meant to be." He gestured angrily at Tie. "And this is how you repay me? By fucking the first bounty hunter who slips under my sensors?"

Tie stiffened behind her. "I'm a hell of a lot more than that, Egan, and you know it."

"Egan?" Cerise looked quickly at Tie over her shoulder and turned to see Regan wince. "Is that your real name?"

Regan's face closed off. "No. My real name is Regan."

Cerise shook off Tie's hands and marched away from both of them. She stopped and stood with arms akimbo and glared at them. "I am so sick of the lies! Finnegan the bounty hunter is really Tie the Super Soldier. But he doesn't tell me until after I've fucked him! Until after I've enslaved him! And now the one solid thing in my life I thought I could trust, you Regan, you've been lying to me since the day we met! Regan is

Egan, Super Soldier." She shook her head in disgust, but it was disgust at herself. "I must be the most gullible woman in the galaxy."

"What do you mean, enslave him?" Regan asked sharply.

"What am I supposed to call you now? Egan?"

He answered her through gritted teeth. "Regan. I told you I was Regan."

"Why? Why the pretense? Your secret is out."

"It's not a pretense!" Regan shouted at her. He grabbed her arm and hauled her over to him. "Regan is my name. It's the name I chose. Egan, Tie, those are Super Soldier names. Not even names. Codes, taken from our serial numbers. We were monsters bred in a lab and they didn't even give us names, Cerise. They gave us numbers. Mine was EG-46872N. And Tie's was T1-45897E. Do you see? Do you see how we named ourselves? When I left the SS, I left it all behind, the name, the number. I am Regan. That is who I am."

Cerise could hardly breathe past the emotion clogging her throat. What had they done to them? Both men had referred to themselves as monsters. But they weren't, they weren't. She raised a shaking hand to his cheek but he jerked his head away.

"Now, what do you mean enslaved him?"

Cerise blinked to clear away her tears. Regan didn't want them. Fine. They'd discuss his past and how he saw her future later. "The Tears, Regan, Carnelian Tears. When I couldn't get him to listen to me, to let me go, I seduced him." She looked into Regan's face as she confessed, determined not to hide what she'd done. She would have to live with the shame for the rest of her life. "I...I deliberately released the Tears, so he would be tied to me. He couldn't turn me over to them, you see. He needs me."

Regan looked as if he'd been stunned. "But the Tears, they're just a myth."

Tie laughed wryly. Cerise looked over where he was leaning a shoulder against the wall watching them. Suddenly she remembered that Regan had known his number. He'd recited it as smoothly as his own. What had they been to each other?

"They are most definitely not a myth," Tie said, his tone matching his look. He stood away from the wall and stared at Cerise hungrily. Her body answered his call, heating again, an ache starting inside her for him. Tie walked over to them and ran his hand slowly in a featherlight caress down her arm. "I crave her. Like a drug. Like the worst Romhead you've ever seen. Without her I go into detox sickness — the shakes, a fever, cramps. When she was on the hulk I had to shoot myself full of airomoxide."

Somehow Cerise found herself in his arms again, the contact making her lightheaded and feverish. She didn't even remember moving. God, she wanted him. Now, right now. She wrapped her arm around his waist and pulled him close. As his hard cock touched her through the thin layer of his loose pants her head fell back and she closed her eyes with a moan.

"And she's the same," Tie whispered as his hand ran down the front of her neck, barely touching her, leaving gooseflesh behind. It was a shadow caress and she shivered as it continued down over her chest and stomach, only their pelvises locked together. "She's as addicted to me as I am to her." He bent down and kissed her throat and Cerise clutched his arms convulsively. She knew they should stop. Regan was less than a meter away, watching them. The thought should have cooled her ardor, but it only fueled the fire. Tie pulled his mouth from her and she gasped. "I will kill for her," Tie whispered, his hand tangling in her hair as he forced her head up, forced her to open her eyes and meet the possession in his gaze. "I will die for her." He turned to look at Regan. "She is mine and I am hers."

Cerise turned to look at Regan as well and she saw his face had gone pale and his eyes even bleaker. She wanted to see his real eyes, like Tie's. She wanted him and she wanted Tie. She blinked at the thought, but it didn't go away. "I can't leave him, Regan," she whispered, "not ever. We belong to each other now."

Regan turned without another word and walked slowly away, disappearing through the hatch onto the bridge.

Chapter Nine

ဢ

Regan sat in the bridge punching a convoluted evasion strategy into the computer. They needed to get to the rebel base on the largest of Mimnet's moons, Quantinium, in the Secundus System. He'd already told the crew of *The Rebel Bounty* to meet them there. They were racing against time. He knew the Amalgamation, knew they'd be disorganized at first in their search for the three of them. Tie, or Finnegan as they knew him, would be a wanted man now and so would his ship. But the chances were good that that information would take a while to reach the rest of the galaxy. They had maybe a day or two to get through the required Smith gates. If they waited to acquire another ship it might be too late. He'd often risked his life and the lives of his crew on such educated hunches, but this was different. Now he risked Cerise's life and he'd never been so unsure of a decision.

His head was viciously pounding. He'd spent the last half hour blocking out everything but what he was working on. His audio filter was on high. He couldn't hear anything outside the confines of the bridge. He wished he could turn off his nose as well. He could still smell them. Smell the sex on both of them, their individual scents mingling into one unique aroma that was driving him mad. The two separate scents had done that to him before, but this one, this combined essence of Tie and Cerise, it was torture to sit here bathed in it. Christ, even the bridge smelled like sex. They must have fucked in here. What was he thinking? Of course they'd fucked in here and probably everywhere else on the ship. He would have fucked her in every position on every surface in every cabin if he had had the opportunity. He closed his eyes tightly against a particularly painful throb in his temple. He'd had the opportunity. He could have had her at any time over the last seven years, but he'd played the honor card on himself. And now here he was, hiding on the bridge while his former best friend fucked her sweet brains out ten meters away.

"Where are we going?"

Regan spun around in the pilot's seat to see Tie standing in the hatch. He'd been able to sneak up on him with his audio off and this headache beating against his skull.

"What?" Regan winced inwardly. He hadn't meant that to sound so angry and defensive.

Tie looked at him coolly. "I asked where we were going...Captain."

His sarcasm wasn't lost on Regan, who just got more pissed. "Well, I thought while you two were so very busy fucking someone should worry about getting away from the bad guys."

Tie sighed and came all the way in, sitting down in the chair next to Regan. He looked tired. Well, hell, he ought to. He'd worked Cerise over pretty good as far as Regan could tell from where he'd sat in that cell listening to them fuck for hours. He'd known then that she was there because she wanted to be, because Tie wanted her to be. The words they'd spoken, the things they'd said to each other in the heat of passion, those were love words and Regan, for all of his lack of experience at love, had recognized them as such. The knowledge left a bitter taste in his mouth. The two people in the whole world he had ever felt...something for and they were so busy fucking each other and falling in love they hadn't even noticed him.

He turned away from Tie, unable to bear the sight of him. Ten fucking years he'd searched for him, only to wish he'd never found him. Life was certainly a bitch, wasn't it? At least for him she always had been.

"Egan," Tie began, but at Regan's glare he held up his hands placatingly. "Sorry, Regan. It's going to take a little getting used to, all right?"

Regan couldn't tell him what it did to him to hear him say his old name in that familiar and beloved voice. He'd dreamed of it, of Tie saying his name, telling him how much he loved him. For more than ten years he'd dreamed of it and he'd woken in a sweat, aching and desperate to find him, to make sure he was alive. Right now he was angry, he didn't want to care. But he did and he hated himself for the weakness. With a growl he gave in to it.

"Are you all right?" he reluctantly asked through gritted teeth, glancing at Tie from the corner of his eye.

Tie looked surprised for a moment and then pleased. "That was going to be my question." He leaned forward and rested his forearms on his thighs, his hands clasped between them. He'd gotten dressed and wore all black from his heavy boots to his tight-fitting shirt. He looked older, meaner, sadder, but still Tie, still trying to get Regan to admit something he didn't want to.

"I'm fine." His voice said the subject was closed, but he knew Tie would ignore it. He always had.

Tie looked out the window, not facing Regan. "I'm not." His head dropped and he ran a hand through that hair. Regan laughed a little and Tie looked at him, hurt. Regan shook his head.

"That hair, where the hell did that come from?" Regan ran a hand over his sleek head. "I got rid of mine. It turned white." Tie's eyes went round and a smile played on his mouth. Regan nodded. "Something to do with the drugs they pumped into me, I think, during the interrogation."

Tie's look turned to pain. "E...Regan, I'm sorry. I didn't realize...I didn't think..." He stopped and shook his head in disgust. "Yes, that's right, I didn't think. I should have known what they'd do to you." He looked away again for a moment then looked back, the lines radiating from the corners of his eyes and bracketing his mouth more pronounced. "I thought if I didn't tell you, then you couldn't be implicated. But that's not the way they work, is it?"

Regan just shook his head and turned his chair to face Tie. "You never understood how they worked, Tie. Eventually they would have terminated you. You did the right thing when you left." It was his turn to look away for a moment. When he looked back he was in control again. "I waited too long. I waited until there was no way out but in a hail of laser fire and death. You were right, I was lucky to get out alive."

Tie leaned forward and clasped his hand over Regan's arm, the contact like a live wire that shot through Regan's system. He'd walked in a fog for ten years and with one touch from Tie it melted away. He felt on fire with all the emotions he'd suppressed. He was suddenly swamped with the fear for Tie, the anger, the loneliness, everything. In desperation he grabbed Tie's arm, clutched it, fighting down the emotional upheaval and Tie put his other hand over Regan's and held on, as if he understood. "I'm glad," Tie whispered looking in his eyes, telling him so much with that look. "I'm glad you got out alive."

Regan just nodded and closed his eyes, savoring Tie's presence, his touch, his smell, the one that only minutes ago he'd been cursing. It took a moment, but he was calm again when he opened his eyes. A kind of calm he hadn't felt since Tie left. This is what Tie gave him—peace. Even his headache was gone. He so desperately needed Tie's peace. "Thank God it was you, Tie," he whispered, overcome with gratitude for fate or whatever drove the universe. "Thank God you were the one who caught her and not someone else."

"Regan," Tie whispered and Regan opened his eyes. When Tie leaned toward him it seemed the most natural thing in the world to meet his lips, to kiss him back, to share his relief and his gratitude. A million memories of Tie assailed him. Memories of things they'd done together, moments

129

they'd shared and things he'd felt only with Tie. The kiss was tender, a foray rather than a thorough exploration and so brief that Regan began to think he'd imagined it as soon as it was over. But the feel of Tie's soft lips still lingered and when Regan licked his lips he tasted Tie's tangy flavor. He felt a bolt of awareness go through him and pulled back sharply. Tie's hand on his arm stopped his complete withdrawal.

"I'm sorry," Tie whispered. His voice was so low and intimate that Regan felt it in his gut and tugged his arm in alarm. Tie didn't release him. "I've waited so long, Regan, I've missed you so much. Give me this. Let me have this for just a moment more." Tie ran a finger down the scar on Regan's cheek tenderly and Regan shivered. "I left so you wouldn't be hurt anymore. Look at me, please." Reluctantly, Regan met his eyes. They were so beautiful. Tie had always hated them, but Regan dreamed of them. The pain filling those eyes now made that awareness burn in his belly again and he looked away, hoping against hope that Tie hadn't seen the emotions swirling through Regan reflected in his eyes.

"Do you ever think about the past, Regan?" Tie asked softly.

Regan shook his head. "No," he lied, dismayed at the roughness of his voice. "The past is over. There's nothing to remember."

"There was us," Tie said, his voice hurt. Regan couldn't stop his instinctive reaction to comfort Tie. But he resisted it. That wasn't his job anymore. "I thought about you all the time. Every day. Every night." Regan's breath hitched at Tie's confession. "I thought about that night."

Regan felt that gentle finger on his scar again and he jerked his head back. "Tie, don't."

Tie's laugh was bitter. "You may look different," he said, "but you still sound the same. Still the same old denial." Tie's hand tightened on his arm. "I won't let them hurt you anymore. No matter what, Regan. I won't let them hurt you anymore." Tie's softly spoken promise filled an empty space in

Regan. It was as if he could feel that strange hope Cerise gave him and the peace and security Tie gave him wrapping him up in bonds that should feel too tight, but instead felt safe. He shook his head, trying to convince himself it was his lack of sleep talking. And worry over Cerise and relief at finally finding Tie alive and well. Too many emotions for a man who had fought so hard to feel nothing for so many years. He'd been right to block those feelings. That way lay madness. This time when he jerked his arm Tie let him go.

"So Skipper, where are you taking us?" Tie asked quietly as he slowly sat back.

Regan was startled, but didn't let it show. It wasn't like Tie to let things go. He'd always worried at Regan's defenses like a dog with a bone. Regan took a deep breath and warily settled back in his own chair. "Secundus."

Tie sat up straight, alarmed. "What? You know that's the first place they'll look for us. They'll think we're going to Quartus Seven, to the Web."

Regan smiled smugly. "Exactly. But we're not going to be where they'll be looking."

"Where exactly will we be?" Tie raised an eyebrow, smiling conspiratorially at Regan's glee.

"A little secret rebel base we've got there." Regan laughed outright at Tie's amazement. "Oh, yes, great hunter. My rebellious friends and I have been hiding right under your nose."

* * * * *

"What the hell do you want?" Ulric Vonner was in no mood to be pleasant. He had a hunter run amok with an escaped bounty, apparently in league with one of the galaxy's most wanted pirates and the trail led right here to his door. He was more than pissed. Having some Amalgamation goon squad with an overzealous and dictatorial Captain in charge show up and try to pull rank on him was not on his top ten list of ways to make this day not quite as shitty as it had been twenty minutes ago.

Captain Ward leaned his meaty fists on Ulric's desk and leaned over in an effort to intimidate him. "I want Finnegan. And Princess Cerise Chessienne. And I really, really want Regan."

Vonner shoved the old-fashioned blotter on his desk so that it rammed the Captain's knuckles, knocking his fists off the desk. The Captain grunted and took a moment to steady himself, looking surprised. It was obvious those intimidation tactics usually worked for him. The Captain glared at Ulric with a vicious curl of his lip. Ulric was unimpressed by the whole show. He stood and leaned his fists on the desk in a mockery of the Captain's earlier stance. His nearly two meter tall frame didn't quite dwarf the other man, but it was enough to make him take a step back. "That is a Christmas list, *Captain*," he growled, with disdainful emphasis on his rank, "and not my department."

"Your hunter absconded with a known rebel criminal, Vonner. He illegally boarded an Amalgamation prison hulk, caused bodily injury to at least six guards, a great deal of physical damage to the ship and he helped not one, but fifty prisoners escape. And it would appear that he has come home to roost." With each crisp word Ulric's wariness increased. Ward widened his stance and crossed his arms over his chest, successfully taking up half of the available space in Ulric's office, before continuing. "And he did it all with the help of one of the Amalgamation's most wanted criminals, the pirate Regan. Unless you would you care to explain that to a tribunal on Amalgama you better make it your problem."

Ulric was good and pissed not to mention worried. He did not need this complication coming down on the Web or his hunters. He had too many irons in the fire right now. He stalked out from behind his desk and got right in Ward's face. "One, the bounty was delivered to the prison hulk as per Bounty Hunters Inc.'s agreement with the Amalgamation. The fact that she later escaped has no bearing on that agreement. Your bosses owe me 150,000 credits. Two, whatever Finnegan did after the bounty was delivered he did on his own time and not as a representative of this company. You have no legal recourse here, either for remediation from me or for criminal charges against me. And three, before you start trying to play with the big boys, Ward, you better learn the rules. And the rules here are that I do the dirty work you and your little lab rats in the SS can't handle. You don't ask questions and you don't rattle my cage. Because if you do, I will make one phone call and you will be the animal control officer on an outlook post. Now, do I need to break that down into shorter words for you, or do you understand?"

Ward took a step forward until he and Ulric were literally nose to nose. Ulric had to hand it to him, he had balls. Not many men had the guts to face down Ulric Vonner when he was pissed off. "We know Finnegan is a deserter from the SS, Vonner. He admitted it to several guards on the prison hulk."

Ulric had to fight to keep his face neutral when inside he was cursing. This just made a complicated situation worse. Ulric didn't like to be surprised with information. He'd known about Finnegan's past, or at least suspected. What he was surprised about was that he'd admitted it. That, more than anything, told Ulric he wasn't coming back. He allowed himself one raised eyebrow in response.

"I find it hard to believe the man worked for you for almost ten years and you didn't know." Ward's stony glare irritated more than intimidated, although it was clear Ward was going for the latter. "Because the situation involves a deserter, the SS is automatically authorized to seize control of the investigation and take all necessary measures to bring the man in."

Damn it, that was what Ulric had been afraid of. He made a dismissive gesture that belied his inner turmoil. "Whatever. Find him, don't find him. He's useless to me now anyway." He

133

narrowed his eyes at Ward. "What concerns me is that I get my money and that you get out of my office."

"Per the authority granted me as investigating officer in this case I request that you allow my men to search these facilities." Ward ground out the request as if it gave him a cramp.

Ulric smiled smugly as he casually turned and walked back around his desk. He enjoyed having the upper hand, if only temporarily. Ulric took the time to sit down and get comfortable before answering. Ward was grinding his teeth to dust by the time Ulric was settled. "Fine. Search the facilities. You may not, per individual rights statutes and the agreement I have with the Amalgamation, search the personal belongings of my staff." He held up a hand as Ward began to speak. "That no longer includes Finnegan and as a wanted fugitive he would be exempt anyway. So I'll have someone meet you at the room he kept here with keys to that door and to his locker." Ulric knew he wouldn't find anything helpful. He'd already searched them thoroughly.

Ulric could see Ward's jaw working with suppressed rage. "He may have contacted someone who works here, or left incriminating information with them."

Ulric smiled coldly. "My hunters do not tend to socialize together, Captain. As a matter of fact I'd be surprised if any of them could recognize more than one or two others by name. Rest assured he has not contacted them."

"Be that as it may —"

Ulric cut him off. "The search restriction is not open for discussion, Captain. Feel free to try to get a Senate order to countermand me, but I doubt you will." Personally, Ulric knew of several Senators who would gladly grant one on less evidence, but he was hoping Ward didn't know that.

Ward looked as if he was going to say something, stopped, debated with himself for one more minute glaring at Ulric, and then he turned and walked smartly to the door. He spoke over his shoulder. "I will divide my men into search teams. We do not require escorts."

"I wasn't going to offer them."

Ulric's softly spoken retort brought Ward up short and he turned to Ulric with a frown. "I will be checking on this agreement you rely so heavily upon, Vonner. You can be sure that if it does not offer you the protection you claim I will know all your secrets before I'm done."

"Oh, I doubt that, Captain. I sincerely doubt that."

Ward walked out the door and Dexter Smith, the Web's resident computer geek, sidled in. With a sharp twist of Ulric's head that set his shoulder-length black hair swinging, he motioned Smith to close the door. Smith started to speak but Ulric held up a hand. He searched through his desk and came up with a small, handheld box that looked like a recorder of some sort. He set it on his desk and pressed a button. Nothing happened in the office, but immediately outside the office door there were several grunts and a few yells.

"High frequency alarm?" Dex looked amused. He didn't wait for an answer. "What gives?"

"Fucking SS and their mutant hearing," Ulric cursed, slamming his fist on the desk. "I hope their fucking ears are bleeding."

Dex laughed, but at a glare from Ulric he stopped and swallowed nervously. "Sorry."

"Put every available hunter we have on Finnegan," Ulric snarled. "When I find that stupid son of a bitch I'm going to personally bash his bloody ignorant brains against the wall. And then..." he paused and took a deep breath.

"And then?" Dex prompted.

"And then...she better be worth it," Ulric finished with a sigh.

Dex grinned and turned toward the door. "From what I hear she is definitely worth it."

"Wait." Ulric rubbed a hand over his face. Now was not the time to act out of character. "Cancel that."

Dex looked back at him, bemused. "What?"

"We don't look for people unless somebody hires us and there's money in it for us and there's no money in Finnegan." He sat back in his chair, frustrated. "So we wait. When he wants us, he knows where to find us."

Ulric felt a headache begin to throb in his temple. Ward was going to be a problem. And Ulric didn't like problems.

Two hours later Captain Ward entered Ulric's office without knocking. He marched over and threw three microsensors on the desk in front of Ulric.

"We found these." His triumph was unmistakable.

Ulric recognized the sensors and inwardly cursed some more. "So? You found sensors." He leaned back in his chair and looked at the soldier sarcastically. "I can take you to our lab and show you a whole drawer full. We use a lot of sensors in surveillance work."

"These are very specific sensors and they are illegal for civilian use. But you already know that, don't you?" Ward smirked at him. It was not a good look.

Ulric sighed. "Why don't you just tell me what you're getting at Captain? I have work to do that is a great deal more important than indulging your theatrics."

Ward's nostrils flared with his anger. "These are very good copies of SS auditory filters, Vonner. They are sold on the black market. We've tracked several SS deserters by following the trail of these black market filters. The Generation 8 standard issue SS filters are designed to last only a few years. A Super Soldier's hearing is so acute he or she can't live without one of these. Eventually they have to find a replacement. If you didn't know you had an SS deserter working for you, why do you have them?"

Ulric looked bored. "I didn't have them, Captain. I don't even know where you found them."

"We found them on level three." Ward's voice was challenging.

Ulric sat up straight, furious. "That level is off limits. It contains nothing but the private quarters of my staff, which I expressly told you were not to be searched."

Ward smiled tauntingly. "We didn't search them all. Only the unlocked ones. This particular apartment door was actually open."

One of the soldiers came into his office then, dragging Dex behind him. Dex was big, at least 1.9 meters, and built like an athlete, but the soldier made him look puny. Ward looked over his shoulder at Dex. "We found them in this man's quarters. He was inside trying to hide them."

Dex looked affronted. His red hair was tangled and his shirt buttoned wrong. "I was not! I was in there changing my shirt when these goons came barreling in and pointed lasers at me, demanding I cease and desist. Cease what? Putting a shirt on?"

Ward started to move toward Dex, but the soldier holding him shook Dex hard, making him stumble so that the soldier ended up between Dex and Ward. "Shut up!" the soldier snarled and then he stood there with one hand gripping Dex's arm, glaring at him. Ward stopped and turned back to Ulric.

"Dex is our resident computer expert, Captain. It isn't all that unusual that he'd have some electronic devices in his rooms. Did you ask him why he had them?" Ulric was trying to stay calm. This asshole was just the type to try to use Dex as a scapegoat when he couldn't produce his quarry for his superiors.

"Fuck no he didn't ask! I tried to explain they're just regular auditory sensors, not SS issue, although I admit I've studied some of the black market versions. I've adapted them for humanoid hearing problems. To enhance hearing, not to filter it." He kept trying to pull his arm out of the soldiers grip and Ulric stood, ready to help. But then something interesting happened. Behind Ward's back the soldier caught Ulric's eye and shook his head almost imperceptibly. It was clearly a signal, not a warning. What the hell was going on?

Ward went on, unaware of the communication between Ulric and the mysterious soldier holding Dex. "Fine. Prove it." He looked calculatingly between Ulric and Dex. "Prove that the filter is not for renegade SS."

Dex shrugged helplessly. "How?"

Ward looked disdainfully at the soldier holding Dex. "Maybe you can actually be useful on this op, Martins. You're Gen8. I got stuck bringing you because the upper echelon was convinced you could track your own. So far you've been useless as a tracker. Let's see how you do as a guinea pig."

Martins didn't say a word and his facial expression didn't change. He was clearly used to the verbal abuse. Dex looked horrified.

"You want me to test it on him? If he really is Gen8, God, it'll kill him. That sensor amplifies sound waves. He needs them muffled."

Ward smiled cruelly. "Well, if the guinea pig dies we'll know you were telling the truth, won't we?"

"Why don't *you* simply put it on, Captain?" Ulric's tone indicated he thought Ward was a coward.

Ward looked back at him, his lip curled in disgust. "I am Gen10, Vonner. Our auditory sensors are more advanced than earlier models. It wouldn't work on me."

"I'm not gonna do it, Vonner, man—"

Dex didn't get to finish what he was saying. Martins interrupted. "Fine."

Ward looked at him coldly. "I wasn't asking your permission, Martins. It was an order." He looked at Dex. "And unless you wish to be taken to the nearest city holding facility for questioning you'll prove your innocence now."

Ulric didn't like it, but he thought that Martins knew what he was doing. "Let's go."

They went to a small room that was used to decode and intercept various surveillance methods, from vids to audio only. Dex set up the test with shaking hands.

"I don't torture people, Vonner. This is torture, pure and simple." He was shaking his head as Martins sat in the chair in front of the console, his face a mask of calm.

Ward was watching the preparations carefully. Ulric distracted him. "What do you hope to achieve here, Ward?"

Ward turned to him. "I know you helped them, Vonner. If these are black market filters it will be enough to bring you to Amalgama for questioning. I think you know more about Regan and the rebels than you claim."

While Ward had his back turned Martins touched Dex on the arm and the two men looked at one another for a moment. Martins nodded slightly and Dex silently asked *are you sure?* Martins nodded again. When Ward turned back to the two men Dex was just finishing attaching the sensor to Martins' ear.

"I'll be bringing you and your entire staff," Ward said, clearly hoping to unbalance Dex. He was disappointed. Martins' reassurances had settled him down.

"I can't insert it under the skin," Dex explained, "I'm not a surgeon and I don't want to displace the one he's already got." He stepped back and there was a wire leading from Martins' ear to a recorder on the desk. "I'm just going to shoot a few tones at him, nothing major. He'll be able to tell you how the sensor is working without undue pain, I think."

"No." Ward's refusal was spoken calmly. "I'll have no way of knowing if he's speaking the truth. You'll hit him with the tone your boss gave us this morning." He was looking at Martins, dislike evident on his face. More than dislike, as if Martins was some sort of lower life form that needed to be exterminated. "If he doesn't leave his filter off the tone will need to get through that."

"I will leave the filter off." Martins' voice was calm, which seemed to annoy Ward.

"Do it," Ward barked, "now."

"I won't," Dex said, his voice strong and determined. "I do not torture people. That's your job, not mine."

"Do it," Martins told him calmly, but Ward had already moved Dex out of the way.

"Fine," Ward said, his voice chillingly flat. "This way I can be sure the test is conducted properly." He looked at the device and obviously had no trouble figuring out how it worked.

Ulric was reminded that these soldiers were bred for intelligence. He'd pegged Ward as nothing but a bully, but clearly there was more to him. Why was he so determined to get rid of Martins? Because there was no doubt in Ulric's mind that that was Ward's intent here. With the right frequency he could cause a brain aneurysm. Ulric had a feeling Ward knew what that frequency was.

Ulric barely had time to form a plan before Ward depressed a couple of buttons and Martins' head flew back, the tendons in his neck stretched to their limits and his face a mask of pain. He made no sound but his knuckles were white against the chair arms.

"That's enough!" Dex yelled. "You can see the sensor isn't filtering! Stop!"

Ward ignored him and pressed another button. He kept pressing it until Martins couldn't stop the scream that ripped from his throat. Ulric grabbed Dex when he tried to go to Martins. There were two armed soldiers stationed in the room with them and Ulric didn't want anyone getting shot.

Martins' screams continued as Ward hit the button three more times. Blood leaked from Martins' ears and nose and Ulric had had enough. He dove for Martins and slammed his open hand down on Martins thigh as he ripped off the wire that connected him to the machine.

"Stop, you're killing him!" Ulric screamed. As soon as the wire tore free, Martins began to convulse, falling out of the chair to the floor. Ulric had to shove Ward out of the way as he fell to his knees beside the fallen man. "He's having a seizure," Ulric said, his voice panicked. He looked up at Ward and caught a satisfied look on the Captain's face. Ulric looked away when Martins suddenly froze for a moment and then went limp. He frantically began to look for a pulse. "Call Doc! We need him now!" he yelled at Dex, but Dex was already on the com.

"It would seem, Mr. Smith, that you were telling the truth," Ward said calmly. He motioned to the two soldiers and they preceded him out the door. "As soon as we know Martins' condition, we'll be on our way. We'll wait outside your office." He let the door close behind him.

"That bastard!" Dex yelled, falling to his knees next to Martins and leaning down to press his ear to his chest.

Ulric didn't bother to explain. He grabbed the com and whispered into it. "I need the antidote for a tranq OD, Doc, immediately. And bring a body bag."

"Yes sir." That was one thing Ulric liked about working with the holographic doctor. He didn't argue over every order.

Dex was looking at him in confusion. "A body bag? But he's not dead."

"As far as the Amalgamation is concerned SS Martins died in this room at," Ulric paused and looked at his watch, "fourteen-hundred hours." Ulric flexed his hand and then turned it over, palm up. The tip of the small needle sticking out of his tranq-ring was red with blood. "I'm going to need a refill."

Half an hour later Ulric watched Ward and his contingent as they left the Web. Ward had accepted Martins' death without blinking an eye. He would pick up the soldier's effects

141

at the city morgue tomorrow and make arrangements for disposal of the ashes. And there would be ashes. Ulric would make sure of it. It wasn't that hard to locate a body in the city. And knowing Ward the arrangements would be further incineration at the city waste disposal facilities. He'd never check to make sure it was Martins in the urn. Ward was so overconfident he couldn't conceive that his plan had failed. Ulric had slammed the tranq into Martins right before Ward hit a killing frequency. He'd gambled that Ward would just assume Martins was weak and succumbed sooner than he'd planned. The problem with believing you're infallible is that it makes you vulnerable.

Now Ulric just had to figure out what the hell Martins was up to and what he was going to do with him. These fucking Super Soldiers were really ruining his day.

Zeri strolled up just as the door closed behind the last soldier. Ulric silently groaned. He didn't want to deal with Zeri's taunting right now. The Web's night shift cook was drop-dead gorgeous with her long, white-blonde hair, lavender eyes and plentiful curves. But with her telepathic abilities she knew just where to kick a man when he was down.

"Finnegan won't fall for it, will he?" she asked innocently.

So it was to be one of those conversations, the ones where she made you beg her to tell you what she knew. Ulric sighed. "I am not in the mood, Zeri. Just spit it out."

She pouted and then smiled. "He's going to sit at the Smith gate, disguised as a crystolium freighter. The Captain figures that if he doesn't catch them trying to sneak through, he'll present an irresistible target to the rebels, who will obligingly show up to play ka-boom."

Ulric grunted as he turned back into his office. "I don't hire people who are that stupid." Zeri laughed behind him. "Be useful. Go to sick bay and see if you can figure out what our newest hunter is up to."

"Oooo, a new victim," Zeri purred and she turned in the direction of sick bay.

Chapter Ten
🕮

Cerise bit her lip as she approached the hatchway to the bridge. Tie had lent her a shirt and with a none-to-gentle shove out of the bedroom had sent her to talk to Regan.

"Whatever he means to you, he means a lot," Tie had told her, holding up a hand as she tried to speak, tried to explain what Regan did mean to her. "I don't need to hear it, not right now. But he does. So go tell him." Tie was so *good*. Every time he did something like that, something selfless and heroic, she hated herself more for what she'd done to him.

So now here she was standing outside the bridge, nervous and tongue-tied like a teenager with her first crush. Oh hell, Regan was her first crush. And then he'd become her first love. And now she'd betrayed that. Betrayed everything he'd meant to her and everything they could have been together. She blinked her eyes rapidly trying to stop the tears and bit her lip harder. She was about to turn away when the hatch slid open and Regan stood there looking at her in exasperation.

"Are you going to come in or are you going to stand out here and cry?" He spoke to her just the same way he had when she'd been eighteen and first arrived on *The Rebel Bounty*. She just stood there, miserable, staring at him.

"Oh for Christ's sake, no one can turn a little fuck into high drama like you can, Princess. Get in here." Regan grabbed her arm and hauled her onto the bridge and the hatch silently slid closed behind her.

"It wasn't just a little fuck," Cerise sniffed inelegantly, "it's a lot of them! Forever! Oh, Regan, I've ruined his life!" She burst into tears and threw herself on his chest and like a thousand times before he held her and let her soak his shoulder with her tears.

Regan sighed. "Ruined his life? Are you crazy?" He spoke softly, his hand gently smoothing over the back of her head. "You are the best thing that has ever happened to him, sweetheart. Trust me, I know."

Cerise shook her head. "No, no, I'm not. I used him. I deliberately seduced him so that I could...could enslave him with the Tears. I'm a monster, a freak and now he's stuck with me forever."

Regan snorted and Cerise pulled back to glare at him. "Don't you get it? He's addicted to me." She spoke very slowly, emphasizing each word. "He can't leave. He can't live without me. Whether he wants to or not."

This time Regan laughed outright. "I can tell you, Princess, that he wants to live without you *not*. A man doesn't say the things he said to you last night if he doesn't mean them. He meant every word."

Cerise covered her face with her hands. "Oh, God, you listened? You heard us?"

Regan let her go and moved to lean his ass against the back of the pilot's chair. He tapped the side of his head with his index finger. "Super hearing, remember? Yeah, I heard."

Cerise leaned against the bulkhead next to the hatch. It was covered with buttons and levers whose purposes she only vaguely understood. She forced herself to meet Regan's eyes. "You must think I'm a galaxy-class slut."

Regan laughed again. Well, he hardly seemed broken up about her betrayal. She couldn't help it, she was getting pissed.

"Hardly. Fucking one guy doesn't even put you in the loose woman category."

"I'm in love with you." Cerise felt a great weight lifted from her shoulders as the confession came calmly from her mouth. "I love you. And I fucked him."

145

Regan looked away for a minute and then turned back shaking his head with a blank face. "No, you don't, because I heard you last night too, Cerise. I heard what you said to Tie and I don't think you're the kind of woman who would lie."

Cerise furrowed her brow, confused. "What are you talking about? Why would I lie to Tie?"

Regan sighed. "See? So you obviously are not in love with me."

It was Cerise's turn to shake her head. "Just because I meant it when I told Tie that I loved him doesn't mean I'm not in love with you."

Regan smiled crookedly. "In love with both of us? I don't think so. You can't love two people."

"Why not? My mother did. She had five husbands when she died and from what I remember and what I've been told, she loved them all." Cerise's pulse was racing. She couldn't believe what she was thinking. But she wanted it, wanted them and she was willing to fight for it. Fight dirty if she had to, Regan had taught her that.

"Cerise—"

She didn't want to hear what he had to say. He could argue around and around her until she didn't know up from down or right from left. She quickly stepped forward so that she was between his legs where he leaned against the pilot's chair and Regan broke off in mid-sentence. Cerise placed her hands on his lower stomach, her fingers splayed upward and she felt all the muscles there coil into a solid wall of hot, hard man.

"Cerise." His voice was a low warning. She ignored it. She pushed her hands up the leather vest he wore, sliding under his crossed arms until he was forced to uncross them. When her palm covered his rapidly beating heart she stopped.

"I want you, Regan," she whispered, looking up at him from beneath her eyelashes. She really wasn't too sure what she was doing. Tie hadn't required a lot of flirting before they had sex the first time and since then he'd required no flirting at all. All she had to do was breathe and he had her down on her back, or all fours, or well, whatever position he was in the mood for.

Regan's hands covered hers, holding them in place. "So, little Princess, you've had a taste of sex and you want to try a new flavor," Regan purred dangerously. "Do I look like harem material to you?"

"You want me. I know you do. I saw it in your face earlier." Cerise was breathless. She'd been close to Regan before, been held by him when they were sparring, or when she was crying. But she'd never been close like this. With this awareness between them that she was a woman and he was a man and all the possibilities that implied. She daringly took a step closer until she was nestled into his crotch and she could feel his erection pressing against her stomach. "You want me now," she whispered and rubbed against the hard, jutting evidence of his desire. Regan's eyes narrowed and his nostrils flared.

"Earlier you were naked. I'm a man, Cerise, and you are a beautiful woman. I'd have to be dead not to be aroused by you." He looked down at the shirt she had on. "And that's not covering much either." It was another tank top because all Tie's shirts with sleeves were far too big. The neck on this shirt sagged over her breasts and the hem hit her just below her ass.

"Kiss me, Regan," Cerise told him. "I'm not good at this flirting. I only know that I want you, that I'm desperate for your kisses and your hands on me."

Regan's eyes burned with intensity and his grip on her hands tightened. "I won't be one of your men, Cerise."

"You already are," she whispered and then she leaned up and into him, slanting her mouth across his.

Regan was so fucking weak he disgusted himself. He should have been pushing her away, but he couldn't, damn it,

147

he couldn't. She felt just as he'd always imagined she would — smooth and sleek and firm. And hot, God she was so fucking hot she was burning him alive. And she could kiss. He guessed he could thank Tie for that. He wished the thought of Cerise and his best friend would cool him down, but instead it drove him wild. All the pent-up frustration of years of wanting her and denying it, of listening to her cry out in pleasure as Tie licked and sucked and fucked her last night came roaring up inside him and he grabbed her and backed her into the bulkhead roughly, his hands moving down to grip her ass and lift her against him. He drove his tongue into her mouth and her flavors exploded on his tongue like spice. Sweet, salty, hot and wet, the smooth curves of her mouth enthralled his tongue and his will to deny her collapsed beneath the onslaught of sensation.

Cerise let out a little moan and Regan felt the reverberations against his chest. He tightened his hold, pressing his cock against the soft heat of her burning through the layers of their clothing. Cerise's hands came up and one gripped his head holding their mouths fused as their tongues dueled. The other arm wrapped around his shoulder and the fingers of her hand dug into his back. She held him as if she'd never let go and he didn't want her to, not ever. This is what he'd dreamed of, lived for, yearned for ever since he turned to see her walk onto his bridge one day, two years after she first came to him. He hadn't been expecting her and when she'd walked in he'd seen her, really seen her, for the first time and lust had nearly driven him to his knees before her. That had been five years ago.

He was manhandling her, he knew it and couldn't stop. He slid his hands down from her ass to her thighs and lifted her legs. She followed the lead and wrapped them around his waist, locking her ankles at his lower back. She clung to him and he feared he held her so tightly she'd snap in two. Instead she broke their kiss with a gasp and groaned as she ground against his cock mercilessly.

148

Regan buried his face in the curve of her neck, panting as if he was running for his life. Perhaps he was. He slid his arm from around her waist and ran his hand up and down her side, teasing, stopping just below her breast. Cerise turned her face against his head and he felt her lips on the bare skin there. The kiss made him weak in the knees and he pressed her back against the bulkhead, leaning on her. The skin on his head was so sensitive, Christ, it was like she was kissing his cock. The pleasure was that intense. He'd never had anyone kiss his bald head before, had never imagined it would feel so good. He shuddered when she moved a hand and lightly caressed his skull.

"I like it, I like the way it feels," Cerise whispered against his skin, her breath hot and moist. "I've always wanted to touch it, to kiss it. It's so different from..." Her thought trailed off but Regan knew what she was going to say — different from Tie. He started to pull away, regaining some of his senses. She was Tie's now, not his. Regan wasn't the kind who could stand aside and take another man's leftovers. It would end badly for all of them. He cared deeply for Cerise and had only just found Tie again. They rode a dangerous edge here and he was apparently the only one who could navigate them all safely around it. Fuck! He was goddamn tired of always being the one who did what needed to be done. Just once he'd like to do what he wanted and damn the consequences.

Cerise must have felt his withdrawal. She grabbed his hand resting on her side and she pulled it over her breast and squeezed, her head falling back against the bulkhead as she bit her lip with obvious pleasure. The feel of that small, perfect breast with the hard point of her nipple pressing insistently against his palm made Regan lower his head until it rested on her shoulder. She dropped her hand and still he couldn't take his away from her, from the sweet mound of flesh he was cupping. He watched as he massaged her gently and Cerise's legs tightened around his waist. He couldn't stop himself from pinching the hard bud between his fingers, rolling it and tugging it softly.

"God, oh God, Regan, yes," she whispered. "Please, please, make love to me. I've waited so long, I've wanted you so long." She pulled away as best she could and began to fumble with the too-large top trying to pull it off. Her words were like laser fire to his gut because he knew he couldn't, wouldn't. She didn't know, didn't understand that their time had gone. She was beyond his reach now more than ever and she would only regret hurting Tie and yes, hurting him as well. Because Regan knew he might never recover if he were to fuck Cerise, if he were to make her his, finally and then lose her. It would be too cruel to both of them.

Regan leaned down and kissed her nipple softly through her clothes. Cerise sobbed and began wiggling in earnest trying to get her shirt off. Regan stopped her by pulling her close again, trapping her arms between them.

"Baby, stop," he whispered into her ear as she struggled, "stop." He could hear the tenderness in his voice, the lonely ache and he hoped she couldn't. If she did she would give him no rest, no peace. She'd hound him until he gave in to her. He'd seen her do it a thousand times with other things and he always gave in to her. And this desire for her was so potent, so powerful he knew he could only fight so long before he surrendered.

He couldn't look at her. Her face was burned in his memory, a favorite daydream. To look at her and see his dream made real would undue him. Christ, he'd always known he wasn't for her, he'd accepted it. Why was it so hard now? Why was turning her away suddenly one of the hardest things he'd ever done?

"Regan," she whispered, as if she could read his mind, "don't send me away. Don't, please." She buried her face in his neck and he felt her tears. "I love you, I love you and I need you." She rubbed her nose against him and he realized she'd moved down to the opening in his vest and was nuzzling the bare skin of his chest. She'd touched him there before, with her hands when they were training, hell, he'd held her when he wore no shirt at all, but this was different. This touch was sexual, desperate, hungry. Her tongue licked along his collarbone and his cock jerked in response, as hungry and desperate as her mouth.

"No," he growled and seized a fistful of hair on the back of her head, yanking her mouth off him.

Cerise was breathing raggedly and her eyes blazed angrily at him. "What is with you people? Why do I always have to beg when I know you want me? Tie said no too and now he crawls to my bed whenever I want him. You will too, Regan, I swear you will."

A burst of bitter laughter escaped. "Is that what you want? You want your men to crawl? I expected better from you." The knowledge that he would crawl if he had to clawed at his pride. She had no clue of the kind of power she wielded over him. He moved to lift her off him and she obstinately tightened her legs around his waist and dared him with her eyes to pry her off. Her jaw was set stubbornly and Regan couldn't help but smile. It became a contest of wills as he gently but firmly pushed to set her down and she desperately clung to him and all the while their eyes never broke contact.

Finally with a sigh she relaxed and looked away and Regan set her on her feet. He took no pleasure in his victory.

"No," she said quietly.

Her hands held his forearms loosely, his hands on her waist. He wanted to hold her just a moment more, not in passion, but just to feel her, just to be close to her. Their bodies were no longer touching but he was close enough to feel the heat radiating off her and he absorbed it gratefully. He could feel a core of ice forming inside that would only grow bigger each day he forced himself to stay away from her. Somehow this slight, unsure, courageous girl—no, woman—had become as necessary to him as breathing. How was he to live now that she was the air that Tie breathed?

"No?" Regan repeated, not sure what she meant.

"No, I don't want you to crawl." She sighed a little unsteadily and Regan could tell she was holding back tears again. "Tie doesn't crawl either and if he does it's mutual." She turned her whole body away from him, still leaning one shoulder on the bulkhead. It was a posture that put up a wall between them and inside Regan let out a howl of loss and rage. "I won't do that to another man, Regan, especially to you. I love you, I respect you." She shook her head and her obvious distress made him want to reach out to her. He did, but stopped his hand before he touched her and she went on, unaware of the battle that raged in him. "I won't force another man to my bed. I love Tie, but I regret what I did. Thank God my instincts were right about him. He's a good man, the best. I couldn't ask for a better lover or a better friend."

She turned back to him suddenly, her eyes bleak. "No, if you come to my bed, Regan, it will be your decision and yours alone. I want you there, so much it frightens me. I need you. You have been the most important person in my life for so long the thought of a future without you is almost unbearable. But I don't want you if I have to force you because that knowledge will always be between us." She leaned forward and kissed him softly on the lips. The contact was chaste compared to their earlier kisses but no less devastating. When she pulled back it was a slow parting, their lips clinging and without thought he followed her, trying to maintain the contact. He came to his senses and pulled away to see her smiling sadly.

"For some reason you've gotten it into your crazy, bald head that you're not good enough for me." She put a finger gently to his lips to silence his protest. "No, don't bother to deny it. You admitted as much with Tie. But Regan, you are one of the finest men I have ever known and I would consider myself blessed beyond compare were you to call yourself mine." She slid her finger caressingly from his lips and they burned where she had touched him. "Don't make me wait too long, Regan. I don't think any of us could bear it."

She turned away and the hatch slid silently open to release her from the intimacy of their confessions.

* * * * *

Tie entered the bridge just a few moments after Regan's summons on the com.

"Exactly where are we?" Tie asked. Regan was looking at the navigational display and Tie went to look over his shoulder.

"Recognize anything?" Regan asked as he sat back in the chair. Tie had one hand on the seat back and when Regan leaned back his head rested against Tie's chest for a split second before he quickly jerked upright again. Regan didn't turn to look at him and Tie felt the old longing and sadness. It was as if their earlier interlude and kiss had never happened. Too many times in the past Egan had retreated in just the same way from any kind of intimacy with him. But Tie still craved him. In a way it was a relief that the new, overwhelming desire he felt for Cerise hadn't obliterated his feelings for Egan. But it was also a curse to still bear an unrequited love and desire for him, to know that he would always love a man who did not return his feelings.

"I'm sorry," Tie murmured sadly and Regan's back twitched it was so stiff. Calling him Regan helped a little. It reminded Tie that this was not the same man he'd known ten years ago. He'd changed his life, changed his name and done so much that Tie knew nothing about. While Tie had been searching for him, his life in limbo, Egan had been reborn as Regan and he'd dedicated his life to destroying the Amalgamation. He'd become a living legend in the galaxy, nurtured a princess and earned the respect of his men. Tie had become a man that he hated, doing work he hated, for a government he hated. With a start Tie realized that he wasn't the same man either. He'd become harder, more ruthless and more selfish.

Tie wanted this man. Whatever name he chose to go by, whatever his mysterious past involved, Tie still wanted him. And the man Tie had become didn't take no for an answer. Cerise wanted Regan too. That had to mean that Regan still possessed Egan's honor, his loyalty and his strength of character—all those things that Tie had loved about him. Cerise wouldn't want a man who lacked those things. And Regan clearly wanted her. There had to be some way they could all have what they wanted.

"What are you sorry about?" Regan asked in a blatant attempt to avoid discussing Tie's feelings. Tie recognized the ploy. It was the same old tactic he'd used before. This time Tie didn't play along. He wasn't going to be meek and accommodating anymore. He wasn't worried that his feelings were wrong or dangerous.

"I'm sorry I made you uncomfortable." Tie put a hand on Regan's shoulder and yanked him back in the chair. He began to knead Regan's tight shoulders companionably. He smiled behind Regan's back. He'd work up to seduction gradually. "Relax. Cerise has fucked just about everything out of me in the last two days. I haven't got the energy to chase you today."

Regan choked on his reply and began coughing. Tie laughed out loud. He leaned close over Regan's shoulder still massaging his back. "That's Secundus, Quartus Seven's on the right." He pulled back. "Do I get the secret codes now? Is there a special handshake I have to learn before we get to the secret rebel base, commander?" He surprised a laugh out of Regan and he felt the other man relax.

"No, no handshake. We'll see about the codes." Regan leaned forward and pointed at the nav screen. "This is where we're headed." He leaned back and Tie took it as an invitation to keep rubbing his shoulders. Regan relaxed into the motion of Tie's hands and Tie smiled. Then he realized where Regan had pointed.

"Mimnet? That planet is completely uninhabitable. It's volcanic, most of the surface is molten lava and it's got a hydrogen based atmosphere. How the hell did you get a rebel base on it?" He shook his head. "No offense, but I'll take my chances with the Amalgamation."

He found a particularly tight muscle in Regan's back and pressed so hard against it Regan grunted. "Christ, Regan you're so tight back here I wonder how the hell you can even move." Tie hollered out the hatch into the galley. "Cerise! Get in here!"

Regan's shoulders hunched as he called for her and again Tie smiled. Oh yeah, he was going to make Regan very uncomfortable. "We do have a comm, you know," Regan said sarcastically.

"Hmmm," was all Tie said as he pressed his thumb against the knot again and Regan yelped.

"What do you want?" Cerise yelled through the hatch. "I'm eating. Jeez, you never let me eat!" She walked through the door carrying a tray with some food on it. "You never told me you had fresh fruit on board. Why didn't I get any of this before?"

Tie reached out and grabbed a grape and Cerise tried to smack his hand but he was too quick. He popped it into his mouth. "You didn't ask and I wasn't going to waste it on a prisoner."

Cerise raised her eyebrows at him. "And since then?"

Tie shrugged sheepishly. "I had other things on my mind."

Cerise snorted and held a grape out to Regan. "Want one?" He started to take it from her but she leaned over and pressed it against his lips. Their eyes locked and she smiled devilishly. He opened his mouth and she pushed the grape inside, rubbing her finger on his lower lip.

Oh yeah, she's going to be a tremendous help in seducing Regan, thought Tie as he watched the exchange. He barely suppressed a laugh at how oblivious the other man was. A few days of backrubs and hand feeding and he was theirs.

Samantha Kane

Cerise held up a gray cube of gelatinous rations with a questioning look. "What the hell is that?" Regan demanded, leaning away from it with a scowl. She laughed.

"I haven't the faintest. I think it's supposed to be some kind of protein." She popped it into her mouth and chewed with a thoughtful look and then swallowed with a nod. "Yep, proteiny."

Tie laughed and Regan grinned. "She always would eat anything. She's got a stomach lined with synth-steel."

"Yeah?" Tie encouraged him. He wanted to know all there was to know about her. He was hungry for stories of her past, of the past she and Regan had shared without him. "What else will she eat?"

"Regan," she said menacingly, but he ignored her.

"Fed her space worm once, she ate it right up."

"No!" Tie laughed. "That's disgusting."

Cerise glared at him. "Everyone ate space worm. We were starving and that's all we could get. We were at the outlooks!"

"Everyone else complained. You gobbled it up and asked for seconds." Regan sounded amused, but also proud.

Cerise finally laughed and shrugged. "I was hungry."

Tie reached out and tugged her earlobe. "You're always hungry."

She smiled and rubbed her cheek against his wrist. "You wear me out. I need to replenish my energy." Tie smiled back at her, but he felt Regan tense under the hand he had on his shoulder.

"Do I need to leave the room?" Regan asked, trying to sound amused, but Tie heard the edge in his voice. He saw Cerise glance at the other man and knew she'd heard it too.

"Nope," Tie said casually, "we're good for a couple of hours. Had a nice hot quickie in the galley a little while ago."

Regan looked askance at Cerise's tray of food. "The galley?" he asked and Cerise giggled. Regan sighed. "I meant

156

to thank you for that, by the way. We were going through the Smith gate and the watch heard you on the com. I think they cleared us out of embarrassment."

Cerise turned bright red. "Oh God, I'm going to have start wearing a gag."

Tie grinned. "No way, baby. I love to hear you scream and moan when I'm fucking you. It's a huge ego boost." He leaned down and kissed Cerise's shoulder. "It's good to be king."

Regan turned to stare at him in astonishment. "Are we going to be blasé about it then?" He turned away, rubbing a hand over his brow. "I'm not sure I'm ready to discuss the princess's new sex life in casual conversation." With exasperation he added, "And there's no king. She's a princess, not a queen."

Tie hit that sore knotted muscle again and Regan arched his back and groaned. "You are way too tense, Regan."

"Oh, are you all right?" Cerise asked, the picture of concern. She got up and put a knee on Regan's chair next to his thigh so she could lean over his shoulder and see what Tie was doing. "Does it hurt?"

Tie saw Regan close his eyes for a moment and then open them to stare at Cerise's breasts, which were even with his face. He moved his leg so he wasn't touching her and looked away, but not before Tie saw the desire on his face. He watched as Regan fisted a hand on his thigh. "It's fine," he said crisply.

Cerise pulled back to look at him in confusion. "That didn't sound fine." She eased off the chair and Regan took a deep breath, but he let it out in annoyance a moment later.

Cerise stepped behind the chair and shoved Tie out of the way. "Here, let me," she said and she began to knead the muscles in the back of his neck with her thumbs, her fingers splayed against his skull. Tie saw Regan shudder and Cerise smile knowingly. Well, well. This just got better and better.

Tie moved to sit in the other chair and grabbed a square of protein. It didn't look pretty, or taste that great, but Cerise was right. They needed to keep up their energy. Would it always be this intense between them? He turned the chair to face the other two. "Cerise, will it always be like this, the desire? Will we always need to fuck every couple of hours, or does the need lessen as time goes on?"

Regan sat up and looked sharply at Tie. "What do you mean 'need'?"

Tie shrugged. "It's like we told you Regan, it's an addiction. If we don't feed it, we get physically sick, mentally...I don't know, confused, disoriented. It hits like a missile, the need just slams into you and it acts like a plasma cannon draining your energy." He looked at Cerise standing behind Regan, her hands on the seat back. She looked pale. "Right, baby?"

Cerise nodded without looking at either man. "Yes...I guess so. I don't know about the weapons analogy, but it does come suddenly and it's fierce." She looked at Tie then, her eyes bright. "It's like a hunger for me. I'm so hungry and only Tie can feed me."

Tie shook his head. "I wanted her before. So much I went against every personal code I had, not to mention breaking all the rules of bounty hunting, just to have her. But after the first time, it became...this. What we have now."

"You wanted her?" Regan asked in a strange voice. Tie looked at him and Regan shook his head as if to clear it. "Of course you did. You had to want her to fuck her in the first place. Didn't he, Cerise?" he asked and Tie looked at her and she was smiling tremulously at him.

"What?" Tie asked, pretty sure he was missing something.

She shook her head. "Nothing. Just...nothing." She grabbed Regan's shoulder much as Tie had done earlier and hauled him back in the chair so she could rub his back some more. "Have you set the course for Quantinium yet?"

Regan dropped his head back and closed his eyes as he sighed in exasperation and Tie laughed. "So we're not going to Mimnet. Isn't Quantinium the largest moon there?"

Regan glared over his shoulder at Cerise. "What? What did I do?" she asked, her hands wide in innocence. "I thought he knew. He was going to have to know."

"You know how valuable that information is," Regan growled at her.

She set her hands on her hips and glared right back. "It's Tie, for God's sake! You know he's not going to tell anyone. Who's he going to tell?" She gestured around the bridge. "We're it! There's nobody else here." She made an inarticulate sound of frustration. "I swear Regan, you are the most suspicious person alive." She pointed at Tie. "I mean, it's Tie. *Tie*. Come on."

Tie interrupted before it became a full-fledged argument. "It's nice that someone around here thinks I'm trustworthy."

Regan turned his glare on Tie. "I know you used to be. I don't know that you are now."

Tie gave him a wry look. "Well, I guess you're about to find out."

Chapter Eleven

❧

"We'll be on Quantinium tomorrow," Cerise whispered to Tie as they lay spooned on the big bed in their cabin. It was still awkward to think of this as theirs and yet she knew with a certainty that that's what it was now. Tie called everything theirs now and it made Cerise happy deep inside. She'd never really had a theirs, only my or yours. She liked having someone to share with.

Tie nuzzled the back of her neck and touched the tip of his tongue to the vertebra just below. It was just a hot, wet little touch but it sent a jolt of heat straight down her back. "Mmm-hmm," he murmured and then rubbed his cheek and nose in her hair. God, she loved that. She loved that he couldn't get enough of touching her, petting her, kissing her, licking her, nuzzling her. Her life had been devoid of loving, or even affectionate, touches since she'd been orphaned. As an adult, even a teenager, she'd been Princess Cerise and most people were afraid to touch her. And as a child she'd been moved around so much after her mother's death that no one really...claimed her. That was what Tie did with each little touch, he claimed her as his. And she loved it. She rolled over to face Tie, snuggling into him, both of them lying on their sides. He tilted his head on the pillow and looked down at her with a tender smile before kissing her forehead and her heart melted.

"Oh, Tie," she whispered, her voice shaky with emotion, "I need you so much." She looked into his eyes a little desperately. "Don't leave me, Tie, not ever, all right? Not ever." She closed her eyes and ducked her head, burying her face in the warm, fragrant curve of his neck.

Tie's arms tightened around her and he drew her closer, wrapping one leg around her thighs so she was almost a part of him. "I won't baby, I swear. I'll never leave you Cerise. Not ever." He waited a heartbeat then said softly. "Not even if you love Regan, sweetheart. If you...want him, that's okay."

"Tie," she said and then couldn't say more. She was breaking inside, hating herself for hurting him. How could she make this better for him? Would he and Regan ever be happy if she took both of them to her bed? Or was she dooming them all to misery with her refusal to give up Regan?

Tie pulled away and lifted her face to his with a gentle finger under her chin. She could see how serious he was. "Baby, I mean it." He sighed and in the near dark she thought she could see him blush and it confused her. "This is harder than I thought," he mumbled, licking his lips nervously.

"What are you trying to say, Tie?" Cerise's heart was pounding in her chest. She knew what she wanted him to say, but also knew it would be too good to be true if Tie wanted what she wanted.

He took a deep breath before he spoke. "I...want him too." He glanced in her eyes and then looked away. "If you want him in our bed...then that's what I want too." He shook his head. "No, that's not right. That makes it sound like I'd be doing it for you and that would be a lie." He looked right into her eyes and spoke plainly. "I want him, Cerise. I want to fuck him. I want to watch him fuck you. I want the three of us to have sweaty, acrobatic, kinky sex for days on end. I just...well, I just want him and you—with me." He looked at her sheepishly. "Crazy, huh?"

Cerise was having trouble breathing. She'd thought to have both men, but not together. They could do that? The images flying through her head were enough to make her wet and the pulse start throbbing in her clit. Oh my God, Tie fucking Regan while Regan fucked her? Or the other way around? She shivered with lust, fire racing through her veins.

"We can do that?" she whispered hoarsely, staring at Tie wide eyed. "How do we do that?"

Tie was looking at her now with an answering fire building in his otherworldly eyes. He rolled her over onto her back and rested on top of her, his weight on his forearms. He leaned down and touched her nose with his. "I can show you how."

Cerise's hand was shaking when she cupped his cheek in her palm. "Have you ever done that with a man before? Or is Regan the first man you've wanted that way?"

Tie hesitated to answer her. The first question wasn't really a yes or no answer and the second…well it could be ambiguous. Regan was and wasn't the first man he'd wanted that way. He'd wanted him as Egan first and still wanted him now that he was Regan. So he could answer it honestly with a yes or a no. He decided to stick with the first question.

"I've never fucked a man before." He winced as he heard the hesitation in his voice.

Cerise picked up on his uneasiness. "Then what have you done with a man before?"

Tie sighed and pulled her close again, finding it easier to tell the story when he wasn't looking at her. The memories had been flooding his mind ever since his earlier encounter with Regan, as well as the longing, the loneliness, the despair. "One night, when I was still in the SS, stationed on Earth, I told a man I loved him and I tried to show him how much."

* * * * *

Earth, Eleven Years Earlier

"Egan?" Tie whispered into the dark of their small barracks room. It was the middle of the night but Tie hadn't slept a wink. They were stationed at the IMF jungle training

162

facility and it was so hot and humid it was even affecting the SS veterans. But that wasn't what was keeping him awake. "Egan?" he tried again. When there was no response he very quietly got up and went to stand beside the other man's cot.

Egan stirred in his sleep as Tie pulled the covers away from him. He didn't fully awaken which surprised Tie. But Tie supposed that on a subconscious level, Egan knew he had nothing to fear from him.

Tie looked down at his best friend's body. He'd seen it a million times—in full battle gear, naked, sweaty, covered in swamp slime or sand or mud, even bleeding and broken—yet it still aroused him. Egan was a big man, like all the Super Soldiers. They were bred that way. It was a natural byproduct of their superior strength and agility, of course, but it also never hurt to have the upper hand in the intimidation department. The Military Sciences Lab thought of everything when developing their most sought-after weapon. Egan's muscles weren't as bulky as Tie's. He was leaner and as a result quicker and more agile. But he could still break an ordinary man's jaw without even using his full strength. Tie could break a femur. They knew—the MSL had made sure. Tie shook his head, trying to dispel the flashbacks from the product testing trials.

Egan stirred restlessly and Tie looked quickly up at his face. He could see his eyes moving rapidly behind his lids, his brows drawn down. He was having a nightmare, but he'd have it like he was trained—silently, repressively. Egan was breathing raggedly and Tie's eyes were drawn to his chest. Broad and covered with black curling hair, it drew his hand as it had drawn his eyes. He lightly ran his fingers around the outline of Egan's pectoral muscles, strong and sharply cut. Centered on each was a nipple, hard and leaning toward pink. His skin was so white against all that black hair, his nipples stark on the pale background. In the moonlight he could see the faint hint of green in his skin. He and Egan had speculated that he'd been bred with some Reptilios DNA, although what

163

for they weren't sure. At some point it would be revealed what advantages that had given him, but for now Egan was apparently on a need to know basis as to his own genetic background and neither the Medical Sciences Lab nor the Interplanetary Military Forces thought he needed to know.

Tie's eyes followed the trail of black hair as it narrowed and became a thin strip down his stomach, the muscles there firm but not as sharply cut as his pectorals. Tie liked the smoothness of his stomach, the clean line of its satin tautness. His bellybutton was a deep indentation there, inviting Tie to dip his finger in, bringing images of other invasions that made Tie's breathing as ragged as Egan's. Finally Tie allowed himself to look down at Egan's crotch. He was wearing standard issue briefs, black and tight down his thighs. He had a hard-on. Tie was surprised. Perhaps it wasn't a nightmare that had him stirring restlessly. Who was he dreaming about?

Egan's leg thrashed down, tangling in the sheet and Tie instinctively reached out and laid a hand on his thigh to still him. Tie's body reacted instantly, his cock going from semihard to thick and pulsing at the feel of the hair on Egan's leg, the firm heat of Egan's thick thigh muscle. Tie forced himself not to clench Egan's thigh, not to fall to his knees and bite into that hot, heavy thigh. He wanted Egan in his mouth. He wanted to taste his flesh and sweat, feel his skin and hair on his tongue. The need was visceral and primitive and almost too much to control. Instead Tie ran a hand softly down that thigh and then grasped it lightly. Egan's legs were more muscular than Tie's. He had the legs of a runner, with large thick thighs and heavy calves. His quickness was part genetics and part training. Every day they ran him, usually short distances trying to increase his speed. Xane was run every day as well, but for distance. Just as Tie lifted stationary weights every day, until he could toss a hovercraft across the compound. They didn't let their merchandise get rusty on the shelf. Only constant vigilance kept the product top of the line and marketable.

Egan moaned in his sleep and his hips thrust up slightly at Tie's caress. Tie's mouth dried up and he quietly lowered himself to his knees next to Egan's cot. He'd only meant to look at him, to drink him in without Egan turning away, uncomfortable with Tie's scrutiny, denying the attraction between them. But he was so tired and so lonely. And then he'd heard today from Xane what Egan had done to get him out of the brig last month. Egan had offered himself as sacrifice. If Tie screwed up again Egan would share his punishment. And Tie had known, as if blinders had been removed from his eyes, that Egan cared about him, no matter how hard he tried to hide it. He was Egan, by-the-book Egan. Fraternization between soldiers was illegal and sexual relations between them could result in termination. But Egan loved him, Tie knew it.

Tie also knew he'd be terminated soon anyway. They wouldn't put up with much more insubordination from him in spite of his high marketability. And before he died he would have Egan. He would die with the memory of being with Egan the last thought he had.

Trembling with anticipation, with fear and uncertainty, Tie leaned down and pressed a soft kiss against the smooth skin of Egan's lower stomach, right above the waistband of his briefs. Egan unconsciously arched into the touch and all uncertainty fled. Tie ran his hand up Egan's thigh and then very gently grasped the edges of his briefs and began to slide them down. He held his breath as the cloth slid lower revealing the sharp angles of Egan's hipbones and the top of the thick bush of pubic hair at his groin. Tie moved a hand between Egan's spread legs and slid it up until he could lift Egan's ass off the bed enough to work the briefs down further. Somehow Egan stayed asleep but his restlessness was growing, as was his erection. After he had the briefs down over his ass, Tie lifted the front over Egan's hard cock and then suddenly they were down around his thighs and all that Tie desired was bared to his gaze.

Tie didn't hesitate. He didn't waste time looking, didn't bother with gentle preliminaries. He just leaned over and took Egan's cock in his mouth. He wanted the whole thing, but realized that it was big, maybe bigger than he could take, but he would try damn it, he would have it all. He pulled back when he started to gag and slid down again trying to relax his throat but it was hard to concentrate. He was awash with sensations, with desire, with an absolute joy that was foreign to him. As he slid down, Egan jerked partially up off the bed with a strangled cry, his hands going to Tie's head. But instead of pushing him off Egan's hands gripped his skull tightly and pushed his mouth down his throbbing cock. He fell back on the bed, still holding Tie to him, panting, his heart pounding. Tie could feel the frantic pulse of that heartbeat in Egan's cock against his tongue. The intimate communication of it made Tie's hips jerk and he felt a drop of moisture leak from his cock. He roughly reached down and jerked his own shorts over his hips, his hard cock bouncing against his stomach as it was freed. Never taking his mouth from Egan he wrapped his fist around the base of his cock and held it tightly, trying to prolong his own pleasure.

"Tie," Egan rasped, his voice rough with sleep and pleasure, "no." His actions belied his words however, his hands holding Tie on his cock, his hips jerking, fucking Tie's mouth. Tie moaned and Egan gave up resisting. It was clear he was still half asleep. Still dreaming, perhaps? Had he been dreaming of Tie?

Tie braced one hand on Egan's thigh and then pulled back against the grip of Egan's hands, sliding up Egan's cock to the heavy, thick head and then sliding back down. Egan's eagerness sharpened Tie's desire-dulled senses. Suddenly he could feel every thickly pulsing vein running down Egan's hard length. He traced them with his tongue and Egan groaned. Tie tasted the musky, salty tang of him, felt the moisture of his pre-cum as it hit the back of his tongue and flavor exploded there. His movements became faster, his own arousal driving his mouth down on Egan faster, deeper into his throat, in rhythm with his hand on his own cock.

Egan's back curled and his head came off the cot, one hand going to the side to grip the edge and the other still on Tie's head, still holding him there on his cock. Tie took deep breaths through his nose as he sucked hard on Egan, the dual stimulation of his taste and his smell pushing Tie higher and higher until he couldn't wait for the fall. Egan was fucking him steadily now, his hips rising and falling with the pull of Tie's mouth, his hands clutching, his head and neck arched back against the bed as he tried to muffle his moans. Tie couldn't get close enough. He couldn't take all of Egan in this position. He pulled his mouth off and felt a hot tide of satisfaction at Egan's low cry of dismay. Egan relaxed suddenly and his body fell back on the cot, exhausted, as if his strings had been cut. His hands covered his face and Tie realized Egan thought he was done, that they were done.

Tie crawled to the end of the cot and kneeled there. He grabbed Egan's hips, hauling him down the cot. When he was at the end, Tie ripped the briefs off and parted Egan's legs with his arms so that they fell around Tie's sides.

"Tie," Egan cried out, his hands leaving his face to grab the edge of the cot again, to hold on. But Tie's pull was merciless. He wanted Egan and he wanted him his way.

"I won't leave you like this, baby," he whispered, moving Egan until his legs were draped over Tie's shoulders. Egan let go of the cot and his hands fisted in the short, black hair on his head, his eyes tightly closed. Tie knew he was fighting an internal battle, but it was useless. Tie had already won. Tie knew when a man was this close there was no stopping. He felt it and he knew Egan felt it as well. Tie kneeled there, his chest heaving with his arousal, his ragged breathing cutting the quiet of the night and stared at Egan as he lay there, submissive, with his eyes closed and his teeth biting so deeply into his bottom lip he was going to draw blood. He made Egan make the decision.

167

After a few moments that seemed an eternity Egan opened his eyes and looked down at Tie. His eyes glowed in the night, the sexual energy arcing between him and Tie. He pulled his hands from his hair and reached one down to slide it along Tie's cheek and onto his head. Then he pulled Tie down until his mouth bloomed over the end of Egan's cock, sucking him in deep and hard and Egan gasped and the fingers on his head tightened as Egan's hips thrust. Tie felt triumphant and smiled around the cock filling his mouth. Egan was his, *his*.

Egan grabbed Tie's head with both hands now, his hips thrusting, his hands driving Tie down on his cock. Tie slid his hands under Egan's tight, firm ass and lifted him higher, sucking and licking and fucking his mouth down hard and deep on that thrusting cock, loving everything—the taste, the texture, the length and thickness. But especially the knowledge that it was at last Egan that he was loving so roughly and with such passion.

"Ah, God," Egan groaned and everything tightened into a knot of longing and tension that had to be released. "Ahhh," he cried out softly as his hips thrust up and he rammed his cock deep in Tie's throat, his hands holding so tightly to Tie's head Tie thought he might leave bruises. His legs tightened as well, drawing Tie closer and Tie felt the first wash of hot cum in his throat. He'd never sucked a man off before, never tasted the thick, hot, salty cum, never understood how much of it there was. He tried to swallow it all, but some escaped his mouth and he felt it slide down his chin and roll teasingly, slowly down his neck. He swallowed voraciously around the cock pulsing in his mouth, shooting more cum in his throat. God, it was good—so fucking good to have Egan coming in his mouth, coming for him. Tie's hips jerked as his cock leaked pre-cum. He was close, just from sucking Egan, from tasting him.

Egan fell back heavily on the bed when he was done ejaculating, his hands falling from Tie. Tie pulled off his cock with a pop, sucking it hard one last time and Egan cried out, his body jerking again. Christ, Tie had to come, he had to. He stood quickly, towering over Egan lying on the cot.

"I'm sorry," he mumbled, fumbling to push down the briefs that had ridden up. He grabbed his cock and felt the first spasm of his orgasm as it ripped through him. He threw back his head with a groan and his cum came in a hot dizzying rush, riding the waves of his climax. He pulled his head up and watched with glazed eyes as he came all over Egan's stomach and chest. The sight made him shudder with a jerk of pleasure, his hips thrusting as the last of his cum shot out onto Egan. When he was done he felt weak but euphoric. This was the beginning. They'd escape together and build a life beyond the outlooks, far from the Amalgamation. They could do anything as long as they were together. Tie leaned forward and gripped the edges of Egan's cot, surrounding him in his embrace and moved to kiss Egan. Egan turned his face away.

"Egan?" Tie whispered, confused.

He heard Egan sigh. "Go to sleep, Tie." Egan sounded sad and very weary.

"What?" Tie couldn't believe he'd heard correctly. After what they'd just shared, that was it? Go to sleep, Tie?

Egan pushed himself up so he was once again lying with his head on the pillow. He put his arm over his face and tried to pull the cover up. He couldn't, Tie was still leaning on it.

"That's it? 'Go sleep, Tie?' You just fucking came in my mouth, Egan. Don't you think perhaps that's something we should talk about?" He tried to keep his tone calm, but it was impossible. The sarcasm and hurt weren't going to help, but he was beyond caring.

Egan moved his arm and the face that stared at Tie was completely impassive. "No, I don't. You caught me half asleep. I don't want it to happen again. End of discussion."

Tie stood up and rubbed his hands over his face, frustrated as always with everything. The goddamned jungle heat, the fucking SS regulations and Egan's recalcitrance. "Why, Egan? Why did you promise them I'd behave from now on or they could re-indoctrinate you as well?"

Egan cursed. "Is that what this is about? Payback? Who told you?" Tie heard the cot squeak as Egan rolled onto his side facing away from Tie. "It doesn't matter. Just behave and nobody will have to be re-indoctrinated, understood? Now go to sleep."

"Why, Egan?" Tie wouldn't give up. If he could only make Egan admit his feelings, then they could talk about the sex, they could move forward, make plans.

Egan sighed again. "Why go to sleep? Because it's the middle of the night."

"Don't be an ass, Egan," Tie growled. He glared at Egan's back.

Egan sighed again and rolled over on his back to stare at the ceiling. "I did it because you're one of my men, Tie. It's my duty to protect you, even from your own foolishness." As he said the last word Egan turned his head to stare at Tie and Tie knew, he knew that there was more to Egan's actions than duty.

"That's a lie," Tie said softly and he saw anger flare in Egan's face.

"Just accept it and for fuck's sake go to sleep."

Never breaking eye contact with Egan, Tie said, "No."

It was Egan's turn to rub his hands over his face in frustration. Tie suppressed a smile. They were starting to mimic each other unconsciously, they spent so much time together. Tie liked it. It made Egan his on some basic level. Egan growled quietly with aggravation. "Yes. I am not in the mood for this right now, Tie."

"I don't really give a fuck, Egan," Tie said casually, his voice low. Most people were asleep except the watch and they wouldn't be able to tell what they were saying anyway, but just in case he wanted to be quiet. They were lucky they hadn't been caught earlier when Egan cried out. And this was definitely not a conversation he really wanted to share.

Egan stared at him in amazement. "You don't give a fuck? Just like that and I'm...what? Supposed to back off and suddenly decide to spill my guts? Forget it." Egan snorted in disgust and started to roll back over.

Tie had had enough of Egan's avoidance and denial. He angrily grabbed the blanket once again covering Egan and tore it off. "Don't you fucking ignore me, or this, again," he growled.

Egan rolled over onto his back and was immediately on the defensive. His arms and legs rose as if to fend off an attacker, one hand fisted and arm cocked. Tie grabbed the fist in his hand and held it tight. "I need to have this out, Egan."

"And I need to fucking sleep, Tie," Egan said sarcastically, "so you can have your little emotional breakdown in the morning, okay?" He was still pushing against Tie's hand with his fist while Tie held it immobile. It became a pissing contest between them, until their teeth were gritted.

With a disgusted sigh Tie wondered what the hell he was doing and backed off. He didn't want to wrestle with Egan, he wanted to fuck him. He'd realized it over a year ago, that he was in love with his best friend. He'd woken up one morning to see Egan shaking him awake and just like that he'd known. Knew that he was the most important person he would ever have in his life. He loved his humor, or more often than not his lack of it, his intelligence, his loyalty and his ruthlessness. Tie loved his broad shoulders and lean muscled body, his thick black hair and those eyes so like Tie's, except his irises were a darker gray, more of a shadow than an outline. He'd wanted to lean up and kiss that perpetually unsmiling mouth and had actually started to do it when Egan pulled back, alarmed. Tie had laughed it off with a lame, "Whoa, still must be dreaming. Sorry." And Egan had accepted it and moved away.

171

But more and more over the last year Egan had caught Tie looking at him with heat and yearning. He'd endured Tie's concern when Egan was hurt in training and the small touches Tie had begun to bestow on him whenever it was safe to do so. Egan had accepted it all, but he'd refused to answer the question in Tie's eyes, refused to acknowledge the feelings Tie no longer tried to hide.

"Egan—"

"No, no more," Egan said, his voice tired and hoarse. He turned away and Tie realized he was fighting tears. He turned back in a moment, once again stoic. He took a deep breath and then shattered Tie's dreams. "I don't...feel that way about you, Tie. I love you, but as my best friend. Please don't ruin that. I can't do this. I can't be what you want." He sat up and his voice turned harsh. "Don't you realize how dangerous this is? I've worked too hard to keep you alive to cause your death."

Tie took a stumbling step back. "We'll run," he said and he heard the desperation in his voice. "We can escape the MSL, the IMF, Earth, the fucking Amalgamation." He spoke quickly, trying to convince Egan, who was looking at him with pity. God! Not pity, anything but that. "We'll go to the outlooks or even beyond. They won't find us, they won't. I love you, Egan. We can have a normal life. You just have to want it. You just have to want it enough." His voice cracked on the last word and he stopped with a gasp that sounded too much like a sob for comfort.

Egan was shaking his head. "I don't want it, Tie. If we just do what we're told, eventually, if we survive, they'll leave us be. They'll let us go and then we can find a place in the galaxy to start over. But I can't run, Tie, I won't. I won't be hunted like an animal and that's what they'll do if we run, you know it. They'll hunt us like animals and kill us. It's that simple. I choose to take my chances here." He stared at Tie for a moment and then deliberately lay back down on his side and pulled the cover up. "Now go to sleep."

And at that moment Tie knew that he was on his own. He would escape and find the life he dreamed of. A life that would include Egan, eventually. But first he would have to break free from the Medical Sciences Lab and the IMF and the Amalgamation. Then he would return for Egan, whether he wanted Tie or not. He quietly returned to his cot and began to plan.

* * * * *

Regan lay on the cot in the holding cell and listened to Tie tell Cerise about their past. He felt as if he'd had a laser through the chest. He reached up and with surprise brushed a tear off his cheek with his fingertips. There was so much Tie didn't know, had never understood. Regan had been trying to protect him. He'd thought he was doing the right thing. Now he knew that Tie had been right all along.

Regan had been so in love with him. Tie had been an idealistic fool, a dreamer in a place that made no allowances for dreams. Regan would have done anything to protect him, including denying his feelings and his hunger for him. But he'd had that night, that one night to sustain him through the last eleven years. Hell, he hadn't bathed for three days after that. He'd left the evidence of Tie's climax on his stomach and chest as long as he could. In the heat and sweat of the jungle he'd gotten some strange looks from the other troops there when he walked by and they smelled him but he didn't care.

They never spoke of feelings or running again. Regan had been so relieved at Tie's apparent submission he'd never thought to question it. Until one morning he woke up alone and the real nightmare had begun. The nightmare of wondering if Tie was dead. At first it had been fear of his being captured, tortured, returned for termination. But the longer he stayed gone the more Regan had become convinced he was dead. Through his own torture, the interrogations, the tagging, he'd been like an android with no emotional programming. Nothing had touched him because he was lost

173

in the black void of abandonment, of being truly alone for the first time he could remember. He had hurt so badly that he shut down so he felt nothing at all. Then one day it had all come roaring back and he'd let it out in a hail of laser fire.

He'd been ordered to terminate a rebel prisoner. The man was unarmed, he'd been caught running, but he wasn't wanted for violent crimes, only sedition. He wouldn't reveal what he knew about the few rebel forces on Earth and in yet another test of loyalty Regan had been ordered to shoot him. He still wasn't sure when he made the decision that he'd had enough. When he was walking over to the prisoner? The day before, when they'd made him run all day long, until he was throwing up with exhaustion and pain? Perhaps it was three months earlier, when Xane had broken his leg so badly he couldn't run anymore, could barely walk and he'd been terminated? Perhaps he never made a conscious decision. He just knew that when it came time to pull the trigger it seemed that if someone had to die it sure as hell shouldn't be the fearless man kneeling on the ground glaring in defiance at the soldiers surrounding him. It was all a blur after that. But when the laser fire died Regan found himself on the run with the rebel, Sasha. They'd cut the sensor from his cheek less than an hour later and caught a freighter for Xy-Three. He'd never looked back.

He'd looked for Tie. He'd still been looking when he came face-to-face with him on that prison hulk, although he'd never really believed he'd see him again. And now that they'd found each other, what were they going to do? Regan rubbed his hands over his face wearily. He'd lost Tie, found him and then lost him again — to Cerise. And Cerise — the one bright spot in his life in the last eleven years, the one thing that had made him think perhaps life was worth living after all. He'd lost her, too. What now? What the hell did he have now?

Chapter Twelve

ℰ

"He was crazy not to love you, Tie." Cerise lay with her head on his shoulder, stroking her hand over his chest soothingly.

Tie hadn't used Egan's name. He wasn't sure why. Eventually Cerise would have to know, but right now…he didn't really feel it was his secret, or his alone, to share.

"Is that why you want Regan, Tie? Because he's former SS and reminds you—"

Tie rolled over and covered Cerise, kissing her neck. "It doesn't matter," he whispered. "All that matters is we both want him."

Cerise looped her arms around Tie's neck and arched her neck. "Do you like that, Tie, what you did to him? Would you like me to do that to you?" Her voice was husky and just a bit hesitant, as if she wanted to but was a little afraid of it.

"Yes," he whispered, his lips running along the curve of her stubborn jaw. "Yes, I'd like you to do that, when you want to. I'm in no rush." He smiled against her fragrant skin as he felt her relax. Her next words had him tensing.

"When you say you want Regan exactly what do you mean, Tie? You mean you want to do that to him?"

"Suck his cock," Tie said distractedly, images of fucking Regan flashing through his mind. Cerise's arms tightened around his neck as he said the words and it took him a moment to understand she was embarrassed. He chuckled. "It's nothing to be embarrassed about," he said matter-of-factly. "That's what it's called and that's what you do. You can say it, you know." He pulled back and looked at Cerise

175

expectantly. She licked her lips nervously and looked at a spot over his shoulder.

"Suck his cock," she whispered, her cheeks turning pink. Tie leaned down and kissed them.

"Yes," he whispered against her cheek as if he were telling her a great secret, "yes, I'd like very much to suck Regan's cock." He mentally added, *again*. "But I'd also like to fuck him," he said aloud. He felt Cerise jerk a little and recognized it as surprise. He looked at her again and gave her a little grin. "Do you know what that means?"

She looked offended for a moment. "Of course I know what it means." She huffed in disdain. "We've been doing it like mad for the last three days."

Tie laughed. "Yes we have," he agreed with another kiss, this time to the sweet little corner of her pursed lips. "But I meant do you know what it means when men fuck each other?"

Cerise avoided eye contact again. "Yes," she said in a small voice. "A...friend explained it to me."

Tie felt his brows lower with suspicion. "Did Regan explain the facts of life to you?"

At that Cerise looked at him with eyes wide in absolute shock. "Regan? You must be joking. He had to leave the room when I asked about it. About men, I mean. You see a friend of ours, in Regan's words, 'fucks anything that stands still long enough'." She smiled with affection as she said it. "And that includes other men. So I asked him about it. When he started to tell me, Sasha had to haul Regan off him and he threw Regan out of the room. Then Conor explained exactly how things worked. As a matter of fact he gave me a great deal of information that day, some of which had nothing to do with the original question."

"Did he show you?" Tie asked, not sure how he felt about this "friend" explaining things to Cerise. He sort of agreed with Regan. And who was Sasha?

At his question Cerise burst into laughter. "Show me? Again, you must be joking. Regan made it very clear to one and all that if anyone so much as touched me they would be killed, painfully and slowly."

Tie leaned down and rubbed his nose playfully against Cerise's. "I'm still here."

Cerise raised her eyebrows at him in mock admiration. "I'm impressed. There aren't many men Regan would allow to live after violating my sanctified body."

Tie laughed softly at her sarcasm. "I shall repent at my leisure," he told her with a lascivious grin as he rubbed his erection against the soft hair on her mons. Cerise exaggeratedly groaned in rapture making Tie laugh some more.

Cerise snuggled up against Tie, her fingers playing in the hair at his nape making him shiver. She smiled softly at him. "So you've never done that? Fucked a man?" She ran her fingers from the soft indentation at the base of his skull down his neck and over the first two vertebrae in his back and it felt like she was igniting little explosions of heat that spread from his spine to the rest of his body. Christ he loved those little barely there caresses. They made him burn for more in an exquisite torture of anticipation.

"No," he said as he arched his back into her touch.

"What about a woman?" she whispered and Tie jerked his head up to stare at her. Every muscle in his body tightened in response to her meaning.

"Yes," he answered cautiously. He needed to make sure she was asking what he thought she was. "Yes, I've fucked a woman like that, in the ass. Is that what you mean?"

Cerise looked into his eyes from beneath a fringe of dark eyelashes, teasing and sultry. "Yes," she said in a husky voice, "that's exactly what I mean."

Tie lowered his body on top of hers, his weight barely held off her by his forearms. He nuzzled his mouth against the

177

vulnerable, soft skin tucked behind her ear. His breathing was rough, disturbing the hair there. "Do you want me to fuck you in the ass?" he whispered and he felt her shiver. "Is that what you want, Princess?"

Her arms tightened around his neck and she buried her fingers in his hair, massaging his scalp. It was his turn to shiver. Cerise turned her head until their lips were touching, her lips a shadow of damp warmth against his mouth. "Yes, Tie. Yes, that's what I want. Show me what you want to do to Regan." He started to kiss her but she clutched her fist tight and the sting as she pulled his hair stopped him. "But first you must call me Cerise. When we're here together fucking, you'll call me Cerise."

Tie leaned down until their lips touched again as Cerise continued to tug on his hair. The pain only heightened his anticipation. "Cerise," he obeyed, the sound less than a whisper on his breath. Her hold on him changed and instead of pulling him away, she was pushing him forward. As their mouths slanted across one another Cerise wrapped a leg around his waist and Tie was lost in her.

Regan put shaking hands over his face. God no, please. He'd tried not to listen, but he was weak. And now this. Did they know what they were doing to him? Did they care?

Cerise wasn't sure what to do. She knew the mechanics of it, but getting there was awkward. Tie broke the kiss and she started to roll over, assuming if one were going to be fucked in the ass one needed to be on one's stomach. Tie stopped her with an odd look on his face.

"What are you doing?" he asked and Cerise could feel herself blush.

"I'm rolling over so you can fuck me."

Tie laughed softly and Cerise frowned at him. "Cerise, baby, I want to fuck you in the ass, I do, but I think we both need a little preparation." He looked ruefully down and Cerise followed his gaze to see that he was hard, but not rock hard.

"Oh," was all she could say. This was something new. Tie was always ready to fuck.

Tie just shook his head in amusement. "I can't go from an emotionally draining confession to hot and hard in sixty seconds, baby." He slid down her body and grinned at her before he leaned in and kissed her stomach. Her muscles seized in arousal at the touch of his lips and the knowledge of where he was headed. "And I'm not wasting a perfect opportunity to kiss your pussy until you're soaking wet and begging for it."

"I'm begging now," she said breathlessly, shifting restlessly beneath him, her hips driving up against his chest.

Tie laughed. God she loved that sound. He sounded content, happy even. She wanted to make him happy. He deserved happiness and she would do whatever it took to give it to him. He slid all the way down until he lay between her thighs and Cerise hooked her legs over his shoulders without being told. He smiled up at her approvingly. "Good girl," he said quietly and then he leaned down and ran the tip of his tongue around her clit. She jumped at the sensation and her stomach dipped as if she were falling through space. The feel of Tie's hands gripping her hips and hauling her closer to his mouth grounded her once again. She buried her hands in his hair and held on, pulling him into her, against her. She loved to feel his soft hair as it fell over her hands and wrists while he was licking her pussy like this. His hands slid under her ass and raised her slightly, his thumbs coming up to hold her lips apart while he licked the valleys of her vulva teasingly. He tongued her inner lips softly before pressing the tip of his tongue inside her and Cerise felt the first moan break from her throat. She could feel Tie smile against her and it was so intimate that she trembled at the force of her feelings for him.

"Tie," she said, her voice high and breathy and trembling like the rest of her.

179

"Shhh," he whispered, his mouth on her, the sound rolling across her. Her hips jerked and he licked her, his tongue dipping inside again on the upward stroke for just a moment. She arched her back and one of his hands slid up her side to her stomach. He let his hand rest there without moving it and it was a comfort to her, an anchor in the storm brewing where his lips and tongue and teeth were swirling over her.

She could feel the slick cream as it began to flow from her, could hear his rumbles of enjoyment and the wet sounds of his mouth on her, eating her. Soon she was wet from her clit to the tight entrance of her ass, her cream running down her crease to tease her there. When she felt Tie's thumb trace the same route she stiffened in surprise and then tried to relax quickly, hoping he hadn't noticed. His thumb came to rest on the sensitive opening in her bottom, rubbing gently. He pulled his mouth away and blew a cool breath across her hot delta. She was panting from excitement, anticipation and perhaps a little fear.

"If you want me to stop, I will," he said softly, not looking at her.

Cerise shook her head as she answered him. "No, I want it, I do. I liked it when you did it before. It felt good. Everything you do to me feels good, Tie." She bit her lip and then decided to be completely honest with him. "I'm just nervous. I'm sorry, but I've never done this, the fucking part." She blew out a frustrated breath. "In the ass, I mean."

She felt Tie's breath huff against her as he let out a small chuckle. "Yes, I know what you mean." He kissed the inside of her thigh. "I'm going to use my fingers to stretch you a little, baby. I don't want to hurt you when I come inside."

Gently he eased the tip of his thumb barely inside her and she gasped at how tight she felt, how large his thumb felt. It was a free fall of excitement again. Not just the pleasure of his invasion, but what it meant, what he was preparing her for. The things he did to her were so marvelous. He made her feel like a woman, a sensuous, desirable woman. She loved it, loved how he made her ache and beg she wanted him so much. His tongue swept up her slit and plunged inside her pussy as he pushed his thumb deeper into her ass and she groaned at how decadent it felt. She felt him moving his thumb in a gentle rocking motion and the sting as he stretched her was just another layer of sensation in a hot swell of arousal.

"God, baby, you're so tight," he groaned, his mouth so close to her she could feel the words against her wet, swollen nether lips. She shivered and then cried out as she felt his other thumb push in next to the one already inside her. It crossed the line from pleasure to pain for a moment and she arched her back instinctively trying to get away from him. He pressed his cheek against her thigh and she eased back down into his touch. He kept one thumb motionless while he began to slowly slide the other back and forth in a small movement that sent spirals of heat curling up her spine. Tie was kissing her pussy, his teeth nibbling on her lips, his tongue dancing along her folds and suddenly Cerise imagined him working Regan's cock the same way as he plunged his fingers in and out of Regan's ass. The image had her moaning and pressing harder down onto his fingers.

"Do you think Regan will be as tight?" she asked breathlessly and Tie froze.

"God, I hope so," he rasped and Cerise moaned again as he thrust his thumb hard and deep.

It was then that Tie heard it—a muffled groan, a slight squeak of the cot in the holding cell. He tuned in to the sounds and they became clearer. He heard the rasp of an indrawn breath, the rustle of clothing and it only took a moment before he understood. Regan was listening to them. And he was jacking off to the sounds of their fucking. Tie nearly swore aloud at the intensity of the desire that flashed through his veins like fire, curling up his cock until it leaked hot and wet against the sheets. He knew he had to fuck Cerise soon because he couldn't last, not with the sight and smell and sound of her combined with the sound of Regan's masturbation. He imagined Regan fisting his cock and pumping it in time to the rhythm of Tie's thrusts and his hips jerked against the bed. God he wished he could tell Cerise what he heard, but if he did then Regan would know he was listening and he'd stop. And Tie desperately did not want him to stop. Touching Cerise, making her moan and gasp while listening to Regan's ragged breaths and guttural moans was the most amazingly erotic thing he'd ever done.

Tie pulled his thumbs from Cerise's ass slowly and she cried out in disappointment. He rubbed one over the wet little entrance and she ground her ass against it, practically purring. He smiled. She was more than ready. He pushed up to his knees and moved to Cerise's side. Her eyes, heavy lidded with desire, followed him. She licked her lips and Tie felt his cock jerk. God, she looked so fucking sexy lying there, waiting for him to fuck her ass—wanting him to fuck her ass. Christ, she was the best thing that had ever happened to him, better than he deserved. She wanted him, loved him, just as he was. She'd let him to do every goddamn thing he'd ever dreamed of doing with his woman and she'd love every minute of it. Why? What had he done to earn the love of this amazing woman? Not nearly enough, he thought, but he would. He'd spend every minute of the rest of his life earning her. And he'd start by sharing her with the man she'd loved for so long, the man they'd both loved for so long.

Tie reached out and rolled her to her stomach. Other than a quick, indrawn breath Cerise said nothing. Leaning over to the side Tie opened a drawer in the wall next to the bed and took out a tube of lubrication. He had some toys on board for long, lonely missions and he used the lube with his dildo and vibrator. He had to close his eyes as he imagined Cerise fucking him with one of his toys. The dildo, he thought, he'd like the dildo buried deep in his ass while she sucked his cock. He breathed deeply, trying to get some control back and stay on course.

"I'm going to fuck you now, baby," he whispered. He heard Regan groan and decided he was going to describe everything he did for Regan's benefit. "I'm going to lubricate your ass and then I'm going to fuck it."

"Yes, God, yes, Tie." Cerise came to her knees, her head and shoulders still on the bed, her arms raised over her head. She thrust her ass into the air invitingly and it was all Tie could do not to ram his cock in as deep and hard as he could in answer. She was so goddamn beautifully submissive lying there, waiting to be fucked. Jesus. Tie opened the lubrication and applied a generous amount to his cock, then took the tube and inserted the tip in Cerise's ass. "I'm just going to squeeze a little inside you, sweetheart." He squeezed gently and some of the lube eased out around the sides. "Tie!" she cried out. He pulled the tube out and threw it across the bed, then moved between her legs. God, he was so desperate to be inside her.

"I've got to get inside you, baby, Jesus, you're so hot for it, so hot for my cock in your ass." He wasn't really sure what he was saying, whatever came into his head at this point. He could hear the cot shifting rhythmically in the holding cell. Cerise was rocking her ass back against him. He placed the tip of his cock against the tight ring of muscles guarding her passage and began to push inside.

"Oh, God!" Cerise screamed. Tie stopped as soon as the head of his cock breached her. She was so tight around him he wasn't sure how he was going to get inside her all the way. Both of them, no, all three of them, were breathing heavily. Tie massaged the cheeks of Cerise's ass, his thumbs manipulating her entrance, tugging gently until he could work his cock in a little at a time.

"Just let me in, little rebel," he murmured, pressing, pressing, each hard centimeter of his cock sliding slowly into her. "So hot, so tight," he groaned as his head fell back on his shoulders and he squeezed her hips so hard he knew he'd leave marks, *wanted* to leave marks. "God. God, baby." He couldn't think anymore, couldn't put together a coherent

Samantha Kane

sentence. She felt so fucking amazing, so tight she was choking his cock and he gasped for breath. He heard a deep, guttural moan from the holding cell, his senses so acute he thought he could hear the glide of Regan's fist up and down his hard cock. His whole body jerked with a violent shudder of arousal.

"Tie, Tie," Cerise sobbed, shoving her hips back. He was unprepared for her move and his cock rammed deeper into her. She screamed and pulled back.

"Cerise," he groaned as he leaned down, resting his weight on shaking hands, kissing her back tenderly. "Slowly baby, fuck me slow and gentle this time. I know you like it deep and hard sweetheart, but that's in your pussy. When I'm in your ass we need to take it slower, not so rough."

She nodded jerkily. "Okay, okay," she panted, her head twisting restlessly on the bed. "Oh, God, Tie, just fuck me. Fuck me!"

Tie laughed weakly as he pulled out and thrust back in, not as slow as his initial entry but still cautious. "You like it, don't you, baby? The perfect princess likes it in the ass."

"God, yes." Cerise moaned loudly as he thrust into her again.

"Tell me," he whispered. He needed to hear it. He always wanted to hear how much she liked what he did to her. And he wanted Regan to hear it. He knew it would drive the other man mad to listen to her talk about how she liked to be fucked. And part of him wanted Regan to know how goddamn good he was at fucking ass.

Cerise knew him so well. She knew what he wanted and gave it to him. "It's so good, Tie." Her voice was a low throaty purr. "Your cock feels so big back there. You're big when you fuck my pussy, you fill me up. But in my ass, God! Every time you fuck into me it's like lightning shooting up my spine and out my fingertips." Her groan was as guttural as Regan's. "Yes, baby, yes, I like it, I love it. I love everything you do to me." She thrust back against him, harder and he obeyed her

184

silent command. His cock tunneled in a little deeper, a little harder with each thrust. "Yes, yes, yes," she chanted. "Harder like that. Fill me up, Tie. Give me all of you."

Tie couldn't have denied her if he'd wanted to. He leaned low over her back, his stomach pressed against her, his nipples grazing her damp skin with each movement. He pressed his nose into the curve of her neck and inhaled her unique fragrance. Just the scent of her across a room could arouse him now. She was imprinted on his brain, his heart, his soul. He gently bit into the tendon of her shoulder and held her in his mouth, the tip of his tongue swirling over her salty skin and she shivered. Then he began to fuck her in earnest. He owned her with each thrust, claimed her and she surrendered. She gave him everything she had, let him possess her and in return he became hers.

With his weight he pressed her down, spread her legs wider, until she was completely at his mercy. His cock pistoned into her tight channel. She was so hot and slick and soft as silk. "I own you, Cerise," he whispered darkly, the possessiveness in his voice dominating.

He heard Regan's ragged breaths.

"Yes, Tie," she said on a sob, opening herself wider, taking him deeply now, her hips tilted, her ass a welcoming hot haven.

The holding cell cot creaked wildly.

"What am I doing Cerise?" he asked thickly as he reached his hands over her head and threaded his fingers with hers. He held her hands pressed to the bed, controlling her, possessing her.

"Fucking me, Tie," she said in a voice trembling with submission and pleasure. "Fucking my ass, Tie."

Regan swore in a harsh, desperate voice.

"And you love it." It wasn't a question, it was a statement of fact and she didn't try to deny it, had already admitted it.

"Yes, yes," she cried, her voice high and breathy.

185

"Yes, yes," Regan's whisper echoed.

"I'm going to own Regan just like this." Tie pushed into her, his movements getting rough as he began to lose control. "I'm going to fuck him just like this, hard and deep. I'm going to hold him down and make him beg, make him cry out in pleasure, just like you, baby, just like you."

"Oh, God," Cerise moaned.

Regan moaned and the cot jerked so roughly on the deck Tie was surprised Cerise didn't hear it.

"Fuck me, baby, make me come," Tie whispered. "Let me hear you come, lover, cry my name."

He reached down with one hand and roughly slid a finger into Cerise's slit, pressing his palm firmly against her hard clit as he rubbed in circles. Cerise cried out hoarsely, her hips bucking and Tie held her down, fucked her hard and deep. In two strokes she fell apart. She screamed his name as she came, thrust that hot, tight little ass up on his cock and he felt the spasms racking her. He thrust two fingers into her pussy. He wanted to feel her orgasm. He wanted to give that hot, empty sheath something to hold on to as she came. She sobbed his name and thrust mindlessly against him.

Regan cried out, the sound quickly muffled. But Tie heard it. He'd cried Tie's name. There was a long, low drawn-out moan as he came. Tie knew he was coming, coming to the sound of Tie fucking Cerise, to the image of Tie fucking him.

"Come, baby, yes, come for us," he told her roughly as continued to fuck her with his cock and his fingers, continued to rub her clit. She was mindless with her climax, crying out both Tie and Regan's names. Tie didn't think she knew what she was saying, but he did. And so did Regan.

The sounds of both his lovers crying out his name, coming for him, pushed Tie over the edge. He thrust into Cerise with a roar and felt his cock jerk over and over as he filled her. "Cerise," he moaned, "Regan." He fucked into her several more times, each thrust forcing more cum out into her gripping ass as she sobbed and pushed against him, offering herself for his pleasure, enjoying his climax, reveling in it.

He heard Regan give a sobbing gasp, cut off in the middle. Then Tie collapsed, barely remembering to roll off to the side so as not to crush Cerise. They lay there beside one another, Tie sprawled on his back, Cerise on her stomach, for several minutes.

"God, that was good," Cerise mumbled as she finally rolled over until she came up against Tie's side. He wrapped an arm around her hauling her half onto his chest as he laughed weakly.

"That is the understatement of the day," he teased.

Cerise snuggled into him. "It just keeps getting better and better, Tie," she sighed. "Keep this up and I'm going to want to fuck twenty-four hours a day, not just every few hours."

Tie looked down at her in mock surprise. "You don't already?" He waggled his eyebrows. "'Cause I sure do." Cerise laughed and kissed his chest. Tie hugged her tightly, listening for any sound from the holding cell, which had become too quiet. "Just wait, Cerise. Wait until Regan is in our bed. Then neither of you will ever want to leave it."

* * * * *

In the holding cell Regan bit his fist and forced his tears back. Listening to Tie and Cerise fuck while fantasizing about him was quite possibly the most intense sexual experience of his life. It was also the most heartbreaking. Because he knew what they wanted could never happen. Regan the pirate, leader of the rebellion, could never be a lesser third, a plaything, in any relationship. But God, how he wanted it. He was so pathetic he'd play the toy if he could only be with them.

187

Chapter Thirteen

ॐ

Entering Quantinium's atmosphere was always a risky proposition and it made Cerise sick to her stomach. The constantly raging ice storms created extremely hazardous conditions and ships had to maneuver using basic controls in order to remain inconspicuous to any sensors that might be monitoring the area. She hid out in their cabin, lying in bed under the dulling influence of a light tranq. She trusted both Tie and Regan to get her down safely — Tie because it was his ship and he knew how to fly it and Regan because he'd done it so many times before. Part of her wanted to be on the bridge to watch them work together. Hell, she wanted to watch them do anything and everything together, but there were only two seats on the bridge and that meant she'd be standing since she was useless when it came to flying in extreme conditions.

She weathered the bumps and stomach churning, unpredictable air currents relatively unscathed thanks to the wonders of a little Rom. Used sparingly, the black market drug could be useful. Go just one little step over the line and you were an addict, a Romhead. Short-term memory loss, lack of focus, extreme weight loss, constant thirst and sometimes hallucinations were all symptoms of Rom addiction. Cerise had seen it too often among the disenfranchised poor of the galaxy who had no hope, no reason not to become a drug addict to escape the futility of their existence in the Amalgamation. Fortunately Regan knew how to administer it properly in order to help her with her anxiety attacks. Tie hadn't liked it, but when Regan had reassured him he'd finally relented, probably because Cerise was already so wound up at just the thought of flying into Quantinium she'd been a trembling, hyperventilating mess. They had to rely on Rom because it was easier to get on the black market than the safer, regulated drugs.

She'd actually fallen asleep by the time they entered the bay at the rebel base. The base was located under an energy dome. Quantinium's extreme cold was lethal to any unprotected creature outside the dome. Along with the raging ice storms and extreme cold the moon's surface was sheer ice a kilometer or more deep. The dome brought the cold up underneath it to a livable temperature, but not warm enough to appear as anything more than a scientific anomaly on sensors, were any to scan the area. It was not enough to warrant a visit from an Amalgamation science team. With an energy dome it was possible to deactivate the dome and evacuate the area within a matter of hours. Portability was an important selling point in rebel equipment.

The moon was covered with one endless jagged shard of mountain range. The base was inside one of the thousands of peaks on the moon. The mountain had been blasted out into a warren of small rooms, interconnected like a maze, all paths eventually leading to the large bay housing the small fleet of rebel ships stationed there. Between the moon's inhospitable weather and the mineral content of the mountain it was almost impossible to get a clear reading of any life inside the mountain from sensors orbiting Mimnet.

Cerise woke up to a featherlight touch on her lips and she opened her eyes to see Tie sitting on the edge of the bed next to her wearing his lopsided grin. She smiled sleepily back and his finger slipped into her mouth. She suckled it instinctively, scraping the tip of her tongue over the edge of his short nail. Tie was still smiling when she heard a noise and looked over his shoulder to see Regan frozen in the hatchway staring at them. Without breaking eye contact with Regan, Cerise released Tie's finger and sat up. Next to her, Tie had also turned to look at Regan. Tie eased his arm around Cerise's waist and pulled her onto his lap. She grabbed the sheet at the last minute and barely managed to cover her breasts and her pubic hair, leaving most of her exposed. For a moment Cerise thought she saw a foreign vulnerability in Regan's eyes but then his familiar, cool demeanor was back in place.

"I contacted Sasha as soon as we arrived." He raised a hand filled with clothing. "He brought something for you to wear."

Cerise smiled broadly at him. "Wouldn't do for the princess to arrive half naked?" she asked teasingly. Regan frowned and Tie laughed.

"Half naked?" Tie asked incredulously. "I think wearing nothing but panties and a borrowed man's shirt is closer to actually naked."

"What do you think Regan?" she asked him, a little worried about his detached manner this morning.

"I think that whatever you choose to do will be accepted by the people here, as always." He sounded completely dispassionate, almost bored.

Tie went very still and then suddenly his hand slid caressingly up her arm and tucked a stray hair behind her ear. "Whatever or whoever?" he asked casually and Cerise realized that yet again there were undercurrents here she hadn't noticed.

"Both," Regan answered as he walked briskly into the cabin and set the clothes down on the end of the bed. He turned without looking directly at them again and walked to the hatch. "I'll wait for you both before debarking."

After he left Tie sighed as he reached for the clothes and dragged them over. He patted her on the behind and pushed her up off his lap. "Get dressed Your Royal Nakedness. Your public waits."

Cerise sighed back at him as she took the gown from his hand. "Tie, please don't be like that. Everyone is going to love you as much as I do." She reached out and took his hand in hers. "Trust me." She could tell from his dubious expression he didn't believe her but he said nothing.

Cerise was sure that everyone would accept Tie once they got to know him. Until then…well it might be a bumpy ride. She knew she'd been the pampered pet of most of the people here for the last seven years, for some even longer than that. The pretty, perfect, perky princess, inviolate and pristine in her virginity. She sighed again. Yes, it might be a little rough going for a while, for Tie at least. She would try to ease his way here, but she didn't think Regan would be much of a help with that.

How was she to make Regan see how good the three of them could be together? Now that they were here at the base again he'd probably hook up with the crew of *The Rebel Bounty* and be gone as soon as his business here was completed. After that who knew how long it would be until they saw him again. She couldn't bear it, the not knowing if he was all right for months at a time. She'd suffered through it in the past, but that was before he'd kissed her, before she knew he shared her feelings, before she'd really known what those feelings were, what they meant. Now she knew, now she ached for him in the way a woman aches for a man, not a child her protector. Even now, when she knew he was only a few meters away somewhere on the *Tomorrow*, she missed him with an intensity that was almost a physical pain.

"Tie, I'm afraid." She blurted it out as she pulled the long gown over her head and it fell around her. She looked at him and saw his resignation.

"So am I." And she knew the admission was as hard for him to make as it was for her to hear.

She looked in the mirror along the wall opposite. They'd sent a gown for her homecoming that was more formal than her normal attire. That meant that there would be a crowd waiting for her. It was long, white with flowing sleeves and a round, low-cut bodice. It was made of a warm, heavy material and there were matching boots, lined with a synthetic fur. The dress had an incredibly soft inner layer that made her aware of her skin as it was caressed by the fabric. Her nipples immediately puckered, but it was hard to tell under the dress.

191

She wasn't sure she'd seen the dress before. Where had it come from? It was much more mature than most of her other clothes. She looked like a woman instead of the young girl who'd left here. Was it the gown or all that she'd been through? She looked over her shoulder and saw Tie gaping at her.

"What?" she asked spreading her hands and looking down for whatever was wrong. The motion made the unfastened dress slide down her shoulders and she had to catch it.

Tie shook his head. "I've never seen you dressed." He grinned at her disgruntled expression. "At least not like that. You're absolutely gorgeous." He walked over to her and leaned down to kiss her exposed back before he looked at her in the mirror. "And you're mine." He slid his hands inside the open back of the dress and his arms went around her, his hands coming to rest on her stomach before gliding up and covering her breasts. Cerise's heart began to race and her breathing became unsteady. Just then Regan appeared in the hatch and once again froze at the sight of them. His eyes blazed with anger.

"Can't you stop fucking long enough to get off the goddamn ship?" He stood glaring at them and Tie's hands slipped out of the dress. He pulled it up over her shoulders again and she felt him lace the ties that bound it in back. The dress suddenly became formfitting, exposing her hard nipples and small waist. Suddenly Cerise saw herself as Tie saw her, as Regan saw her now. She was an alluring, desirable woman, long and lithe and fuckable.

Tie was breathing heavily behind her and she looked into Regan's face. He was perusing her from her bare feet to her low neckline. "You'd best put on your boots," he said in a voice that was suddenly low and intense. He picked them up from where they lay on the deck and carried them over. Cerise moved to sit on the bed and Tie went to his knees before her. Without exchanging a word, Regan handed him each boot as

192

Tie slid them up her legs and laced them, the two as subservient as retainers. The way they served her, cared for her, made Cerise ache inside. She wanted them so much.

She put a hand on Tie's cheek as he gazed up at her and then she looked at Regan. "Regan," she whispered. He took a step back, the spell broken.

"Here," he said, pulling something out of his pocket. He dropped it in her lap. "Put it on. You've a right to wear it now."

Cerise held it up and drew in her breath in shock. It was a Carnelian matewaist, a long, thin jeweled chain worn as a belt to signify that a woman was mated. They were considered old-fashioned now, very few women wore them and most of those were ancient. There were just too few people who considered themselves Carnelian nowadays. This chain had one jewel. It was for the newly mated. As a Carnelian woman acquired more husbands, jewels would be added. The stone anchoring the chain was a dark red Carnelian.

"Where did you get it?" Cerise whispered as she ran reverent fingers down the delicate chain. She looked up at Regan but his face was closed. "Why?"

He shrugged negligently. "I can't remember. I thought it would be a nice touch when you finally took a husband. Very traditional and royal. The people will love it."

His answer took some of the joy from his gift. It was just another of Regan's ploys to make her queen of the universe.

"That's bullshit." Tie spoke harshly. "I don't even know what the damn thing is, but if it has significance to Cerise then you bought it for her because you knew that."

Cerise jerked her head up to look at Regan. His eyes were narrowed and he stared hard at Tie, clearly pissed off. Her heart leapt with happiness. Tie must be right, or Regan wouldn't be so mad.

"Thank you," she said softly and Regan's sharp gaze cut to her. He gave nothing away, but she knew that the matewaist was a special gift for her. Had he bought it hoping to give it to her when the two of them mated? If so, it was one of the greatest gifts she'd ever received because it brought her hope.

"Don't read too much into it, Cerise," he said softly. "Don't build dreams on it."

"Too late," she whispered and Regan closed his eyes in frustration. Cerise glanced at Tie and he was looking at Regan with such hunger that it made Cerise tremble.

"It's a Carnelian matewaist, Tie," she told him, her voice breaking. "It signifies that I am a mated woman."

Tie's eyes widened in shock and he stared between Regan and Cerise. "Do you mean me?"

Regan snorted in disgust. "You are too stupid to be king."

"Fuck you," Tie said happily as he took the chain from Cerise and looped it around her waist. "I got first dibs. You'll have to settle for pirate sex slave."

Cerise choked on a laugh as Regan tried not to smile. "In your dreams," he told Tie and he turned away before he saw Tie and Cerise exchange knowing grins.

A few minutes later, the three of them stood ready to walk down the gangplank to the bay. Cerise could hear a cacophony of excited voices. The bay was full. Everyone had come out to welcome her home. She hadn't been on Quantinium for months. She looked at Regan, tall and commanding beside her, fierce in his black leather, his vest accentuating the strong muscles of his chest and arms and throat. He only had the middle button of the vest closed. The black hair on his chest spilled out over the low, open neck and Cerise shivered as she imagined rubbing her nipples against that hair. Suddenly Regan turned as if to say something to her but the words never came as his eyes locked on hers. She let every ounce of her hunger for him show. She reached out a hand and slowly placed it on his chest right on that mat of hair and she trailed her hand down into the open vee of the vest.

The hair was soft, not coarse. Regan's hand came up and slapped down on hers, stopping the motion.

"Cerise," he growled, chastising her. She refused to be disciplined like a child. She curled her fingers into his pectoral muscle, her nails digging in and his lips parted. She relaxed her hold a little and scraped her nails across his chest, fighting against his restraining hand only a little. He was letting her mark him.

"You're mine," she whispered harshly and his eyebrows rose as his mouth closed and his nostrils flared. She wasn't sure where this harsh, almost violent possessiveness was coming from. She only knew that the thought of those women out there watching her men made her crazy. "Don't forget it. If you need a woman to fuck, it will be me. Do not send for one like you usually do when you return from space. I will not tolerate it."

Regan's eyes grew wide in astonishment. "You will not tolerate it?" he asked incredulously. "Who are you to dictate who I can and cannot fuck?"

Cerise's fingers ran over his aroused nipple and she smiled triumphantly. "I am your princess, Regan," she told him softly, "and the woman who loves you." She leaned closer and Regan swayed toward her unconsciously. "And I will cut out the heart of anyone who tries to take you from me."

Regan was breathing hard, his face a mask of outraged arrogance. "You do not own me," he said harshly. "No matter what you think, you do not own me."

He pulled back from her and she let her hand fall gracefully to her side. She cocked her head and looked at him knowingly. "I own you as surely as you own me, Regan. Body and soul."

His face showed his struggle as he fought the truth of her words. "Tie." He seemed to think the one word was argument enough.

Cerise deliberately misunderstood him. "Yes, as surely as Tie owns us as well."

Regan paled and his gaze flew to the other man beside her who had been a silent witness to their exchange. Tie stepped up next to her now and turned her to face Regan with his hands on her hips. He snuggled up behind her and placed a seductive kiss behind her ear. "I'm afraid she's right, Regan. Fuck anyone else besides Cerise or I on this station and I will kill them." He didn't give Regan time to answer. He stepped back, all business. "Shall we go?" he asked Cerise politely and offered her his hand as he stepped out onto the steep gangplank.

She smiled and took his hand, following him. She felt a thrill of possession chase down her spine as Regan silently stepped to her other side. She imagined how they would look to the people awaiting their arrival. These two big, strong, dominant males, both dressed all in black as they flanked their small, delicate princess all in white. It was an amazingly arousing image.

Tie was shocked by the number of people filling the bay. He'd had no idea there were so many here on this frozen rock. How did they feed them all? Clothe them? Who was in charge? As soon as they caught sight of Regan and Cerise the crowd went wild, shouting their names and cheering. Tie let go of Cerise's hand as people surged around them. Regan and Cerise kept walking, but Tie stopped and stepped back into the shadows cast by the *Tomorrow*, still unnoticed by most of the people.

Regan was surrounded by people all shoving papers at him for his signature and demanding decisions be made about everything from sleeping quarters for new arrivals to a shipment of munitions. With a start, Tie realized Regan was in charge. He wasn't sure why he was so surprised. He'd always been a leader, protecting those in his care. Regan handled it all with sharply barked orders, the pen thrust into his hand signing papers as he walked. He kept the other hand on the small of Cerise's back, guiding her, protecting her. It was a practiced move, unconscious and unnoticed by observers.

Cerise was being adored. There was no other word for it. They flocked to her like moths to her flame. She smiled and hugged them, kissed babies, let old women weep on her shoulder. Little girls brought her presents and the men all watched her with hungry eyes. The last made the hairs on Tie's nape rise with agitation. He wanted to stalk out there and claim her, but something held him back. He didn't want to call it fear, but search as he might he couldn't give it another name. He was afraid — afraid that there was no place for him here with Cerise and Regan.

Suddenly Cerise stopped and looked around. Her movements became frantic until she turned and saw him in the shadows. By then Regan had stopped as well and was ignoring the people clamoring for his attention. He turned to look at Tie and raised a hand to motion him forward imperiously. When Tie didn't immediately obey, Cerise walked back to him. By now the crowd knew something was amiss. They strained to see what the princess was doing, who she was smiling at. The bay grew quiet as she stopped about a meter from him and held out her hand. Her smile beguiled Tie as much as it did the masses. He stepped out of the shadows and took her hand, smiling back at her. They would do this together.

Cerise started forward again holding Tie's hand and the crowd surged forward, all shouting at once to know who he was. One look from Tie and those crowding closest fell back to a safe distance. Immediately the whispers of *Super Soldier* began. As soon as they reached Regan's side he turned back to his advisors and began walking again as if nothing untoward had occurred. Regan's hand once again went to Cerise's back and Tie felt a wave of contentment wash over him. This was right, the three of them together.

197

Cerise laughed and hugged and expertly avoided pointed questions about Tie. She stumbled over an overly enthusiastic little boy at one point and Tie caught her against him, the two of them laughing over the incident. Immediately the buzz in the bay grew louder and more insistent. Clearly they had figured out that she and Tie were intimate. Good. He wanted everyone to know that she was his now. He didn't miss the unfriendly looks cast his way by many of the younger men. When he set her from him and looked away, he caught the hungry look on Regan's face before the other man shielded his thoughts behind his ever present mask of cool detachment. Tie just grinned cockily at him and Regan's nostrils flared with annoyance as he turned back to one of his toadies.

"Thomasina!" Cerise cried as she surged forward into the crowd to hug an old woman. Tie followed and the crowd parted. In a moment Regan was at her other side. The two men kept the curious crowd at bay.

The old woman cackled merrily as she touched the matewaist at Cerise's hips. "Princess! So you've come into your Tears then, eh?"

That caught Tie and Regan's attention as well as Cerise's. "What do you know of the Tears, Thomasina?" Cerise asked eagerly.

"Well now, I'm Carnelian aren't I?" The old woman was offended, but the twinkle never left her eye.

Regan rolled his eyes. "Everyone is Carnelian it would seem, old woman. What do you know of the Tears?"

She ignored Regan with an insouciance shared only by the ancient. "I've been waiting for you to grow up," she told Cerise with a sly grin. "Finally brought the pirate to heel, eh?" She sniffed and then a look of confusion passed over her features. "No, no, not him, not yet," she mumbled and then she turned to Tie. Her grin returned. "Ho, now, so I'm guessing this fine, brawny lad is the one that brought your Tears." She laughed in delight. "That must have been quite an experience." She shook her head in consternation. "I always

198

thought it would be this one." She gestured with her head at Regan, who wore a thunderous expression.

"The Tears," Regan reminded her through gritted teeth.

She ignored him again to inspect Tie. "So, laddie, can't get enough of our little princess now, eh? I can see it runs strong in you both, the bond." She finally spared a glance for Regan. "The Chessienne women have always attracted the fiercest warriors. It runs in their blood and like calls to like. The late princess Jordianne had five husbands, all soldiers or warlords the lot of them." She sighed like a young girl as she smiled coquettishly at Tie. "There was a day old Thomasina here had six of her own and not a one left unsatisfied." Her eyes glazed for a moment with memories.

Tie laughed. "That I believe, my lady," he said, bowing with a flourish that had her blushing. "What say you and I chuck the royal and run off together?"

"Tie!" Cerise exclaimed with a disgruntled look as she put her hands on her hips. Tie laughed harder at her jealousy. He liked her jealous. It made him want to take her somewhere and show her she had nothing to be jealous about.

"I think you've done enough running," Regan said darkly and Tie cut his eyes to the pirate, who wouldn't look at him.

Thomasina laughed again. "As if I could satisfy one such as you, lad! No, you'll have to stick with Princess Cerise."

Cerise bit her lip, looking worried. "Thomasina, you must tell us what you know about the Tears. I don't know very much. We need to find out if...well if what we're feeling is normal and what happens next. Can you help us?"

Thomasina looked taken aback. "Don't you know your own power, dearie? Didn't anyone tell you about the Tears?"

"Who, Thomasina?"

At Cerise's question the old woman opened her mouth to answer and then closed it with shock. She had no answer. She patted Cerise's arm. "I should have realized. I am sorry, my dear. Of course I'll tell you what I know."

Regan turned to several people waiting impatiently behind them. "Bring the old woman." He walked off without waiting to see if his order was obeyed.

Tie sighed and looked at Cerise who was looking after Regan. Tie turned back and frowned at the two men who had come and were about to take Thomasina's arms and they hurriedly backed off. "My lady," he said respectfully and offered her his arm. She smiled with delight as she took it. He held out the other arm to Cerise who was watching them with an amused expression and with an exaggerated, flirting flutter of her eyelashes she took it. She tugged Tie after Regan who was waiting for them impatiently a few meters away.

"Come on. You know how impatient he is. I swear." Her exasperated tone amused Tie, but on a deeper level he was struck speechless by the intimacies of the situation. Tie did know how impatient he was. Yet, no matter his impatience or the hundreds of details demanding his attention he waited for them. Not just for Cerise, but for Tie as well. Because when they arrived Cerise reached Regan's side first, but he didn't move until Tie had emerged from the crowd. He didn't turn away until he was sure Tie was with them. They moved again as one, Regan matching his steps to their much slower pace as Thomasina hobbled along beside Tie.

* * * * *

They entered Regan's office, a large chamber with several anterooms. The chamber had a large rectangular table surrounded by chairs and couches lined the walls. The furniture was plush and expensive, an indulgence. But Regan felt as a respectable pirate he ought to surround himself with some obvious booty. And he liked things plush and expensive.

He watched Tie and Cerise seat Thomasina on a couch and Cerise sent one of the people milling about off, probably for refreshments. He hoped she'd ordered food. The rations on the *Tomorrow* had been barely palatable and he was starved. How did Tie live like that?

200

Regan sat down at the head of the table with a sigh as more papers and requests were brought to his attention. He was so goddamn tired. He hadn't slept a wink last night and the flight into Quantinium had been exhausting. Then he'd had to watch Tie claim his woman for the entire world to see and act as if it wasn't slicing his pride and his heart to ribbons with each step they took across the bay.

Suddenly a new voice cut across the room. "Get back you vultures! Give them some space, for fuck's sake. They just got back. Who gives a damn who sleeps where? If they're old enough send them to my bed." Conor shoved a pinch-faced bureaucrat out of the way. "Get out! Everybody out!"

Cerise jumped up and squealed. "Conor!"

The tall rogue barreled through the dispersing crowd and grabbed her in a bear hug. "Darlin'! Damn if you didn't have me worried." He set her on her feet and wagged a finger in her face. "Do not do that again, understood? I think poor Regan lost all his hair for real over your misadventure." Suddenly Conor stepped back and surveyed Cerise from head to toe and back again appreciatively. "Hey, now, Amalgamation prison hulks must not be as bad as they say. You're lookin' all right, darlin'."

In the blink of an eye Tie was on his feet and shoving Cerise behind him. Conor stumbled back a step at the dangerous look on Tie's face.

"Jesus, what the fuck are you?" Conor asked in surprise.

"Tie!"

Regan stood as both he and Cerise said Tie's name warningly. Cerise had her arms wrapped around Tie, holding him back.

"Tie, trust me, you will be very unhappy if you hit him," Cerise tried to reason with him.

Regan jumped to the pertinent information. "Tie, meet Conor Stanislaus."

201

Samantha Kane

That froze Tie in his tracks. His eyes grew wide as he stared at Conor who looked nervously back. "Is that a good look or a bad look?" Conor asked no one in particular, looking ready to run.

Tie turned to Cerise and she nodded her head sheepishly.

"Why didn't you tell me?" Tie asked her incredulously. "'I didn't start naming things after it,'" he mimicked in a high voice. Regan had no idea what he was talking about but Cerise clearly did, as she blushed. Tie turned back to Conor.

"Mr. Stanislaus, I am very honored to meet you." Tie was all earnest admiration as he held his hand out to Conor.

Conor looked at Regan for reassurance. Regan nodded and Conor took Tie's hand. "I've figured out what you are," he gestured at his eyes, clearing recognizing the Super Soldiers' telltale eyes. "But who are you?"

Cerise stepped out from around Tie. "Conor, this is Tie. He's the bounty hunter who captured me."

Conor looked at them all in disbelief. "Huh?"

Regan and Tie sighed simultaneously, which made Regan frown and Tie smile.

"I'm also the bounty hunter who rescued her from the prison hulk," Tie told him as he quirked an eyebrow at an amused Cerise.

Conor sat down at the table. "Clearly this story requires that I sit. Will it also require whiskey?"

Cerise laughed and hugged him again as he sat there. "No, silly. It's very simple really. You see Tie captured me on T-Sdei Delta and then—"

Regan interrupted. "Everyone out." At his simple, quiet command the room emptied in record time and the door shut behind the last person out. Regan smiled. It was good to be the badass pirate.

202

He noticed that Thomasina had ignored his command and still sat on the couch. That was just as well. She hadn't told them what she knew yet.

Conor's eyebrows were high on his forehead as he regarded Regan. "That bad, huh?" Regan nodded. Conor turned back to Cerise with his eyes closed and a pained expression. "Okay, hit me with it."

"Regan," Cerise said admonishingly, "it's all turned out for the best, so it's not that bad."

"Has it? When did that happen?" Regan asked casually as he sat back down. Tie was glaring at him with his arms crossed.

"Quit being such an asshole." Tie's voice was angry, but Regan could hear the hurt underlying it. It stung that he'd hurt Tie.

"Did he just call you an asshole?" Conor asked in absolute amazement. "And he's not dead?"

"He couldn't kill me if he tried," Tie said with a disgusted snort.

"Oh, I might manage it," Regan countered with a feral grin.

"Stop it, both of you," Cerise told them and Regan felt like the asshole Tie had accused him of being.

Conor was watching the exchange with an almost comical look of disbelief. "Is this some kind of joke?"

Regan sat with a sigh. "I wish it was."

Just then old Thomasina reminded them she was there with another cackling laugh. "Oh my, pirate, you've got it bad."

Regan narrowed his eyes at her. "What exactly do you mean by that?"

She gestured vaguely in the air. "The Tears, the Tears. They're affecting you, laddie, all right. Won't be long now."

She had everyone's attention. "No, Thomasina, Regan and I haven't..." Cerise paused, stumbling over her explanation. "I mean, I haven't used the Tears on him."

Thomasina frowned. "What do you mean? You haven't taken him to your bed?"

Cerise blushed but shook her head.

Thomasina waved her hand dismissively. "Doesn't matter. When he's around you give off the scent. His body's reacting to the Tears on you both." She turned to look at Tie. "Which is interesting. I've never before seen a man take the Tears as his own."

"What Tears? What are you talking about? I know you've cried over Regan before, Cerise," Conor said ingeniously. Regan's gut clenched at his words and he quickly looked at Cerise who was staring at him in horror.

She turned to Conor and punched him in the shoulder. "Conor Stanislaus! You promised you wouldn't tell him!"

Conor shrugged. "Something has obviously happened in the last few days and I want to know what it is."

Tie finally spoke. "Cerise tried to enslave me with her Carnelian Tears after I captured her." He was looking at Cerise as he said it, but turned to Conor with a face devoid of expression. "Since we're clearly going to take you into our confidence that means she had sex with me. What she didn't know was that we would become addicted to one another."

Conor blinked rapidly. "Carnelian Tears? I thought that was a myth."

Thomasina spoke at the same time. "Enslave? What are you talking about?"

Regan chose to focus on the old woman. "Tell us what you know about the Tears."

Thomasina sighed and shook her head. "I don't know what nonsense you all have been listening to. The Tears aren't about enslavement. They're about bonding. They have no effect on the unwilling."

"What?" Cerise gasped.

"You can't release the Tears with someone you aren't compatible with and the Tears won't affect any man who isn't willing, who isn't meant for you."

Cerise sat down with an ungraceful thump on the chair Tie shoved under her. Regan suddenly realized he was standing and he didn't remember doing it. His hand was gripping the edge of the table so tightly his knuckles were white. "Start at the beginning," he growled and for the first time Thomasina looked a little frightened of him.

"The Tears bond lifemates and that's all they do. When the bond is forming its very intense, like with these two." She gestured at Tie and Cerise and then at Regan. "And you."

"We have not bonded." Regan spoke very clearly, his tone indicating that that subject was closed. "Are they or are they not addicted to one another? Will they die without the other?"

"Die?" Thomasina's voice was horrified. "What nonsense is that? Of course not! I've lost six husbands and I'm still here at one hundred and eleven!"

Cerise was shaking her head in shock. "I don't understand."

Thomasina got up from the couch and slowly walked over to sit in the chair next to Cerise. She took the younger woman's hand in hers. "My dear, what's happened is natural to our kind. When you meet a man with whom you are compatible then you instinctively release the Tears. It merely...enhances the attraction, the connection. For some the bond is so intense that they can read each other's thoughts, although that has not happened for hundreds of years." She smiled. "For most it simply means that you are going to be on your back a great deal for quite some time." She patted her hand. "Your young man was willing, Princess. You've done nothing wrong."

Cerise slumped back in the seat with stark relief as she sniffled. A tear rolled down her cheek and Tie dragged a chair over next to her. He turned her to face him and took her hand, his elbows resting on his knees so that their faces were even. "Very willing, Cerise. I was very willing. God, I'm sorry, baby. I'm sorry about the way I reacted. I'd never felt like that, not since…" He sighed. "The minute I got a good look at you, heard your voice, it started for me. I wanted you," he tapped his chest with his fist, "deep in here. I recognized you. Do you remember? I said that our paths were meant to merge, that *you* were my path." He ignored Conor's indrawn breath. Cerise nodded tearfully. "That hasn't changed. Even when I thought you were an addiction, I never regretted it. I was yours the minute I touched you in that kitchen on T-Sdei Delta." He held out his hand and it was shaking. "This, this is about how much I want you and need you, not like a drug, but as my woman, my mate, my everything." The two looked at each other as if the others weren't even in the room.

Regan had to sit he was shaking so badly. Tie had released her Tears, not him. All along he'd thought he was the one that she loved. He could see that now. He'd thought she loved him, but she'd had to use the Tears on Tie. The assumption was that as real as it seemed, theirs was a false bond. But it wasn't true. Regan, he was the false one, a childhood crush, not her true love. He put a hand to his chest and rubbed against the pain there, feeling like he'd been cut open and his heart ripped out.

Cerise wiped her cheeks dry with the back of her free hand and Tie reached up to catch one that she missed. The moment was so tender that Regan felt like an intruder. He had to close his eyes against the knowledge that he would always feel that way now.

"Why did all my mother's husbands die then?" Cerise asked, her voice still a little shaky from crying.

Thomasina shrugged. "Some because they hunted down your mother's murderers and died in the process." She looked at Cerise sadly. "Some because they loved her and had no wish to live without her. You Chessienne women seem to inspire that in your men."

Cerise looked back at Tie, biting her lip. "You won't die without me," she whispered. "If you want to leave, you won't die without me."

Tie just shook his head at her as if she were an idiot. "Yes, I will." He ran his fingers through her hair and gripped the back of her head, bringing her forehead to his. "Yes, I will," he whispered. He kissed her tenderly and Cerise clung to his shoulders. They broke the kiss and smiled at each other.

When they turned to look at him Regan was numb. He didn't know what they wanted. Couldn't they see he was dying here?

"I will die without you," Tie said, his eyes on Regan's. Regan tried to ruthlessly tamp down the small flare of hope that sprang up in his chest.

Thomasina laughed and settled into her chair. "Yes, won't be long now."

Chapter Fourteen
ꙮ

Conor was still in shock as he walked down a corridor, heading back to his room. He'd received some information from the Cintealios that was for Regan's eyes only and he'd secured it in the safe there waiting for his return. It was rather late, most people were in bed, but Regan insisted he wanted to catch up on everything before he slept. Conor sighed. He knew that there were other reasons for Regan's reluctance to go to bed—namely that Cerise was sleeping with that giant hulk of a Super Soldier. Conor shied away from using the word fucking when it came to little Cerise. He'd been willing to accept it when Regan finally decided to quit playing the martyr, as everyone had known he would eventually. But to accept that their pretty little princess was...well, you know, with that scary-ass bounty hunter? Christ, that guy was big. Conor seriously did not want to get on his bad side. He looked as if he could rip Conor's head off with one hand without spilling his drink in the other. He was lost in thought as he rounded a corner and came to a stop as it took a second for the scene before him to register.

The two people he'd been thinking about were busy doing the thing he'd been reluctant to think of them doing. Right there, in the corridor. And...Christ, it was so...Conor was thunderstruck. It was primal, rough and so goddamned beautiful it made Conor's breath catch in his throat.

The two were on their knees facing the wall and the bounty hunter had Cerise up against it. Her hands anyway. She was spread wide, her hands braced against the wall, her head throw back in obvious ecstasy. Her feet, still in their boots, lay on the floor alongside the massive thighs of the large man fucking her, her skirt pushed up around her waist and held there by his hands on her hips. He raised and lowered her down on his cock and Conor could see it gleaming wet in the low light as it slid out of her. The hunter, Tie, his head was lowered as he watched his cock fuck in and out of her. Conor jumped, startled when Tie's ragged whisper cut through the night.

"I couldn't wait, baby. Christ, I needed to fuck you." He leaned down and kissed her neck and Cerise tipped her head to the side to give him better access.

"Tie," she cried as he fucked into her. Conor could tell it was deep and hard and his own cock throbbed in response.

"That's right," Tie whispered hotly as she ground down on him, "fuck me, Princess. Fuck your mate." They continued to move against one another in a powerful dance that had both panting. Cerise was moaning loudly, biting her lip and Conor felt his cock leak. God, he was frozen. He knew he should walk away, but he couldn't. Jesus, Regan had had two days of this locked up on that little ship with them.

"Your clit's hard," Tie whispered, licking the back of Cerise's neck and Conor realized one of his hands had moved around and was between her legs. "Shall I make you come, baby?"

"Tie, please," she cried, her hands coming off the wall to reach above and behind her, to cradle Tie's head against her neck. The move arched her back, and the graceful line of her long torso was like a work of art, her small breasts thrust forward enticingly. Tie wrapped one arm around her waist while the other still worked between her legs. She spread her legs wider and his hips began moving faster, harder. He pulled her back until she was almost in his lap and his hips angled to thrust deep into her. It was an amazing feat of strength, Conor knew — he'd fucked in almost every position imaginable. Tie was completely supporting Cerise's weight and yet he was fucking her smoothly and effortlessly.

Suddenly Cerise went stiff and cried out hoarsely. Tie turned them suddenly and pushed her down with his chest against her back. Her hands fell from around his neck to the floor and he covered her, one hand slamming down next to hers, the other still between her legs as he pounded into her. It was a rough move and Conor realized Tie wasn't as in control as he'd seemed. He knew a moment of worry, should he interfere? Was Cerise all right? And then she let out a muffled scream and Tie stroked deeply into her and held there as he groaned and shuddered. Conor's cock jerked as he watched the two of them climaxing simultaneously, lost in the throes of passion. In his release Tie leaned closer into Cerise and when his hips relaxed and he sat back down on his haunches he brought her with him, still buried inside her. The hunter wrapped both arms around her tightly and buried his face in her neck.

"I love you, baby, I love you," he murmured and Conor suddenly felt dirty, like a lascivious voyeur.

"Oh, Tie," Cerise said softly and Conor could hear the emotion making her voice quaver, "I love you so much. So much." She turned her head toward him and buried her hand in his hair holding him close.

Conor started to back up quietly but froze when he heard her next words.

"Bring me Regan, baby. I need him."

What did she mean? How did she need him? Conor knew he must have misunderstood.

"We both need him, sweetheart," Tie answered. Conor's heart thudded in his chest. "It won't be long, Cerise. He'll be in our bed and we'll have all that we desire."

Conor escaped as quickly as he could. He didn't want to hear any more.

* * * * *

Cerise stepped onto *The Rebel Bounty* where it sat docked in the large bay the day after their arrival on Quantinium. She'd looked just about everywhere before finding someone who'd told her Regan had gone to the ship. She was a little nervous about seeing him. The information they'd gotten from old Thomasina yesterday had seriously upset him and she was determined to find out why. She'd thought it was good news. What had disturbed him?

She'd dressed for the occasion. The gown she'd worn yesterday had given her a thirst for more attractive clothes than the boyish ones in her closet, so she'd gone in search of Conor. He was another one who was acting funny. Cerise sighed. She wasn't sure how Conor felt about Tie. Tie had gone with her to Conor's room—it was so cute the way he thought every man was out to fuck her—and Conor had barely been able to look at him.

"Well, come on," Conor had grumbled and he'd dragged them to a little burrow full of women's clothes for sale. Conor knew everything that went on in this station. Everyone told Conor everything. He just had one of those faces. The women there welcomed him with hugs and propositions and he accepted them all, making Cerise smile while Tie looked on in amazement. They had been thrilled to hear Cerise wanted some new clothes and made quite a few suggestive remarks to Tie about his influence on her new "desires". He'd laughed and flirted almost as much as Conor and Cerise had been thoroughly disgruntled until he'd dragged her into the changing area behind a curtain and kissed her silly while undressing her. She'd been aching and breathless when he left her alone so she could try on her clothes.

She'd picked her favorite new dress to wear today. She wasn't one to put off until tomorrow what she could do today. She smiled to herself as the thought brought Tie to mind and his faith in Conor's book and the little ship where she'd learned to love him. The dress was made of soft, synthetic dusky purple suede. It had a similar shape to the white dress she'd worn yesterday, tight with a low round neckline and long full sleeves, but it was short. It came only to the middle of her thighs and made her a little self-conscious, but Tie had

211

practically ripped it off, his eyes blazing with heat, when he'd seen her in it the first time. It, too, had matching boots, a necessity on this cold moon. They were the same warm purple cloth and were very high, up to her thighs, leaving only a few centimeters of thigh exposed between the boots and her dress. The boots had a folded edge at the top and crisscrossed ties running up the sides. Conor had grinned appreciatively and declared them "very pirate-like". Good. Maybe Regan would see her and fall to his knees with lust. She actually snorted out loud in amusement at that.

Conor had taken Tie to meet some of the people in charge around here. If Tie was to be accepted as her mate, her consort or king or whatever the hell he was going to be, then he needed to start meeting important people and taking on some responsibility. They'd talked about it briefly yesterday in Regan's office. Tie knew Cerise was going to talk to Regan and he'd agreed it might be best if she did it without him. Regan seemed more willing to open up to her when she was alone with him.

Cerise stopped in the hatchway that led to *The Rebel Bounty's* bridge. She scanned the relatively small room, although it looked huge compared to the bridge on the *Tomorrow*. There were several members of Regan's crew here and they all knew Cerise. But like everyone else around the station they seemed uncomfortable around her today, as if the fact that she was fucking Tie made her a different person than she'd been a week ago. A few said hello without meeting her eyes and several blushed as they suddenly got too busy to talk. She spotted Regan on the far side of the bridge and when she saw who he was with her blood boiled. Some little Aboolan whore was hanging on his arm, her hand rubbing the bare chest that just yesterday Cerise had claimed as her own. She didn't even notice men scurrying out of her way as she marched across the bridge and grabbed the woman by her long, blonde hair. The little whore screamed as Cerise hauled her away from Regan and threw her into the bulkhead. Regan stood there staring at her with his mouth agape in shock.

212

"That belongs to me," she snarled at the whore and started to turn away. The woman flew at Cerise, grabbing her arm and slamming her back against the bulkhead. Cerise screamed, more in anger than pain.

"I've heard about you, *Your Majesty*," the Aboolan mocked. "And I know you can't handle Regan, even if you are fucking that SS," she hissed.

Cerise was incensed. She was Princess Cerise Chessienne, by God, and no one, no one, talked to her that way. She came off the bulkhead with a snarl. The Aboolan knew how to fight. She came at Cerise with a right hook before she thought Cerise had her balance, but Cerise was able to block the punch with her arm. The impact knocked her down to one knee. She saw a foot coming at her and tucked under, rolling away. The foot never made contact. Cerise watched Regan grab the woman by the hair and nearly break her neck he jerked her off her feet so hard. One look at his face and Cerise almost felt sorry for the vicious little bitch. The woman started screaming. Cerise stood up as Regan forced the Aboolan to her knees in front of Cerise.

"How dare you fucking touch her?" he growled at her as she whimpered in his hold. "Apologize. Now."

The entire bridge was silent as they watched the drama unfold. Sasha took a tentative step forward. "Regan," he said quietly, calmly, "she's just a foolish little whore. Let her go now."

"Apologize," Regan said, shaking the woman roughly. She screamed again, clearly frightened of Regan's legendary temper and then she started babbling an apology. Right then Conor raced onto the bridge followed by one of the crew. He barreled into Regan, taking him into the bulkhead with a crash. Regan let go of the girl and she scrambled to her feet and fled without a backward glance.

"Regan!" Conor yelled at him, imprisoning him against the bulkhead, holding Regan's arm painfully high against his back. "What the fuck is your problem? She's a woman, for Christ's sake." Regan tried to twist in his arms, still half-mad

213

with rage and Conor used his free hand to push the side of Regan's face against the cold synth-steel in front of him. It was clear that Conor wouldn't be able to hold him for more than a second or two. His hold on Regan forced the other man's arm into an incredibly awkward position, one that gave him no advantage, or he'd be free already. "Calm down, you stupid asshole," Conor barked, struggling against Regan's superior strength.

Tie rushed onto the bridge. When he saw Regan held against the wall he didn't hesitate as he stalked over to Conor with a growl and punched him viciously in the side.

"Tie, no!" Cerise screamed, suddenly coming out of the shock that had held her immobile. "It's all right! Regan's all right!" She flew over and covered Conor with her body where he lay crumpled on the deck. Tie stood there over Conor with his fists clenched as his nostrils flared angrily and he breathed his rage heavily.

"Tie," Regan said quietly. He was leaning back against the bulkhead, breathing as heavily as Tie, as though he'd run a race.

Tie looked at him and took a step toward him. "Are you all right?" he asked, his voice vibrating with tension.

Regan straightened and ran a shaking hand over his head. "I'm fine. Conor was trying to knock some sense into me. I deserved it." He put his hands on his hips and looked down at the deck, clearly still trying to get himself under control. "I saw her attack Cerise and I...," he shook his head, "I just lost it." He looked at Cerise. "I'm sorry, baby."

Cerise's heart was pounding at the look on his face, at the endearment. He seemed surprised after he said it and then his face shuttered as if he'd revealed too much.

Tie growled and Cerise looked back to him where he raged behind her. "Who? Who attacked Cerise?" He took two steps and hauled her to her feet as he began running his hands over her arms, then went to one knee to run them up and down her legs. "Are you all right?"

His hands slid under the short skirt of her dress and Cerise gasped at the feel of his hands on her bare flesh. She pushed ineffectually at his hands. "I'm fine, Tie, really," she assured him hastily and she looked up to see Regan staring hungrily at Tie's hands on her exposed legs.

Cerise barely heard the thunder of booted feet as the rest of the crew evacuated the bridge without a word.

Conor sat up gingerly. "No, really, don't worry about me. I'll be fine. I'm just bleeding internally. Nothing to worry about."

"Oh, Conor," she said apologetically as she turned and squatted down next to him. The next thing she knew Regan was hauling her back up.

"Are you trying to give him a peep show?" Regan snarled, running his free hand over his head again. Cerise blushed. She wasn't used to such short skirts, hadn't considered the view she was giving Conor. "What the hell are you wearing?" Regan asked, obviously aggravated.

Well, that just pissed Cerise off. "This is the new dress I just bought and wore especially for you, you big dummy."

Regan was taken aback. "For me?"

Tie helped Conor up. "Sorry," he said as he watched Cerise and Regan. He leaned against the bulkhead and casually crossed his arms. "Looks good, doesn't she?"

Regan's brow furrowed in displeasure. "She looks too damn good. Do you want every man on this station chasing her around?"

Tie just raised an eyebrow in amusement. "Yeah, that'll happen with me sleeping in her bed and you nearly ripping the head off anyone who so much as looks cross-eyed at her."

Regan turned away dismissively. "That is a gross overstatement. The woman attacked her."

That made Cerise recall what she'd seen when she'd arrived on the bridge. "What the hell were you doing with her?" she asked furiously. "I told you yesterday that if you need to fuck somebody it better be me."

"Whoa," Conor said backing up with wide eyes and hands held in front of him defensively. "Way too much information here, Princess darlin'." He turned to leave.

"I can talk to and fuck, anyone I feel like fucking," Regan snarled as he spun back around to face Cerise.

Tie straightened angrily from the bulkhead. "Don't you fucking talk to her like that."

Conor turned back around with a sigh. "At the risk of life and limb, I feel the need to referee."

Cerise was glaring at Regan who was glaring at both her and Tie, who was glaring at Regan too. They all ignored Conor.

Conor stepped closer. "Tell them, Regan."

That got Cerise's attention. She looked at Conor. "Tell us what?"

Conor looked at the silent Regan with exasperation. He turned to Cerise and Tie. "Does Regan know how you both feel?"

Tie narrowed his eyes at Conor. "What do you know about how we feel?"

Conor took a cautious step back. "I happened upon you and Cerise in the corridor last night."

"What?!" Cerise shrieked. No wonder Conor had been acting so funny this morning. She felt her face heat with embarrassment and her hands flew up to cover her red cheeks.

Tie breathed deeply for a moment, his lips thin. "Get an eyeful?" he asked sarcastically.

"It wasn't on purpose," Conor hastened to assure him as he took a little side step that placed him behind Regan. "And I got an earful too."

Tie took a step toward him and Regan put a hand on his chest to stop him. Both men froze at the contact. Tie looked down at the hand on his chest and started to raise his hand as if to cover it there and Regan snatched it away.

"Okay," Conor said slowly, "that answers that question." He stepped around so Regan could see him. "Now it's your turn."

"Shut the fuck up." Regan turned as if to walk off and Conor grabbed his arm. Regan spun and Cerise thought for a moment that he was going to hit Conor.

"Don't take it out on me." Conor was clearly at the end of his patience. "Another hit like the one your buddy here gave me and I won't see another frigid sunset on this rock." He threw Regan's arm away in disgust. "He's the one, isn't he? Jesus, even I've figured it out. He's the one you've been searching for all these years. The one you were looking for when you found me."

Cerise felt a crushing weight on her chest and struggled to breathe. She looked at Tie and saw how shocked he was. He hadn't known either.

"Goddamn it," Regan barked as he stormed away from them all and punched the bulkhead hard enough to put a dent in it.

"Egan." Tie said it softly but that one word spoke volumes.

Cerise stumbled back and leaned on one of the captain's chairs, weak with dawning horror. Tie hadn't used a name, but she realized how stupid she'd been. His story, the man he loved, it was Regan. And they'd been searching for each other for the past ten years or more. Only she'd gotten in the way.

"Egan, why? Why didn't you tell me?" Tie's voice was full of pain, regret, longing.

"Regan," the pirate said automatically, not looking at any of them, "it's Regan now."

Cerise had to look away from them. The two men she'd thought were hers. She'd believed she would bring them together, but she was keeping them apart. She looked at Conor and he was staring at her with sympathy on his face. She closed her eyes, unable to bear it.

"He's the one," Cerise whispered and she opened pain filled eyes to look at Tie. "He's the one that you love."

"Cerise," Conor began, but Regan quietly cut him off.

"Get out, Conor. You've done enough damage here."

Cerise didn't spare another look for Conor as he left. She watched the guilt steal over Tie's features. "I didn't tell you, baby, because I wasn't sure how he felt. It wasn't my secret to tell, not completely."

Cerise choked out a laugh. "No, no I guess not." She looked at Regan, who was struggling to maintain his cool detachment. His goddamn blank look. How many times had she seen that look when a moment between them got too heated, too personal? She hated that goddamn look. She was as weak as a babe, but forced herself to stand up straight, shaking so hard she thought she might fall over. "I'm sorry."

Both men looked at her in confusion. "What are you sorry for?" Regan stepped toward her and Cerise instinctively took a step back. He stopped, his face blank again.

"I've ruined it," she told them as she backed toward the hatchway. "The reunion. You two have been looking for one another for years and when you finally find each other I'm in the middle. Stupid little Cerise, who felt so guilty about ensnaring poor Tie." She tried to choke back the sob but it escaped her best efforts. She put the back of her hand to her mouth. When she was in control she spoke again. "I'm sorry, Regan. It must have been very uncomfortable for you, this attraction between us, when all along you were in love with Tie." She covered her face with both hands until she felt warm hands cup her shoulders. She jerked away and opened her

218

eyes to see Tie looking at her sadly, his hands in fists at his side.

"Baby, please, let me explain," Tie said softly and when she laughed she heard the hysteria in it. Regan took another step in her direction and she backed up rapidly.

"No explanations necessary. I did it. I released the Tears. I never gave you the chance to tell me you loved someone else." She looked at him feeling betrayed. "But you could have told me afterward. You could have told me after Regan came. But you didn't." She looked at Regan and saw the same guilt on his face that was clouding Tie's. "Or you could have told me." She closed her eyes in pained embarrassment. "Oh, Tie, all that talk of how you wanted Regan, how I wanted him. You had so many opportunities to tell me. Now I'm the fool."

"No, Cerise." Tie reached for her, but she couldn't face them anymore. She turned and ran for the hatch, running from a future in shreds.

* * * * *

Tie started to follow Cerise but Regan grabbed his arm stopping him. "You won't catch her or find her," Regan said sadly with a shake of his head. "She knows this station well enough to hide as long as she wants. And everyone here will protect her."

Tie ripped his arm from Regan's grasp, suddenly furious with the other man. "Why the hell didn't you tell me? Tell us?"

"Tell you what?" Regan asked calmly, turning to some papers on the console in front of him as if nothing were wrong.

Tie wasn't going to let him get away with it, not this time. He spun Regan back around and held him with a hand on each arm. Regan's head whipped up and he glared at Tie.

"Why didn't you tell me you looked for me?" Tie's voice was calmer, but there was still betrayal and confusion in it.

Regan closed his eyes as he sighed deeply. "To what end, Tie?" His voice became mocking. "Now that you've found

219

your princess, Tie, you should know that I've been searching for you for the last ten years. I was wrong to turn you away. And, oh, Cerise, same to you, baby. Just wanted to say sorry." He snorted in disgust. "Yeah, that would have been great timing."

Tie was shaking his head. "That's not how it would have gone down, Regan and you know it. Both Cerise and I are in love with you and have been for a very long time. If you had told us how you felt, about both of us..." Tie didn't have to finish the sentence. He could see the knowledge of what might have been in Regan's eyes. "It can still work for us Regan, all three of us."

Regan's gaze was haunted. "No, it can't Tie. You heard the old woman yesterday. I never brought her Tears, Tie. You did. But I never did."

Tie shook him roughly. "Don't be an idiot. You never let yourself touch her sexually, Regan. If you had the Tears would have come for you, too." Tie let go and stepped away as realization dawned. "What are you afraid of Regan? That you might have to let someone love you? You might have to admit you care?"

Regan scoffed. "Hardly. I've cared for her for the last seven years. I cared for you back on Earth. How many times did I get you out of the brig?" His hand swiped the papers viciously to the floor. "Don't tell me I don't know how to care."

"Those things were easy, Regan," Tie said softly. "You kept your distance. You watched over us, you made sure we were safe and warm and protected. But you never loved us, Regan. You never let yourself love us. You never took the chance. We could have had it all, Regan. We could have had it for the last ten years if you'd left with me, if you'd taken a chance on me, on us. You could have had it with Cerise for the last seven years. But you keep running and running. What are you running from? Why won't you let us love you?"

220

"Because I'll lose you!" Regan yelled furiously. "These times, the life we live, the Amalgamation, always the fucking Amalgamation out there ready to take it all away. I lost you once, Tie. I almost lost Cerise." He covered his face with his hands and then ran them up and scrubbed the top of his head in frustration. "I've always known that it will never last, Tie," he whispered raggedly. "This life we have has always been high risk. We aren't even really men, are we?" He shook his head. "Love, happily ever after, family, stability, those things were never meant for the likes of us." He smiled sadly at Tie. "At least not for me."

Tie was shaking. "I might have agreed with you a week ago, Regan, but not now." Now he had Cerise, had felt her love for him in her soft touch and hungry lovemaking. And now he'd found Regan. No, that life *was* for them if they wanted it enough.

"A week ago my life was centered around you, or rather, around Egan." Regan's eyes opened wide in shock. "I've spent every spare moment I had in the last ten years looking for you. I put my life on hold. Hell, I stopped living. I had no one and nothing, just a job I hated that helped fund my search for you. I kept telling myself that when I found you, then I could live again." Regan started to speak, but Tie cut him off. "If I—" he shook his head. "No, if *Finnegan* had found you then, I'm not sure what might have happened between us."

He took a deep breath and admitted what he'd only realized in the last two days. "I stopped living and you lived as you never did before." Tie smiled ruefully. "You had a new identity, people under your protection, a life as the hero of the rebellion. You had moved on. I never did. Not until Cerise." Tie looked away and bit his lip to stop its trembling. "I would have resented you, Regan. I would have resented the life you've found." He looked back, cleared his throat. "But then there was Cerise. She made me realize that there were still things to live for, even if you couldn't be one of them. She made me start living again and when I saw you on that hulk and later on the *Tomorrow*, I was ready, Regan. I was ready to live again, not just with Cerise, but with you."

"We are men, Regan." He smiled crookedly. "Or so Cerise assures me." He walked over and cradled Regan's cheek in his hand as the other man looked at him with a mixture of hope and despair. "And we deserve happiness. I'm not going anywhere, Regan. Not this time. I will make you happy. Cerise will make you happy. And you will make both of us very happy." Tie leaned in and kissed Regan softly, his lips barely touching Regan's. Regan stood there trembling and Tie was humbled that he could reduce this incredibly strong man to such a show of emotional weakness. He pulled back from the kiss and ran his thumb across Regan's sculpted bottom lip. Unconsciously Regan's tongue slipped out and the tip touched the pad of Tie's thumb. Tie's yearning for Regan, never far from the surface to begin with, clawed its way up his throat. "I have loved you for as long as I can remember," Tie whispered, "and I will love you until I turn to dust." He met Regan's confused, desperate gaze. "You just have to want it, Regan. You just have to want it enough," he echoed his words from long ago and watched the memory fill Regan's eyes. Then he turned and walked off the ship.

Chapter Fifteen

❧

Cerise stumbled as she came through the hatch onto the bridge. Regan didn't rise to help her. She'd backed away from him today, twice. In horror, disgust, anger, he wasn't sure but none of it was good. She'd come looking for him and he wasn't about to drive her away. It was late, the lights on *The Rebel Bounty* were dim and the bay outside the bridge shield was dark as well. He was aggravated that she'd apparently been walking around the station at night by herself and drunk from the looks of it. Didn't she realize what could have happened to her?

"So the mighty pirate Regan is still hard at work plotting, eh?" she drawled, straightening as she self-consciously pulled the short skirt of her dress down. Regan's heart began pounding out a pulse thumping dance in his veins until his fingers and toes tingled and his cock rose steadily, throbbing in time to it. Christ, he'd nearly had a heart attack when he'd watched her stalk across the bridge in that tight, tiny little dress with those cock-teasing, thigh-high boots today. And now here she was back again and each wide step she took drove the dress higher and his pulse faster. She looked around with wide eyes and said with mock sincerity, "Oh, dear, I hope I haven't interrupted your plans for the evening. Say a quick fuck with some little Aboolan whore?"

Regan cocked a brow at her, forcing his breathing to stay normal at the sound of her sweet voice saying fuck. "When I fuck, it is anything but quick."

Cerise put her hand to her heart and faked shock. "Oh my God. Are you actually going to talk to me about fucking?" She sauntered over to examine the myriad buttons and gauges on the bulkhead across from where he sat and only stumbled once. "That's mighty big talk, by the way, for a pirate who won't even touch my knickers."

A burst of laughter broke unexpectedly out of Regan. "You wear knickers?"

Cerise turned with a smile and leaned back against the bulkhead. "You got me. Tonight I'm bare as a newborn baby." She started to lift the hem of her dress and Regan's heart stopped briefly and then began beating so quickly he felt lightheaded. He leaned forward, not sure if he was going to stop her or encourage her but she stopped suddenly with a little moue of regret. "Oops, I forgot. You're not interested in seeing anything I've got under there." She let the dress drop and put her hand on her hip looking at his obvious arousal with satisfaction.

Regan sat back with a grin at her womanly maneuvers. She was good. She'd definitely learned a thing or two in the last week. "Where's Tie?"

Cerise shrugged nonchalantly and turned back to the bulkhead. Regan wasn't fooled. He'd seen the hurt in her eyes. "I have no idea. He didn't bother to tear the station apart looking for me." She'd been pressing buttons—thank God the ship was powered down—but stopped. "Did you two have a nice reunion after I left?"

Regan knew what she was really asking was if he and Tie had fucked. "He stayed long enough to rip into me for not telling you both how I felt. Then he left. I haven't seen him either."

Cerise spun to face him. "Really?"

Regan smiled softly. "Really."

She licked her lips and Regan literally felt the motion along his cock. It startled him. She did it again and the sensation on his cock made him squirm in his seat. Christ, he'd dreamed about it for so long now his imagination was working overtime. "I wouldn't mind if you fucked him." She looked up then, into his eyes and her hot, hungry gaze made him break out in a sweat.

"Cerise, you don't understand," he said, clutching the arms of the captain's chair.

"What? How men fuck? I understand." She stepped away from the bulkhead and tipped her head to the side as she regarded him with a knowing little grin. "In the ass. Tie showed me. I liked it. I think you would too."

Regan groaned and closed his eyes, no longer trying to hide how she affected him. "Do you?" he rasped as he opened his eyes.

She wandered closer and let her hand trail along the tops of the chairs and the console as she worked her way over to him. "Mmm-hmm," she murmured. He watched her as she came to a stop in front of him. She deliberately rested her hands on his knees and leaned over to look directly into his eyes. "Yep, I definitely think you'd like it. Tie is very good." She blinked and the smile she gave him made flames lick up his body.

Regan choked, his breath caught in his throat at her sultry statement. Cerise spread his legs wide and stepped between them, snuggling up into the vee of his thighs. Regan knew he should stop her. She was drunk and confused and hurt. Was she here to hurt Tie? Or to hurt him? But he just couldn't make himself push her away. He'd pushed and pushed for seven long years and God, he was tired of pushing. The truth of Tie's earlier accusation that Regan had been running from them for years stung like salt on an open wound. Well, he wouldn't run. Not yet. Not right now.

"Don't bother to say anything," Cerise said as she bent her legs and lowered herself just enough to press her mons against the erection clearly outlined by his tight leather pants. Regan's head fell back against the back of the seat as his hands gripped her thighs and slid up onto her hips pulling her closer, tighter.

Cerise shuddered in his hands. "Oh Regan, yes, please," she moaned, rubbing against him. It wasn't enough. He needed her even closer. He wanted her bare pussy rubbing on him. He'd waited so damn long to look, to touch.

"This will be better, sweetheart," he murmured. He sat up and pushed her back a little. He pressed his left leg between hers and used his knee to nudge her legs wider apart. The action pushed her skirt up until it rode just below her ass. He let his hands slide up her bare skin, the dress riding higher and higher. First he got a glimpse of her strong thighs, braced apart. He stopped when he realized she'd spoken the truth earlier. She had nothing on underneath her sexy little dress. His palms traced the jutting bones of her hips, his thumbs gliding into the crease between thigh and hips. She moaned and thrust her hips into his hands and his cock jerked. He pushed the dress up impatiently, anxious to see her.

When he saw her naked pussy he groaned. She had a springy bush of dark hair, the pale lips peeking through as if coyly flirting with him. His first thought was *mine*. He placed his hand on her flat stomach, his thumb just touching the top of her pubic curls. He ran his thumb lightly over the hair there and she gasped. He looked up at her then, quirking his head to the side. Her face was tight with desire, her eyes bright, burning at him, lavender beacons on the dimly lit bridge. Her little up-tilted nose and sweet mouth were everything he'd dreamed of. He moved his hand down, caressing her stomach and mons until he slid his thumb in between her labia and felt the hard bud of her clitoris. Cerise's breathing was harsh, her chest rising and falling rapidly as she spread her legs wider to make room for his hand between them. Regan rubbed his thumb in a circle over her clit and Cerise moaned. Her hand came up to grip his wrist tightly and Regan was struck by the contrast of his white hand against her dark curls. He watched his thumb circle and Cerise's grip on his wrist tightened. Suddenly he could feel that thumb on his cock, circling the slit in his head. He felt a drop of moisture seep from his cock and slid his hand down further until he felt the cream coating

226

Cerise's entrance. The dual sensations were maddening, arousing him beyond anything in his experience. How was this possible, that he could feel what Cerise was feeling as he loved her?

"Cerise," he moaned.

"Regan, Regan," she whispered, her voice low and throbbing like the pulse in his cock. She slid her hand up his arm from his wrist and he pulled his thumb back to her clit, dragging her moisture forward to lubricate his caress. Her thighs began to shake as her hand slid up and over his shoulder until she cupped his nape and pulled him to her descending mouth.

The kiss was tender at first, telling him everything he'd been so afraid to hear. But she turned hungry and ferocious. Her teeth nipped him, her tongue thrust ruthlessly into his mouth in the same rhythm her hips were dancing against his hand.

Regan pulled her forward and down until she straddled his thigh, her weight riding his leg. She pulled her mouth from his and gasped. She began to hump his thigh and he could hear her juice against the leather of his pants. Christ, it made him fucking wild. Cerise, hot and wet and riding his leg. He moved to the edge of the seat and hauled her closer until her thigh ground against his hard cock. Regan buried his lips in her neck as they sat there and thrust against one another, grinding almost painfully. But it felt so good and it was so good to feel. Cerise wrapped her arms around his head, holding him to her as she smoothed a hand over the sensitive skin of his scalp and it was his turn to gasp. He slid his hands up, from her hips to her ass and then higher, to the small of her back, pushing her dress up. He passed over her matewaist, but his brain barely registered it. Knowing she was exposed, that anyone who came through the hatch would see her sweet little naked ass humping him like mad and the wet streak of her cream on his leather-clad thigh, drove him mad and he bit her shoulder.

227

"Yes," she hissed, throwing her head back as she gripped the back of his skull tightly and pressed him to her. He sucked hard on her tender skin, wanting to devour her and she shivered and moaned.

He broke the harsh kiss and his breathing was ragged. "Do you like it like that, baby? Do you like it rough?" He'd never dreamed, never imagined that Cerise would like that.

"Yes," she moaned. "Take me hard and rough, Regan. Fuck me wild."

"Christ, Cerise." His voice was a guttural rasp in his throat. He wanted to, God, how he wanted to, but he couldn't. It was Cerise and she was drunk and she was Tie's.

He licked the tender skin that was rapidly bruising. He should feel like a brute, but all he felt was satisfaction that he'd marked her. He closed his eyes and mind against this further proof that he was more animal than man. He slid his hands back down to her ass and moved her hips against him. "I've wanted you, Cerise. I just...I need you to know that. I want you to know that. For years now, I've wanted you."

"When? How?" Her questions came out harsh and low, her breathing ragged.

Regan huffed out a humorless laugh. "Forever it seems." He shook his head. "No, I remember when I suddenly realized you were a woman and not the orphaned little princess they brought to me. You'd just worked out and you came marching onto the bridge dripping with sweat, that little tank top clinging to you, demanding something unreasonable," she laughed softly in his ear, "and it hit me so hard I almost fell at your feet. Instead I barked at you to get the hell off my bridge and we had another fight. That was five years ago."

Cerise thumped him on the back, hard. "Five years? You idiot. Could have had me, Regan. Could have had me then."

"What would have happened to Tie, then, Cerise?" Regan's voice was low, but she heard him. She stopped moving on his thigh.

"I don't know, Regan," she whispered against the side of his head and he shuddered. "I don't have all the answers. I only know what's already happened, what's happening now. Be in the now with me, Regan. I need you now." He started to shake his head, but Cerise stopped him with a firm grip on the back of his skull that made him moan. "You were the first man I ever wanted. The only man, until Tie. I saved myself for you, Regan, until I had to let go. Let go, Regan. Let go for me."

He pulled her closer and held her tightly. "I almost lost you, baby," he whispered. "What if—"

Cerise cut him off. "Do you remember when I wanted a dog? I cried and told you that I needed something to love that would love me back. You knew then, didn't you? Because you told me that sometimes we can be loved and not know it. And for a second I hoped that you meant you loved me. But then you made some cynical comment about how the masses loved their little princess. And you told me to stop sniveling like a baby. But the next day you bought me that little android dog."

"Finnegan. We lost it in the Outlooks." Regan rubbed his nose in her hair. It was so silky, so soft and sweet smelling. He'd always wanted to touch her hair.

Cerise laughed softly and then she kissed him behind the ear and the skin was so sensitive there that he shivered as he broke out in goose bumps. "Finnegan," she murmured. "Conor was so mad." She shook her head. "But I understand now. You didn't name him for Conor. You named him for Tie."

She began moving on him again, slowly undulating her hips, rubbing her sex along his thigh. "I remember everything, Regan." Her voice was a low throb in his ear. "Every moment we've spent together. And I've wanted you for all of them. Every single second we spent together I wanted you, even before I fully understood exactly what I wanted. I need *you* to know that. I need you to understand that what I'm feeling isn't new. It isn't the Tears, Regan, or curiosity. I love you and I need you. Please, Regan, please."

He remembered, too. And he was ashamed because he had known. He'd known how she felt and he'd played on it, making her need him. And he'd known how he felt, too. He'd known he was in love with her although he'd refused to admit it, even to himself. And now she was Tie's and he still couldn't admit to more than wanting her, could he? He still couldn't let himself go. But he needed to give her what she wanted. Was he atoning for making them both suffer for so long? He didn't know and he didn't care. He only knew he couldn't let her go.

"Come for me, love," he murmured. He drove one finger roughly into the crease of her ass, pushing the succulent cheeks apart as he delved deeper until he found the tight rosebud at its center.

"Regan," she groaned, but her head was shaking against his shoulder. "I need cock, Regan, your cock," she told him. She bit his earlobe hard and he was so startled his finger pressed inside her tight ass as his hand convulsively gripped her. "Oh yeah," she moaned, her head falling back on a sigh. "Fuck me, Regan," she demanded, "fuck me now."

"No, no fucking, just this, just my hands on you, making you come." He moved her hips, pressing her pussy against his thigh, his finger working her ass gently. He pulled the finger out and glided it down to capture some of the cream coating her inner thighs. She was weeping for it now, cream dripping from those rosy lips, coating the leather on his thigh, her thighs, her bush. When his finger was slippery with her juice he glided it back up and into her ass, a little further than it had been before. She moaned deeply.

"God, baby, I want your cock in my pussy and that finger in my ass, just like that," she murmured and Regan's cock jerked hard as if demanding he satisfy her. Had Tie taught her to talk like that, to ask for exactly what she wanted without artifice or shame? It was the most arousing thing he'd ever experienced, hearing Cerise ask him for what they'd both been dreaming of for years.

His free hand slid from her hip up her bare back, pushing the dress high and holding her tightly to him with his hand between her shoulder blades. He sat up straighter, her pumping hips working her pussy against his thigh and her leg against his cock at just the right angle. They both groaned. He licked a path from the pulse in her neck to the soft indentation between her collarbones and then along the low neckline of her dress. She tasted salty with want, musky with her own spice. Her skin was so smooth against his tongue he wanted to bite her again, to eat her up until her taste, her touch, her texture were a part of him.

"Pull it down," Cerise panted, her words breaking through the fog of lust clouding his mind. "The dress, pull it down and suck my breasts, my nipples. Eat me alive, Regan," she demanded breathlessly. It was as if she could read his mind, knew exactly what he wanted and he briefly marveled at the connection between them. Had it always been this strong? He wasted no time obeying her. With a shaking hand he undid the tie on the back of her dress and it bagged loosely, falling off one shoulder. He started to pull it down, but then reversed, freeing both hands to shove it up and over her head. He threw it aside and leaned back to look at her.

She was gloriously alive, sitting there on his lap. She was completely naked except for those amazing, thigh-high boots on legs a kilometer long and the matewaist he'd given her riding low on her bare hips. He'd pulled back far enough that she had to let go of him and she rested her hands on his thigh as she pushed back, riding him slowly, watching him intently. Her feet arched so that only her toes rested on the floor and her knees spread wide, rising as high as her hips in their soft, purple suede. Regan leaned back in, his hands going to her calves, lightly gliding up the boots, the sensation of the smooth suede against his rough palms making him shiver. He let his hands run up the boots, then over their tops onto bare thigh. He paused and then continued up, caressing hips, stomach. He let one finger trace the chain around her hips, the carnelian dangling alluringly above her cunt, pointing the way and then his hands finally came to rest over her small, perfect breasts.

When he held his palms against her breasts he had to take a deep breath. He'd imagined them almost every day for the last five years, ever since he'd noticed her as a woman. He knew they were small, her clothing revealed that much. His hands, white as they were, were darker than her delicate, pale skin and in the low light of the bridge they glowed with that otherworldly green shimmer that horrified him. But here...here it seemed right. It looked strong and possessive against her, his color dominating her as he wanted to.

He watched as he pulled his hands slowly down, revealing her breasts fully. They were indeed small, but solid, warm and pliable. They weren't perfectly round. Instead they were heavier on the bottom, the nipples tipped up enticingly. Dark pink, hard nipples that made his mouth water. They were a color found in the most breathtaking of nature's creations—hibiscus blossoms and roses, the swirl at the heart of a seashell, the warm recesses of a woman's vulva. Slowly Regan glided his hands around Cerise's back, arching it, as his mouth descended and he tasted one of those nipples for the first time. He groaned at the sheer, unadulterated pleasure of Cerise's breast against his lips, her nipple between his teeth as he flicked his tongue against it. She tasted of heaven, of hell, of all things in between. She tasted of sex and passion and dreams fulfilled.

"Regan," she whispered as her arms cradled his head to her. He hauled her close, closer, until he could grind his cock against her leg and suck her gorgeous breasts and feel her naked ass in the palm of his hand as she rode his thigh. It was an overload of sensation and he was drowning in it. She sobbed and thumped a fist on his back and he realized how hard he was sucking on her nipple and stopped. He pulled back and licked it soothingly.

"I'm sorry," he whispered, running his nose over the wet, turgid tip. He could see that it was red, plump and hard from his attentions. He groaned and pulled her in, ground his cock against her.

"Liked it," she panted, "want more."

"You always want more," a deep voice said and Regan turned to see Tie filling the hatchway.

It was every fantasy Cerise had been harboring for the last week. She was naked, riding an aroused Regan, the lust practically vibrating off Tie. God! She loved being naked for both of them, hot and wet and aching. It was the most exciting thing she'd ever experienced. She slid down Regan's hard, leather-clad thigh and she could feel how wet her pussy was. Her arms went around his chest and she rubbed her nipples against his vest. His hands automatically held her to him, one on her ass and one on her back. Damn his hands felt good. His touch was lighter than Tie's, a tease against her overheated skin. One minute he handled her as if she'd break, the next he was biting her and nearly sucking her nipple off. The combination was exhilarating.

Suddenly feeling his bare chest against her breasts became the most important thing in the world. She desperately needed to feel his hair rubbing on her nipples, his heartbeat thudding in time next to hers. Cerise began to frantically pull at Regan's vest. "Off," she demanded. Regan tried to stop her but she wouldn't be denied. Damn it, he was hers, or she was his. It didn't matter, she wanted him and he would take her. "I want to feel you, damn it," she growled, leaning in and biting his neck. Regan let out a surprised yell and rammed a hand into her hair trying to yank her off. She sucked hard on the skin as he had on her and his grip changed, holding her to him.

She dimly heard Tie chuckle right behind her and she broke out in gooseflesh, a shiver racing across her skin. "She's a little hellcat when she fucks," Tie said quietly.

Regan was panting and Cerise could feel the indecision in him. He wanted her, she knew it. And she knew he wanted Tie too, his reaction earlier told her that and the reaction he was trying to control now. No, there was more. She could feel his heartbeat pounding in *her* chest. She could feel his arousal as if it rose between her legs.

She carefully broke the kiss on his neck and licked it slowly, lingeringly, enjoying him as if he were a tasty treat. He was a tasty treat, all sweaty and hot and tangy. She'd noticed that about both men. They had a smell, a taste that was unique to them both. As if it were hardwired into her DNA, it called to her. "Mmm," she murmured and felt Regan shudder in her arms. "I want to taste you all over, to suck you all over." She ground her pussy on his thigh and gasped as her hard clit rubbed on the warm, wet leather.

"Fuck her," Tie told Regan, his voice quiet but hard, uncompromising. "You owe it to her." Regan began to protest but Tie cut him off. "You've got her so aroused I can smell it, feel it, practically taste it in the air. Are you going to leave her like that? Are you that cruel a tease?"

Cerise continued to pet and lick Regan as she felt him relax by increments, until he was warm and amenable against her. Her body mimicked his, relaxing against him. "No," he murmured into her hair, "no, I'm not a tease." Cerise hid her triumphant grin against his shoulder as she began to unbutton his vest. His hands closed over hers, stopping her and she looked up questioningly.

"Are you sure?" he asked her quietly. "You can still go and I won't hold it against you, darling. Tie is here now. If you need someone you can have him now, if you'd rather."

Cerise's heart nearly broke at the desperation in his face, even as his voice stayed calm and soothing. She tugged her hands free and finished unbuttoning his vest. As she slid it off over his shoulders with a lingering caress she gazed into his eyes and said with absolute certainty, "I'm sure."

His chest was as broad as she remembered, as muscular and fascinating as it was the first time she saw it bare, when she was just seventeen and he was determined to teach her to defend herself. She ran her hands over his hot, smooth skin and his soft, curly chest hair. His nipples were dark brown, flat and hard. Cerise was beyond asking permission, beyond shyness. She leaned down and licked one of those impertinent nubs, rubbed her nose in the soft hair surrounding it and breathed in the scent of him.

"You both smell so good to me," she murmured, rolling her face against Regan's chest, feeling his heartbeat with her cheek. "I can feel your scent down to my toes. It's primal, the way it makes me feel." She pulled back as she was struck suddenly with understanding. "It's part of why I thought I was addicted to Tie, the way his smell made me feel almost drunk." She leaned forward again and breathed in deeply, taking Regan into her lungs. "You're spicier than Tie, sharper. You make the top of my head explode." She bit down gently on Regan's nipple and he jerked under her with a gasp. She chuckled and flicked her tongue on him.

"What," Regan paused breathlessly and swallowed, "what does Tie smell like?"

"You tell me," Cerise countered teasingly. "Can't you smell him?" She felt Tie move in closer behind her, felt Regan's heart accelerate under her hand.

"Musk," Regan whispered. "Tie smells exotic. He makes me think of deserts and the hot sun, silk and sex."

Cerise's breath was caught in her throat. That was exactly what Tie smelled like. She'd used those exact words before, when describing it to Tie. Her heartbeat began racing erratically. "Regan?"

His hand smoothed the hair on the side of her head and applied a little pressure until she looked up at him. He was so intense. His face was taut with desire, his longing a tangible thing swirling around all of them on the bridge. "Can't you feel it, Cerise? Can't you feel me? Inside?" He rested his forehead against her temple, kissed her jaw. "Or is it only me? I can feel what you feel Cerise. The physical sensations I mean. I know, just…know how Tie smells to you. I can smell him too. I know how my hands feel on you. When I touch you," he ran his hands up and covered her breasts and Cerise shivered, followed closely by Regan, "I can feel it too." He looked at her, puzzled and a little concerned. "What is this? Is it just me?"

Cerise's breathing was ragged, frightened. She shook her head. "No, no, it's me too, I can feel you. I just thought…I thought it was my imagination, how much I want you. My daydreams coming to life. But it's more, Regan, it's what you said. I can *feel* what you feel. You're," she thumped a fist on her chest, "you're in here."

Regan grabbed her fists in his hands, pressed them to his heart. "Is it like that with Tie?"

"No," Tie spoke from behind Cerise and she watched as Regan looked up at him. For a moment she saw the flash of heat in his eyes, the naked desire for Tie and then she felt it inside and she groaned. She didn't feel threatened by it, didn't resent his desire for Tie. Instead she reveled in it, in the way it made him feel and the way it made her feel. It was good, so damn *good*.

She heard Tie take an unsteady breath behind her. "I can't feel the physical, but I can feel her emotions. I always know what she's feeling. It's how I knew there was something wrong on the bridge today. I felt her anger, her fear." He stepped right up behind her then, his chest supporting her head, his hard cock rubbing on her back. "Just as I can feel her desire now. I know she enjoys the heat between us, Regan. Our mutual desire for one another pleases her." His hands cupped her shoulders and then glided down her arms. He wrapped his hands around her wrists while Regan still held her fists against his chest. She was bound between them, naked, hungry and involuntarily her hips thrust against the hard thigh beneath her. Tie chuckled, his cock right between her shoulder blades and Cerise couldn't stop her moan as she rubbed the back of her head against his chest. "Yes," Tie whispered, "she likes it very much."

"It's the Tears." Regan's voice was a low growl and it traveled along her nerve endings until it made her nipples and clit throb in distressed arousal. She whimpered and rubbed that aching clit on Regan's thigh, making her breath hitch. "The old woman said the Tears could enable men and women to read each other's minds. This is a form of that, I think."

"Then you know. You know she makes the Tears for you, Regan."

Tie started to pull his hands away, his chest and cock leaving her as he began to step away. "No!" Cerise struggled against Regan's grip, wanting to hold Tie behind her while she clamped her thighs around Regan's leg.

"Cerise," Regan said again, shaking her gently until she looked at him. "Do you want us both, right now?" She heard Tie's indrawn breath behind her and she was suddenly flooded with his feelings. Desire, anguish, hope, love—they washed through her until she was shaking. She realized then that Tie had locked those feelings away for so long, but here, now, he couldn't hide anymore. This was everything he'd ever dreamed, to have the two people he loved more than anything in the world. God! She wanted them so much she hurt. She felt so empty, so lonely inside. She needed them, needed them, needed them.

"All right, darling," Regan murmured, kissing her temple, her nose, her chin and she realized she'd spoken out loud. "Yes, yes, baby," he reassured her.

Tie stepped away and Cerise sobbed at his abandonment, but he quickly pulled her off Regan and spun her to face him. He kissed her violently and she felt the need in him, the need to possess, to claim her. She opened for him and let him take what he needed, let him drive her passion higher until it was a desperate ache within her. Halfway through the kiss she felt Regan's hands on her. He cupped her ass and then caressed her back. She realized he was running his hands over Tie's arms wrapped around her and the answering flood of emotions from Tie and physical sensations from Regan had her gasping, lightheaded. Tie broke the kiss with a groan.

"Get undressed, Tie," Regan murmured as he kissed the curve of her shoulder and moved against her. With a moan of pure delight she realized he was naked behind her. "We need to fuck our princess."

Chapter Sixteen

ઐ

Tie had never heard such wonderful words. Regan was theirs at last. He stripped his shirt off quickly as he watched Regan's hands glide over Cerise, caressing her breasts, her stomach. Regan ran a hand lightly between her legs, teasing her with light caresses.

"Spread her legs," Tie growled. Regan froze for a moment and looked up at Tie. "Spread her legs and fuck her with your finger. I want to watch." Cerise groaned and her head fell back on Regan's shoulder. Tie watched the light from the console gleam on Regan's sleek head as he bent and nuzzled Cerise's neck. Slowly, Regan ran a hand down and pressed it against the inside of her right thigh, hooking his bare foot inside hers on the floor and sliding her leg wide. Tie's chest was rising and falling erratically, his breaths coming faster as he watched the slow tease.

Cerise took Regan's free hand in hers and brought it to her cheek, closing her eyes as she rubbed against his palm. Between her legs Regan's hand began an excruciatingly slow glide back up to her pussy. Tie was clenching his teeth, hands fisted at his sides by the time he watched Regan's long finger enter Cerise. She was panting now, holding onto his arm desperately. Regan fucked in and out of her several times and Tie could see her wetness on his finger.

"Tell me how she feels." Tie roughly tore at his clothes, frantic to join them, skin to skin.

Regan's forehead rested on Cerise's shoulder and his voice was muffled as he spoke. "She'd so goddamn hot and wet and tight, Christ is she tight. How do you fit in here Tie? You're so damn big and she's so small."

"That's what makes it so damn good," Tie answered with a satisfied smile.

Cerise laughed weakly. "Speak for yourself."

Tie was about to step forward but at her words he stopped, dismayed. "Oh my God, Cerise, why didn't you tell me?" He was horrified. Had he been hurting her all this time?

Cerise lifted her head from Regan's shoulder to gaze at Tie blankly for a moment. "Tell you...Oh Tie, I was joking, honey." She gasped and squirmed as Regan fucked two fingers into her and Tie's cock jumped. "Feels good," she panted. "When we fuck, you fill me up and it feels good. Better than good. Ah, God, Regan," she ended on a moan.

Regan looked over her shoulder at Tie, his gaze tracing him from head to foot. Tie stood there and let him look. He could feel his cock stretch to impossible lengths as he watched Regan fondle Cerise while his eyes devoured Tie. He wanted to fuck them both, in every way imaginable. "Is that what you like, baby?" Regan whispered to Cerise loud enough for Tie to hear. "You like how big Tie is? His strong shoulders, muscular arms and legs, a cock so big it won't all fit in your mouth, will it? Is that what you like?"

"Yes, yes," she answered breathlessly. "And you, always you, Regan."

Tie took a moment to see them, all of them. Cerise was so fucking sexy standing there with her legs in those amazingly sexy boots spread wide, thrusting down on the fingers fucking her. The matewaist that proclaimed her his gleamed in the faint light of the console. Regan had an arm wrapped around her, one hand massaging her breast while the other fucked her. He could see the top of Regan's bare chest and his wide, muscled shoulders. One of Regan's naked hips peeked out from Cerise's side, his long, muscular leg braced beside hers. Regan was nibbling on Cerise's ear as she writhed and moaned against him. He saw Regan jerk at a particularly enthusiastic wiggle of Cerise's hips and Tie knew it was because she was grinding her ass against his erection.

240

"Enough." Tie's voice was a wicked rasp and he shivered as he felt the effect of it on Cerise. He looked at Regan and immediately the other man froze warily. "I want to see Regan. Come to me, Cerise. Come." He held out his hand and beckoned her imperiously. He was enjoying playing the master here, although he was a little shocked Regan would let him. Shocked and thrilled.

Regan slid his fingers out of her as slowly as he'd pushed them in and she groaned and bucked in protest. "Don't worry, darling," he crooned softly in her ear, "we'll fill you again soon."

Cerise sobbed. "Regan," she cried, "Tie," and Tie's gut twisted with a desire so elemental he felt his entire world shift. Regan gently pushed her toward Tie and Tie took her hand and pulled her into his embrace, first turning her to face Regan so her back was against his front then wrapping both arms around her.

Regan stood there unashamedly. The fierce, self-confident pirate was very much in evidence as he relaxed under their scrutiny. His hands were loose at his sides, his head tipped to the side with an enigmatic smile while they stared at him. He was fucking amazing, better than Tie remembered. Tie had bulked up since he'd left the SS He was bigger, stronger than before. Regan had gone the other direction. He was still very muscular, but it was lean muscle, sleek and savage. His thighs were still the impressive thighs of a runner, but not quite as big as they'd been a decade ago. He reminded Tie of a predatory jungle cat. All in all he was sleek and dangerous and heartbreakingly familiar.

At last Tie let himself look at Regan's cock. It was large, wide and long, the head a light pink, rosy now in his arousal. The blue veins running up and down the length of his cock were mesmerizing in their clean and vivid lines. His pubic hair was black, like the hair on his chest and once, the hair on his head. His scrotum was heavy, framing the base of his cock. Tie had to choke back his groan as he remembered the taste and feel of Regan's cock on his tongue.

His skin glowed with the green shimmer that made him seem so exotic, so foreign.

"I love his skin, too."

Tie was taken aback for a moment at Cerise's murmured comment. Had he said that out loud? No, it was the Tears.

"I look like a reptile," Regan scoffed. "I hate this damn green glow."

Cerise shook her head and moved out of Tie's arms. He let her go. "Mmm, no, baby. You look like magic, like you'd taste cool and delicious." She hadn't gone far and Regan was forced to step forward to meet her. She smiled at him, catlike, as she laid her palm flat on his chest. She ran her hand down his stomach and Tie could see the muscles rippling in the wake of her caress. "But something's not right," she murmured, almost to herself. "Tie?"

"His eyes." Regan still wore the contact lenses that made his eyes a dull mud brown.

Cerise stood back nodding. "Yes, that's it. Take them out Regan, let me see you. The real you."

Tie held his breath. Those contacts represented the past— the past where Regan had to hide who he was and what he felt. If he removed them he would be admitting everything. Was he ready for that?

Slowly Regan raised his hands and removed the contacts one by one. He looked up when he was done and Tie's breath caught in his throat. He'd forgotten how damn beautiful his eyes were. The gray iris was faint. It looked like a spring storm cloud lost amid the startling white clouds filling the sky. Regan held the contacts out to Cerise and Tie felt his eyes fill. Cerise's breath caught on a sob as she absorbed his emotion and he could feel that she too was moved beyond words. Regan's face was serious, unsure, hopeful. Yes, they all knew what this meant. Suddenly Cerise knocked the lenses from his hand to the floor and threw herself into Regan's arms.

"Never wear them again, Regan, promise me."

Regan buried his face in her neck. "Never, Cerise. I swear."

Cerise laughed tearfully. "Fuck me now, damn it. I've waited long enough."

She started to wrap her legs around Regan's hips but he wasn't ready for it and stumbled. Tie quickly moved up and caught her, raising her up, holding her secure in Regan's embrace. The two kissed passionately and Tie knew that he wanted Regan to enter Cerise first, alone. He wanted him to know how amazing she felt when she was loving you. Without asking, Tie reached down between Cerise's legs and found Regan's cock. He was hard, his skin soft, the shaft pulsing with life and arousal. Regan groaned deeply at Tie's touch, his hips jerking. Tie's wrist brushed Cerise's dripping pussy and he swore. "Christ, she's so wet."

Cerise laughed on a moan. "Of course I am. You two are naked and planning on fucking me. That's the only foreplay I need, trust me."

"Less talk," Regan growled, "more fuck."

Cerise raised her hips allowing Tie to move Regan's cock to her entrance. Tie kept his fingers there as she began to lower herself onto it, feeling Regan's cock as it was swallowed by her eager pussy. He couldn't control his groan which matched the one coming from Regan. Cerise cried out and tried to ram herself down on the thick shaft, but Tie caught her hips and wouldn't let her.

"He's too big, baby, too wide. You've got to take him slowly. He's bigger than I am that way."

"Oh, God, oh God," Cerise panted. "I want it all, please."

Tie wasn't sure who she was talking to, him or Regan, but it didn't matter. Regan's hands gripped her ass with her arms wrapped tight around his neck and he began to thrust slowly and rhythmically into her, a little deeper each time. The three became lost in the sounds of a deep, wet fuck, moans of pleasure, kisses and caresses. Tie was plastered against Cerise's back, supporting her, her head on his shoulder as Regan moved her up and down on his cock, his hips pumping. Tie could feel every penetration as she was pushed into him. He was kissing her neck, her shoulders as he fondled her breasts and pinched her nipples. Before long he found his own cock pressed down between her ass cheeks, rubbing against her, bumping into Regan's cock as he pulled out and then thrust back in.

"Yes, that's it, fuck her," he murmured his eyes closed in pleasure.

"Fuck her with me," Regan whispered and Tie opened his eyes to see Regan staring at him with undisguised lust. "I want to feel your cock rubbing against mine inside her, Tie."

Cerise groaned. "God, yes, that's what I want too. Please Tie, please."

Regan pulled out of her and Cerise cried out. "Fuck her pussy first, Tie," Regan rasped. "She's so goddamn wet it will help you get into her ass."

Tie's breathing was ragged, his heartbeat thundering in his head. This was it. This was the moment he'd been waiting for. He lifted Cerise slightly with his hands under her arms. Regan held her high, his hands still on her ass, while Tie moved his cock into position. "Put her down on me," he panted. The first touch of her pussy was like fire on his burning cock and he gasped. She always felt like this, so good and tight and hot and wet and his. He shivered as she began to fuck him.

"Tie, Tie, Tie," she chanted. "You feel so good. You and Regan, so good."

It was Regan's turn to kiss and caress her while Tie fucked her. He couldn't help it, his strokes became hard and deep and Cerise muffled a scream against Regan's shoulder.

"Tie," Regan warned.

"She fucking loves it," Tie growled. "She loves to be fucked hard and deep, rough. Ask her."

Cerise was thrusting down on Tie as hard as he was fucking her. Regan grabbed a handful of her hair and yanked her head back. The action made Cerise's pussy spasm on his cock in pleasure and Tie exhaled roughly. "Is he right, baby? Do you like to be fucked hard?" Regan's voice was low, deep and dangerous. It made identical chills race up Tie and Cerise's spines.

"Yes, Regan," Cerise answered frantically. "I told you, fuck me wild. Wild!" The last word was a shout as Regan bent his head and bit her nipple as Tie rammed his cock deep into her. She came apart in their arms and Tie pulled out of her quickly, while she was still coming. "No!" she screamed.

"Fuck her while she climaxes, Regan. Feel it," Tie ordered. He stepped back, his legs unsteady as Regan lifted Cerise and slammed her down on his cock. She screamed and he continued to fuck her hard and deep as she writhed and begged for more.

"That's it, Cerise," Regan growled, "come for us, Christ yes, wild like that. Scream for me." He was watching his cock piston in and out of her and then bent and sucked her breast deeply into his mouth. She sobbed and her hips convulsed against him. Regan dropped to his knees, controlling her squirming body effortlessly. "I want to watch you come all night for us, Cerise," he said softly, slowing his thrusts, gentling her. "Tie's going to fuck into your ass now, while I stay snug in this pussy, yes, baby? And then we're going to fuck you hard and deep. Both of us."

Tie kneeled down behind Cerise. When he reached for her he noticed his hands were shaking. He fisted them tightly for a moment and met Regan's understanding gaze. The other man held his hand up and Tie saw it shaking in the shadows. They shared a smile.

Samantha Kane

"You'll need to pull out while I enter her," Tie told Regan softly. "Her ass is already tight, I've only fucked it once before. It might hurt her if I were to try to enter while you were filling her, making her tighter."

"You're right," Regan murmured and he gently lifted Cerise. Tie watched Regan's cock slide out of her, slick and still hard. It made his mouth water, his ass tighten and his groin ache. Regan kissed Cerise's temple. "I'll be back," he told her softly and she laughed weakly.

Tie moved in and rubbed his cock in all the sweet cream flowing from Cerise so freely. He ran his cock up and down, spreading her moisture from her weeping entrance to the tight rosebud beckoning him mercilessly. God, she got so wet when she fucked, it was heaven. When he thought they were both lubricated enough he put his cock at her entrance and pushed. He met with resistance, her portal tight and unwelcoming.

"Don't you want me to fuck you, baby?" he whispered in her ear and Cerise moaned and shuddered. "Open for me, Cerise. I want to feel your hot, tight ass wrapped around me. Relax and open for me."

He felt some give and pushed hard, forcing the head of his cock into her ass. She gasped and cried out and Tie had to stop, gritting his teeth at the effort. Christ, she was so tight he wasn't going to last a minute. But he had to. He had to feel Regan in her, feel Regan's cock sharing their woman, fucking her for the first time. His breathing was labored and he felt as if he'd run for kilometers as he silently counted in his head, focusing on the numbers and not the incredible, tight heat enveloping the sensitive head of his cock. Suddenly he felt more give in her ass, felt her relax and push against him. He looked down and saw Regan's hands holding her, spreading the cheeks of her ass wide as his cock slipped in deeper. Regan was watching over her shoulder as Tie entered her and Tie was thrilled at his obvious enthrallment with Tie's cock.

"Do you like what you see?" he asked Regan roughly, pulling slightly back and then fucking deeper into Cerise. She

246

was trembling in their arms, moaning, thrusting back against him, taking him and loving it. That was one of the best things about fucking Cerise, how much she loved everything he did to her.

"Yes," Regan answered simply. "You have a damn fine cock and you know it. I like watching it fuck Cerise."

"Oh, God," Cerise moaned and Tie agreed.

"Your turn," he told Regan in a voice laced with heat and impatience. "Fuck her. Now. With me."

The entire situation seemed unreal to Regan. He'd dreamed of this for so long, fucking Cerise, fucking Tie, admitting his feelings for them. Now that it was happening he felt like an observer, removed from the intensity of the moment. The feeling lasted for all of a few seconds until Tie adjusted his position and Regan's cock rubbed against Cerise's wet pubic hair. Then his emotions came rocketing back at him and he couldn't breathe for a second as they assailed him.

"Regan, please," Cerise whispered, her hands gripping his skull tightly, holding his forehead to hers. "Please, make me yours, be part of us."

He slid his hips forward and his cock slipped inside her. He threw back his head with a groan as Cerise gasped. Damn, she was so fucking tight, even tighter than before. Thank God she was so wet, or he'd have a hard time getting inside her. Even as he thought it his hips thrust again instinctively and he was halfway home. Tie whimpered behind Cerise and the sound was so needy, so aroused that it made Regan smile in satisfaction.

"You feel so damn good," Regan whispered, lowering his head and fucking into Cerise a little deeper, a little harder. Tie was biting his lip holding absolutely still as Regan worked his way in.

"Yes, I do," Cerise whispered back, shaky amusement in her voice. God, she was so amazing, so wonderful. And now she was his—his and Tie's. He'd never imagined that he'd feel so good about sharing her with another man, but this was Tie. This was right. This was meant to be. Here, now, he could finally understand what they'd all been talking about, Conor and Cerise and Tie, about paths merging and finding your way. Everything in their lives had led to this moment, this union.

He thrust into Cerise all the way, swallowing her cry in a hard, hungry kiss. She opened her mouth and took him as she'd taken his cock, willingly, lovingly. He tasted and tasted, ate and ate at her mouth. He couldn't get enough of tangling his tongue around hers, feeling her small, sharp teeth, her smooth cheeks, tasting the wine and her own unique flavor. And all the while he kissed her he fucked her. Fucked her and Tie. Because with each thrust and retreat he felt his cock glide along Tie's inside her and it was so amazing he had no words for it, no frame of reference. It was unlike anything he'd ever known and it made him feel alive and loved and all powerful. He could well understand why Tie and Cerise had assumed this was addiction because he never wanted to live without it again.

Cerise broke the kiss with a keening cry and Regan felt her walls squeeze him tight as she came. He realized as he held his cock deep inside her and let her ride out her orgasm, rubbing her clit against him, that Tie had yet to move. He looked over Cerise's shoulder and saw Tie staring at him, his look so hungry and possessive Regan's stomach tightened and he had to clamp down on his rising climax.

"Move in counterpoint to me," Tie told him, his voice a bass thrum beating along Regan's nerve endings. Tie pulled out slowly and as he thrust in again, Regan pulled out. Cerise cried out and tried to move but Tie held her hips. "Let us love you, baby," he murmured, kissing Cerise's shoulder. "You just enjoy the ride."

The feelings, both physical and emotional, became so intense Regan couldn't speak as they fucked Cerise. They were so in synch with one another's needs. Each move was choreographed perfectly, each sigh in harmony with the others. Regan couldn't get close enough. He was pressed chest to pelvis against Cerise, her heartbeat pounding against his chest, her breath bathing his neck, her hands clutching his back, nails biting into him. The pain made it so real, so electrifying. He tried to wrap his arm around her but Tie was pressed just as closely to her, so he wrapped his arm around Tie, buried his hand in Tie's hair. Tie groaned and leaned into Regan's hand.

Suddenly Regan felt a soft, wet touch on the scar on his cheek. He opened his eyes and met Tie's gaze millimeters from his own. Tie waited a moment and when Regan said nothing he licked the scar again, slower than before, from one end to the other. It was tantalizingly erotic. When he was done Tie kissed the scar softly. "I'm sorry," he said so softly Regan barely heard him. "I'm so sorry, Regan." His voice broke and Regan tightened his fist in Tie's hair and did the only thing that made sense. He kissed him with all the forgiveness and love in his heart. He loved this man as much as he loved Cerise. He'd spent most of his life loving him and knew he would never stop.

The kiss froze all three of them. Cerise moaned. "Yes, God yes," she said and Regan could feel her sincerity, how much she wanted them to be together, not just like this inside her but in every way. And he knew they would. He knew he would never deny Tie again.

At her words Tie's kiss became demanding and reckless. He sucked and bit at Regan's lips and Regan returned his fervor. Damn, damn, damn. Tie tasted as good as Regan remembered. He had a sharp dark flavor, like plums, ripe and earthy. His mouth was big, his lips soft. His tongue was a constant torment, driving Regan mad with pent-up desire and emotion. It seemed natural when he felt Cerise's lips against the corner of his mouth, when Tie's tongue slipped across his lips to Cerise's and back again. Soon the kiss was a tangle of three mouths, three tongues, a chorus of sighs and moans.

"Don't cry, baby, don't cry," Cerise whispered and Regan realized she was talking to him. She and Tie licked at his cheeks and he knew he wasn't going to last. It all felt so good, everything. Regan gasped and gripped Cerise's hips, or rather Tie's hands on her hips and he began to thrust wildly, hard and deep. Cerise screamed, but he knew it was pleasure and not pain that drove her.

"Yes, yes, yes," Tie chanted, fucking into her with him, sliding against him and Regan lost the battle. He felt his release shoot deep into the heated recesses of Cerise's womb, heard her scream again as her strongest orgasm of the night clamped down on him. With shock he realized that it was his voice crying out her name. He'd never come like this, never. He had no control over the waves of pleasure crashing through him, the emotions boiling over inside him intensifying the physical sensations of his orgasm.

"Fuck," Tie groaned and then through the thin wall separating them Regan felt the heat of Tie's climax, his semen filling Cerise just as Regan's was and Regan's cock jerked against Tie's making both of them cry out.

When it was over no one moved for several minutes. They were all breathing harshly, clinging to one another, wet with sweat and other things that made Regan immensely satisfied to think about. Finally Tie spoke.

"We're not going anywhere." Regan looked up to see Tie gazing at him tenderly. He remembered their conversation earlier today. He was hit with the realization that he wasn't alone anymore. He'd always been so afraid to love, to need anyone that he'd forced himself to be always alone, always lonely. But from now on there would always be someone there for him, waiting for him, loving him. He knew he could be stubborn and reckless, his temper was legendary, but he also knew none of that mattered to these two people. They loved him and always would. Christ, he would do anything for them, anything. No one and nothing would ever harm them as long as he lived.

"I would die without you," he said, finally answering Tie's statement from the night before. And he meant it.

"That is so sweet," Cerise said against his shoulder. "Now get out of me."

They separated from Cerise with a great deal of groaning and laughing.

"My knees may never work again," Regan joked as he stood and helped Cerise up and she playfully punched him in the shoulder.

"Oh, God," she suddenly shrieked ramming her hand between her legs, "I'm leaking! My new boots!"

Tie laughed so hard he couldn't get up, so Regan took advantage and grabbed Tie's shirt from the floor, shoving it between Cerise's legs.

"Hey!" Tie yelled, jumping up and grabbing for it. Cerise spun away behind Regan and laughed as she wiped herself off.

Regan just shrugged with a smile. "That's what you get for being too slow. Oh and for not wearing leather." He scooped his vest off the floor and put it on.

Tie just laughed and shrugged back. "Anything to save those boots. If I had my way she wouldn't take them off for the next two months."

Regan wrinkled his forehead as if he were thinking about it, then shook his head. "No, I'd rather suck her toes while I fuck her." He motioned with his hands, "You know, with her legs straight up, over my shoulders."

Cerise groaned and threw the shirt at Tie, who caught it with a grimace. She began hopping around on one foot while trying to wrench the boot off the other. "Quick, help me get this damn thing off."

251

Regan laughed again and realized with a shock that this was the most he had laughed in...Christ, he couldn't even think of another time.

He shook his head and her and clicked his tongue. "Next time. And it's going to be in a bed. I'm too old for this shit."

Cerise laughed and threw herself into his arms. He was pulling on his pants and had to let go to catch her, nearly stumbling as the pants fell down around his ankles. "You're a Super Soldier, you idiot. A good hard fuck on a little synthsteel shouldn't affect your superman abilities." She kissed him wildly, enthusiastically, not in passion but in play, with love and it stole Regan's breath. This was a different kiss from the others they'd shared and perhaps more devastating. She ended the kiss with a playful bite on his upper lip, then sucked it and let go with a pop. When she pulled back her smile fell and she placed one hand on his cheek. "What's the matter, lover? Are you all right? I didn't hurt you did I?"

Regan shook his head and buried his face in her neck, breathing her in, memorizing the moment. He belonged. He belonged to her and she to him and Tie, always Tie. As the thought went through his head he felt lips on his shoulder and a presence at his side. He looked up at Tie next to them. He'd dressed, except for his shirt which he held in a ball in his hand.

Tie smiled roguishly and Regan's heart skipped a beat or two. "Get dressed you two, or I'm not waiting for a bed. I want to fuck again. Right now. I don't care who. So hurry up or last man, or woman, standing naked gets it."

Regan's laugh was a little shaky as Cerise snuggled against him and laid her head on his shoulder. "That's not really an incentive to hurry up, Tie," he said and watched Tie's eyes glow with desire, his pupils dilating more in the low light.

"Does that mean what I think it means?" Tie asked softly as Cerise nipped his earlobe. Tie leaned in and kissed him in that incredibly sensitive spot behind his ear and then licked a delicious path with just the tip of his tongue along Regan's bare skull.

Regan shivered at their attentions, at the sensations boiling inside him—his, Cerise's and Tie's. "I'm not running anymore, Tie," he whispered. "I can feel you now, too. Can you feel me?"

Tie nodded as he continued to kiss Regan's bald head. Christ he loved that. "Yes, baby," Tie whispered, "I can feel you, too." He nipped the skin and Regan groaned. Tie chuckled wolfishly. "That's how I knew how much you'd like that." He smiled. "I think the old woman, Thomasina, was right. Somehow, I've got the Tears, too. And so do you Regan. The bond, it's between all three of us now."

"Mmm," Cerise murmured, rubbing her nose along the outer rim of Regan's ear. "Does this mean you two are going to fuck? Because I definitely can't wait to see that."

Her words made Regan instantly hard, an image of Cerise watching him and Tie fuck blazing across his mind.

"That's my girl," Tie said as he pulled away.

"No," Regan corrected him as he set Cerise back down and patted her ass. "That's our girl."

Chapter Seventeen

ॐ

When they were dressed Cerise couldn't hide a huge yawn. Tie scooped her up in his arms and she snuggled in close to him. "I need to rest before round two."

They'd just left *The Rebel Bounty* and were crossing the dark bay when Regan saw Conor approaching. They stopped and waited for him.

Conor actually blushed when he reached them. Regan realized what they must look and smell like. Pure sex. He just grinned. He was feeling too good to be ashamed. When Conor just stood there staring at Cerise held against Tie's bare chest, Regan cleared his throat. He raised an eyebrow when Conor's gaze snapped back to him guiltily.

Conor gulped. "Sorry. I didn't mean to interrupt. It's just that something just came in on the comm that I thought you should hear."

Regan frowned. "Why was it brought to you? Why not to me?"

Conor coughed nervously. "I, ah, think they tried to find you and then thought perhaps they should bring it to me instead."

Regan sighed. Well, so much for keeping this secret for five minutes. He should have known better than to expect perfect privacy in the small confines of the base.

"If it was important they should have interrupted us." He was annoyed and let it show.

"Regan," Tie said smoothly, "don't shoot the messenger. He came to interrupt. Didn't you Conor?"

"Do not hit me again," Conor said to Tie, backing up behind Regan. "I'm a lover, not a fighter."

Tie laughed. "Tonight, so am I."

Conor blushed again at his remark and Regan sighed impatiently. "Take the princess back to your quarters, Tie. I'll join you as soon as I can."

Tie's eyes burned a hole right through him, setting fire to his blood, making his cock ache and his stomach lurch in anticipation. "Promise?" Tie murmured seductively and Conor and comm messages faded away.

"Yes, Tie. I promise." Regan heard the need, the desire in his voice and marveled at it, marveled at the change that just an hour in their arms had wrought in him. Tie turned and walked away and Cerise blew him a sleepy kiss over Tie's shoulder. Regan reached out and pantomimed catching it and Cerise smiled and then laid her head back down and closed her eyes.

"Who are you and what have you done with the mighty pirate Regan?" Conor joked. "Big, scarred, scary guy? Bad-tempered, killing people with a flick of the wrist and a snarl?"

Regan turned back to Conor with a scowl. "Shut up Conor. I am not in the mood."

Conor laughed as if that were a great joke. "Looks like you are definitely in the mood," he said and that sent him off into great guffaws again.

Regan was getting irritated. His scowl turned to a glare. "Conor, either give me the message or rue the day. I am standing here in the cold when I could be sharing a bed with two very warm, enthusiastic lovers for whom I have been lusting for more years than I care to remember. My mood is quickly souring."

Conor held up his hands defensively. "Okay, okay. Sorry. It's just I've never seen you like this. You're...almost human."

Regan's back went stiff. He remembered Tie's words, let them give him confidence. "I am human. I am a man."

255

Conor looked at him in confusion. "Well of course you're human. And I know what a man looks like. You're definitely it. I just meant you always try so hard not to show any weakness. It's good to see you're just as susceptible as the rest of us."

Regan was taken aback for a moment. Had he misunderstood Conor all these years? Did he really think of Regan as a man? "Conor," he asked carefully, "do you think of me as a monster? An animal?"

Now Conor looked shocked. "What the hell are you talking about?" He got angry. "Did Tie say something? He's one to talk. He's a fucking giant ape. Who's he calling an animal?"

Regan shook his head with a grimace. "No, no, not Tie. He's the one who made me see that I've been wrong." He looked at Conor with new eyes. "Thank you. Thank you for your friendship. I'm sorry I thought the worst of you."

Conor shook his head with wonder and *thunked* his ear with the flat of his palm incredulously. "I'm sorry, did you just apologize? To me? You *have* been possessed. We need a priest or something."

Regan laughed, finally understanding how much Conor's humor and irreverent personality had meant to him during his lonely years. But his weak moment had passed. Thank God no one but Conor was around to see it. "No, we don't. Now give me the message or Tie's punch this afternoon will seem like a love tap."

Conor smiled. "Ah, there's the nasty bastard we all know and love." He rubbed his hands together gleefully. "There's a nice, juicy Amalgamation crystolium freighter just sitting all alone at the Smith." Conor frowned. "But we haven't got a lot of time. It's due to ship out in a matter of hours." He shook his head. "Never mind. You're busy playing loverboy. I'll tell the men we can catch the next unprotected freighter."

That caught Regan's attention. He wasn't about to lose the ground he'd gained over the last ten years by letting sex interfere with business. "What do you want to do with this freighter, Conor? Blow it up?" His heart was racing. He needed to show everyone that this situation with Tie and Cerise didn't change a thing. He was still Regan the pirate, damn it and he blew up crystolium freighters for a living. Tie and Cerise would be fine. He'd send word to them, let them rest for the night and see them when he got back.

Conor looked at him and waggled his eyebrows. "I'm a man. Of course I want to blow it up."

* * * * *

"God damn it!" Tie swore as he crumpled the note in his hand.

"Tie?" Cerise rose sleepily from under the covers looking deliciously rumpled. Tie gritted his teeth as he thought about how much he'd been looking forward to fucking her awake with Regan. Wouldn't happen now, the bastard. *I'm not running anymore Tie*, he'd said. Like hell he wasn't.

"Tie?" Cerise blinked the sleep from her eyes, concern marking her brow.

"Regan's run off to blow up some damn crystolium freighter," he growled. He shook the crumpled paper at her. "He sent a note. A goddamned note!" He threw it across the room, but it was too light to go far and its pathetic flutter to the floor in mid-flight only fueled Tie's anger. *"Everything will be fine. You and Cerise rest up for when I get back,"* he quoted. He let lose a frustrated howl of rage and kicked a chair which made a much more satisfying thud than the flight of the crumpled note.

Cerise was kneeling on the bed now, shivering. "Tie." The sound of the fear in her voice made him take a deep breath and get it under control.

"I'm sure everything will be fine," he said with a sigh. "I'm just pissed that he took off without a word. He left us here waiting for him. As if we were something that he could compartmentalize like his lists and his comm messages. Oh, Tie and Cerise? Just reschedule them for later this evening. I must go and blow something up." Tie bit his lip while he stood there with his hands on his hips staring at the ceiling for a count of twenty. Ten years he'd spent learning to control his emotions. He was known for his calm, logical, emotionless demeanor, damn it. Three days back in Regan's company and he was kicking inanimate objects. Oh, yeah, and punching people. He still winced a little at how he'd hit Conor yesterday. But the guy could sure take it. He was tougher than he looked.

He looked back at Cerise. She was studying him in silence, warily. "All right, I'm better now. Still pissed, but no longer in the mood to kick things."

Cerise tried unsuccessfully to smother a grin. "That's good to know." She gave up and laughed. "Oh, Tie, you wouldn't be you if you weren't always yelling, kicking, or fucking."

Tie looked at her in shock. "What the hell does that mean?"

Cerise shrugged happily as she arranged the covers around herself, snuggling into their warmth. "Just that you're very emotional. I like it. I like always knowing how you're feeling, that you're not afraid to show it. I've spent most of my life around people who were determined to show no fear. But also no love, no hate, no extremes on the emotional spectrum. You are a breath of much-needed fresh air. I love that about you." She motioned him over. "Come here. I'm cold."

Tie walked numbly over to the bed. "But I'm not like that. I'm a cold, logical, ruthless hunter. That's who I am now."

Cerise laughed as if he'd told a great joke. "What? Who told you that?" She shook her head. "Silly, you don't honestly believe that do you?" She looked at his face and hers showed dawning realization. "Oh my God, you do. Tie, honey, that's not you at all. It's never been you."

Tie's mouth thinned. "In the restaurant, on T-Sdei Delta, you believed it then. You believed I would hurt that boy."

Cerise looked stricken for a moment. "Yes, yes I did. But you wouldn't have, would you? I know that now. You knew it at the time, didn't you?"

Tie thought for a moment and then nodded slowly. "Yes. I remember thinking it was a good thing none of you realized that I'd let you kill me before I'd harm a hair on his head."

Cerise slumped in relief. "You see? That's not the thinking of a cold, ruthless hunter." She came back up on her knees and placed her palms on his chest. He wrapped his arms around her and she snuggled close. "That was the real you. You were playing a part, but it was never who you are. With me, with us, you can be yourself. That emotional, volatile part of you is what makes you Tie. You love unconditionally, you protect instinctively." She looked up at him, her eyes sultry. "You claim me thoroughly when you fuck me, Tie. You invade every particle of my body and my soul and you won't let me back away. It's never just fucking with you, Tie. When we make love you pour every ounce of your soul inside me and beg me to take it. And I do, I will, gladly, every time. I love you. I love how wild you are. I love how you love me, how you love Regan. I love your loyalty, your fierceness," she pulled his head down and kissed one eyelid then the other, "your superhuman qualities." She pulled away from him and lay down on the bed, her legs spread suggestively. "Make me take it, Tie," she whispered and he did.

Two hours later Tie and Cerise finally got up and dressed since they couldn't sleep. She poured herself into black leggings and a long, black, body-hugging jacket that buttoned up the front from hip to neck over a little black tank top. She wore heavy-duty black combat boots. All in all she looked dangerous, tough and sexy as hell. Tie thought about stripping it all off her and fucking her again, but she was all business.

Tie had a little more trouble getting dressed. "I've worn these pants every day for almost a week and I don't need to tell you what I've been doing in them." He was disgruntled and sounded it. She wanted emotion, she'd get emotion. "And there is no fucking way I'm wearing that shirt until it gets washed."

Cerise burst out laughing, which only made him more irritated. "Poor baby," she crooned walking around him running her hand across his shoulders and down his chest, inspecting his naked form appreciatively. His cock acknowledged her appreciation with some appreciation of its own, which made her laugh again. Tie relaxed and smiled. "Do you have some other things on the *Tomorrow*?"

Tie nodded. "I'm pretty sure I've got a decent change of clothes. I left most everything back on Quartus Seven." He raised his eyebrows wryly. "You were supposed to be a quick hunt. Two days at the most."

Cerise gave him a smug smile. "Best laid plans, sweetheart. You know the saying." Her smile turned rueful. "But, probably not a bad assumption. I'll be the first to admit I got lucky."

Tie pulled her into a playful hug and growled as he nipped her neck. "Very lucky. Repeatedly. Over and over and over…"

Cerise laughed and tried to push him away. "I get it, I get it! No wait, I mean I got it! I got it!" They both laughed as he let her loose. She picked up his old pants and threw them at him. "Put these on for now. We'll go straight to the ship and get you some clean clothes, okay? Then we'll find some more for you, although we may have to find someone to make them. I can't think of anyone as big as you on the station, not even Regan." She closed her eyes and sighed dreamily. "Well, his shoulders aren't as big as yours anyway."

Tie snorted. "No, his shoulders aren't, but his cock is."

Cerise's eyes popped open in mock innocence. "I didn't say that!"

Tie waggled his brows suggestively. "No, I did."

Their banter continued as they walked through the maze of the station toward the bay and the *Tomorrow*, but underlying it was a thread of tension that neither acknowledged. They were worried about Regan and Tie didn't like it. Something was bothering them. Was it something they sensed from him?

Once they reached the ship Cerise wandered over to the galley looking for something to eat while Tie rummaged in his cabin for some clean clothes. When he came out she was nibbling desultorily on a tray of fruit and protein squares.

"Hmm," Tie said as he came up behind her and stole a grape. "Have we discovered something you won't eat yet?"

Cerise didn't take the bait. Instead she turned to face him with a worried expression. "How do you think he is?"

He didn't need to ask who. "He's fine. He's done this sort of thing before, hasn't he?"

Cerise chewed on her bottom lip. "Sure, he's blown things up, gone on dangerous missions, but that's not what I'm worried about." She frowned. "I mean, do you think he's reacting the way we did after we fucked the first time? Last night was the first for him, you know, the first full-blown taste of the Tears. You and I had a very hard time with it."

And there it was, what had been niggling on the edge of Tie's brain. Jesus, was Regan going through the same sort of withdrawal as Tie and Cerise had? And if he was, how much danger was he in because of it? Tie took a moment to search inside himself. That restless tension took on new meaning. It was mild compared to his initial reaction to Cerise, but it was desire, no, need for Regan that had his nerves jumping.

"That stupid, idiotic, shit-for-brains," Tie swore. "We told him about it, we told him what the Tears did to us and he took off anyway." He spun away in frustration and punched the bulkhead. It creaked in protest. "I'm going to kill him when he gets back."

Cerise came up behind him and rubbed his back soothingly. "No, you're going to fuck him, just like I will. Because by then he's going to need it very badly."

Tie ran his hands through his hair in frustration. "Okay, okay." He blew out a calming breath. "Getting upset won't solve anything. Fuck!" He paced around the confined space of the galley. "I've got to contact Vonner on Quartus Seven."

"Who? Why?" Cerise asked confusion.

"My boss, or former boss I guess." Tie headed toward the bridge. "He's not exactly a friend, but he's been there for me. I owe him. I need to let him know I'm okay and I won't be back."

Cerise scurried after him. "Isn't that dangerous? What if they're scanning his comm?"

Tie settled into the pilot's chair as Cerise threw herself into the navigator's chair beside him. "He's got a secure line at the Web, Bounty Hunter's Inc.'s headquarters, just for situations like this. He might be able to give us some intel on who's looking for us and what the situation is. He's going to chew my ass off since this mission went total goatfuck, but," Tie shrugged, "nothing he can do about it now." Tie programmed the secure line into the communication unit and engaged the scrambling mode as an extra precaution. "I just need to do something." He paused and looked at her. "If I don't I'll sit here and go crazy worrying about Regan."

Cerise touched the back of his hand briefly in understanding. "I know."

"Vonner." The disembodied voice came over the comm and Tie could hear how pissed Vonner was. Before he could say anything Vonner spoke again. "This is a secure line for the use of Bounty Hunter Inc. personnel only. Are you an employee?"

That was the code that transmissions may be monitored. Tie was glad he'd engaged the scrambler. "Hunter K-58." He gave Vonner his unrecorded employee number, the one he'd been given when he was hired. Only Vonner knew those numbers. He'd memorized them for situations just like this. "I wish to terminate my contract immediately." Tie waited to see if Vonner would hang up. He didn't.

"Acknowledged." Vonner spoke slowly and it was clear he had more to say. Tie waited. "You've become a very popular hunter. There are many who wish to engage you."

"I'm retired." Tie kept his answers short. Vonner was telling him that they were looking for him. He wasn't going to make it easy.

"Is your last bounty secure?"

Tie was surprised at Vonner's question. Why did he want to know about Cerise? "Affirmative."

"Acknowledged. Bounty off apprehension list."

Ah, BHI wouldn't be taking that commission again. That was good to know.

"There's a pirate at the top of the list you might be interested in."

What the fuck? How did Vonner know about Regan? "I'm retired from bounty work. I've taken a position as personal bodyguard."

"Acknowledged and understood." Tie heard Vonner shuffling some papers. "Is this job on a freighter?"

Tie's blood ran cold. "Negative."

"If I were offered that position, I would refuse it," Vonner said coldly. "I don't like the class of people they let on those freighters nowadays."

What was Vonner saying, that there was someone on the freighter that was after Tie and Cerise? Or after Regan? They'd wanted Cerise expecting Regan to come for her. Now there was a freighter conveniently sitting at the Smith to tempt Regan out of hiding.

"A friend has gone there about a job. He thinks the crystolium market is going to blow wide open." Tie could see Cerise sitting on the edge of her chair, gripping the armrests. She knew exactly what they were dancing around.

There was silence on the other end of the line. Finally Vonner said, "He will find the mining trade has taken a turn for the worse. The Amalgamation controls that market now."

Christ, he was telling Tie they'd set a trap there. Tie's hand was shaking as he ran it over his face. "It may still be possible to reach him before the job interview." Tie almost broke the connection then, but stopped at the last second. "Thanks, Vonner, for everything."

"Acknowledged. Do not return for your personal effects. The environment is...unstable."

"Acknowledged." Before Tie even finished he heard the line go dead.

"Have you got a munitions supply room on this station?" Tie asked Cerise. She was pale and shaking next to him.

"Yes." She stood up and began running off the ship. "Follow me." She stopped suddenly and Tie nearly ran into her. "I'm going with you."

"No fucking way—" Tie began.

"I will die without you." Cerise told him flatly, her voice calm, her eyes determined. "And don't forget, Regan taught me how to fight."

Tie didn't like it, but he didn't have time to argue. He nodded once and they set off running again.

* * * * *

Vonner ended the call. He didn't think the secure line could be monitored. Dex was just too good for that. But it never hurt to be careful. He sat and thought about what he'd learned from Finnegan. So the princess was safe and under his protection, as was the pirate. Interesting, but not unexpected. Unfortunately it sounded as if the pirate had slipped away from that protection and was in trouble. And Finnegan was going to ride to the rescue, probably alone. Vonner shrugged and went back to work. Not his problem. He'd done more than was required already.

Five minutes later he threw his pen across the room with a curse. Finnegan may have terminated the contract, but god damn it he was still Vonner's. With a sigh he stood up and headed out of his office for sick bay. He still wasn't sure he could trust the SS, Martins, but what the hell. This was a total goatfuck already.

Martins was sitting in the back playing chess with Doc, who was looking a little green. That meant he was losing. Vonner stopped short. Doc was a computer-generated hologram and it was nearly impossible to beat him at chess. Vonner reevaluated his decision to trust the Super Soldier. In the end he decided that his intelligence didn't necessarily make him an enemy. It might make him a very valuable ally.

"Are you going to stand there staring all day, or are you going to tell me what you want?" Martins asked casually as he moved his knight. "Checkmate." He sat back with a smirk as Doc stared at the board in disbelief.

"That makes three times you have beaten me," Doc muttered. "That is impossible. I must recheck my analytical thinking chip."

"Ward's sitting on a crystolium freighter at the Smith, waiting for Finnegan and his bounty to make a run for it."

At Vonner's bald statement Martins froze and pinned Vonner with a cold, assessing gaze. A chill raced up Vonner's spine. This was one dangerous son of a bitch. How had he missed that?

Martins stood immediately and began walking to the door. He said nothing, no acknowledgement of the information or his intentions whatsoever. Vonner stepped into his path, stopping him. "Are you going to kill him?"

Martins' face showed nothing. He must be one hell of a poker player. "Probably."

Vonner relaxed as Martins showed no aggressiveness at his questioning. "You don't seem like the revenge type."

Unexpectedly Martins grinned. It didn't exactly relieve the scary factor, but it made him seem more human. "I'm not." He sighed. "Ward is my mission. The...people I work for are very interested in who he works for."

Vonner tipped his head to the side. That was interesting intel. "They're not the same people?"

Martins shook his head. "The discrepancy is rather worrying." He moved to the bed he'd been occupying and grabbed the jacket Con O'Rourke, supply handler at the web, had lent him. "If Ward is unable to give me the information I need, then he becomes a liability."

Vonner crossed his arms and leaned against the end of one of the empty beds. "You in any kind of shape to resume this 'mission'?"

Doc spoke up from the back of the room where he was reviewing the chessboard with increasing agitation. "No, he's not. He must remain here for at least another day or two."

"Sorry, Doc," Martins said as he shrugged into the coat. "No time for a rematch." He grinned conspiratorially at the hologram. "And just for your information, I'm perfectly healthy. The ear has been healed for the last two days."

Doc looked up in astonishment. "What? But you said — "

Martins laughed. "I'm SS, Doc. I heal at twice the speed of sound."

Vonner looked at him wryly. "Then what have you been waiting for?"

"I had to wait for you to decide to spill your guts."

Vonner's laugh was more of an astounded snort. "I didn't have anything to spill until today. And, get ready, here are more guts for you. There's a certain pirate and a wanted SS deserter who are walking right into his trap."

Martins looked at Vonner in astonishment. "Regan's on the freighter?"

So, Martins knew about Regan, too. Curiouser and curiouser, Alice. "According to my source, yes." Martins made for the door but when Vonner stood up quickly he stopped again. "He is not to be touched. I've given my word."

"Who, Regan?" At Vonner's nod, Martins looked at him for a moment and then seemed to come to a decision. "I had two missions and they just merged paths." He shook his head at Vonner's warning look. "No, I'm not supposed to kill Regan. I'm supposed to make contact with him."

"What the fuck is going on?" All of Vonner's senses came to full alert at Martins revelation. Whatever was going down was going to have big consequences in their little quadrant of the galaxy and Vonner did not want to get caught in the crossfire.

Martins shook his head again. "No can do, Vonner. That's a strictly need-to-know basis and you don't need to know. I will tell you this. Stay out of it. It's going to get messy and you don't want to get near it. Yet. When the time is right, you'll know." He walked toward the door and then stopped again. "Your assistance might be required in the future. Will it be available?"

Vonner sighed. He knew it. He'd known this whole goatfuck was going to blow up in his face. "Yes," he paused and held up a hand at Martins' smile, "on a very discreet basis."

This time Martins' smile was as chilling as his blank face. "I know how to keep secrets, Vonner. Let's just hope you and your people can."

Vonner's eyes narrowed on Martins. "I can keep a lid my people. No one will know you're alive and well and wreaking havoc in the galaxy."

Martins laughed in genuine amusement. "You don't mind if I borrow a few things, do you? I'm in sore need of some equipment."

Vonner sighed again. "If you mean weapons, yes I mind." He crossed his arms and glared at Martins as the other man just stood there waiting. With a curse Vonner whipped out his communicator. "Con, Martins is on his way. He needs a full outfitting."

"Roger," Con acknowledged.

"Thanks, Vonner, for everything." Martins turned to go and then looked back sheepishly. "Just remember when I'm gone, Vonner, that I had to do it. Computers are vulnerable, you know." Then he looked back at Doc and said, "It's been nice beating you, Doc." Then he slipped out the door.

As Vonner watched Doc froze just as he was getting ready to say something. His image shimmered and then blinked several times before becoming solid again.

"What do you want, Vonner?" he asked as he glared at him. "I'm busy."

"Doing what?" Vonner asked, resigned.

Doc paused in consternation. "I don't know."

Vonner sighed and headed out to find Dex to order a full computer scan of the facilities. Fucking Super Soldiers.

Chapter Eighteen

ॐ

Regan could not believe how quickly the situation had deteriorated. Somehow they'd gotten pinned down in a service corridor on the crystolium freighter. The rest of *The Rebel Bounty*'s crew, led by Sasha, was trying to find an escape route behind them. Regan, Conor and a few others were holed up at the corner of the L-shaped corridor trying to hold off the IMF troops pursuing them. If Tie were here he'd know exactly how to get the fuck off this rusty piece of shit. But no, Regan had to leave him behind like a goddamn fucking idiot. One of the crew went down in a burst of laser fire and Regan screamed in rage.

"Get him back! Get him back," he hollered at two young crewmen who weren't being much help in the shooting department. They could play medic for a while. They scrambled forward and Regan had to yell again. "On your bellies, you fucking idiots! Do you want to get shot?" He breathed a little easier when they managed to haul the injured man back behind the lines and peel his singed clothing off the still smoking wound. The soldiers weren't shooting to kill. Why not? What were they hoping to achieve?

Regan was out of breath. Christ, he was never out of breath. He mentally amended that. The only time he could remember being out of breath was when he was fucking Cerise with Tie. He felt similar now. The airomoxide must be wearing off. Shit.

"Remind me again, asshole, why you decided it was a good idea to go on a dangerous mission when you knew you were going to be going through detox?"

Conor's sarcasm had a bite to it today that it normally didn't hold. Regan could hardly blame him. What was supposed to be a little hit-and-run had turned into a major goatfuck. They'd been waiting for them, an entire platoon of IMF, it seemed. Regan was so disgusted with himself he wanted to hit something until it bled. He should have seen the trap, a pretty little target like this just sitting like a fat duck at the Smith in the last system he'd been tracked to. He would have seen the trap if he hadn't been so caught up in his personal life. No, not his own personal life, his own personal shit. So what if he went a little soft over Cerise and Tie? So what? It didn't mean he wasn't still Regan. But he'd had to run off and prove what a bad-ass rebel pirate he was. Shit and god damn.

Regan took aim and missed his target by a mile. His hands were shaking so badly he nearly dropped the gun. Fuck, fuck, fuck. He should have listened when Tie and Cerise told him what it was like. He'd assumed he was tougher than they were. He leaned back against the bulkhead and pounded his thick skull against it three or four times.

"And that's supposed to help how?" Conor snapped at him. "Is it Morse code for get us the fuck out of here?"

"Regan!" The laser fire coming at them came to an abrupt halt as the voice boomed down the corridor at them.

Conor looked at him in dismay. Clearly he hadn't figured out it was a trap. Regan nodded grimly and shrugged. "What?" he yelled back, using the cease-fire to look back down the corridor. Sasha was waving frantically from the end, pointing to a missing panel in the bulkhead. They'd managed to cut it out and even now Regan could see several crewmembers scrambling down into the space.

"You're not getting out of this, Regan," the voice yelled. "You surrender now and we'll let your crew go. You have my word."

Regan rolled his eyes at Conor who looked just as disbelieving. Regan motioned Conor and the others down the corridor toward the impromptu escape hatch. Conor shook his head vehemently, pointing first at himself and then at Regan, indicating he was staying.

"Fuck that!" Regan yelled back, stalling for time while silently arguing with Conor in sharp hand motions. Conor answered by giving him the finger. Nice. "How do I know you'll keep your word?"

"You got me, Regan," the voice laughingly replied, grating on Regan's nerves. He really wanted to kill this guy. "But if you surrender yourself, maybe I won't blow up this ship with you, your crew and the two hundred civilians I've got locked in the cargo bay below decks."

Conor's eyes got very big and Regan got a sick, sinking feeling in his gut. This just went way beyond goatfuck. "What the hell are you talking about?" he yelled, now frantically motioning Conor back. *You've got to rescue...cargo bay*, he mouthed at Conor.

Lying, Conor mouthed back. Regan didn't think so. This guy sounded like he meant business.

"Ticktock, Regan," the voice said in an irritatingly cheerful tone. "I've got the ship wired now and most of my men off. They'll chalk it up to the big, bad, Regan, who has started to blow up innocent civilians now. That won't make you very popular will it? Or your little rebellion."

"And how will it be different if I surrender?" Regan called out as he watched Conor war with himself and finally begin to back down the corridor to the hatch. Regan could see the anguish on his face at leaving him alone there, but it had to be done. Regan smiled at him. It wasn't much, but it was all he could do now.

"If you surrender it'll just be the ship. I'll still blow it, but I'll let everyone off first. Then I can arrest you for blowing it up, caught in the act by me. The trial will be quick and the execution public. It's good PR and you'll make a fine example."

271

Conor hesitated as he heard the asshole brag. Regan just shook his head and rolled his eyes again at this guy's conceit. He waved Conor in and as Conor's head disappeared from sight Regan felt a calm settle over him.

"I'll surrender when I have reliable confirmation that the cargo bay is empty and my men are off the ship." He knew whoever this guy was he wouldn't agree to that. But always start negotiating with more than you realistically knew you could get. Because, really, what were negotiations but not so cleverly disguised stall tactics? Everyone knew it.

"Regan, Regan, Regan," the voice chanted, sounding so disappointed Regan almost felt guilty for a minute. "You know I can't do that. You're a notorious pirate. Oh and I almost forgot, you're also a deserter from the SS. EG-46872N, I'm placing you under arrest for desertion and high treason." There was a pregnant pause. "Now is when you step out with your hands up."

Regan's stomach twisted into a knot so tight he doubled over. Shit, this wasn't fear or anything like it. It was desire, lust, slamming into him. He fell to his knees and groaned at the pain. Why now? There was nothing in this situation to warrant his physical reaction. Was it the Tears? He couldn't think for the blood pounding in his head, sending heat and torturous awareness through him. Clearly the airomoxide had worn off.

* * * * *

On board the small cargo ship they'd commandeered on Quantinium, Cerise screamed. She and Tie were sitting on the bridge with four or five other people who'd volunteered to accompany them when the news of Regan's situation spread. There were at least fifty others crammed into the bay below decks, armed to the teeth. No one had heard anything from *The Rebel Bounty* since it had left in the middle of the night.

"Cerise!" Tie yelled and leaped over to where she'd slumped down on the deck.

She couldn't stop the sob that escaped. "It's Regan! Did you feel it? He's hurt, or hurting, I don't know! Something's wrong! Can't we go faster?" Her insides felt like someone had stabbed her with a hot poker. It was the same thing she'd been feeling on the prison hulk when Tie finally came for her. The feeling faded, leaving a shadow behind, as if someone was muting the pain.

Tie took several deep breaths next to her and then helped her up. "Yeah, I felt it too. We must be picking it up through the connection from the Tears. I recognize it. Jesus, we've got to get in there." He handed her off to someone who lowered her into one of the vacant chairs on the bridge. Tie went back to the computer and continued with what he'd been working on when she'd collapsed. "I've almost got the schematics memorized. I've reprogrammed the security system. It's similar to the one on the hulk, when I rescued you. It worked there, it ought to work here. I don't think they're expecting anyone else to show up."

A few minutes later he looked up at Cerise, worry etched on his brow. "I don't think you should go, Cerise. You don't look good. You're tied to closely to him. I can't risk you, too."

Cerise dug deep to find the strength to stand and face him determinedly. "I'm going and that's that. Not just to get Regan, but everyone else. They're mine, Tie, my responsibility. This rebellion is under my leadership. If my people are in danger I'm going to damn well help save them." The bridge had gone deathly quiet at their exchange.

"You are not responsible, Cerise. You did not send them on this mission." Tie was trying to be reasonable, but she could hear the fear in his voice.

"No, but that trap was for me, for us and you know it. They got caught in the crossfire."

Tie was silent for a minute. "They knew Regan would come, Cerise. It's why they put the bounty on you, to catch him. This trap was for him and me, too. If you were caught in the net that would be icing on the cake."

Well, that was lowering, but when she thought about it, it made sense. "Fine. They want you two. What they are going to get is my foot up their ass. I'm not just some darling little princess who is going to wave from the victory parade, Tie. If you and Regan want me to lead this resistance then you've got to stand back and let me lead."

All heads on the bridge turned to Tie to see what he'd say. God, let it be the right thing. Cerise could clearly see that they were ready to take Tie's lead here. He was the big, bad Super Soldier bounty hunter. If he said Cerise was too weak to go on this mission, then they would treat her like that forever. And she didn't think she could live like that. Not without coming to resent Tie.

"Can you shoot that thing?" He nodded at the energy bow she'd secured to her waistband. She wore the arrows, small silver balls that would expand into piercing arrows, around her torso on a bandolier.

"Better than most." Her heart was pounding. *Please, please, Tie*, she silently begged with her eyes, *don't shut me out.*

"You will stay behind me at all times." He held up a hand as she started to agree. "And I'm assigning someone to be at your back, too. Understood? You are not to put yourself in danger unless it can't be avoided. No heroics."

She glared at him. "I have no intention of putting myself in danger. I'm not a soldier. I'm not here to be a hero. I'm here to get them out. Period. And you need every able body you can find."

Tie sighed and in one quick, wide step was in front of her, gathering her close to him in a fierce hug. "You're too important Cerise—to me, to Regan, to the resistance. You are everything good and right left in this galaxy. It's not that I don't think you can lead. It's that I think you lead too well. You'd throw yourself in front of an energy sword for every single person on that ship and we all know it. I'm just saying, don't. Please." His next words were soft, but she was sure everyone on the bridge heard them. "I'm selfish, Cerise. I've finally found you and Regan and I want what we've only just begun. I want a life, a real life, with the two of you. Please understand."

She pulled back so she could look into his eyes. "Don't worry, Tie. I want that life too and I'm not going to let the Amalgamation steal it from us. Not this time."

Twenty minutes later they were making their way cautiously down the corridor on the second deck. They'd docked at the emergency refueling port on the starboard side close to the stern. As on most ships it wasn't used much, so it had minimal security and was located far from the main decks. The hatch had been easy to jimmy open and within minutes they'd all climbed silently aboard. Tie had designated a young man named Theo as his second-in-command. Theo had military training, special ops he'd said, but he'd seen very little action before deserting and joining the resistance. His honesty had impressed Tie, as had his training. Tie took point and Theo fell back. Cerise was in the middle of the group, shadowed by a woman named Esmerelda who was a former gang member from T-Sdei Delta. She was taller than Cerise by about fifteen centimeters, with short, black, spiked hair and a scar that went from the corner of her left eye down her cheek and onto her neck. Her eyes were as black as her hair. She carried identical Icsantheze daggers. The twin half-meter, curved, golden blades with their pale green streaks glowed in their open weave scabbards across her chest. She looked as if she knew how to use them. Tie had just looked at Esmerelda and pointed to Cerise. The woman had nodded once and been glued to her back since.

Laser fire came from out of nowhere and Esmerelda threw Cerise back against the bulkhead and plastered her body over Cerise's. Cerise was annoyed, but also humbled. Yet another stranger willing to die for her. It was a heavy responsibility and one she hoped she lived up to. Tie yelled and everyone took cover. The firing stopped immediately.

"Tie?" A voice came from the shadows.

"Conor!" Cerise yelled, struggling to get out from behind Esmerelda. "Where's Regan?" Cerise searched inside herself. She could still feel Regan, knew he still lived. He was still hurting, but not so bad now. So where was he?

"Cerise? What the fuck are you doing here? Do you realize what's going down here?" The last question was hissed at Tie as Conor and the crew from *The Rebel Bounty* slid silently out of hiding and converged on their group.

"Yes," Tie hissed back, "we are well aware of what's going down. They set a trap and you fell right into it like big, fat idiots. Now where the fuck is Regan?"

"We left him behind." Sasha shoved his way in between Tie and Conor. Cerise gasped and Tie growled. "At his insistence," Sasha continued. "He's stalling for time so we can find the damn cargo bay. The IMF bastard up there claims to have locked up two hundred civilians in the cargo bay and he's going to blow this ship to kingdom come with all of us on it." He nodded politely to Cerise. "Beggin' your pardon, Your Highness."

"Tie?" Cerise knew he'd know what to do. She consoled herself with the knowledge that a good leader knows when to lead and when to get the hell out of the way and let someone more qualified take over.

"Cargo bays are on Deck One, just below us, starboard bow." No one who'd been on the ship with them on the way here questioned his knowledge. They'd seen him memorize the ships schematics. Conor, however, looked askance at him. Tie shrugged. "I have a photographic memory. It wasn't hard to track down the identity of the freighter at this particular Gate and download the information we needed."

Conor looked grudgingly impressed. "Then what's the fastest way down there?"

Tie closed his eyes for a moment. "About seventy-five meters down the corridor here there's a maintenance shaft between decks. Take the ladder down and then continue on for another twenty-five meters dead ahead. Starboard you'll see the entrance to the cargo bay." He opened his eyes. "I don't know how they've sealed it. Chances are you'll have to blow it. Do you have someone who can do that? And the equipment?"

Conor's look was sarcastic. "Considering we came here to blow it up, yeah, I guess we can handle that."

Tie gritted his teeth. "I see one wounded. Any more?"

"No, sir," Sasha answered respectfully. "But Hearn's pretty bad. I was about to send them back to *The Rebel Bounty.*"

"Are you sure the way is clear? Where are you docked?" Tie was listening, but at the same time Cerise could see him calculating various scenarios in his head as he surveyed the alert rebels in the corridor.

"We came in at the loading dock, disguised as a cargo vessel. Don't know if it's still clear. It was when we came on, but then again they wanted us to think so."

"Then belay that order. Have them take Hearn to the *Ice Crystal.* It's the small cargo vessel we arrived in, docked at the emergency refueling station, one hundred meters back. I need some of your crew to go with them to monitor the situation outside." He pointed to one of the volunteers who'd accompanied them. "You, take them back the way we came and help them with that." He turned to Conor. "Conor, I need you to take the rest of your men and half of ours and find the cargo bay. I'd be surprised if it's not heavily guarded. Those civilians are their ace in the hole."

Conor didn't hesitate. "All right. Sasha, pick volunteers and move out. I'll follow. Bivens, make sure you have what we need to blow that bay open." He turned back to Tie. "Regan's on Deck Five. They've got him holed up in a dead end. The leader is some little bastard with a Napoleonic complex. He's gloating and taunting Regan, pretending to negotiate our release. He claimed that most of his people were off the ship already. We didn't run into any on our way down here, so he may be telling the truth."

"Off where?" Tie demanded. "I didn't see another ship out there. Were there any in the loading dock?"

Conor nodded. "Several midsized cargo vessels like *The Bounty*. They could hold that many I think."

"How many?" Tie asked.

Conor just shrugged. "Too hard to tell. Even Regan was stumped. The laser fire was precise and heavy at times, but it still could have been anything from a few men to...fifty maybe? In that small space, who could tell?"

"Theo," Tie called quietly. The young man glided silently up to them. "Take the rest of our men and go to the loading dock. You saw the plans. Can you find it?" At Theo's nod Tie continued. "We need those ships. Make them available." He looked back at Conor. "When you get the cargo bay open get those people to the loading dock and on those vessels as quickly as possible. I've got an itch between my shoulder blades that says this ship is set to go off on a timer. We're on the clock and it's ticking. Move."

"I'm on it," Conor said as he turned away. Cerise called to him.

"Conor, be careful." Conor saluted her with a jaunty wave and took off running down the corridor.

In a matter of minutes only Tie, Cerise and Esmerelda were left in the corridor. Tie turned to her and Cerise knew what was coming. "No."

Tie ignored her. "Cerise, I want you to go back to the *Ice Crystal*. I'll get Regan and meet you back there."

She was shaking her head even as he spoke. "No. We're going with you."

Tie looked behind her. "Take her back."

Cerise spun around and dared Esmerelda with her eyes to try it. The other woman slowly shook her head. "With all due respect, sir, I'm going to have to agree with the Princess. You need someone to watch your back." She sighed. "I guess that would be Her Royal Highness and me, since you sent everyone else off."

"God damn it—" Tie snarled, but Cerise got right up in his face.

"Forget it. I'm not leaving you vulnerable. We're all there is to get Regan off this ship safely. The longer we stand here arguing about it the more danger he's in. So let's do it." Cerise pushed past him and began walking. Tie hauled her to a stop.

"You are one stubborn woman," he said angrily and let go of her arm to point in the opposite direction. "And we need to go that way."

"Well, then, go!" Cerise said shoving him forward. She saw Esmerelda hide a grin as they fell in line behind Tie's ground-eating strides.

* * * * *

Regan took another deep breath in through his nose and let it out slowly through his mouth. It was a very simple technique to relax, but it seemed to be working. He was sitting on the deck leaning against the bulkhead just around the bend in the L-shaped corridor. He held out his hand and saw that it was only shaking slightly, a big improvement over the convulsive tremors that had seized him a few minutes ago. He could feel waves of soothing energy bouncing gently against him and then sinking in. At least that was what it felt like. It had to be Cerise and Tie. Did they know what was going on? Where were they?

"Ticktock, Regan," the IMF bastard called out and Regan had to grit his teeth and count to ten breathing deeply. Trying to relax while that piece of shit taunted him was becoming a Herculean task.

Through the muddle in his brain Regan snatched at an awful thought floating around there. "Are we on a timer?" he called out, fishing for information. He honestly didn't think he'd get an answer and was surprised when he did.

"Ah," the hated voice called out, "not as dumb as your average Gen8 are you? Yes, we're on a very tight schedule, Regan and it's getting tighter."

Fuck, fuck, fuck was all he could think. If he contacted Conor on the comm the IMF forces out there, however many there were, would figure out the others had gotten away and were even now trying to rescue the people in the cargo bay. But if he didn't...Christ, he had to tell Conor. The crew had to get off this ship.

"Conor?" he spoke quietly into his comm-tab. "We're on a timer. Get off this ship. Repeat, get off this ship. Now."

"What did you say?" called out the voice. "Who are you talking to? Your little friends racing to the cargo bay?" Regan went cold as the bastard laughed. "They won't make it in time. They'll never be able to offload that many people before the ship blows."

"Regan?" Conor's voice came from the comm and Regan could hear voices in the background shouting. "We're getting ready to blow the cargo bay doors. Tie is on his way." Before Regan could answer, Conor delivered the most disturbing news. "Cerise is with him."

The shaking began in earnest again, a mixture of fear and exaltation. He'd see them soon! Christ he needed to see them, to touch them. But then fear left him cold. They were walking into this trap. For him. And he couldn't let them. If it came down to him or them, he chose them.

"Conor, tell them to go back, to get off the ship. This guy is going to blow it. Tell them they've got to get off."

"Close down this comm. Now." Tie's voice cut off Conor's answer and Regan's heart began to pound in his chest. Tie's voice was like water on the fire that was consuming him. Even with the anger in it, Tie's voice soothed him and sent shivers down his spine. Oh, this was bad. Regan knew Tie was right, it was foolish to reveal so much on an open channel, but he had to convince them to get off.

"Tie, for God's sake get her off. Get her off the ship. I don't care about me, but the two of you..." He closed his eyes for a second as pain slashed through him. "If something happened to you because of me I'd never forgive myself."

"How touching." That goddamned voice was closer, just around the corner it sounded like.

"Regan, shut up," Tie's voice barked on the comm. "We've had this discussion before. That is not an option." Regan heard Cerise say his name in the background, her voice shaky, and his chest felt so tight he put a hand there and rubbed at the pain.

"Tie, please," he begged, not even caring that everyone else could hear. "Please take Cerise and leave."

"Too late." Tie's voice was no longer on the comm, but echoing down the corridor from the other end. The end which the little IMF bastard was in, making Tie and Cerise perfect targets.

"No!" Regan yelled scrambling to his feet and flying around the corner.

When the hit came he didn't feel it, not really. Just a burning hot sensation for a moment and then nothing. Regan hit the deck as he was knocked back, his last thoughts of Tie and Cerise. Were they all right? Would they get off in time?

"You fucking speared him!" Tie yelled, locking every muscle to keep from running to Regan's side. There was an SS next to him, one Tie didn't recognize. Regan lay on the deck. It looked as if he were unconscious. God, Tie hoped he was. That had to hurt like hell. A huge spear was lodged in his shoulder. It had gone all the way through and he lay unevenly on the deck, the tip of the spear holding his left side up.

The SS had his laser pointed at Tie and Cerise and Esmerelda. Esmerelda had literally picked Cerise up from behind to keep her from running to Regan. She'd spun around holding Cerise so that her back was to the SS. He'd have to shoot Esmerelda to get to Cerise. Cerise was sobbing hysterically, frantically trying to jerk out of her arms.

"I didn't want to kill him," the SS said reasonably. He motioned at Regan with a jerk of his head. "He hasn't served his purpose yet. With that lodged in his shoulder it should slow him down. Now that the two of you have joined us, this will be perfect." He slowly went to one knee next to Regan. "Drop your weapons and back up, to the central traffic circle at the lift doors." Tie hesitated and the laser was pointed at Regan's unconscious head. "SS are hard to injure and harder to kill. Lucky for me I know how to do both. Do it now or I will kill him."

"You're going to kill him anyway." Tie spoke calmly, but inside he was a fiery ball of impotent rage. How the hell was he going to get Regan and Cerise off this ship safely? He was going to have Regan's head when this was over. No way was Tie going to let that SS bastard kill him. He wanted to do the job himself.

The smile the soldier gave him was chilling. "But there's always hope, isn't there? Even now you're desperately trying to think of a way to get all of you off this ship. As long as there's hope, you'll do what I say."

Tie felt like a rat in a trap. He was right, damn it and they all knew it. Tie slowly lowered his laser rifle to the deck and stood up again, taking a step back. The soldier laughed derisively. "Am I supposed to believe that's the only weapon you're carrying? I'm Gen10, moron. I don't fall for that kind of stupid trick." He motioned with his laser. "The rest. Now."

Tie was grinding his teeth. At least he knew where this guy was coming from now. Gen10, Jesus, they were fucking crazy. The indoctrination process for those bastards was so brutal that if they survived, nine out of ten were borderline psychotic. They were fanatically loyal to the IMF and the Amalgamation, however, so that was not considered a negative side effect. Tie's optimism, pretty low at this point already, took a nosedive. He slowly reached back and pulled the hilt of an energy blade from the waistband of his leggings. He threw it to the floor. The Gen10 just kept looking at him. Again slowly, he reached down and pulled an Icsantheze dagger from its hidden scabbard in his boot. He tossed that on the pile. "That's all I've got."

"You travel light, hmmm?" The Gen10 motioned with his chin at Esmerelda. "Now the Amazon."

Esmerelda looked at Tie. He knew she'd do whatever he told her. He didn't want her trying to protect Cerise unarmed, but he wasn't willing to let her die a meaningless death, either. He nodded.

"I'm going to put you down, Your Highness," Esmerelda said in her deep, husky tones. "I want you to stay in front of me, understood?"

Cerise was crying hard, but managed a nod. When Esmerelda let go she crumpled to the ground sobbing. It took a moment for Tie to realize what had been bothering him, other than the obvious, about this situation. She didn't sound like Cerise. He'd heard Cerise cry before and it didn't sound like this. This sounded hopeless and helpless. She looked broken and utterly defenseless lying there. The only reaction Tie couldn't control was a blink of his eyes. Cerise was anything but helpless. She was up to something, God bless his scheming little mate.

Esmerelda slowly pulled her daggers from their sheaths and tossed them on top of Tie's weapons on the deck.

"Back up to the traffic circle," Gen10 said, not even bothering to order Cerise unarmed as well. It was all Tie could do not to grin at the soldier's idiocy. So easily fooled by a few tears.

Tie backed up a few steps and stopped, waiting. Esmerelda helped Cerise to her feet and supported her back down the hall. Once they had passed him Tie started moving again, keeping his eyes on the Gen10 all the while. His laser never wavered from Regan's head.

Tie reached the large central opening on the deck and moved to the middle. Several dead-end corridors came off the large space, like a sunburst. Esmerelda and Cerise had retreated all the way across the open space and Cerise lay in a heap at the entrance to one of the corridors. Esmerelda slid slowly to the side until she stopped at a forty-five degree angle to Cerise, in front of another corridor. Tie saw what she was doing. If they spread out it would be harder for the Gen10 to cover them all. It probably wouldn't work, but Tie eased over to another corridor, directly across from Esmerelda.

"On your knees, hands behind your heads," the Gen10 called out. Tie waited a beat trying to figure out if he could see the three of them. "Do it, now!" he yelled and Tie went down to his knees and put his hands behind his head. He knew the position. God knows he'd made enough bounties assume it. Across from him Esmerelda did the same. Cerise was still crying weakly on the floor between them. Suddenly a scream ripped out from down the corridor and Tie started to come to his feet in panic.

"Get down!" the Gen10 snarled and Tie fell back down, his heart pounding.

"What are you doing to him?" he demanded hoarsely. He couldn't see them anymore, couldn't see down the corridor. Why had he moved over here? Damn it, goddamn it!

"Get up," he heard the Gen10 order Regan in disgust. Regan groaned painfully and then Tie heard a shuffling noise coming down the corridor. When the Gen10 emerged he had an arm wrapped around Regan's throat, his hand holding tight to the spear, grinding it into his shoulder. His other hand still held the laser to Regan's head. Regan was conscious now, but pale, the shoulder bleeding heavily. He stumbled and was yanked back up by the spear. He couldn't stop another groan of pain.

Cerise was sobbing hysterically again. "No, no, don't hurt him! Don't hurt him! I'll do whatever you want, I swear. Just don't hurt him!"

"Well, well," the Gen10 sounded amused, "isn't this interesting? The beautiful princess in love with the pirate. Does she know what you are?" He shook Regan and he gasped, refusing to answer.

Tie answered for him. "Yes, she knows what we are."

The Gen10's eyes spun around to him and Tie was frozen by the disgust there. The Gen10 shook his head. "Caught, because of a woman." He seemed to want to talk, so Tie just sat there and listened. "You know you were the hard one to find." He smiled in appreciation. "We couldn't find you anywhere T1-45897E. You just vanished, poof." He shook Regan again, hard and Tie cringed at the tight scream that Regan cut off. "This one, he was so easy. We knew almost immediately that Regan was EG-46872N. He murders his fellow soldiers and disappears, only to have a new pirate scourge plague the galaxy in the company of the very same rebel he'd helped escape. It didn't take a genius to put two and two together."

"That's good for your sake," Regan managed weakly. Tie grinned at him.

The Gen10 pushed hard at the spear and Regan bit his lip until it bled, unsteady on his feet. "Unfortunately, although we knew who he was, his people are incredibly loyal for some reason. We couldn't capture him." He looked over at Tie. "We knew you'd end up together eventually. Everyone knew you were lovers. It was only a matter of time."

"We weren't lovers," Tie corrected him.

"Yes, we were," Regan said weakly and Tie looked over at him, saw the emotion there and he nodded.

"Yes, we were."

The SS looked over at Cerise who was crying quietly now, her arms wrapped around her stomach. Tie looked a second time. She'd unbuttoned her coat. She was holding it closed, covering the bandoliers. The Gen10's smile was cruelly satisfied. "And now we've got the rebel princess. The three of you will make a touching scene when you hang in Amalgama."

Cerise doubled over sobbing weakly, her hands sliding from her sides until they were lost underneath her. Tie watched her performance in awe. She was fucking brilliant. But time was running out.

Chapter Nineteen

ഇ

Martins watched the pretty little princess collapse as she surreptitiously tried to get to the energy bow and arrows she'd slowly been working free from her bandoliers. She was good, damn good. He smiled. He could definitely see the attraction she held for the two SS out there. She had Ward completely fooled. He thought her a silly, helpless, little nothing. The Amazon kneeling to her left made a sudden move as if to go to the princess, drawing Ward's eyes away from her. Oh, yeah, she knew what she was doing, too. He recognized the cut on her face as the sign of the Gunslingers, the baddest of the bad gangs on T-Sdei Delta. What the hell was she doing risking her life for the cause? It was out of character for a Gunslinger and therefore interesting. Martins mentally shrugged. Perhaps he'd be able to study her more later — or perhaps not. They could all end up as space debris in a few minutes.

Martins sighed as he watched the princess's painstaking efforts to get the bow and arrows out without alerting Ward. He'd hoped he'd be able to stay out of it, but it was taking her too long. She needed another diversion. Martins would just shoot Ward himself but his angle was all wrong. Ordinarily he wouldn't worry about tagging the pirate too, but his orders were to make contact and leave him breathing, so that's what he'd do. The pirate was, after all, necessary for their plans.

Martins stepped out of the shadows next to the lift. The SS kneeling on the floor, Vonner's hunter, noticed him first. Before he could give the alert Martins motioned him to silence with a hand signal straight out of the SS handbook. It startled the guy so much he obeyed without thinking and Martins had to smother a grin. Training was a bitch, but when it paid off it was worth it.

"I wouldn't buy your tickets for the execution just yet, Ward," he said in a flat voice, stepping over to a new set of shadows in the corridor directly behind the Captain.

"What the fuck?" Ward said, spinning around and backing closer to the collapsed princess so he could keep Martins, the hunter and the Amazon in his sights. Martins almost laughed aloud at how easy it was to herd him where they wanted him. "Martins?"

"The same." Martins casually raised his laser rifle and sighted it on Ward, his finger on the trigger.

"I should have known it was too easy to kill you," Ward spit out. "Vonner will pay, painfully, for lying to me." He dragged the pirate closer to him by the spear and pressed the gun into his temple hard, forcing his head to the side at an awkward angle. "Drop the gun or I'll kill him."

"Go ahead," Martins said in the same flat voice. "He's not my mission. You are."

"No!" the hunter said in a panicked voice from where he was kneeling. Martins ignored him. He was too emotionally invested here. Martins wrote him off immediately as useless in this situation.

"What mission? What the fuck are you talking about?" Ward demanded.

"Where are the rest of your men?" Martins asked, moving to his left slowly, pulling Ward's eyes with him. He had the soldier's undivided attention. Good.

"I don't need them to take care of this pathetic crew of rebels," Ward scoffed. "I sent them to the ship to report our successful capture."

"Want all the credit for yourself, hmmm?" Martins asked, taking one quick step forward, forcing Ward to stumble back a step in surprise. Ward's face twisted in anger. "Or is it that you're not actually following the same orders as everyone else?" Martins continued. "Have you got your own agenda here, Ward? Whose orders are you following?"

Ward was pissed off. He hadn't yet realized what was going on. He honestly didn't think that three Gen8's and a former gang member could beat him, let alone a hysterical rebel princess. Martins had known he'd react like that. His arrogance had always been his weak spot.

"Who are you working for, Martins?" Ward countered. "It's obvious you are the one here with a separate agenda."

Martins tsk tsked. "Now I could tell you, but then I'd have to kill you." He paused a moment as if in surprise. "Oh wait, that's what I'm going to do anyway."

While they'd been talking the princess had been stealthily getting her weapon out and loaded. She clearly knew what she was doing, which eased Martins' mind. She was all business. He loved having a woman in that position. They handled the stress of these situations far better than most men. If it was the hunter over there they'd all be dead.

Ward laughed, genuinely amused. "You think you're going to kill me?" He snorted in disgust. "I should tell you who I'm working for just for laughs and then watch the information die with you when I kill you."

Martins went still, still sighted on Ward. "We already have the information. You were just to confirm. Then it's goodbye. You're a liability now. A pest that has to be exterminated."

"If your boss thinks that he has the upper hand he is sorely mistaken," Ward purred. "My superiors will soon have control of the Amalgamation Senate. Then it's only a matter of time until this galaxy is under their complete control, enforced by a loyal IMF. You're too late, Martins." Ward's look was calculating. "I'm sure there's room for someone as ingenious as you. I'll put in a good word. I'll even let you have some of the credit for this capture. You could be a major mover in the new order."

"I like the chaos of the status quo," Martins said. "And you just confirmed what we already knew. Thanks."

Martins could see the princess standing in firing position behind Ward. She was locked and loaded, her arrow notched. She was using a silver shaft—smart girl. An amateur would have gone for an exploding copper shaft. She must be pretty confident in her own ability. At that point Martins had no choice but to trust her judgment. Ward had all his senses trained on Martins now. If Martins fired Ward's reflexes were quick enough to use the pirate as a shield. The princess had a better chance because Ward wasn't expecting the shot to come from that direction. And if she missed, at least she'd distract him long enough for Martins to get a shot off.

She was watching him, obviously unsure if he was going to fire. He lowered his weapon sharply, confusing Ward and giving the princess a clear go-ahead.

She nodded and in the next instant Martins realized the hunter wasn't as useless as he'd appeared. He leaped up and seized Ward's wrist, twisting hard. Ward wasn't prepared for the attack, he'd been so focused on Martins and Martins heard the bone snap. Ward fired and the laser harmlessly struck the deck above. Ward's scream of pain was cut off when the princess's arrow went through his neck until the tip poked out his throat. He crumpled to the floor, his brain stem neatly cleaved in half by the arrow.

It all happened in an instant—two, three seconds at most. Cerise was in a fog. She'd been blocking Tie and Regan so hard she felt empty. They'd been bombarding her—Tie's emotions a jumble of fear and rage, Regan's physical pain nearly bringing her to her knees. She'd slammed some kind of mental door on them, but as she watched the SS, Ward, the stranger had called him, go down the door opened and she stumbled on the first step as she ran over to Tie and Regan. Tie had Regan in his arms, tenderly holding him up, trying not to touch the spear in his shoulder.

"Is he all right?" she cried, reaching for Regan, but pulling her hands back, afraid of hurting him.

"I'm fine," Regan gasped. "Christ, don't ever scare me like that again."

"Me?" Cerise was dumbfounded. "Me? You idiot, you're the one who was speared and held hostage, not me."

Regan's legs gave out and Tie lowered him to the deck. Cerise covered her mouth with her hands, smothering her sob of dismay.

"You two," he continued, his voice weak. "Should have left. Followed orders."

"I don't take orders from you," Tie said firmly, taking his knife from Esmerelda. Cerise hadn't even seen her collect the weapons. Tie looked at Regan and smiled wickedly. "At least, not outside the bedroom." Tie began to cut away Regan's vest.

"Haven't," gasped Regan, "been in bedroom yet."

"Oh my God, listen to you two!" Cerise yelled. "He's bleeding to death, Tie! Do something besides flirt with him!"

The stranger stepped up. "He'll be fine in a few hours, all better in a few days. He's a super soldier. It takes more than a little spear to put us out of commission." He looked down at Ward's dead body, shaking his head. "That's why you should never underestimate the pretty girls, Ward," he said wryly. He looked back up at Cerise. "Good shot, by the way."

"Great shot," Tie corrected him, feeling around the spear. Regan winced and clenched his teeth but said nothing. "Who the hell are you?"

"Martins, Gen8," the stranger replied.

"Yeah, I got that," Tie said sarcastically. "But who are you? Or better yet, whose side are you on?"

Martins crouched down beside Regan. "We're going to have to shove it all the way through. He can't be transported with that thing sticking out of his shoulder."

"No!" Cerise felt her stomach heave at the fear and pain radiating from her two men. My God, to push the spear through would be agony for Regan.

Suddenly the freighter was rocked by an explosion below them.

"What was that?" Cerise asked in a panic.

Tie was grim. "Hopefully it was the cargo bay doors and not the start of a chain reaction." He looked at Regan. "Are you ready?"

Regan nodded. "Do it." He looked at Cerise and she could see the pain in his eyes. "I'll be all right, baby. He's right, we heal fast. And we don't have enough time to debate. I have no fucking idea how he's got this ship wired. We're on borrowed time now." He closed his eyes and laid his head back on the deck. "Just do it."

"I'm on your side." Martins answered Tie's earlier question. "So tell your girl there to take the rifle off me and I'll hold him while you shove it through." Cerise looked over at Esmerelda in surprise and saw that she had Martins covered with Tie's discarded rifle. Tie nodded and Esmerelda lowered the gun.

"What do you want me to do?" Cerise asked, kneeling at Regan's head.

Tie looked up at her in concern. "This is going to be rough, Cerise. Are you sure?"

Before Cerise could answer Martins looked at Tie in disbelief. "She just saved all our asses by killing a Super Soldier with one expert bow shot after pretending to be hysterical for at least ten excruciatingly long minutes. And now you think she's going to get squeamish?"

Regan cracked a smile with pale lips, never opening his eyes, while Tie looked chagrined. "Good point," Tie mumbled and Regan chuckled.

"That's our girl," Regan whispered. He reached his good arm over his head and Cerise took his hand. He squeezed hers gently.

"Okay," Martins said as he rolled Regan onto his side. Regan groaned and Cerise nearly ruined everything by

292

throwing up. She swallowed the bile in her throat and prayed for the strength to get through this. Martins went on. "I'm going to kneel here and support his back against my legs while you pull. Princess, I want you to support his head the same way." They got in position and Cerise saw Tie wipe his hands on his pants nervously. "Make it quick," Martins said and Tie nodded jerkily.

He leaned forward and took hold of the spear and Cerise felt Regan tense. "I'm sorry, baby," Tie whispered and then he pulled hard, driving the spear three-quarters of the way through the shoulder. Cerise had to dig the toes of her boots into the deck to keep from being moved by the force of Regan's body as Tie pulled. Regan screamed and Tie pulled hard again. Martins grabbed the end of the spear behind Tie's hands and pulled and the spear came out with a sickening sucking sound that made Cerise gag. Tie threw the spear and it clattered across the deck. He jerked off his shirt and tore it in two and pressed the pieces against both sides of Regan's shoulder.

"Ah, God, Regan. Regan? Are you all right?" Tie sounded as if he was going to cry and Cerise realized she already was.

Regan nodded weakly. "Now..." he coughed weakly, "get us off this fucking deathtrap."

Tie carried Regan in the lift down to deck one. Martins talked fast on the trip down.

"You all need to lie low," he told them, which caused Regan to snort sarcastically. "What I mean," Martins explained flatly, "is no more blowing up Amalgamation freighters." He sighed. "The people I work for want to work with you. You've created quite a support network in this quadrant of the galaxy. At this point your efforts should move to political, nonviolent change. With the right support, you could be a viable opposition party."

"Who do you work for?" Tie demanded.

Martins sighed. "I can't tell you that. Not yet. Things are unstable, to say the least. Let me just reassure you that my superiors are at the highest level of both the political and military branches of the Amalgamation."

"Why should we believe you?" Cerise asked. The question was moot. She already believed him, but she wanted to hear his answer.

"Because I could have killed all of you back there. It would have been expedient and solved a great big problem if I'm the enemy. Instead, I helped you." He looked hard at Cerise. "Do you want to be queen of the galaxy so much that you're willing to ignore an olive branch that could save millions of lives? When I say my superiors are willing to work with you, I mean an end to corruption. Some of the issues on your agenda could become reality. No more forced labor. Reintroduction of displaced populations." He looked at Tie and Regan. "Cleaning up the IMF and cutting off funding for certain Military Sciences Lab programs, like extreme indoctrination and termination of faulty subjects."

"You realize we can't control the insurgents in other parts of the galaxy?" Regan's voice was barely a whisper, but they all heard him. "Our support here is tenuous at best. We have minimal contact with groups elsewhere. Why single us out?"

Martins smiled and the effect was strangely unsettling. Cerise thought that somehow a smile just wasn't supposed to look like that. "You underestimate your influence and your popularity. You may not control the rebels throughout the galaxy, but they will follow your lead. At least some of them. And that's enough for now."

Cerise sighed and exchanged glances with Tie and Regan. Their looks clearly said it was Cerise's call. Great, *now* they were willing to let her lead. She looked back at Martins. "No." Martins actually looked shocked for a moment before his face became unreadable again. Cerise shook her head. "Other than not killing us we've been given no reason to trust you, or whoever it is you work for. So no, no *official* truce." Martins gave her a very small smile, just the corner of his mouth tipped up, but for one startling moment he seemed not only human, but devastatingly handsome. Cerise actually felt a warm glow at his obvious approval. She blinked and the smile was gone.

"Unofficially?" Martins asked.

Cerise gave him what she hoped was a stern, calculating look. "Unofficially, there are things you could do to persuade me. If we're to be a viable opposition party, then Tie and Regan must be pardoned. They are my consorts and as such are an integral part of any government, or political party, that I may lead. They are royalty now, do you understand? And the entire galaxy will know it within a matter of weeks." She looked at Regan and he smiled grimly. She continued. "We will rethink any active resistance but we will not stop recruiting or training recruits. In return, the Amalgamation will put all political bounties, trials and executions on hold. We will not demand you release political prisoners at this time. At the end of six months I want assurances of good faith from your superiors and a scheduled face-to-face meeting."

Martins considered. "It could take years to make that happen." His look gave nothing away.

"You heard me," Cerise replied coldly, meeting his gaze confidently. "You have six months."

Regan spoke again, his voice hoarse. "I have certain obligations that must be met. I will do so, but I will consider putting further action on hold." He looked hard at Martins. "If at any time I feel that the princess is in danger because of this agreement, I will not hesitate to break it."

"What agreement?" Martins asked sarcastically with a raised brow.

Tie spoke up. "I feel the same, but I will include Regan in that. Someone has been going to a lot of trouble to catch him. I want that to stop. Now."

Martins tilted his head to the side and regarded all three. "They are under the mistaken impression that he is the force behind this rebellion. Once word gets out that you are a triumvirate of power, their efforts will cease, or will be focused elsewhere."

Regan closed his eyes and took a deep breath. "That's what I'm afraid of." He squirmed in Tie's arms. "Tie, put me down."

Tie hesitated. "Can you walk? Because I can carry you."

"I want your hands free in case we run into any hostiles."

When the lift stopped Tie lowered Regan's feet to the deck. Regan leaned against the wall for a moment and Cerise noticed his shoulder wasn't bleeding as badly as before. "The bleeding is slowing down," she said as she lifted a corner of Tie's torn shirt to peer at the wound. It looked ragged and incredibly painful. "Why can't I feel your pain?" she asked, searching but not finding a trace of the pain that had burned through her earlier. She couldn't remember when it had receded. Surely before they had to pull the spear through?

Regan shook his head. "I'm not sure. I think the physical sensations you get from me have to be wrapped up in some strong emotions. If I keep my emotions in check, you don't get the message." He chuckled humorlessly. "At least this damn shoulder is keeping the Tears at bay."

"God damn it," Tie growled, "what were you thinking to take off like that? We told you what would happen after the first time."

"So Carnelian Tears aren't a myth?" Martins had been watching their exchange avidly.

"No, they aren't a myth." Tie spoke curtly. "But the reality is far from the myth. Do we look like slaves to you?" He narrowed his eyes and raised his eyebrow and Martins held up his hands defensively.

"Just asking. Not slaves, got it." Martins was all business again. "So we have a deal?"

Tie, Cerise and Regan nodded. Martins stepped off the lift and backed toward the shadows. "In six months, then." In the blink of an eye he was gone.

Cerise shivered. "He gives me the creeps."

"He's Gamma Project," Regan said, weaving a little as he stood up. Cerise rushed over and wrapped an arm around his waist and he leaned heavily on her.

"Let me," Tie said, moving toward them, but Regan waved him off.

"I told you, I want your hands free. I'll be fine. We'll be fine."

"I've got him," Cerise told Tie firmly.

Tie smiled. "Yes, you do. Finally."

They moved off down the corridor toward the loading dock.

"So, what is Gamma Project?" Cerise asked, struggling to help Regan as he stumbled along.

Tie answered quietly from in front of them. "An experiment by the Military Sciences Lab. Gammas were trained to be emotionless, rational, get the job done at all costs. Not the extreme indoctrination they've been using on Gen10's and later generations, but something different altogether. It was a small group of specifically bred Gen8's, separate from the rest of us. No one knows exactly what they did, but the program was considered a failure. First, purely rational thought processes meant that the Gammas didn't always obey orders, not unless they thought it was the correct thing to do under the circumstances. They had very little loyalty — to the Amalgamation, the MSL, or the IMF. And, rumor has it, they learned the hard way that bottling up all those emotions will come back and bite you in the ass. I heard several just went apeshit at different times, offing themselves and whoever was in the vicinity."

"Jesus," Esmerelda muttered from behind.

"I thought they terminated all the Gamma subjects," Regan said, his voice rough as he gritted his teeth. They'd made a sling out of Cerise's tank top and she could see him holding his arm tightly against his chest, trying not to jar his shoulder.

Tie shrugged. "I guess not. Which is interesting. Makes you wonder who the hell is running the show."

"Who do you think Martins is working for?" Regan asked. It was obvious he was trying to keep his mind off his shoulder.

"My guess is Krys Xan, or Cartiere." Tie waved them to a stop and peered around a corner. It was clear and he motioned them on again.

"Halcion Cartiere? The head of the IMF?" Esmerelda asked in disbelief.

Cerise pondered it for a moment. "It makes sense. They've been awfully quiet about this revolution of ours. And we've heard some murmurs that all is not well in Amalgama. There's talk of overthrowing Xan. And Cartiere publicly refused to order troops into the mines in the Xy System when the workers went on strike for more food last year."

"If it is Xan or Cartiere," Regan growled, leaning against a bulkhead to catch his breath, "I don't find that comforting. When the leader of the Amalgamation and the head of the Interplanetary Military Forces have to look to a motley group of insurgents for support this is not a good sign."

Tie came over and checked his shoulder. He was apparently satisfied with the way it looked because he nodded and stepped back. "On the other hand, bringing the insurgents over to their camp, ending violent resistance in the galaxy and becoming the saviors of the previously malcontent could help to subdue the grumbles in Amalgama." He looked at Cerise. "Any thoughts?"

Cerise shook her head. "Not right now. All I know is that if it seems too good to be true, it usually is. And what Martins offered seems too good to be true. All we can do is wait and see what happens, because he was right about one thing. If accepting this olive branch could possibly save millions of lives and bring about political change, then I'll do it."

Tie pointed down the corridor. "The loading dock is that way. Cerise, you and Esmerelda get Regan on a ship. I've got to cut this freighter loose from the Smith gate. If it blows, it'll take out the entire gate."

The freighter jerked and shuddered, throwing all of them down on the deck. Regan groaned.

"We're moving," Esmerelda said, crawling over to Regan and helping Cerise lift him up again.

Tie smiled. "My guess is our new friend Martins realized the same thing. His timing is perfect."

"Creepy," Cerise said with a grimace and Regan chuckled.

"Some people would say what we can do is creepy." Regan sounded breathless, but, unbelievable as it was, stronger.

"You mean the mind, emotion thing?" Tie asked, gesturing between the three of them. "That's different. That's the Tears, the bond."

"Creepy," Esmerelda said flatly.

"Are you feeling better?" Cerise asked Regan in amazement. "Already?"

He nodded. "We told you, we heal fast. It still hurts like a bitch, but I can tell the bleeding has stopped. I've got some feeling back in my hand and arm. They were pretty numb for a while."

"Fucking amazing." Esmerelda was obviously impressed. "Can anyone sign up for that shit?"

Tie laughed. "Sorry. You have to be bred in a lab to have our amazing superhuman powers."

"Regan? Where the fuck are you guys? Did you cut this rusty piece of shit loose?" Conor's voice was pissed as it came out of the comm. "We are ready to go, now. So get your asses down here."

"We're on our way to the loading dock, Conor," Tie told him. "Find us a fast ship. Send the others off now."

"Conor," Regan added, "we'll meet you at the rendezvous point near T-Sdei Delta. That's where I want to offload those civilians. Put them down one ship at a time, with one crew member on each ship. Tell the crew we'll get them at the pick-up location in two days."

"All taken care of," Conor came back a moment later. "The last ship is heading out and your orders have been sent. I'm waiting for you on a sweet little cruiser that was hidden down here. Hurry up and let's get the hell out of here before the evil cavalry comes."

Cerise laughed. "Roger that," Regan said with a grin at Cerise. He held out his arm and she tucked herself against his good side. "Let's go."

* * * * *

Tie stayed on the bridge to oversee the evacuating ships. Conor and two of the men they'd brought with them from Quantinium were with him. Tie and Cerise had insisted that Regan go lay down in the captain's cabin. His shoulder felt fine, just a little sore. Okay, a lot sore, but he wasn't a goddamn invalid.

The woman, Esmerelda, followed them to the cabin door. Regan turned to her with a raised brow and she stopped, her eyes going wide with alarm and indecision.

"He told me to stay with her," she offered before Regan even spoke.

He smiled coldly. "I'm pretty sure he didn't mean while I was with her."

"You're hurt," she blurted out and then looked even more alarmed as the smile fell from his face.

"If I didn't think I could protect her from any threat on this ship, I'd be the first to order you into this cabin with us. Trust me when I tell you that I am feeling well enough to make your presence in there very uncomfortable." He turned and grabbed Cerise's hand, pulling her into the room behind him.

Esmerelda looked confused. "What does that mean?"

"It means we're going to fuck," Regan told her right before he closed the hatch in her face.

"Oh goody," Cerise said from behind him and Regan turned to see her unbuttoning her jacket. His smile returned with a vengeance. She paused and regarded him sternly. "Are you sure you're up to this?"

Regan tried to move his speared arm. He stopped and left it in the sling with a slight grimace. "You're going to have to be on top." He held his shaking hand out for her to see. "But I need you, baby, bad."

Cerise left off her buttons and came and undid his pants for him. She pushed them down over his hips and his cock was hard, rising high against his stomach. "Oh, God," she breathed. She backed up rapidly and ripped at her jacket, buttons flying.

She wore nothing underneath but the bandoliers and her matewaist. When she started to take them off Regan barked out, "No!" and she left them on with a grin.

She sat down on the bed and unlaced her boots, throwing the first one off in her haste to get undressed. "You like the bandoliers, huh?" she laughed.

"I like," Regan said with a hungry growl. He palmed his cock and masturbated while she watched. She licked her lips and threw the other boot, then tugged frantically at her pants. "Hurry," Regan panted, "I want to come inside you. But, Jesus," he bent forward at the pleasure just touching himself in front of her was giving him, "I'm close. Not even that fucking spear could take away all of it. I've been hard for hours."

"Get on the bed," Cerise ordered as she stood up and kicked off her pants. Christ she was so fucking gorgeous. How the hell had he stopped himself from having her all these years? Her breasts were firm and sweet, framed by the black bandoliers with the shining balls that would expand into energy arrows. Her nipples were already hard, dark pink in their arousal. The bandoliers draped across each shoulder and then dipped down past her slim waist to rest on her hips.

He walked slowly past her and let his hand trail softly from her stomach down to the tight curls between her legs. "You're wet. How long have you been aroused, Cerise?"

She shivered as his fingers slid down into her curls and then out again as he moved to the bed. "Since you fucked me last night," she moaned. "Since Tie fucked me the first time. Since the day I looked at you while we were sparring two years ago and saw you had a hard-on for me."

Regan sat down on the bed and scooted back. Cerise came over and piled the pillows behind him and he leaned back against the wall. She went to the end of the bed and pulled first one of his boots and then the other off, tossing them away as she had her own.

"I wish you had said something," Regan told her, aching for all the years they could have been together like this.

Cerise reached up and grabbed his pants. He rested on his good arm and raised his hips so she could tug them off. "I was afraid," she said quietly. "Afraid you didn't want me, at least not for more than a fuck. I was always so unsure of your feelings. And, I guess I wasn't ready." She got up on the bed and climbed up his body on all fours, like a cat. He could almost hear her purring. She stopped and lowered her head to nuzzle his cock and Regan groaned and thrust his hips at her, but he raised her head with a hand in her hair. "I'm ready now," she whispered.

Regan laughed weakly. "So am I and that's why sucking me is going to have to wait. I need to be inside you, Cerise, deep. I want your pussy right now. I'll take your mouth later."

Cerise continued up until she straddled his hips.

"That's my girl," Regan growled as he put his hand on her waist and adjusted her.

She sank down slowly onto his cock and Regan had to bite his lip to keep from crying out at the sheer bliss of her. She was hot and wet and tight and everything he'd ever wanted. He could feel her saturating him from the inside out. The essence of her filled his veins and his lungs, made his fingers and toes tingle, his mouth water. Everything about her was food for his starving soul. She took him to the hilt, her wet pussy resting against him. They stayed like that for a minute or two, just soaking each other up, grinding gently. She tightened her inner muscles, hugging him, milking him and he gasped. "Fuck me, baby," he groaned. "Fuck me hard."

Cerise moaned as she rose above him, letting his cock slide out until only the plump head remained inside her heat. "Oh, God, Regan, your cock feels so good. Did you know? Did you know it would feel this good?" She drove down on him as she spoke and shuddered with pleasure.

Regan shouted as she slammed back down on his cock. "Fuck, yes, that's the way I want it baby. Hard, take it hard." She pulled up and slammed back and he saw stars. She was so wet and the fuck sounded as good as it felt. "I knew how sweet it would be to fuck you, Cerise. I dreamed about it at night. I must have jacked off five thousand times to fantasies of you doing this." He leaned forward and bit her nipple and Cerise cried out and her pussy trembled around him.

"Fuck me, Regan," she said in shaky voice. "God, just fuck me."

He chuckled against her breast and sucked her nipple a few times. "I am, baby, I am," he whispered as he leaned back against the wall. His shoulder throbbed, but it was lost in the throb of his cock, his blood pounding through his body and pulsing until it was all one long, glorious aching beat. He slid down to get more leverage for his hips against the mattress and then held tight to her hip as he thrust up into her.

"Ah," Cerise gasped and fell forward, resting her hands on the bunk on either side of his chest. She leaned forward and licked his nipple and he held his breath. She nipped at it and his breath came out in a rush. When she sucked it into her mouth he groaned.

She worked his nipple for a minute or two and he held still, letting her, but finally he had to move again. He thrust up into her and she came off his nipple with another gasp. Then she began to fuck him back and the top of Regan's head nearly came off.

"Kiss me, kiss me, kiss me," Cerise chanted low and Regan pulled her head down to him, licked her mouth open and delved inside. He wanted to weep at how good she tasted, at how wonderful it felt. He moved inside her, his tongue, his cock and got lost in her. It wasn't until Tie spoke that he even realized someone had come into the room.

"This is not helping my concentration," Tie groaned. "I can feel everything you guys are doing up there on the bridge. I had to leave because they were all giving me strange looks."

Regan broke the kiss, but couldn't answer Tie. He couldn't think, couldn't breathe. He could feel his climax, which had been hovering in the background, roaring up, overtaking him when Tie's presence registered and suddenly he was fucking Cerise in front of Tie, Tie was watching, Tie wanted him...

"Tie, Tie, Tie," he groaned, not sure what he wanted or what he was saying. His cock felt so good buried in Cerise, so hard and hot cocooned in her soft, tight, wet heat. And Tie was here.

Tie fell to his knees beside the bunk. "I know, baby, I know," he murmured, leaning in and kissing Regan's sore shoulder. "She feels so good, it's so amazing inside Cerise. Let her take you, Regan, give it all to her. She wants it."

Tie's voice was low and rough and hot, his breath burning across Regan's shoulder as he whispered there. It felt like a brand and the heat from Regan's cock slammed up his spine and down his legs and then he was coming deep inside Cerise and she was crying out, climaxing around him. And all the while Tie was there murmuring those amazing things. His orgasm seemed to last forever, until he was drained and spent and fell back against the bunk, boneless.

He lay there for several minutes trying to catch his breath and make sense of the world again. Cerise lay against him, her head on his good shoulder and he could feel Tie's hair and occasionally his lips, from where he still knelt beside the bed. Tie was kissing and caressing both he and Cerise, on the back, the hip, the arm. It was soothing and yet not. A gentle, steady arousal and Regan could feel his blood heating again.

"Someone needs to be on the bridge," Tie murmured softly, "but it's not going to be me. I need to fuck."

Regan laughed and liked the way Cerise's body moved on top of him with his laughter. It was incredibly intimate. He wrapped his good arm around her and squeezed. "Get off me so I can go see what's going on."

Tie stood up next to the bed. He was still shirtless and Regan admired his smooth, broad chest, the way the light played across the planes of all the ridged muscles in his abdomen and the thin strip of light hair that disappeared into his clothes. Tie stripped off his boots and pants without preamble. Regan's heart caught in his throat when he saw Tie's cock, so long and hard and strong. The ridge running the length of his cock along the underside was prominently displayed as his erection reared along his stomach. Regan let himself imagine how it would feel inside him. "I'm coming in," Tie warned softly, "so if someone's getting out they better do it fast."

Cerise rolled off Regan. "I'll go," she said softly. Regan turned to her in surprise and she smiled ruefully. "You've been waiting over ten years. Enough is enough already."

But it wasn't right. Something inside him told him that. He didn't want his first time with Tie here, on a strange ship, without Cerise. "No," he said and hated the flash of hurt he saw in Tie's eyes. "Not here, not now." He couldn't explain it properly, so he just rolled off the bed. Tie stepped back to give him room and Regan wrapped a hand around his arm, shivering at how good Tie's skin felt against his palm. He looked at Cerise. "I'm not ready for people to know that I'm hiding in the captain's cabin fucking Tie." He turned back to Tie and saw confusion and hope. It was better than hurt. "When we get home, then we'll figure this out."

He let go and walked over to pick up his clothes and dress while Tie climbed on the bed with Cerise. In mere moments he heard Cerise gasp and then moan. Regan spun around to see Tie on top of Cerise, buried between her legs, fucking her while he held her hands down on the bed over their heads. The muscles in his ass flexed with each thrust, his arched back enticing in its curve. Tie looked at Regan over his shoulder. "I wanted to feel her still hot and wet with your cum." Tie closed his eyes and shuddered. "It's good, damn good."

"Tie," Cerise moaned, her head thrashing from side to side as he pumped into her ruthlessly.

"I'm going to fill you some more, baby," Tie whispered as he licked and nibbled on her shoulder. "Can you take it?"

Cerise was shaking her head but chanting, "Yes, yes, yes," when Regan opened the hatch with shaking hands and let himself out. Once he was in the corridor he could still hear them, still smell them, still feel each thrust of Tie's cock as if he were Tie and Cerise at the same time. He had to lean against the bulkhead until his legs were steady. This was going to be a long trip.

Chapter Twenty

ᔍ

It took three days to escort the evacuating ships to T-Sdei Delta and oversee the offloading of the passengers in such a way as to not draw the attention of the planetary authorities. They had to do it one ship at a time at different locations. Regan was worried that some of them would talk, but soon realized he needn't bother. According to the civilians they'd rescued, the rebels were now the heroes of the moment. It was good PR, but he was still nervous about the unwanted attention. All of his crew members made the rendezvous point and he breathed easier as they set a course for Quantinium.

As usual entering Quantinium's atmosphere and landing at the base was a harrowing ride, although the little cruiser handled extremely well. Regan wasn't sure who it had belonged to docked there on the freighter. He sincerely hoped it wasn't Martins, or the Gamma SS may have had more difficulty than he'd counted on getting off the freighter. Cerise refused any drugs for the trip and she handled it pretty well. Considering that Tie was fucking her senseless at the time it wasn't much of an accomplishment, but it was good to know there were alternatives to drugging her when they had to make a rough landing.

Christ, between him and Tie, Cerise had hardly left the captain's cabin in three days. Regan felt a little guilty about that, but Cerise seemed to take it in stride. He didn't know how she handled the two of them. She was such a tiny little thing and he and Tie were definitely not tiny, in any way. But she took it and begged for more. Just the thought of how many ways they'd fucked her in the last three days had him hard and ready again. He didn't think he'd ever get enough of her, or Tie for that matter. He and Tie had only been able to fuck

Samantha Kane

Cerise together once on the ship. One of them had been on the bridge almost every moment to oversee the mission.

He knew that now that they were back on Quantinium, Tie would want to fuck him. He hated to admit, even to himself, that he was nervous. But after waiting so long, what if it wasn't what Tie had dreamed of? Regan had never fucked another man, he honestly didn't know if he'd like it, or would be any good at it. He wanted Tie, but did he *want* Tie? Fuck, this is why he hated having too much time to think. He loved Tie. He knew that. But how would his crew and the rest of the people here react to the two of them having an intimate relationship, one which included Cerise, their perfect princess?

Regan rubbed his hand along his smooth skull. He knew it was a nervous gesture, but it was also unconscious. He never knew he was doing it until he was doing it. He rarely played poker because of it. The bridge hatch slid open and he glanced over his shoulder to see Tie smiling at him.

"Okay, she's ready."

The three of them were the last ones left on the ship. Regan's assistant Delroilinda had brought them all clothes and Cerise was taking forever to get dressed. He smiled thinking about it. Now that she had some pretty clothes she was turning into a typical woman. He was so far gone he actually enjoyed standing around waiting for her.

Tie was wearing a new outfit too. Regan had ordered it the day they'd arrived on Quantinium. It looked more regal than the hunter uniform he'd worn. The leggings and boots were the same, but he now wore a black jacket that was held closed with an elaborate sash. The jacket had no collar and a long vee opening in front that showed a great deal of Tie's smooth, muscled chest. It fell to his thighs with deep slits on the sides and the wide sleeves ended just below his elbows, showing off his heavily muscled forearms. Even in the more formal clothes he looked dangerous and sexy as hell.

Tie noticed Regan looking at his new jacket and grinned as he looked down at himself. "Pretty nice, huh?" Tie

308

considered Regan's signature leather vest. "We need to get you one of these," he declared running a hand down the front of his jacket. "You need to go more aristocratic bureaucrat than pirate, especially if the Martins' deal goes through."

Regan glanced down at his vest with a frown. "You don't think I look good in this?" He glared at Tie. "Cerise has always loved these vests. What's wrong with my vest?"

Tie laughed and walked over to Regan. He reached out a hand and stopped just a centimeter away from touching Regan's chest where the vest was unbuttoned and gaping open. He seemed to be waiting for Regan to say no, but the word wasn't there. Regan wanted Tie to touch him. He needed him to, to reassure him that this was right. Tie had stopped laughing. Regan didn't look at his face, but instead concentrated on his hand hovering there. When Tie finally moved his hand Regan stared at it as it slowly approached his chest and then sank against it one finger at a time. Tie's palm slid against him and Regan felt his heart stumble. Tie gently caressed that small area of Regan's chest left bare by the vest.

"There's nothing wrong with your vest," Tie whispered. "I was wrong. This is you. This is…perfect."

Tie's fingers pulled back and then he skimmed them over Regan's injured shoulder. The wound had closed, but it was still red and raw-looking. He knew he was going to have one hell of a scar. The muscles were taking a little longer to heal than he liked, but as Cerise said, it was a spear, not a needle. She and Tie were determined to baby him and he was equally determined to resume his regular schedule as soon as they got back.

"How does it feel?" Tie asked him, running his fingers over Regan's shoulder and down to the exit wound in his back. The light caress made Regan shiver and Tie smiled.

"It hurts." Lying to Tie wouldn't work, so Regan didn't even try. "But it feels better by the hour. I'll be fine. Hell, I'm fine now. By tomorrow I'll be able to do a little physical therapy on it and in a few days it will be good as new."

"You're going to have a scar." Tie kept circling his fingers around the wound lightly and Regan was getting hot, his blood humming in his ears. At least his question of whether or not he wanted Tie in that way was being answered, with a definite yes.

"I know," he answered. "Will it bother you?"

Tie stopped his fingers. After a pause he ran them down Regan's arm and then took his hand. He leaned down and kissed Regan's shoulder, his tongue flicking out softly and Regan's cock jerked.

"No, it won't bother me," Tie murmured.

Cerise appeared in the hatch. "Oops. Am I interrupting?" she asked teasingly, sashaying onto the bridge.

Tie pulled away from Regan with one last smoldering look. Regan felt the heat of it from his toes to the top of his head. "No," Tie said, turning to Cerise with a welcoming smile. "I was just kissing it to make it better."

"I don't think that's where he wants you to kiss him for maximum healing efficiency." Cerise didn't try to mask the amusement in her tone.

"You naughty pirate wench," Tie said suggestively.

"Yo ho ho," Cerise sang merrily and Regan laughed out loud.

"What do you think of your wench's new dress?" Cerise asked, spinning around in front of them.

Regan liked it, very much. It was green, a really dark green. It made her skin glow and her eyes look amazing—a deep, rich, purple. It hugged her curves until just past the top of her sweet ass and then it flared out, as if shyly hiding all her secrets under there. The top was modest, except in the way it tightly clung to her. The neckline was high, the sleeves long. As in almost everything she wore, her nipples stood out hard and mesmerizing atop the small, delectable mounds of her breasts.

"I like," Regan said hoarsely, Tie's attentions and Cerise's desirable body arousing him immensely.

"It screams 'princess'," Tie said, walking around Cerise in a circle as he pretended to listen to the dress. "No wait, it says I'm a princess who is fucking a pirate and a bounty hunter. Don't mess with me. I eat Super Soldiers for breakfast."

Cerise looked down at the dress with a concerned frown. "I had no idea this dress talked so much. It better keep its mouth shut once we get to the bay."

Regan's laughter burst out in surprise. Cerise and Tie looked at him with identical pleased grins. "Let's go, before someone comes looking for us and hears more than the dress talking." Regan walked up and took Cerise's elbow as he guided her off the bridge to the gangplank. "You are such a bad little princess," he murmured in an undertone as the three began to descend down to the bay. He could hear the muffled sound of hundreds of voices. "I always liked that about you."

"And now?" Cerise asked tartly. "Do you like it now?"

"No," Regan said louder as they reached the bottom of the gangplank and cheers rose from the crowd. "Now I love it."

Tie was again shocked at the crowd and the reception they received, only this time he was treated as one of them, as much a leader, as much royalty, as Cerise and Regan. It shook him. He felt a sense of belonging and acceptance here that he had never had before, not as a soldier and not as a hunter.

He saw immediately that Regan was going to try to brazen it out. As before he was inundated with clambering flunkies demanding decisions and with endless papers to read or sign. With a sigh he moved to Regan's bad side, protecting his shoulder from getting jostled. The arm was out of the sling, but still only at about fifty percent. Tie's abrupt movement and size startled the people pressing in on them on that side and

311

they jumped back. Esmerelda and Theo took the opportunity to move in and act as bodyguards.

Tie put his arm around Regan who stiffened momentarily and then relaxed into the familiar gesture. Tie felt a warmth, a pressure expand in his chest at Regan's reaction. He wasn't pushing Tie away. Did that mean he was willing to acknowledge their new relationship here, in public? Before he could consider the question further, Regan made it moot. He turned into Tie, so his shoulder was tucked into the safety of Tie's one-armed embrace. The move was so obviously intimate that Tie heard several people around them gasp.

Cerise took Regan's free hand, concern clouding her features. "Are you all right, darling?" There was a pause and then a burst of confused whispers flew across the bay like wildfire.

Regan nodded a little stiffly. "Yes, I'll be fine, but let's hurry this along. I'd feel better if I could relax in my office and deal with all of this one issue at a time."

Tie didn't need to be told twice. "Es," he said to Esmerelda, whom he had forged a rather close working relationship with over the last few days, "you and Theo are doing great. Keep them away." He looked around and spotted Regan's assistant standing a few meters away, waiting. "Delroilinda, take names and concerns here. Schedule the most pressing issues for later this evening. We'll deal with them over dinner. Everyone else can be fit in over the course of the next few days."

Delroilinda looked startled for a moment and glanced at Regan and Cerise briefly. At their calm acceptance of Tie's right to give orders she fell back into efficient assistant mode. "Of course, sir." Loudly she announced. "If you wish to speak with the royal family about anything it must first be cleared through me. Over here, please."

Tie hustled them through the crowd as quickly as he could, but all three of them had to acknowledge the welcomes and well wishes from the people assembled there. At one point

Tie had to kiss a baby. What the hell was that about, for Christ's sake? Finally they reached the relative safety of the corridor leading to Regan's quarters.

"I thought I was going to my office," Regan drawled. Tie wasn't fooled. He could hear the amusement and excitement in Regan's voice.

"Not yet," Tie said, pulling Regan a little closer. Regan didn't resist and Tie could feel his cock getting hard in anticipation. "How's that shoulder?"

Cerise was practically skipping along beside them. Clearly she knew what was about to happen too. They were home. Regan had said they'd talk when they got home. Tie didn't want to talk. He chose to believe by "talk" Regan had meant "fuck". It made perfect sense to him.

"It's all right, thanks to you," Regan answered him. "The pain meds are working, but if too many people got a good shove in like that one guy when we hit the crowd, I'd be hurting." He straightened the arm and frowned. "It's still awfully fucking weak though. This is taking way too long to heal."

"Well, we'll work it out. You can lie on your back, or be on top," Tie said soothingly and Regan came to an immediate halt.

"Excuse me?" he asked incredulously.

Cerise cleared her throat. "I'm, ah, just going to go ahead and get the hatch," she said before scampering down the corridor.

Tie turned slowly to Regan. "I'm going to fuck you. Now. Today. I've waited so long I can't even remember how long. I'm not waiting anymore. You said wait until we get home — we're home."

Regan showed the first signs of anger. "I said we'd talk about it. And it would be nice if you'd let me do that, talk about it. I'm not one of these people you've been ordering around with impunity the last few days, who seem to want

313

nothing more than to jump to do your bidding. I'm Regan, damn it, I give the orders around here."

Tie felt a muscle twitch in his jaw as it tightened in anger. "Fine. If it makes you feel better order me to fuck you. Then when it happens, you can take the credit."

Regan jerked out from under Tie's arm. "I'm going to my office. When you're ready to talk with something besides your dick, call me."

Tie didn't give a damn about being careful with Regan after that. He grabbed his good arm and yanked him into a tight embrace, wrapping his arms around Regan's back, trapping him. Tie grabbed the soft, sleek back of Regan's head and pulled Regan's lips to his. He ground out the next sentence with their lips touching, Regan straining his neck to break the contact. "My dick has been waiting to 'talk' to you as far back as I can remember. We've talked and talked and talked and I still want to fuck you so bad I'm rabid with it. So you will go into your quarters and you will strip and I will have my cock up your ass within the hour." Tie's voice turned brutally seductive. "And Cerise will be with us, watching."

Regan's breath was sawing from his lungs, the hot bursts against Tie's lips making his cock jerk in time. Tie fit his hips to Regan's and felt the other man's arousal, hard and throbbing along his own. It was heaven and Tie had to close his eyes for a minute and lean his forehead against Regan's. Regan had stopped fighting. He rubbed his head against Tie's in a rough caress that revealed his own inner turmoil at the erotic contact.

"Kiss me, baby. Kiss me and tell me you want it," Tie whispered, seeking Regan's mouth.

"Tie," Regan whispered and Tie could hear his indecision, his excitement, his fear.

"We just want to love you, Regan. Why are you making it so damn complicated?" Tie couldn't keep the frustration out of his voice.

Regan turned his head, but kept his cheek pressed to Tie's. "What if it's not what you've dreamed of, Tie? What if it isn't enough, for either of you?"

Tie ached at the insecurity in Regan's voice. He was so strong all the time, responsible for so many, that to discover this kind of vulnerability in him broke something in Tie and then rebuilt it, a little different than it was before, but stronger, deeper. He gently resettled Regan against him, sliding one arm under Regan's bad one. They were suddenly pressed together from chest to thigh and Tie shuddered and felt an answering response in Regan. Regan's arms went around him tentatively.

Tie nuzzled Regan's neck right below his ear, making him shiver. Tie smiled triumphantly against Regan's skin and nibbled a little. Regan's tremors increased. "Let me make it good. I'll make it good for you, you know I will," he whispered. He'd already noticed how much Regan liked his hot, suggestive, little whispers when they'd been fucking Cerise. Tie licked a path up the tendon along Regan's shoulder to his neck and Regan groaned. "Yes, see? See how good Tie is to you?" He moved his mouth to Regan's. Regan's lips were parted and his tongue darted out to lick them as Tie rubbed his lips across their warm, damp, plump folds. "Mmm," Tie groaned at the flick of Regan's tongue, "that's nice, baby." He paused and pulled back just enough to look into Regan's eyes, which were dazed and glassy with need. "Already this surpasses my dreams, Regan. The feel of you hot and ready in my arms. I will never get enough of you, never." Tie pressed his lips to Regan's, hard and demanding. He wasn't asking, he was taking—taking what was his, finally.

Regan surrendered, but in so doing he fought for control. His hand fisted in Tie's hair roughly, pulling the strands and sending a shock of heat straight to Tie's cock. Regan bit his lips and thrust his tongue into Tie's mouth, claiming that space as surely as he'd taken Tie's heart so long ago. Tie opened his mouth and let Regan have his way. Christ, he wanted to fuck Regan, but if Regan wanted to fuck him first that was fine.

315

Someone's cock was going to be buried balls-deep in the other one and Tie didn't really care what went where as long the three of them were together.

Regan sucked Tie's tongue into his mouth with a growl, drawing deeply on it and Tie felt the suction in his cock. It made his knees weak and he spun around and slammed his back into the bulkhead, taking Regan with him. Regan pressed his leg between Tie's and pulled weakly at Tie's hip with his bad arm. Tie followed the command and slid down just enough to ride Regan's heavily muscled thigh. Tie fell out of the kiss with a deep moan, his head hitting the bulkhead almost as hard as his back had a moment ago.

Tie felt a soft touch on his shoulder and looked dazedly to his left to see Cerise standing there. Her cheeks were flushed and her pupils large and dark with arousal. She spoke quietly. "You two might want to take this into our cabin before the clothes start coming off." She made a small gesture behind them. "You have an audience."

It took a moment for Tie to process what she was saying. Her presence there, while he and Regan were so lost in the throes of desire, spiked his need higher and hotter. God, he wanted her with them. He wanted her touching them when they fucked. An image flashed through his head and he spoke without thinking. "I want you to suck his cock, baby, while I fuck him."

"Christ," Regan whispered, burying his head in the curve of Tie's shoulder and biting him. Tie cried out, thrusting on Regan's leg. Cerise made a sweet little whimper in her throat and Tie felt Regan tense and then he jerked his hips and ground his cock against Tie's hip.

"Get out of the fucking corridor," a voice snapped at them and Tie instinctively moved, putting himself between Regan and Cerise and the threat. He glared over his shoulder and was shocked to see Conor bearing down on them, a small crowd of people gaping at them from the bend in the corridor about ten meters away.

Cerise's laugh was a little shaky. She reached out and took both Tie's and Regan's hands, pulling them toward the open hatch. "Sorry. Sorry. We just…you know. God, come on." She yanked and Tie stepped quickly to the hatch. He wrapped an arm around Cerise and pulled her between his legs to walk her backward through the hatch while he wrapped his other arm around Regan and leaned down to kiss him again. Regan bit his lip with a feral smile.

Regan turned back to the gaping onlookers. "Get out," he said calmly and the corridor was empty, except for Conor, in a matter of seconds.

Conor crossed his arms and looked at them in annoyance. "That's it. From now on, no fucking in the corridors. I mean it." The three ignored him as they tumbled through the hatch, a tangle of arms and legs and lips. Conor called out as the hatch door closed. "Did you hear me? Fucking newlyweds—" His voice was cut off as the door closed.

Regan knew what he needed to do. He knew what Tie needed, what he needed to give him.

"Fuck me, Tie," he whispered as Tie once again had him plastered to the bulkhead, Tie's hands running up and down the inside of his spread thighs, so close to his cock it burned and jumped for his touch. Tie was kissing one side of his neck, while Cerise was nibbling the other side. It was sheer heaven.

Tie leaned in and pressed his hand over Regan's leather-covered cock and Regan thrust into the heated palm holding him. "Are you sure?" Tie asked softly, rubbing his nose against Regan's cheek.

Regan nodded. "Yes, I'm sure." Tie pulled back to look at him and Regan realized Cerise had taken a step away and was looking at them with an odd mixture of happiness and sadness. He wanted to explain how he'd been feeling, what had made him run before and why he wasn't running anymore. Tie must have felt something in his body, because

317

he, too, took a step back and gave Regan some room, looking at him steadily. Tie seemed so solid, so trustworthy, so completely true that Regan wondered how he'd ever denied him.

"I was afraid," Regan told them honestly. He ran his hand over his bald head and smiled ruefully when he realized what he was doing. He looked at Tie. "For so many years it was, 'don't touch or die'. I spent so long pushing you away to save you, to protect you and I guess in my completely screwed up head I began to associate touching me with...bad things. Bad things would happen to anyone who wanted me, who touched me." He looked at Cerise. "And when I met you, that crazy idea was still firmly lodged in my subconscious." He shook his head, feeling that the explanation was unsatisfactory. "I know here," he touched his temple, "that's bullshit. But in here," he touched his chest over his heart, "there's a fear that knots my stomach every time one of you says you love me, or you want me."

Regan pressed his hands to the bulkhead at his sides at hip level and hung his head. He had to tell them the rest. "And I've been afraid since the prison hulk. I've been afraid that giving in, loving you, would make me less." He looked up, his concentration intense, his voice trembling. "I was Regan. I loved no one and no one loved me. I was fearless and fearsome. I needed to believe that. Believing it helped me gather the reins of this unruly rebellion and pull it into something that will make a difference." He looked at Cerise. "It helped me keep you safe." He looked at Tie. "It helped me bury the fury and pain of losing you." He shook his head again. "I've been afraid of what will happen if I stop believing it."

Tie moved in, but stopped at the quick shake of Regan's head. "No, not yet. Let me finish." He sighed and relaxed against the bulkhead, reaching up to gently massage his sore shoulder. "I realized, slowly, over the last few days that admitting I loved you both didn't make me weak, it made me

318

stronger. But I'm a stubborn bastard and I wasn't ready to throw in the towel yet." Tie chuckled at his admission and Cerise smiled, bringing her clasped hands to her chin and gazing at him over them with love. "That was it," he whispered, unable to look away from her. "That look, that love. God, Cerise, do you know what you have given me, by loving me so much?" He held out his hand and she eagerly came to him. He pulled her in and buried his face in her hair, hugging her tightly.

Tie came forward then and wrapped an arm around Cerise while he rested his forearm against the bulkhead next to Regan's head. "Cerise is the key, Regan. We couldn't find each other, not even when we were together back on Earth. In her way, Cerise and her love changed us both. She was the signpost that altered our paths and brought us to each other." Regan was nodding, unable to speak for the emotion clogging his throat. What Tie said next shocked and then soothed fears he'd been unable to voice. "I know you've wondered if I love you, Regan, or if I'm still in love with Egan. Just as you are not the man you were, I am not the man I was. Time, experience and, yes, Cerise, have changed us both." Tie pressed his lips to Regan's skull and Regan shivered at the streak of heat that burned through him. "The man I was left Egan. The man I am will never leave you, Regan. I love you more than my own life, my own happiness."

Regan whispered brokenly, "Yes." It was all he could say.

Cerise put a hand on his cheek and turned his face to her so she could kiss him. The kiss was tender and spoke loudly of the love she bore him, them. It humbled him.

"I don't know what made you two love me for so long, what made you wait for me. But thank God you did. Thank God." His voice was thick with emotion and he didn't want to talk anymore. Wryly, he thought that should make Tie happy.

Regan kissed Cerise as Tie began to make love to his head with his mouth. It was the most erotic thing he'd ever felt. Tie's lips kissed his scalp and his tongue licked. Regan

319

couldn't control his shaking arousal. Regan pressed Cerise's lips open and thrust his tongue into her mouth. He was immediately enveloped in her taste, her scent, her heat. Her tongue was sinuous and smooth as it danced with his, her teeth sharp as she softly bit his tongue. She sucked in his lower lip and bit it at the same time Tie took a nibble of his scalp and Regan cried out, jerking at the dual, fiery caresses.

Tie pulled away. "Come," he ordered gently. Regan obeyed and was surprised to find he felt no weakness in doing so. Tie unbuttoned and removed Regan's vest, being so careful of his sore shoulder that Regan had to stop him and kiss him. Again he was filled with the essence of his lover, as he had been when he kissed Cerise. He had never known such complete possession with a kiss as he experienced with Tie and Cerise. Cerise could be aggressive in her kisses, but Tie dominated with this one. He held Regan's head between his hands and positioned it as he liked as he plundered Regan's mouth with his tongue, deliberately setting a pace that foreshadowed what was to come. He filled Regan's mouth completely and Regan felt his ass grow tight as he imagined Tie's cock doing the same there. It was a powerful image and he moaned into Tie's mouth.

"I'll go," Cerise said quietly and both men jerked back from the kiss.

"What?" Regan asked, his voice disbelieving, hoarse with desire.

"You two have waited so long to be with each other," Cerise said as she stepped toward the hatch. "It should be private." She turned to go, but before she could hit the button to open the entryway, Tie grabbed her arm and spun her into his embrace.

"Oh, no, pretty." He wrapped his arms around her tightly and tucked her in between his legs, then thrust his hips into her. Cerise's head fell back and she moaned and Regan grinned in agreement. Yes, Tie's cock did that to him, too. Tie laughed and continued. "I've taken your virginity," Tie whispered hotly as he stepped back and pressed a hand to her mound, "here." She gripped his arm and gasped. "And here," Tie went on, sliding his hand around to her ass and squeezing. Cerise groaned. Tie pulled her into his arms again and then outlined her mouth slowly with his index finger. "But not here. Here is for Regan."

Regan was shocked. "What? You mean you never...?" He couldn't believe it. He hadn't initiated it, knowing that not all women liked to do that. He assumed when she didn't try again after that first time, right after they got off the freighter, that she'd done it with Tie and didn't like it. He'd never dreamed she'd never sucked cock before. He hadn't realized until that moment how much he wanted to be the first with her in something. He didn't begrudge Tie what he'd done with Cerise, at least not anymore. But this was a gift he hadn't let himself wish for.

Cerise blushed as Tie laughed wickedly. "Oh, I wanted to. But something just kept postponing it." He thrust against her again and sighed. "Oh, yeah, that kept getting in the way." He laughed self-deprecatingly. "I wanted to get in her pussy or her ass too much."

"Tie!" Cerise scolded, punching him in the arm.

Regan glided up behind her and pulled her arm slowly and gently behind her back, holding her prisoner. Her breathing ratcheted up and her legs spread instinctively. Regan felt a pulse begin to pound in his cock. "Don't get angry, baby," he soothed with a kiss on the back of her neck, "I understand. Your pussy and ass are so sweet I haven't been able to think of anything but fucking them for almost a week." Cerise groaned and Regan nibbled her neck with his lips and then bit her on the nape of her neck, not too hard, but clearly in a dominant move. She shuddered from head to toe and Regan's eyes nearly crossed as she pressed her ass back against his cock. "Oh, yeah, sweet heaven, baby," he crooned and then licked the spot he'd bitten. "Are you going to open up for me, Cerise? Are you going to take my cock in that pretty mouth?"

"Yes," she whispered and Regan felt a drop of pre-cum slip out of his cock. The feeling made him grit his teeth. Everything, absolutely everything with Tie and Cerise was more than it had ever been before. His whole body was so fucking sensitive. Then he remembered he was getting shadowy reflections of everything Tie and Cerise were feeling. It had been more powerful on the ship from Quartus Seven, but Regan liked this mellow feeling better. It hummed behind his emotions and physical sensations, heightening them, but not taking them over.

"The feelings, the...creepy exchange," Regan said breathlessly, unable to think of a better description. "They're a lot mellower now for me. What about you two?"

"Okay," Cerise said with a shiver, "yeah, that's what it is, why everything seems amplified." She groaned and rubbed herself against the two men. "God, that feels good. Not crazy, like on the ship, but just...good." She paused. "Can we call it something else besides the creepy exchange?"

Tie snorted with laughter. "It feels better than good." He snaked a hand around Cerise and with a hand on his ass pulled Regan's hips tight against her. All three of them groaned. "Tears, we'll just call it the Tears."

Cerise nodded, bumping into Regan's chin. He jerked his head to the side, but the pain was inconsequential compared to the pleasure.

Tie stepped back abruptly and began to pull off his clothes, fumbling in his haste. "Fuck. Now," he grunted as he yanked off a boot.

Cerise scrambled to undress, but got stuck on the buttons running down the back of her dress. Regan laughed and pulled her to him and began to unbutton them. Tie looked at him over Cerise's shoulder and the look was so hot Regan began to sweat. "That's taking too long," Tie growled and Regan watched, fascinated, as Tie put one hand to his cock and stroked along its length. God, that cock — it had Regan's mouth watering and his ass clenching. He took hold of the two sides of Cerise's partially undone dress and ripped. Buttons flew everywhere and, because his strength was unevenly distributed, the dress tore down one side, a chunk of it hanging by loose threads.

"Regan!" Cerise yelled, spinning around as she tried to look behind her. "My new dress!"

Tie grabbed her shoulders and yanked the sleeves down her arms. "We'll buy you twenty new dresses if you'll get out of this one and suck his cock."

Cerise stopped protesting with wide eyes. She stepped out of the dress. "Fuck the dress," she muttered and Tie and Regan both laughed.

Cerise and Tie turned to him with narrowed eyes. "You're still wearing clothes," Cerise accused. "I gave a dress to the cause. Strip."

Regan looked down at his pants and boots ruefully. "I'd love to sweetheart, but," he gently waggled his lame arm, "I'm handicapped."

Tie took one hand and Cerise the other as the led him to the bed. "Sit," Tie ordered, pushing him down gently. When he was seated they removed his boots. It was so sweet, so domestic that Regan got choked up again. Christ! He was never going to make it through the afternoon without humiliating himself with tears.

When his boots were off, the other two stood before him. Tie, not surprisingly, was choked up by lust and emotion. "Oil, or some kind of lubricant?" he asked. "Have you got any?" The question had the blood fleeing Regan's brain for other, tenderer regions. He nodded.

"In the medicine chest, in the bathroom." He gestured to the right. "I've got some massage oil." Even the sound of his own voice rumbling out from deep in his chest gave Regan pleasure.

"Get his pants off," Tie ordered Cerise as he backed toward the bathroom. He spun around and strode purposely into the small, adjoining area.

Cerise winked at Regan as she pushed him back to lie on the bed and he grinned back in understanding. God, it was sheer heaven to share such intimate moments with her at last. He undid his pants and lifted his hips as Cerise tugged them down. "This makes the second time you've had to undress me to have your way with me."

Cerise looked at him archly with an amused smile. "Is that what I'm doing? And here I thought you were getting your way. After all, you're going to be in the middle."

Regan closed his eyes with a shudder of longing.

Tie returned from the bathroom with a small bottle of oil. When he saw Regan naked on the bed he threw the oil down next to him on the sheets and prepared to dive on top of him. Cerise recognized the signs.

"Tie, no!" she yelped, jumping up to put a hand on his chest, stopping him. "His arm. Don't throw yourself on top of him, you'll damage something and then we'll have to wait again."

Tie shuddered as he stopped his forward momentum and his muscles protested. "God, Regan, I forgot. You look so...and I just forgot everything else in the need to touch all of you, to feel you beneath me."

Cerise saw Regan give a little shiver of desire as his stormy eyes shone brightly in the light of the cabin. "Yes, on top of me," he told Tie and held out his hand.

Tie wasted no time climbing on the bed gently and lowering himself over Regan. The two men groaned as Regan's legs fell open and Tie nestled between them. Cerise's heart began to pound in her chest and she felt a flush of desire sweep up her chest to her face. Tie lowered his forearms to the bed and pressed his stomach and chest against Regan's and

Cerise saw him bite his lip as Regan arched his neck and swallowed deeply at the sensation.

They were beautiful, amazingly, stunningly beautiful together. Separately they were gorgeous, irresistible even, but together they blew her mind. Regan with his luminescent skin, sleek skull, lean muscles and his muscular thighs hugging Tie's slim hips. And Tie, his tight, sweet ass clenched as he rubbed against Regan, the muscles in his long back undulating with his movements, his golden skin and shining caramel hair so warm against Regan's cool shimmer.

Cerise shivered with desire. She wanted to touch them. No, she *needed* to touch them. Almost as if they could feel the growing hunger in her, Tie turned his head and Regan opened his eyes and looked at her.

"Come," Regan whispered and he held out his hand palm up, inviting her into their embrace. "Come and love me."

Tie turned back to Regan and after looking at his face for a moment he leaned down and began to tenderly kiss Regan's neck and shoulder. Regan's hips jerked at the first touch of Tie's lips and Cerise broke free of whatever had been holding her back. She approached the bed on unsteady feet and took Regan's hand. His fingers closed tightly around hers as he closed his eyes again and arched his neck into Tie's kisses. Cerise climbed on the bed, careful not to jostle Regan's shoulder too much.

Tie licked a path along Regan's collarbone and Regan moaned. "Oh, God, that feels so good." He licked his lips and Cerise's nipples got so hard they ached. Regan kept talking. "I thought about this, about what your mouth would feel like on me, Tie, as I watched you make love to Cerise."

"What does it feel like, lover?" Cerise whispered, encouraging him to talk more. She loved to listen to her two men make sex talk. It was devastatingly arousing and pushed her to the edge to hear what they liked, what they wanted, how they felt.

"I—" Regan broke off with a little cry as Tie leaned down and ran the flat of his tongue over Regan's hard nipple. "How can I describe paradise?" Regan asked in a hoarse whisper. "When you both touch me, when you kiss me, I'm lost. Lost in the essence of you, the feel of you, the smell of you, the touch of you. You become part of me and I become part of you and it feels so damn good I want to cry."

"Regan," Tie said, his voice shaky. He raised his head and pressed his lips to Regan's softly. Regan didn't want soft. That became clear when he lifted his head from the bed and pressed his open, seeking mouth hard against Tie's. Tie's hands came up to frame Regan's face as the kiss turned almost desperate.

Cerise couldn't wait any longer. She had to be a part of them. She crawled over and straddled Tie's ass, her knees resting on the bed just outside of Regan's waist. She was spread wide and pressed her wet, throbbing pussy against Tie's ass, rubbing there. The smooth skin over hard muscle felt so good against her sensitive lips she groaned and so did Tie as he broke the kiss with a gasp.

"Damn, yes, baby," he told her as he thrust his ass up into her. "Hump my ass, just like that."

Regan's good arm came around Tie's back and his fingers pressed deeply into the muscles there, pulling him back down. "You hump my cock," he whispered and a sigh mixed with a groan escaped as Tie obeyed.

Cerise leaned down and began to lick and nibble Tie's warm, salty skin. Her hands caressed his back as she kissed each vertebra there, starting at the top. She moved down until she kissed the last little bump in his back, just above the crease of his ass. She couldn't resist dipping her tongue into the sweet little dimple at the top of the crevice. Tie nearly came off the bed.

"Fuck!" he shouted, as he spread his legs, pushing Regan's wider. Cerise could tell it took every ounce of Tie's control not to buck against her mouth. She placed both hands on his ass cheeks and squeezed and Tie groaned like a man in pain.

"Did you like that?" she purred, smiling, thrilled that she could make a man of Tie's strength lose control. She dipped her tongue in again, sliding it down a little further, into the incredible heat of his crease which was damp with perspiration. She tasted the sweat there and her eyes nearly rolled back at how good it was.

"Yes," he hissed. "God," he shook his head, "I've done that to others, but never had it done to me. Now I understand why they enjoyed it so much."

Cerise slapped his ass, hard and this time Tie did buck, but his accompanying groan wasn't one of pain. "You will not speak of past lovers while you are fucking us," Cerise told him sternly. "Do you understand?"

"Yes, your highness," Tie ground out and Regan grabbed a fistful of his hair, angling Tie's head until he looked into Regan's eyes. "When you fuck us, you will call her Cerise."

Tie's breathing escalated and Cerise could feel the trembling in his legs. He was wild with lust. She and Regan were just holding him in check, but for how long? The thrill that chased down her spine at the thought was delicious. How she wanted to see Tie lost to the desire, unable to hold back, as he'd been that first time with her and so many times since. When he threw his control away and fucked like a wild man he made her scream. She wanted to see him make Regan scream. Cerise's pussy actually spasmed at the mental image.

"Yes, Regan," Tie whispered, repentant. "Cerise, she is Cerise."

"Good boy," Regan growled and then pulled Tie's head down for a voracious kiss. Regan's hand snaked down Tie's back until he palmed the sweet curve of his ass. Cerise moved her hand down and caressed Tie's inner thigh as he shuddered. She placed little licking kisses down the center line of his ass and Tie actually whimpered against Regan's mouth.

At the sound Regan's fingers tightened, pulling until his crease widened just a bit and Cerise obeyed his unspoken command. Her tongue dipped in and ran down the length of his ass, the tip pressed tight against him. When she reached the tight, puckered hole in the center she paused briefly and ran her tongue around it. He tasted salty, with the essence that was pure musky Tie. Tie cried out and she smiled against him as she moved on.

Cerise couldn't believe what she was doing. But it felt good to her and obviously felt good to Tie and was clearly what Regan wanted. She could find no embarrassment, no hesitation inside herself. This was right, she and Regan loving Tie was right, the three of them loving one another in whatever ways pleased each other was right. There was no wrong between them and she knew there never would be.

Tie's ragged breaths cut through the air as he struggled to speak. "If...if you want to fuck me first, Regan, I'm on board with that." He cried out as the flat of Regan's hand came down sharply on his ass.

"Oh, no, lover," Regan purred, thrusting his hips up against Tie. "I want your cock in my ass. I've waited ten long years for it. I want your cock in my ass while Cerise sucks me hard and deep. You promised. And you will live up to that promise. Both of you."

Cerise's mouth began to water as chills of excitement raced across her skin. "Yes, Regan," she answered softly, making sure she sounded appropriately submissive. She liked this game.

"Yes, Regan," Tie echoed her, in a soft, obedient tone that nearly brought Cerise then and there. God, she *loved* this game.

Tie couldn't believe how incredibly turned-on he was at playing the submissive for Regan. The thought of he and Cerise being Regan's toys was mind-bendingly erotic.

"Get the oil and prepare me for your cock," Regan ordered him in that silky, commanding purr that made Tie's balls pull up tight with lust. With a shudder Tie felt his cock harden to impossible lengths. Tie sat back on his heels and then reached for the oil which had rolled over next to Regan on the bed.

"Cerise, get over here and put your mouth on me," Regan continued, his voice raspy and Tie looked up to see him staring fixedly at the oil in Tie's hand. When Tie pulled his hand back and began to uncap the small bottle Regan demanded, "What are you going to do? Tell me."

Cerise moved from behind Tie and for a moment he missed her warmth. Then she crawled up next to Regan and straddled his chest. Tie could see Regan's fingers playing along the matewaist she always wore now. Regan groaned as she pressed that hot, wet pussy that had recently ridden Tie's ass against Regan's chest and rubbed. Tie had to close his eyes and swallow hard to keep from reaching forward and shoving a finger inside her to feel her velvet soft, slick walls, to test how hot and wet she was. The idea that he and Regan, together, getting ready to fuck, was arousing her made Tie ache with the need to fuck.

He cleared his throat. "I'm going to pour oil on my fingers and down into the crease of your ass and then I'm going to finger-fuck your ass. First with one finger, then two. When you can take three comfortably, when you're fucking them and it feels good, then I'll replace my fingers with my cock."

"Oh, God," Cerise moaned as she leaned forward along Regan's stomach until her mouth hovered over his hard cock. "I want to watch. I want to see you fuck him."

"Wait," Regan ordered, his voice harsh. Both Tie and Cerise froze. Tie's heart beat a rapid, panicked tattoo in his chest. Had Regan changed his mind?

Regan wiggled and adjusted his position, shoving two pillows behind his head. "Cerise, lean back more," he murmured, "I want to eat this pussy while you two work me."

Tie released the breath he'd been holding and he could hear how shaky it was. He clenched the fist not holding the small bottle of oil, trying to control the wild need coursing through him. It was taking over, driving him, just as it had that first time with Cerise. "I'm going to lose it," he whispered. "I can't hold on much longer."

Regan looked at him tenderly, but his voice was firm. "You'll hold on as long as I tell you to. I'll tell you when you can lose control."

Surprisingly Tie could feel his body accept Regan's domination before his head could protest. His breathing evened out, although it was still heavy and the throbbing beat in his cock became a soft, insistent pulse. "Yes, Regan," he whispered and he knew that Regan could see the heat, the desire burning in him. But Regan just smiled as he pulled Cerise's pussy to his mouth.

Cerise was leaning over, reaching for Regan's cock, when his tongue licked a long path through her slit. She gasped and braced one hand against Regan's stomach as she arched her back and thrust against the mouth feasting on her. Tie could hear how wet she was. "Take him, Cerise," Tie told her. "Take him in your mouth. Show me." Cerise was trembling and Tie didn't know what to do, how to help her. Without thinking he leaned down and took the head of Regan's cock in his mouth, sucking gently. Regan's hips came off the bed and he tore his mouth from Cerise with a gasp. Tie pulled back and Regan's cock fell from his lips, so hard it bounced and then lay rigid along Regan's stomach. "Like that," Tie whispered, seducing Cerise with his words as much as he'd seduced Regan with them. "Love it, Cerise. Kiss it, take it. Do what feels good. Can't you feel it?"

"Yes," Cerise gasped, "yes, I can feel it and it's killing me. God it feels so good." She leaned in then and took half of

330

Regan's length into her mouth and her cheeks hollowed as she sucked hard, pulling her mouth down to the head and then sliding up again. Regan groaned.

"Yes, baby, suck it just like that. Perfect." Regan's voice was rough, the sound racing along Tie's nerves. Cerise set a slow pace and with each bob of her head she took more of Regan until almost his full length was sheltered in her warm, wet mouth. Tie closed his eyes and deliberately sought out the connection. He found it amid the multitude of sensations bombarding him. There, he could feel the pull on his cock, the heat of her mouth and her saliva surrounding him. He groaned with Regan.

"I can feel it," he told them, his hips thrusting in time with her suckling.

"Hurry, Tie," Regan ground out. "Fuck me. I can't last long with her sweet mouth tormenting me. And I want you inside me when I come."

Tie felt the same urgency. He adjusted Regan's legs so his knees were bent and splayed wide. He wasn't high enough. Tie looked around and found two more pillows lying on the floor next to the bed. He reached down and grabbed them. "Lift your hips," he told Regan. "I need to put these pillows under you to raise you up."

"Off," Regan growled, his fingers pressing deeply into Cerise's hips as she devoured him. "Get her off, so I can move." Tie reached down and fisted his hand in Cerise's hair, pulling her up sharply. She came off Regan with a cry of dismay.

"No, baby, relax. I'll give him back. I just need to raise him up, Cerise, so I can fuck him. Let me fuck him, baby." Cerise scrambled up, panting. Regan lifted his hips and Tie shoved the pillows under him and then pressed him back down. "There. Take him, Cerise, suck him." Cerise crawled back on top and without a word swooped down to take Regan in her mouth again, as if he was water, air, the very sustenance her body craved. Regan pressed his face in between her legs, pulling her hips down, in the same desperate way.

With shaking hands Tie tipped the bottle over Regan's crease and watched the oil drip and then run down toward the tight hole he needed so badly. He quickly placed his finger against Regan's ass, catching the oil. He smeared it around his anus and all over his finger and then he pushed inside with no warning. He stopped at the first knuckle when Regan's hips shot off the bed and he cried out.

"Tie!" Regan sounded like he was strangling.

"Too much?" Tie asked, concerned. "Do you want me to stop?"

"Not if you want to live," Regan growled. "That feels so damn good. How far in are you?" Regan pressed his head back in the pillows and closed his eyes tightly.

"Only to the first knuckle."

"Thank God," Regan said on a shaky sigh. "That feels so good and I was hoping there was more."

Tie chuckled. "Oh, there's more, baby. I've got lots more for you." He pulled the finger out until only the tip still nestled snugly in the tight space. More oil gathered on his finger and then he slowly, firmly, pressed it all the way in. Watching his finger disappear into Regan's ass was one of the most erotic things Tie had ever seen. Regan's groan of pleasure was surely one of the most arousing things he'd ever heard.

"More, Tie," Regan panted, pressing down on his hand. "I want more."

Regan couldn't focus on just one sensation. The taste of Cerise on his tongue, the feel of her mouth on him, hot and wet and sucking, the knowledge that his was the first cock to breach that space, were enough to drive him crazy with need. But Tie, his finger moving in and out of Regan's ass, his hard cock pressed tight to Regan's thigh, that pushed him beyond need, beyond desire. He was in a place he'd never been, where everything in his whole world centered on the feelings the three of them created together.

He was in a loop of pleasure, experiencing his own and shadowy reflections of what Tie and Cerise were feeling. He knew Cerise loved the feel of his cock in her mouth, loved the width and length and heat of it, the salty taste on her tongue, the vein pulsing from head to root. It was almost as if the cock was in his mouth and he suddenly desperately wanted to suck Tie. Later, next, after this round he'd take Tie in his mouth and learn his taste and the texture of his cock. The thought made him groan and he gripped Cerise's hips harder, pressed her pussy against his open mouth and thrust his tongue inside her. And groaned again. She was so hot and tight. Her lips, her walls, were all swollen with arousal and she was so wet, so deliciously sweet and spicy feeding him her cream. Cerise bucked against him with a cry around his cock as he rubbed the tip of his tongue over the rough patch of sensitive tissue inside her.

Because of the Tears and their connection Regan knew a second before he did it that Tie was going to thrust two fingers inside him. He tensed and Tie stopped.

"Relax, baby," Tie crooned, "relax and let me in. It will be good, Regan, so good. Tie will make it good. Let me in."

Regan unconsciously reacted to Tie's voice, relaxing and the fingers pushed deep inside him. There was a slight sting that faded as Tie pulled them back and thrust them in again. Pleasure bloomed in its place. Then Tie hit a spot that had Regan crying out and bucking, fucking those fingers desperately.

"Oh, yeah, baby, like that," Tie whispered. "I've got you now."

Regan couldn't respond. Every instinct inside him demanded he fuck something, that he dominate it and fuck it and make it come. He voraciously ate at Cerise's pussy, licking, sucking, fucking her with his mouth and fingers. He shoved two fingers in her pussy as he tormented her clit and then pushed his thumb, slick with her cream, into her ass. He moved his fingers to the same rhythm Tie was using in his ass and his head nearly exploded at the eroticism of it.

"Regan!" Cerise cried out, pulling off his cock. She was panting, fucking his mouth and fingers, beyond reason as she reached for the climax only he could give her. She arched her back so her hard, sensitive nipples were rubbing along his stomach with each thrust. He felt the carnelian on her matewaist tapping against his chest with each move. She tried to move back down to suck him again, but Regan stopped her.

"No, baby, hold off. I don't want to come yet and I'm too close. Wait until Tie is inside me."

At his words Cerise whimpered and Tie pushed a third finger into him. Regan felt only pleasure this time and fucked against Tie's hand, showing him how much he liked what Tie was doing. He couldn't speak, his mouth was buried in Cerise and he felt her inner walls trembling with her oncoming release.

"Finish her, Regan. Finish her, so she can watch me fuck you." Tie's voice rasped out, raking Regan's nerve endings. He was so far gone that he'd lost control of his auditory sensors. He could hear the pounding of Cerise's and Tie's hearts, their breath screamed through him and the sounds of fingers fucking wet, slick flesh rode him hard past the point of any control.

Cerise shattered. The feel of Regan's hands and mouth on her, the desperate edge to Tie's voice and the anticipation of watching her two men fuck for the first time brought her climax. She felt her muscles clamp down on Regan's fingers and as she cried out Tie roughly tipped her head up with his free hand and crashed his mouth down on hers.

Cerise hung on as she was bombarded with overwhelming pleasure. Her fingers dug into Regan's thighs as she kissed Tie back wildly, biting his lip and moaning in ecstasy. Regan kept his fingers rubbing over the most wonderfully sensitive areas inside her. The fullness of being filled both front and back was bringing on smaller explosions within her and Cerise simply let it take her, throwing aside her control and trusting Regan and Tie to catch her.

When it was over she saw flashes of bright lights behind her closed eyelids and she was dizzy and off balance.

"Whoa, girl," Tie said softly and he braced her as she collapsed against Regan.

She buried her nose in Regan's springy nest of curls, right next to his cock and when she opened her eyes she could see them both, Regan's cock right in front of her and Tie's resting along Regan's inner thigh. Both were hard, the heads swollen, Tie's flushed red with his arousal and Regan's almost purple under his deep green shimmer. She realized the green in his skin became more pronounced when he was aroused. She longed to pull the heat and hardness of both of them into mouth.

"Can I suck you both, at once?" she asked breathlessly. "I want to do that sometime."

Regan was kissing her inner thighs tenderly, but froze at her words. "Fuck, yes," he said hoarsely and then he gently bit her thigh, making her shudder as the pleasure rose in her again.

Tie choked out a laugh. "And she's back. That was a quick recovery."

Cerise raised her head just enough to rub her nose in Regan's pubic hair. He smelled so wonderful, he and Tie, she'd never get enough of it. And now their scents mingled together, Regan smelled like Tie and Tie smelled like Regan and they both smelled like her and the result pushed some button in her, something that made everything fall into place.

"I love you," she whispered, overwhelmed, "I love you both so much."

"Cerise," Regan said, his voice breaking at the end, with emotion, with pleasure, with something unspoken. Tie leaned down and kissed her back, rubbing his hand down over her back and ass and Regan groaned. "God, that pressed you deep inside me, Tie, pushed you against my cock. I need it. I need you to fuck me. Please, Cerise, sweetheart."

Cerise could tell he wasn't fully in control of what he was saying anymore. She knew that place, the one where Tie's hands and cock were all you could think of. She climbed off Regan and he cried out in denial. Cerise lay down next to him and ran a caressing hand over his chest, rubbing her palm in circles over one of his hard nipples. Leaning up she pressed her lips to his and spoke as she rubbed her mouth gently back and forth, tasting herself there on his damp lips. "We'll fuck you, baby. Is that what you want? Watch him, Regan. Watch him fuck you."

Cerise pulled back and Regan raised his head off the pillow to glare at Tie. "Fuck me, now."

Tie's eyes were burning, his pupils dilated, soaking up the light in the room and reflecting it back. He was so sexy, kneeling between Regan's splayed thighs, one hand on Regan's knee and the other pressed tight to Regan's ass, three fingers deep inside. Cerise saw the muscles of that arm flex and Regan winced, his hips jerking. Tie let his other hand slide slowly down Regan's leg until he let go and wrapped his fist slowly around his own cock. "Is this what you want?" he asked silkily, stroking himself.

Cerise watched a drop of pre-cum slide out of his slit and over his head. Out of the corner of her eye she saw Regan lick his lips and her pussy clenched.

"Yes, damn it," Regan growled, "give it to me."

"Say it," Tie demanded. "Tell me I can lose control now."

Regan smiled darkly. "Not until you're inside me. Once you're inside, I'll let you do what you like. But you have to give it to me first."

"Oh, God," Cerise breathed. She was so turned-on by the two of them she thought she might come again just watching them. She scooted closer and thrust her pussy against Regan's hip.

He looked down at her, his smile triumphant. "You like this, don't you? You like watching Tie and me."

"Yes," she moaned. "God, Tie, fuck him, please. I can't take much more."

Tie laughed and pulled his fingers out of Regan. Regan shuddered deeply, his hips instinctively thrusting, seeking. He needed to be filled. Cerise could sense his need, his desperation for Tie and his desire for her as well. He wanted her mouth on him again.

"I'll suck you at the end, baby," she whispered, kissing his chest, "when you're ready to come."

Regan looked at her in shock. "How did you..."

Cerise laughed, the sound low and throaty. She liked it. It was sexy. She liked being sexy. She gave Regan a knowing smile. "The Tears. I own you now, remember? I know everything."

Regan smiled back. "Do you now? Everything?" His smile vanished and his head fell back as he gasped. Cerise looked down and she saw the head of Tie's cock pushing into Regan.

"That's right, Regan, take me inside," Tie told him roughly. "You want it, you got it."

Regan spread his legs wider and brought his head up, his look intense and hot enough to burn. "Show me. Show me how you fuck me."

Tie's nostrils flared as he answered Regan's look with one of his own. He didn't say a word, he just reached out and hooked his hands beneath Regan's knees and lifted his legs. It brought Regan's hips and ass up and Cerise could clearly see Tie's cock inside Regan. Tie flexed his hips and his cock went deeper.

"Ah, God, Tie," Regan groaned, "that's perfect. Do it. All of it."

Tie braced his knees and pulled his cock out until just the tip remained. Cerise held her breath. She knew what was coming, felt the anticipation of both her men thick in the air. After a breathless moment Tie thrust and the length of his cock disappeared into Regan. Regan cried out, his hips jerking and he fell back on the pillows.

"Move the pillows," Tie barked at Cerise, his control held by a thread. He shook his head. "I'm sorry, I'm sorry." He looked at Cerise and saw the understanding there. It was a relief, a balm. She knew him so well, she understood him and what he needed, what he wanted. "I can fuck him better if his back is flat on the bed. And I don't want to hurt his shoulder."

"Do it," Regan rasped. He raised himself up again, his arms shaking. His eyes met Tie's and Tie could see his own desperate need reflected there. Cerise pulled the pillows from behind his back and threw them to the floor.

Tie barely waited for Regan to lie back before he pulled out and thrust in again. Regan was so tight, so hot and slick with the oil. He felt so fucking amazing. Tie was glad he'd never fucked another man. This was for Regan, only for him.

"Does it feel good?" he made himself ask. If it didn't he'd make himself stop. He would.

"Are you fucking insane?" Regan asked with a disbelieving bark of breathless laughter. "It feels better than good. Christ, Tie, fuck me now."

"Say it," Tie demanded.

Regan took several deep breaths and deliberately scooted down the bed a little, pressing closer to Tie, pressing Tie deeper. Tie shook with his desire, with the effort to hold back. "Take me, Tie. Do what you want. Lose control."

Tie dropped Regan's legs and grabbed his hips. His heart was trying to pound its way out of his chest, out of his cock, as he pulled back and then thrust hard and fast. He set a punishing pace, but Regan wasn't protesting. Tie was holding him so hard he knew he'd leave bruises and got a primal satisfaction from knowing that tomorrow Regan would look down at his hips and see Tie's fingerprints there, his mark of ownership.

Cerise was plastered to Regan's side, kissing his chest. She looked like she wanted to crawl inside Regan's skin. Her obvious arousal and enthusiastic participation in this fuck made it perfect in every way. Even as long as he'd wanted Regan, Tie knew that if Cerise wasn't here it wouldn't be the same. It wouldn't be as good and it wouldn't mean as much. Was that the Tears talking? Maybe. Did it matter? Not to Tie.

"Tie, Tie," Regan groaned as Tie pressed deep inside him, hitting that spot guaranteed to drive a man wild. Tie wanted Regan as wild as he was.

"You feel so goddamned good, baby," Tie growled, yanking on Regan's hips to pull him closer and wrapping Regan's legs around his waist. Tie rose higher on his knees, angling down and Regan cried out. He had one arm wrapped around Cerise, his hand buried in her hair as she sucked his nipple and his bad arm was lying by his side. Tie watched him fist his hand in the sheets until his knuckles turned white as Tie fucked him hard and deep. "You like it hard, like Cerise," Tie panted. "I like to fuck you two like that."

"Yes, God, Tie, yes," Regan said breathlessly. His ass flexed against Tie, pulling his cock in, refusing to let it go without a fight when Tie pulled out. The tight friction nearly had Tie undone. He couldn't last, he couldn't. He had to come in this ass, he had to fill Regan. Tie reached down and wrapped his hand around Regan's hard cock. He ran his thumb over Regan's leaking slit, spreading the warm liquid over the ultrasoft head.

Regan's shoulders curled up from the bed. "Tie," he gasped, "no. I won't last if you do that. I'm going to come."

"Good. I want to watch you come before I do. I want to see you come in Cerise's mouth." Tie turned his gaze to Cerise, who had raised her head from Regan's chest. The smile she gave him was sultry and hungry and Tie let go of Regan's cock and leaned over and gripped the back of her head. "Suck him now. Suck him off and then I can come inside him." He pulled gently but firmly and Cerise let him drag her head down to Regan's cock.

Cerise opened her mouth wide and swallowed Regan whole. Regan shouted with pleasure when she did and Tie felt his cock jerk at the sight. Cerise ran her fingers through Regan's pubic hair until she reached his scrotum. She lightly ran her finger along the line in the sac and Tie felt Regan shudder. Then her hand moved further down, cupping his balls in her palm while she slid her index and middle fingers to either side of Tie's cock, so he was nestled between them, still inside Regan. Tie had to pull back slightly to give her room. The feel of her hand there was thrilling. She wanted to feel him fuck Regan. God, she was amazing.

"Cerise, Jesus," Regan whispered. "Is she...is she doing what I think she is?" His last two words were gasped out as Cerise sucked his cock deep into her throat.

Tie thrust sharply, involuntarily, into Regan. Cerise's touch had him desperate to move again. "Yes," he hissed, "she's feeling me fuck you."

Cerise pulled off Regan for a moment. "Move," she ordered him. Just the one word, then she swallowed Regan again. Regan was writhing on the bed, fucking into her mouth, forcing Tie in and out of his ass with his movements. Tie didn't need to be told twice. He began to fuck Regan, slower than before and not as hard because Cerise's hand was there and he didn't want to hurt her. Her fingers caressed his cock as it came out of Regan and again as he slid back in. The dual sensations of her fingers and Regan's tight, hot ass had Tie teetering on the edge of orgasm almost immediately.

Suddenly Regan's good hand reached down and held Cerise to him, his cock buried deep in her throat. "Cerise!" he shouted and his back and neck arched, the tendons standing out in stark relief. Tie could feel Regan's muscles contracting around him as he came. Tie pressed deep and held there, closing his eyes tightly at the pleasure-pain of trying to hold back his own climax. Cerise choked a little, but didn't pull away, or at least Regan didn't let her. She recovered and Tie opened his eyes to see her swallowing deeply again and again.

When he was done, Regan's muscles relaxed as if a string had been cut. He collapsed against the bed, his hand dropping from Cerise's head. She let go of him with a gasp and pulled deep breaths into her lungs for several seconds. Then she dove on top of Regan. "Regan," she cried and straddled his stomach as she held his face in her hands and kissed him wildly. Regan hugged her to him with his good arm and Tie heard what sounded like a choked off sob. Regan's shoulders were shaking.

Tie could feel every muscles straining as he tried to control himself. He wanted to give Regan a minute or two to recover, so that he could feel and watch Tie fuck him. He wanted Regan to see it, to know that he belonged to Tie now.

"Cerise, baby, move to his side," he told her as gently as he could, his voice a low rumble.

Cerise obediently slid off to Regan's side and broke the kiss. Both she and Regan were breathing hard, as if they'd run a race. They looked down at Tie with identical expressions of love and desire. There were tears on their cheeks. Yes, it was that intense, that emotional for Tie as well.

Tie leaned over and deliberately placed his hands on either side of Regan and Cerise scooted a little further over. She wrapped a hand around Tie's biceps and the muscle there trembled at her touch. Tie adjusted his position a little, settling his hips snugly under Regan's ass, his cock hard and hot inside the other man. The new position brought them almost face-to-face and from the corner of his eye Tie saw Cerise lie down on her back so that her head rested right next to Regan's and he could look into her eyes as well while he fucked Regan. How did she know to do these things? How did she know just what would drive him over the edge? The Tears, of course. The Tears.

"Fuck him," she whispered and Tie couldn't wait anymore. His balls were already pulling up and he could feel his orgasm rising. He looked into Regan's face and the love and acceptance there shook him to his very core. He pulled out and thrust and Regan's lips parted. On the next thrust, Regan's hips parried and his ass tightened around Tie.

"Regan." There was a warning in the word, but Regan didn't heed it. He just smiled darkly and did it again. "God, God," Tie chanted, his thrusts growing hard and deep again.

"That's right, Tie," Regan whispered enticingly, "Give it to me. Give me everything you've got."

Tie was shaking his head, trying to deny his climax, not wanting this to end.

"Yes, Tie, yes," Cerise told him and she tenderly smoothed an errant lock of sweat-drenched hair off his cheek. That touch did it. Tie gave a ragged shout and pressed deep as his cock pulsed forcefully. Regan cried out as Tie's semen hit his prostate, making him shiver and grip Tie tightly with his legs and ass. Regan, Regan, Regan, Tie thought. At last, you're mine at last.

When it was over, Tie laid his head on Regan's chest and wept. He cried for the wonder of it, of what they'd found here. He cried for the years they'd been apart, for the men they had been and the men they were now, the men Cerise made them. He cried because they loved him and because he was allowed to love them.

Chapter Twenty-One

❧

"I..." Regan had to stop to clear his throat. "I need to get cleaned up." He paused for a moment, drawing a deep breath. "And I need to breathe. Tie, get off me. You must weigh two hundred kilos."

A laugh burst from Tie where he had his face pressed to Regan's chest and Cerise's heart leapt. Tie had been so overwrought she'd been worried. But the storm had passed, as all Tie's storms passed.

Tie pushed himself up and gingerly moved his hips. Regan gasped softly and Cerise looked down to see Tie's cock, still half-hard, easing out of his new lover. She couldn't contain a little shiver of excitement at the sight. Regan's arm tightened around her. "Like that, do you?" he asked, breathless but amused.

"Oh, yeah, I like it," Cerise agreed as she watched Tie roll off the bed and walk over to the bathroom. She leaned over Regan, propping a fist on his stomach and resting her chin on her fist. "He's awfully nice to look at, every centimeter. Don't you think?"

"Awfully nice," Regan agreed. Cerise cut her eyes to his face and saw he was watching Tie as hungrily as she was. She smiled. She liked sharing her passion for these two men with them. She liked that she could talk to Regan about Tie and Tie about Regan and they understood what she was feeling. They felt it too.

"Are you two talking about me?" Tie yelled from the bathroom.

"Of course we are," Cerise yelled back and he laughed.

She moved her hand and rested her cheek on Regan's stomach. His skin was still warm and damp with perspiration from their exertions. She turned her head slightly and licked him, savoring his salty, spicy flavor.

"Cerise," he moaned, "give me a minute. I'm worn out, used up."

Cerise chuckled and pushed off him to sit up. She scooted over a little and sat crossed legged next to him. "All right, all right, old man. One minute and then you have to pleasure me again." Cerise ruined it by giving a huge yawn even as she finished the sentence and Regan laughed. Cerise felt giddy, she was so happy. She hadn't heard Regan laugh so much in all the years she'd known him. And Tie certainly hadn't been a laugh a minute when they met. She'd done this. She'd brought them all together and gave them back laughter.

Tie came out of the bathroom with a damp cloth and handed it to Regan. "Here. I've got to go clean myself up." His smile took away any sting in his words. Regan took the cloth and Tie reached out and ran a finger tenderly down the scar on Regan's cheek before he turned away. Cerise got a lump in her throat.

"Here," she said, grabbing the cloth. Regan tried to grab it back.

"Cerise, I can do it myself," he protested. He started to sit up and then cringed and fell back, a hand on his shoulder. "Damn, what did you two do to me?"

"Oh, baby, are you all right?" Cerise bit her lip as she leaned over and tentatively reached out to touch the still angry-looking, red wound. Regan grabbed her hand.

"I'll be all right, sweetheart, but let's not aggravate it further. I'll put a cool pack on it in a minute."

Cerise looked at him with narrowed eyes for a moment, but decided he was telling the truth. She nodded and then reached down and tried to pull the pillows out from under his hips. Regan lifted his hips and then dropped back to the bed.

Cerise grinned at him. "Spread 'em," she said, waggling the washcloth over him. Regan narrowed his eyes, but bent his knees and spread his legs. Cerise gently washed him off, turning the bath into a series of sensual caresses. By the time she was done, Regan was getting hard again.

She was concentrating so hard on Regan she didn't hear Tie come back. "Next time you get to clean me off, too," he said in an amused voice as he lay down next to Regan, resting on one elbow with his head in his hand. He caressed the other man's taut stomach.

Regan laughed weakly. "You two are going to kill me."

Cerise balled up the washcloth and threw it toward the bathroom. The two men watched as it fell a couple of meters short. Regan just shook his head and Cerise shrugged with a grin.

Regan turned to look at Tie. "So what did you hide next to the bed?"

Tie looked alarmed for a second, then sheepish. "I've got a gift for you."

"For me?" Regan asked, surprise in his voice.

"No, I mean yes." Tie laughed self-consciously as he sat up and reached down next to the bed. He shook his head. "For both of you. I've got a gift for both of you." When he came up he held two packages tied with bright paper and string.

Cerise felt her face light up. "A present? For me? Is it clothes?"

Regan laughed. "You are becoming impossible. How many clothes does one woman need?"

Cerise raised an eyebrow. "I have no idea, but a princess needs many, many clothes."

Tie handed her one of the small boxes. "It's better than clothes." He handed Regan the other. Regan turned it over and over in his hands, looking bewildered.

Samantha Kane

Cerise leaned over from her sitting position and looked into his face. "It's a present. You know? You open the paper and there's a surprise inside just for you?"

Regan looked at her wryly. "I know what a present is. I just didn't expect one." He turned to Tie, chagrined. "I don't have anything for you."

Cerise was horrified that she hadn't thought of that. "Oh my God, I don't either. And I'm so selfish I didn't even think of it. Oh, Tie!"

Tie gave them both an impish grin and leaned back over the bed. He pulled up a present that looked identical to Regan's. "That's all right, I got one for me, too."

Cerise laughed. "Only you would buy a present for yourself. You open yours first."

Tie shook his head. "No. You open yours, Cerise." She hesitated, although she really, really wanted to. What was better than clothes? Tie smiled and waved his hand, indicating she should open it.

Regan laughed again. "Go on. You know you want to."

Cerise pulled off the string and tore open the paper. She lifted the lid on the small box she found. Inside was something wrapped in soft cloth. She pulled it out and gave Tie a puzzled look.

"Unwrap it. Gently." Tie looked as excited as Cerise and he kept looking between she and Regan.

Cerise unwrapped the cloth and nestled inside was a large carnelian, almost identical to the one she wore on her matewaist. Cerise had to swallow deeply before she could speak. "It's another carnelian, for my matewaist." She held it up for Regan to see. "Look, darling, for you."

Regan looked stunned. "Tie…" His voice was choked up with emotion.

Cerise rose to her knees immediately and spun her matewaist around until the stone already attached dripped

346

down her stomach. She held out Tie's gift to Regan. "Put it on, Regan. Put it on and be my mate."

Regan reached out slowly and took the stone from her hand, holding it as if it would break. "Cerise...are you sure?"

Cerise crawled over to him and wrapped her arms around his neck, hugging him close. "I'm sure," she whispered in his ear. He hugged her back and then set her away from him. He bent low and attached the stone to a large link in the chain. He fumbled a little and Cerise bit back a smile.

When he was done he smoothed the chain and his stone was next to Tie's as they both draped low against her stomach. He rose and took both of Cerise's hands in his. "You are mine." The statement was simple, the emotion behind it wasn't.

"Yes," Cerise said softly, as her eyes filled with tears. "Yes, I am. It feels like I always have been."

Tie kneeled next to them and reached out to touch Regan's carnelian. "It's perfect. I knew it would be perfect." He put his arm around Cerise and pulled her close, then kissed Regan, just behind his ear. "We're perfect."

"Rather high opinion of yourself," Regan teased, rubbing his head against Tie's, his voice still choked up.

"Yep," Tie agreed, kissing Regan softly on the cheek. "Now open yours."

"You open yours at the same time." Regan cleared his throat and tried to be all business.

Tie grinned. "Deal." He let go of Cerise and reached for his box, as Regan pulled the string off his. Cerise settled back to watch them, but couldn't stop herself from glancing down at her two-stone matewaist repeatedly. When Regan had the paper off and was about to open the box, Tie stopped and watched him.

When he had the lid off Regan just stared into the box, his expression unreadable.

"What is it?" Cerise couldn't stop herself from asking. She was on fire with curiosity.

Regan pulled a necklace out of the box. The chain was made of heavy gold links and there was a gold disk dangling from it. Regan laid the disk in his palm and traced its surface with his finger. It had one large carnelian off center and two smaller carnelians off to the side.

"This is Cerise," Tie said, pointing to the large carnelian, "and these are you and I." He ran his finger over the two smaller carnelians.

"Because she is our sun," Regan whispered, "the one who gives us life. And we will follow her forever."

Tie squeezed Regan's good shoulder. "Yes, yes, exactly. I knew you'd understand, Regan." Tie finished opening his box and he had an identical necklace inside. He put his on and then took Regan's from his hand and placed it around his neck. "She belongs to us and we belong to her."

Regan gripped the necklace in his fist, against his chest. "And to each other." He looked up at Tie. "We belong to each other, as well."

Cerise was crying so hard she couldn't speak. God, oh my God. Until this moment she'd still harbored doubts, though she'd refused to face them. She'd been afraid they didn't really love her, not like they loved each other. But she knew now, she could see it on their faces, they meant it. They would love her and protect her forever. Without her, they would have no center.

"Tie," she cried and she threw herself in his arms. He caught her and held her to him so tightly she couldn't breathe and didn't care.

"I love you, Cerise. You gave me a life I had only dreamed about, a love that I never thought I'd find. I am yours and you are mine."

"I love you, Tie. I love you." Cerise was so overwhelmed they were the only words she could find.

"Tie," Regan spoke softly next to them. Tie opened one arm and wrapped Regan in their embrace and Cerise turned so that she had an arm around each of them. "I love you both, Tie and Cerise. You are my future, my path, my everything. You are mine and I am yours."

"Yes," Tie whispered, "You are mine and I am yours."

Cerise tilted her head up to Tie and he kissed her deeply, with hunger and possessiveness. Suddenly Cerise felt a feather light, damp stroke against the corner of her lips. She broke the kiss and turned to see Regan. He leaned down and kissed her tenderly. When he pulled away Cerise saw that Tie hadn't moved back. His mouth was right there, right next to theirs. Without speaking, in perfect accord, all three came together, lips, tongues, breaths mingling. It was the most erotic and romantic kiss Cerise had ever shared.

Regan pulled away first and Cerise came away from the kiss in a daze. He smiled at her, full of sensual promise and lay back on the bed. He patted the space next to him and Cerise crawled over him to curl up there, her head on his good shoulder.

"So how are we going to do this?" Regan's voice was serious, his Regan the Pirate-making-plans voice.

"Well," Tie drawled as he leaned down and kissed Regan's chest right over his heart, "I thought that this time you could fuck me while I fucked Cerise." He slid down and lay next to Regan opposite Cerise and lightly bit Regan's nipple.

"Hmm," Cerise said, running her hand through Tie's hair and wrapping her leg around Regan's, "I'd like to suck someone's cock again, although they don't have to come in my mouth."

"I meant how are we going to do this mate thing," Regan responded wryly, "and lead the rebellion. But I'm willing to entertain those suggestions later."

Cerise chuckled. "Oh, sorry. I've got sex on the brain, which I blame entirely on you two."

Tie snuggled in next to Regan and began kissing his jaw. "Guilty as charged," he said between kisses.

"I'd really like to talk about it," Regan replied and his tone made Cerise lean up on one elbow to look at him.

"All right." She took a deep breath and thought for a minute. "I'm entirely comfortable with the situation. I am Princess Cerise Chessienne. Carnelian tradition dictates that a woman have more than one husband. I choose you two." She looked at Regan and he nodded, but his expression said he was waiting for more. "It would seem that over the last few days we've broken some rules of our previous relationship and established others." She moved to sit cross legged again.

"You can say that again," Tie muttered with a wicked grin and Cerise reached over Regan to punch him in the arm.

"I meant that you two seem to want and value my opinion on political matters. Am I wrong?"

"No, you're not wrong," Regan agreed, taking her hand. "I value your opinion very much. I realized that you've been at my side for the last seven years. You've been a very big part of making this rebellion more than a few malcontents grumbling and shooting indiscriminately. You know as much about the current political situation as I do. I want you at my side, as equals."

Cerise felt that lump of emotion threatening to choke her again. "That means almost as much to me as this," she told Regan, touching the carnelian at her waist. He placed his hand over hers with a tender smile.

"Well, I know nothing about politics and I'm afraid I wouldn't do well in that arena." Tie sounded disgruntled, but underneath it Cerise could hear his uncertainty.

Regan sighed and turned to Tie with a lop-sided grin. "No, politics is not your forte, although as a royal mate you'll have to learn some finesse."

"Thanks," Tie responded sarcastically and Regan tried to brush his fingers against Tie's cheek, but it was his bad arm and he winced. Tie made a sympathetic face and grabbed Regan's hand instead, giving it a squeeze.

"Tie is very good with people," Cerise defended him. "Look how he won over everyone here."

"You're right, he is. I hope we can use that to our advantage," Regan agreed.

Tie was mollified. "Thank you."

"Since this is the time for confessions," Regan said haltingly, "I guess I should mention that I haven't particularly liked the battle training and missions for the last few years." Cerise looked at him with wide eyes. She'd had no idea. He seemed so at home barking orders at the men and, well, blowing things up. Regan sighed. "Tie was right. I've become a bureaucrat. And I like it. I'm much happier organizing things and keeping a tight rein on the finances. Fewer temper tantrums."

Tie sat up abruptly. "Does this mean I get to be General King Tie?" He rubbed his hands together. "I get to train the troops and play war games and strategize and oversee security?"

"You're better at it." Regan's voice contained no animosity, just fact. "That was apparent on the freighter." Tie whooped, but Regan interrupted. "And there is no king."

Tie leaned down and kissed him. "I'll settle for General, but you're still our pirate sex slave."

Cerise smiled sleepily and lay down next to Regan again. "There, see? Everything is settled." She had to stop to yawn noisily. Regan pushed her head back down on his good shoulder.

"Go to sleep, princess," he told her with a kiss on her brow.

Cerise yawned again. "I think we're going to miss dinner." Her words were getting slurred.

"I'll tell Delroilinda to reschedule," Tie whispered, leaning over and kissing her head. "You need some rest."

"Mmm," was all she could say before she drifted off, the scent of Tie and Regan filling her head, Regan's necklace nestled under the palm of her hand.

* * * * *

"Cerise?" Tie's whisper woke her in the middle of the night. The room was dark and she was nestled into the curve of Regan's side, her head still on his shoulder. Tie was leaning over her shoulder.

She turned her head and smiled sleepily at him. "Hmmm?"

"Is it tomorrow?"

She was still half asleep and his question made no sense. She shook her head and then Regan turned and nuzzled her cheek.

"Finnegan, begin again," he quoted quietly, his voice rough with sleep, *"but he always said tomorrow, I'll begin again tomorrow."*

And Cerise remembered. She remembered Conor's book and remembered the conversation she and Tie had had on the *Tomorrow*.

"Yes, Tie," she whispered as she leaned back into him and he kissed her neck, "tomorrow has arrived."

The End

Also by Samantha Kane

ɞ

A Lady In Waiting
Brothers in Arms 1: The Courage to Love
Brothers in Arms 2: Love Under Siege
Brothers In Arms 3: Love's Strategy
Brothers in Arms 4: At Love's Command
Brothers in Arms 5: Retreat from Love
Ellora's Cavemen: Jewels of the Nile II (*anthology*)
Islands

About the Author

ॐ

Samantha has a Master's Degree in History, and is a full-time writer and mother. She lives in North Carolina with her husband and three children.

Samantha welcomes comments from readers. You can find her website and email address on her author bio page at www.ellorascave.com.

Tell Us What You Think

We appreciate hearing reader opinions about our books. You can email us at Comments@EllorasCave.com.

Why an electronic book?

We live in the Information Age — an exciting time in the history of human civilization, in which technology rules supreme and continues to progress in leaps and bounds every minute of every day. For a multitude of reasons, more and more avid literary fans are opting to purchase e-books instead of paper books. The question from those not yet initiated into the world of electronic reading is simply: *Why?*

1. *Price.* An electronic title at Ellora's Cave Publishing and Cerridwen Press runs anywhere from 40% to 75% less than the cover price of the exact same title in paperback format. Why? Basic mathematics and cost. It is less expensive to publish an e-book (no paper and printing, no warehousing and shipping) than it is to publish a paperback, so the savings are passed along to the consumer.

2. *Space.* Running out of room in your house for your books? That is one worry you will never have with electronic books. For a low one-time cost, you can purchase a handheld device specifically designed for e-reading. Many e-readers have large, convenient screens for viewing. Better yet, hundreds of titles can be stored within your new library — on a single microchip. There are a variety of e-readers from different manufacturers. You can also read e-books on your PC or laptop computer. (Please note that Ellora's Cave does not endorse any specific brands.

You can check our websites at www.ellorascave.com or www.cerridwenpress.com for information we make available to new consumers.)

3. *Mobility.* Because your new e-library consists of only a microchip within a small, easily transportable e-reader, your entire cache of books can be taken with you wherever you go.

4. *Personal Viewing Preferences.* Are the words you are currently reading too small? Too large? Too... ANNOYING? Paperback books cannot be modified according to personal preferences, but e-books can.

5. *Instant Gratification.* Is it the middle of the night and all the bookstores near you are closed? Are you tired of waiting days, sometimes weeks, for bookstores to ship the novels you bought? Ellora's Cave Publishing sells instantaneous downloads twenty-four hours a day, seven days a week, every day of the year. Our webstore is never closed. Our e-book delivery system is 100% automated, meaning your order is filled as soon as you pay for it.

Those are a few of the top reasons why electronic books are replacing paperbacks for many avid readers.

As always, Ellora's Cave and Cerridwen Press welcome your questions and comments. We invite you to email us at Comments@ellorascave.com or write to us directly at Ellora's Cave Publishing Inc., 1056 Home Avenue, Akron, OH 44310-3502.

COMING TO A BOOKSTORE NEAR YOU!

ELLORA'S CAVE

Bestselling Authors Tour

Discover for yourself why readers can't get enough
of the multiple award-winning publisher
Ellora's Cave.

Whether you prefer e-books or paperbacks,
be sure to visit EC on the web at
www.ellorascave.com

for an erotic reading experience that will leave you
breathless.

5567658R0

Made in the USA
Lexington, KY
23 May 2010